Born in Canada in 1966, Susanna Kearsley has been writing since the age of seven. She read politics and international development at university, has worked as a museum curator, and has had two short novels published in the US. She lives in Ontario.

Susanna Kearsley is the second winner of the Catherine Cookson Prize which was set up in 1992 to celebrate the achievement of Dame Catherine Cookson. The prize is awarded to a novel that features the strong characterization, authentic background and storytelling ability that have been the outstanding qualities of Catherine Cookson's work.

Mariana

Susanna Kearsley

CORGI BOOKS

MARIANA
A CORGI BOOK 0 552 14262 X

First publication in Great Britain

PRINTING HISTORY
Corgi edition published 1994
Corgi edition reprinted 1995

Set in 10/12 Linotype Sabon by
Phoenix Typesetting, Ilkley, West Yorkshire.

Corgi Books are published by Transworld Publishers Ltd,
61–63 Uxbridge Road, Ealing, London W5 5SA,
in Australia by Transworld Publishers (Australia) Pty Ltd,
15–25 Helles Avenue, Moorebank, NSW 2170,
and in New Zealand by Transworld Publishers (NZ) Ltd,
3 William Pickering Drive, Albany, Auckland.

Printed and bound in Great Britain by
Cox & Wyman Ltd, Reading, Berkshire

All day within the dreamy house,
    The doors upon their hinges creak'd;
The blue fly sung in the pane; the mouse
    Behind the mouldering wainscot shriek'd,
Or from the crevice peer'd about.
    Old faces glimmer'd thro' the doors,
    Old footsteps trod the upper floors,
Old voices called her from without.

TENNYSON: *Mariana*

For Susan Shepherd
Who led me down
the road less travelled.

Chapter One

I first saw the house in the summer of my fifth birthday.
It was all the fault of a poet, and the fact that our
weekend visit with a favourite elderly aunt in Exeter
had put my father in a vaguely poetic mood. Faced with
an unexpected fork in the road on our drive home to
Oxford, he deliberately chose the left turning instead
of the right. 'The road less travelled by,' he told us,
in a benign and dreamy voice. And as the poet had
promised, it did indeed make all the difference.

To begin with, we became lost. So hopelessly lost, in
fact, that my mother had to put away the map. The
clouds that rolled in to cover the sun seemed only an
extension of my father's darkening mood, all poetry forgotten as he hunched grimly over the steering wheel. By
lunchtime it was raining, quite heavily, and my mother
had given sweets to my brother Tommy and me in a
vain attempt to keep us from further irritating Daddy,
whose notable temper was nearing breaking point.

The sweets were peppermint, striped pink and white
like large marbles, and so effective at hindering speech
that we had to take them out of our mouths altogether
in order to talk to each other. By the time we reached
the first cluster of village shops and houses, my face and
hands were sticky with sugar, and the front of my new
ruffled frock was a stained and wrinkled ruin.

I've never been entirely certain what it was that made
my father stop the car where he did. I seem to remember

a cat darting across the road in front of us, but that may simply have been the invention of an imaginative and overtired child. Whatever the reason, the car stopped, the engine stalled, and in the ensuing commotion I got my first watery glimpse of the house.

It was a rather ordinary old farmhouse, large and square and solid, set back some distance from the road with a few unkempt trees dotted around for privacy. Its darkly glistening slate roof sloped down at an alarming angle to meet the weathered grey stone walls, the drab monotony of colour broken by twin red brick chimneys and an abundance of large, multi-paned windows, their frames painted freshly white.

I was pressing my nose against the cold glass of the car window, straining to get a better look, when after a few particularly virulent oaths my father managed to coax the motor back to life. My mother, obviously relieved, turned round to check up on us.

'Julia, don't,' she pleaded. 'You'll leave smears on the windows.'

'That's my house,' I said, by way of explanation.

My brother Tommy pointed to a much larger and more stately home that was just coming into view. 'Well that's *my* house,' he countered, triumphant. To the delight of my parents, we continued the game all the way home to Oxford, and the lonely grey house was forgotten.

I was not to see it again for seventeen years.

That summer, the summer that I turned twenty-two, is strong in my memory. I had just graduated from art school, and had landed what seemed like the perfect job with a small advertising firm in London. My brother Tom, three years older than myself, had recently come down from Oxford with a distinguished academic record, and promptly shocked the family by announcing his plans to enter the Anglican ministry. Ours was not a particularly religious family, but Tom jokingly maintained that, given his name, he had little choice in the matter. 'Thomas Beckett! I ask you,' he had teased my mother. 'What else could you expect?'

To celebrate what we perceived to be our coming of age, Tom and I decided to take a short holiday on the south Devon coast, where we could temporarily forget about parents and responsibilities and take advantage of the uncommonly hot and sunny weather with which southern England was being blessed. We were not disappointed. We spent a blissful week lounging about on the beach at Torquay, and emerged relaxed, rejuvenated, and sunburned.

Tom, caught up on a rising swell of optimism, appointed me navigator for the trip back. He should have known better. While I'm not exactly bad with maps, I *am* rather easily distracted by the scenery. Inevitably, we found ourselves off the main road, toiling through what seemed like an endless procession of tiny, identical villages linked by a narrow road so overhung by trees it had the appearance of a tunnel.

After the seventh village, Tom shot me an accusing sideways look. We had both inherited our mother's Cornish colouring and finely-cut features, but while on me the combination of dark hair and eyes was more impish than exotic, on Tom it could look positively menacing when he chose.

'Where do you suppose we are?' he asked, with dangerous politeness.

I dutifully consulted the map. 'Wiltshire, I expect,' I told him brightly. 'Somewhere in the middle.'

'Well, that's certainly specific.'

'Look,' I suggested, as we approached village number eight, 'why don't you stop being so pig-headed and ask directions at the next pub? Honestly, Tom, you're as bad as Dad—' The word ended in a sudden squeal.

This time, I didn't imagine it. A large ginger cat dashed right across the road, directly in front of our car. The brakes shrieked a protest as Tom put his foot to the floor, and then, right on cue, the motor died.

'Damn and blast!'

'Curates can't use language like that,' I reminded my brother, and he grinned involuntarily.

'I'm getting it out of my system,' was his excuse.

Laughing, I looked out the window and froze.

'I don't believe it.'

'I know,' my brother agreed. 'Rotten luck.'

I shook my head. 'No, Tom, look – it's my house.'

'What?'

'My grey house,' I told him. 'Don't you remember, that day the cat ran onto the road and Daddy stalled the car?'

'No.'

'On the way back from Auntie Helen's,' I elaborated. 'Just after my fifth birthday. It was raining and Daddy took the wrong turning and a cat ran onto the road and he had to stop the car.'

My brother looked at me in the same way a scientist must look at a curious new specimen, and shook his head. 'No, I don't remember that.'

'Well, it happened,' I said stubbornly, 'and the car stalled just here, and I saw that house.'

'If you say so.'

The car was running again, now, and Tom manoeuvred it over to the side of the road so I could have a clearer view.

'What do you think it means?' I asked him.

'I think it means our family has bloody bad luck with cats in Wiltshire,' Tom said. I chose to ignore him.

'I wonder how old it is.'

Tom leaned closer. 'Elizabethan, I should think. Possibly Jacobean. No later.'

I'd forgotten that Tom had been keen on architecture at school. Besides, Tom always knew everything.

'I'd love to get a closer look.' My voice was hopeful, but Tom merely sent me an indulgent glance before turning back onto the road that led into the village.

'I am not,' he said, 'going to peer into anyone's windows to satisfy your curiosity. Anyway, the drive is clearly marked "Private".'

A short distance down the road we pulled into the car park of the Red Lion, a respectable half-timbered pub with an ancient thatched roof and tables arranged on a makeshift terrace to accommodate the noontime crowd. I stayed in the car, preparing to take my shift as driver, while Tom went into the pub to down a quick pint and get directions back to the main road.

I was so busy pondering how great the odds must be against being lost twice in the same spot, that I completely forgot to ask my brother to find out the name of the village we were in.

It would be another eight years before I found myself once again in Exbury, Wiltshire.

This time, the final time, it was early April, two months shy of my thirtieth birthday, and – for once – I was not lost. I still lived in London, in a tiny rented flat in Bloomsbury that I had become rooted to, in spite of an unexpectedly generous legacy left to me by my father's Aunt Helen, that same aunt we'd been visiting in Exeter all those years earlier. She'd only seen me twice, had Auntie Helen, so why she had chosen to leave me such an obscene amount of money remained a mystery. Perhaps it was because I was the only girl in a family known for its male progeny. Auntie Helen, according to my father, had been possessed of staunchly feminist views. 'A room of your own,' Tom had told me, in a decided tone. 'That's what she's left you. Haven't you read Virginia Woolf?'

It was rather more than the price of a room, actually, but I hadn't the slightest idea what to do with it. Tom had stoutly refused my offer to share the inheritance, and my parents maintained they had no need of it, being comfortably well off themselves since my father's retirement from surgical practice. So that was that.

I had quite enough to occupy my time, as it was, having shifted careers from graphic design to illustration, a field I found both more interesting and more lucrative. By some stroke of luck I had been teamed early on with a wonderfully talented author, and our collaboration on a series of fantasy tales for children had earned me a respectable name for myself in the business, not to mention a steady living. I had just that week been commissioned to illustrate a sizeable new collection of legends and fairy tales from around the world, a project which excited me greatly and promised to keep my busily employed for the better part of a year. I was on top of the world.

Ordinarily, I'd have celebrated my good fortune with my family, but since my parents were halfway round the world on holiday and Tom was occupied with Easter services, I had settled for the next best thing and spent the weekend with friends in Bath. On the Monday morning, finding the traffic on the main road too busy for my taste, I detoured to the north and followed the gentle sweep of the Kennet river towards London.

It was a cool but perfect spring day, and the trees that lined the road were bursting into leaf with an almost tropical fervour. In honour of the season, I drove with the windows down, and the air smelled sweetly of rain and soil and growing things.

My arthritic but trustworthy Peugeot crested a small hill with a protesting wheeze. Gathering speed, I negotiated a broad curve where the road dipped down into a shallow valley before crossing over the Kennet via a narrow stone bridge. As I bumped across the bridge, I felt a faint tingling sensation sweep across the back of my neck, and my fingers tightened on the wheel in anticipation.

The most surprising thing was that I wasn't at all surprised, this time, to see the house. Somehow, I almost expected it to be there.

I slowed the car to a crawl, then pulled off the road and stopped altogether, just opposite the long gravel drive. A large ginger cat stalked haughtily across the road without so much as glancing at me, and disappeared into the waving grass. Three times in one lifetime, I told myself, even without the cat, was definitely beyond the bounds of ordinary coincidence.

Surely, I reasoned, whoever owned the house wouldn't mind terribly if I just took a casual peek around . . . ? As I hesitated, biting my lip, a flock of starlings rose in a beating cloud from the field beside me, gathered and wheeled once above the grey stone house, and then was gone.

For me, that was the deciding factor. Along with my mother's looks, I had also inherited the superstitious nature of her Cornish ancestors, and the starlings were a good luck omen of my own invention. From my earliest childhood, whenever I had seen a flock of them it meant that something wonderful was about to happen. My brother Tom repeatedly tried to point out the flaw in this belief, by reminding me that starlings in the English countryside were not exactly uncommon, and that their link to my happiness could only be random at best. I remained unconvinced. I only knew that the starlings had never steered me wrong, and watching them turn now and rise above the house I suddenly made a decision.

I grabbed my shapeless green anorak from the seat beside me and stepped out of the car, nearly tumbling into the ditch in my eagerness. I wasn't exactly dressed to go visiting, I admitted, tugging the anorak on over my jeans and rough sweater – but that couldn't be helped. I ran a hand through my hair in a hopeless attempt to smooth the short, unruly curls, but the damply blowing wind spoiled my efforts.

Now, I thought, what excuse to use? Directions? A glass of water? Trouble with the car? I glanced back at the dented and battered Peugeot and nodded. Car trouble, I decided. Anyone would believe that. Mentally rehearsing my lines, I crossed the road and started up the gravel drive. A cracked and weathered signboard bearing the words 'Strictly Private' in faded red paint, hung dejectedly from a nail in a nearby tree. Undaunted, I soldiered on, hoping that my footsteps didn't sound as crunchingly loud to the people inside as they did to my own ears.

The house looked exactly as I remembered it – the same red chimneys with their clay chimney-pots, the same symmetrically-positioned white windows, four panes over four; the same rough-hewn grey stone walls under the steep slate roof. The only thing different was the door. I had always imagined it to be brown, but now

I saw that it was clearly dark green, standing out in sharp contrast to the massive stone portal that surrounded it.

My knocking echoed heavily with a dull and hollow sound. Three times I bruised my knuckles against the heavy wood, before finally conceding that no-one was coming to answer the door.

Which meant there was nobody home. And, I told myself happily, since there was nobody home, it followed that no-one would be disturbed if I went round to the back of the house and looked in a few windows. Having thus rationalized my trespassing, I retraced my steps to the drive and followed it round the north side of the house.

Here the drive ended abruptly at a squat, low-slung stone building with a weedy thatched roof. Presumably this had once been the stables, but the bumper of a car protruding from one of the open stalls left no doubt as to its present use.

The view from where I stood, looking across the level farmlands and gently undulating downs, broken here and there by clusters of dark green trees and wild shrubs, was truly beautiful. There was no yard as such, although a tumbled heap of stone a hundred feet or so behind the house looked as if it might once have been part of a boundary wall. And though I had counted three oaks, a fruit tree and several shrubs at the front, the only bit of vegetation growing close against the back wall of the house was a solitary poplar with gnarled bark, its silvery green branches trembling in the breeze.

There was another dark green door here, with an old-fashioned latch, and another double row of white-painted windows. Beneath what I assumed must be the kitchen window, someone had piled a precarious stack of ancient flower pots, their sides encrusted with thick black moss from lack of use. I stretched on tip-toe and leaned closer, cupping one hand against the glass to shield my eyes against the reflected glare of the sun. It *was* a window to the kitchen, or perhaps the pantry. I could just make out a shelf of tinned goods and an old porcelain sink. I was angling my head for a better look when a man's voice spoke suddenly out of the air behind me.

'He's not there.'

It was a friendly voice, with a faintly un-English burr to it, and had come from some distance away. But I didn't register any of that immediately. I spun round, startled, and sent the pile of flower pots crashing to the ground.

At first I could see no-one, but as I stood there staring the figure of a man detached itself from the tumbled stone wall and came across the grass towards me. He was a young man, perhaps five years my senior, dressed in rough working clothes and wearing leather gauntlets that looked oddly medieval and out of place.

'I didn't mean to frighten you,' he apologized. 'I just thought, if you're looking for Eddie, he's not there.'

He was quite close now, close enough for me to clearly see the combination of auburn hair and flint-grey eyes that is, somehow, so distinctively Scottish. He smiled, a friendly smile that matched the voice.

'Are you a friend of Eddie's?' he asked.

I shook my head.

'A relative, then.'

'No.' To my credit, I blushed a little. I had a hunch my tale of phony car trouble would not make it past those shrewd grey eyes. 'No, I don't know the owner. Will he be back soon, do you know?'

The man tilted his head to one side and gave me a long, measuring look that rather reminded me of my brother.

'I hope not,' he said evenly. 'We buried him last month.'

'Oh, I'm sorry.' I blushed deeper. 'I really am sorry.'

'No harm done.' He shrugged. 'You're just having a poke about, then?'

My face, by this time, was crimson, and I had a feeling that he was enjoying my obvious discomfort. It took a moment, but the full importance of what he'd just told me finally sank in, and I abruptly forgot my embarrassment.

I lifted my eyes quickly. 'Is the house for sale, then?'

'Aye. Did you want to have a look at it?'

'I want to buy it. I've waited twenty-five years for this house.'

The man raised a russet eyebrow, and for some absurd reason I found myself babbling out the whole story of 'The House and I', to which he listened with admirable patience. I can't imagine he found it very interesting. When I'd finished my childish narrative, his level gaze met mine for a second time, and the resemblance to my brother was even more pronounced.

'Well, then,' he said solemnly, 'you'd best see Mr Ridley in the High Street. I've not got my own keys with me, or I'd show you round myself.' He stripped off one gauntlet and extended a hand in greeting. 'I'm Iain Sumner, by the way.'

'Julia Beckett.' I must have altered my expression at the sight of his hand, because he smiled again, looking down at the tiny lacerations marring his skin.

'Brambles,' he explained. 'They'd choke out my garden if I didn't thin them back. It's not painful,' he assured me, pulling the glove back on. 'I'd best be getting back to my work. Good luck with the house.'

'Thank you,' I said, but he was already out of earshot.

Five minutes later I was sitting in the offices of Ridley and Stewart, Estate Agents. I confess I don't remember much about that afternoon. I do recall a confusing blur of conversation, with Mr Ridley rambling on about legal matters, conveyances and searches and the like, but I wasn't really listening.

'You're quite certain,' Mr Ridley had asked me, 'that you don't want to view the property, first?'

'I've seen it,' I'd assured him. To be honest, there seemed no need for such formalities. It was, after all, my house. My house. I was still hugging the knowledge tightly, like a child hugs a present, when I knocked on the door of the rectory of St Stephen's, Elderwel, Hampshire, that evening.

'Congratulate me, Vicar.' I grinned at my brother's startled face. 'We're practically neighbours. I just bought a house in Wiltshire.'

Chapter Two

'Where does this one go, miss?'

The fair young mover's assistant hoisted an upholstered chair as easily as if it were a child's toy, and paused in the hallway for directions.

I was busy rummaging in one of the tidily packed boxes, trying to locate my faithful old teapot before the kettle I'd put on the kitchen stove came to a boil. I glanced over my shoulder, distracted.

'In my bedroom,' I told him. 'First room on your right at the top of the stairs. Aha!'

My hand closed over the familiar contour of the teapot's handle at the same instant that the kettle burst into full boil with a piercing whistle. Switching off the gas ring I spooned some loose tea into the pot, filled it with water and set it on the back of the stove to brew.

'Miss Beckett?' That was Mr Owen, the head mover, with another assistant in tow at the back door. His cheerful round face was pink with exertion. 'We've got your kitchen table here. Thought it might be best to bring it through the back – I'd hate to make a mark on that panelling in the front hall.'

I moved obligingly out of their way, pulling a box or two along with me.

'I've just put some tea on,' I said, 'if you and your men would like a cup. Oh.' I looked around, suddenly remembering. 'I haven't got any cups unpacked yet.'

'Never you mind, miss.' Mr Owen winked good-naturedly. 'I've got a box of disposable ones in the truck. Always come prepared, I do.'

The fair-haired young assistant was back again, looking perplexed. 'Are you sure you mean the *first* door on the right, miss? It doesn't look like a bedroom to me – it's awfully small and has an easel or something in it.'

I clapped a hand to my forehead and smiled in apology.

'Sorry, I meant the *third* door on the right. The big bedroom on the north side of the house.'

'Right, miss.' His face cleared, and he was off again.

'Always a bit of a panic, isn't it?' Mr Owen slid my table into position against the pantry wall. 'You'll get it sorted out soon enough. Right, I think that's all the furniture. Just the boxes left. I'll nip out and get those cups for our tea, then, shall I?'

He was a bit of a marvel, certainly the most organized man I'd ever met, and well worth the extra money I was paying for his services. When I'd bought the house three weeks ago, I hadn't given much thought to the matter of moving my belongings from London to Exbury. But when I returned to my flat in Bloomsbury and started packing up, I soon realized that professional assistance was called for. Apart from my prized Victorian bedroom suite – another inheritance from Aunt Helen – there was my lounge and kitchen furniture, all my studio supplies, my drafting table, and the few hundred books I'd picked up at sales and second-hand stores during my years in London. On the recommendation of a close friend, I had called Mr Owen, and he had come charging like a modern knight to my rescue.

In my flat, the neatly taped and labelled packing boxes had looked huge and overpowering. Here in the house, they were barely noticeable, dwarfed by the sheer proportion of the architecture and the spacious, sunlit rooms. I had been pleased to find the interior of the old house every bit as appealing as the exterior, and well suited to my traditional tastes.

One entered through the front door into a large front hall, panelled in richly burnished oak. 'Seventeenth-century', Mr Owen had pronounced at a glance, 'and very good quality.' Directly ahead, a heavy oak staircase set in the centre of the hall ascended several steps, paused for breath at a square landing, then executed a sharp ninety-degree turn to the left and continued its climb to the first floor. Doors to the sitting-room and the study opened off the hall to the left and right, respectively, while to the right of the staircase a narrow passage led through to the kitchen. Dining-room, kitchen and old-fashioned pantry occupied the back half of the ground floor, their large, bright windows looking out over the rolling green plain with its fresh sprinkling of early spring wild flowers.

There were four bedrooms upstairs. The large one, running the full length of the north side of the house above study and pantry, had been the obvious choice for my own use. It even had its own working fire-place, along with a sizeable cupboard nestled in the space under the attic stairs. I had selected the small back bedroom for my studio, and was content to leave the two front rooms unfurnished for the time being, to serve as storage areas until I was completely set-tled. Between my studio and my bedroom, opening onto the wide landing, was a full bath – quite a luxury to find in an older home.

There were a few cracks and creaks, naturally, some protestations from the pipes, and dampness had crumbled the plaster round the upstairs windows, but there was nothing that couldn't be put right, in time.

'It's a lovely old house you've got here,' Mr Owen said, affirming my own thoughts as he took a seat on the packing crates beside me and passed me a polystyrene cup. 'Built in the fifteen-eighties, you said?'

'That's what the house agent told me.' I nodded. I poured out strong tea for the mover and his two perspiring helpers, then settled back on my makeshift seat to enjoy my own steaming cupful. 'I don't know much about its history, I'm afraid.'

'Oh, the village folk will fill you in there, I've no doubt,' said Mr Owen sagely. 'Old houses like this always have a past. Interesting, most of 'em. You'll learn more over a pint in the local than you will out of any history book.'

'I'll remember that.'

The two younger men drank their tea in respectful silence, waiting patiently for Mr Owen to finish chatting and give them the signal to return to work. Eventually, after his second cup of tea, he rose to his feet. At precisely the same moment, a terrific bang echoed in the front hall, and I jumped in my seat.

'Just the front door, miss,' one of the younger movers explained. 'The hinges swing inward, see, and the latch is none too sturdy. Strong gust of wind'll blow it open.'

Mr Owen promptly examined the door, fitted the inside handle with a protective cover to avoid further damage to the panelled wall behind, and suggested I buy a new lock as soon as possible. 'Can't be too careful,' was his fatherly advice.

It took the three men less than an hour to unload and distribute the remainder of my belongings, and at half-past-two I found myself standing in the front doorway, giving a final wave to the retreating van and feeling, for the first time, very unsure of myself. And very much alone.

The enormity of what I'd just done suddenly struck me, with a force that neither my brother's outright scepticism nor my parents' gentler lectures on the telephone had been able to achieve.

I could do my work just as well from Exbury as I could in London, I'd told everybody. In fact, I would probably be more productive in Exbury, away from the distractions of the city. And property was, after all, a sound investment. The fact that I was exchanging a familiar environment and an established circle of friends for a community of strangers had never seemed to me to be very important. Until now. I felt a tiny pang of longing for my third floor flat, and for my neighbour Angie, down the hall, who could always be counted on for a cup of coffee and gossip in the mid-afternoon.

The longing vanished in an instant, though, as I turned from the hall into the study. It was a lovely, peaceful room, with dark panelled walls, rows of empty bookshelves smelling faintly of lemon oil, and a cosy-looking fireplace that corresponded to the one in my bedroom upstairs. Earlier that morning, sunlight had come spilling in through the curtainless window, falling in wide, slanting squares across the brown leather upholstery of my old sofa. Now the light was indirect, and dimly restful. Apart from the sofa, the only other pieces of furniture I'd added to this room were a matching armchair in front of the fireplace, and a simple walnut writing-desk and chair. At the moment, they were buried beneath the boxes of books and papers I'd brought with me.

It was tempting to begin my unpacking in here, but

I knew from experience how little it took to distract me. A favourite old book, joyfully discovered in the middle of a box, would mean my spending the rest of the afternoon in blissful, unproductive oblivion. Better to leave the study for last, I reasoned, and begin in the most logical and practical place – the kitchen.

I shut the study door reluctantly and retreated to the back of the house, where for the next few hours I attacked the packing boxes with a fervour that would have made my mother proud. The hard work left me, in the end, covered with dust, and longing – like the mole in my favourite children's story – for a breath of the fresh spring air.

With Mole's impulsiveness, I swung the back door wide and wandered outside, welcoming the gentle breeze that played upon my skin and lifted the curls from my damp forehead. I rubbed my palms on the legs of my jeans to get the worst of the dirt off, and stood for a moment with my hands on my hips, enjoying the feeling of well-earned freedom.

My gaze fell upon the tumbled pile of stones where Iain Sumner had been standing on the day I'd bought the house, and I altered my course towards it, interested.

It was some thirty yards or more distant from the house, well outside my own property line, and while it was therefore unlikely to have been part of a fence, it was far too symmetrical to be a natural feature. As I drew closer, I saw that the stones were arranged in an 'L' shape, the longer side of the 'L' running parallel to the back wall of my house. In places, the wall was not much shorter than my own height of five-foot-three, and in the shelter of the 'L' someone had carefully broken and cultivated the earth to make a garden. The dark soil was neatly furrowed and newly fertilized, ready for planting.

'So you've bought it.'

For the second time I jumped, and turned, at the sound of Iain Sumner's voice. He was not a small man, and it was a mystery to me how anyone could have crossed the yard behind me without my hearing them. Recovering quickly, I was able to greet him with my most brilliant smile. He was wearing a rough brown sweater over heavy work trousers, and a brown cap with a stained brim. He pushed the cap back on his head and his grey eyes smiled back at me.

'You've bought the house,' he repeated. It was a statement, not a question, but I answered it anyway.

'Yes.'

'Well, you've been all the talk of the village these past few weeks, I'd best warn you. Mr Ridley let out that you were an artist, and from London, so everyone's fair curious.' He grinned. 'If you don't have a few disreputable, bohemian friends to invite down for weekends, you'd best get some, else the whole village will be disappointed.'

I laughed. 'I'm afraid they'll find me very boring. And I don't have any bohemian friends.'

'Not even a disreputable relative?'

'They all moved to New Zealand. My parents are out there now, actually, on holiday, so the only person likely to visit me in the near future is my brother,' I confided. 'And he's a Vicar.'

'Ah. Well.' He accepted the information graciously, tilting his head to one side. 'What do you think of my garden?'

'Very nice,' I said honestly. 'This is your land, then?'

'No.' He shook his head. 'It belongs to a friend of

mine. I just do this as a favour to him. There's only room for a few flowers, nothing much.'

'And brambles,' I added, remembering his hands.

'Aye,' he grinned ruefully. 'And brambles. Goes along with the gardening, that does.'

I reached out a hand to touch the stone wall, liking the feel of the sun-warmed roughness beneath my fingers.

'What was this place?' I asked him.

'Used to be a dovecote, they tell me, for keeping pigeons. Not much left of it, now.'

'Is it very old?'

'As old as the house, I believe. Maybe older.'

'The people who lived here were farmers then, originally?'

'Tenant farmers, maybe.' He shrugged. 'The land you're standing on is manor land, and always has been to my knowledge.'

'I've an interest in old houses,' I confessed, still caressing the weathered stone with an absent hand, 'especially this one. I'd love to learn more about its history.'

'Ah,' he said, smiling, 'you're talking to the wrong person, then. I've not been here more than five years, myself. Vivien's the one you should ask.'

'Vivien?'

'Aye.' His eyes softened. 'Vivien Wells, at the Red Lion. A regular walking encyclopedia, she is. If she doesn't know it, it's not worth knowing.'

I wasn't really listening, because as I'd raised my head my attention had been captured by a solitary horse and rider who had appeared just over Iain Sumner's shoulder, in the distance. They were standing in the shadow of an oak, watching us. The horse was a large, powerful grey and the rider was a man, dressed in dark clothes, but they were too far away for me to see them clearly.

Iain Sumner narrowed his eyes. 'Is something wrong?'

'What?' I brought my gaze back to him guiltily. 'Sorry. No, I was just looking at that man.'

'What man?'

'That man on the horse, behind you,' I said, pointing.

He turned to look, but the shadow under the oak was empty.

I shook my head. 'He's gone now. A big man, on a grey horse.'

'Might have been Geoff,' Iain said slowly. 'That's manor land. Though I don't know that he has any greys in his stable.'

'It's not important,' I told him.

'Perhaps not.' He smiled. 'Well, I'd best leave you in peace. I just came back to get my spade.'

He retrieved the forgotten tool from its resting place in the corner of the wall and, wishing me a good evening, pulled his cap down over his eyes and strode off towards the road, whistling.

After a final look round, I went back into the house where, unable to recapture my previous energy, I ignored my earlier resolution and settled myself in the study. After unpacking nearly two boxes of books, I came across a dog-eared copy of Wilkie Collins' *The Moonstone*, and it was well past midnight when I finally dragged myself upstairs, bathed, and fell asleep exhausted, with the shadow of the poplar tree lying like a guardian across my bed.

Chapter Three

It wasn't difficult to locate Vivien Wells the next afternoon, in the bar of the Red Lion pub. This was the same pub where Tommy and I had stopped to ask directions all those years ago, its Tudor beams and plaster looking slightly cleaner than I remembered beneath a new thatched roof. Inside, the main bar was low-ceilinged and intimate, a little threadbare, perhaps, but comfortable, the old floor covered with a worn carpet that deadened the sound of conversation.

Apart from a small group of old men clustered around a corner table, I was the only other customer enjoying the pub's congenial atmosphere at that hour of the day. And of the two people keeping bar, only one was a woman.

Vivien Wells was tall and healthy-looking, close to my own age, with long honey-coloured hair, honest blue eyes and a quick dimpled smile. I liked her on sight.

She slid a gin and tonic across the bar to me and leaned her elbows on the scarred wood, tilting her head appraisingly.

'Iain said you were pretty,' she remarked without malice, and I shifted awkwardly on my stool.

'He said you were an encyclopedia,' I offered.

She laughed in genuine amusement. 'Praise indeed. And how are you enjoying Greywethers?'

I quirked an eyebrow. 'I'm sorry?'

'Your house,' she elaborated. 'That's its name.'

'I thought it was called Braeside. That was the name on the deed, surely?'

'Eddie's invention that,' she told me. 'The last owner. He thought it sounded grand, despite the obvious fact that we haven't a brae round here for miles. No, it was just plain Greywethers, when I was growing up, and that's what everyone still calls it.'

'Greywethers.' I tried the feel of it on my tongue. 'It sounds very romantic.'

'Uninspired, really.' Vivien Wells smiled at me. 'It's just an old name for the stone they used round here for building. Sarsen stone. You know, like the ones at Stonehenge. There used to be hundreds of them littered across the downs, and builders just took what they wanted.'

'Oh.'

'You've had your eye on it some time, Iain tells me?'

I nodded, wondering how much of my foolish story he had told her. Not much, I wagered, remembering those impassive, flint-grey eyes. Iain Sumner had not impressed me as the gossiping type.

'I saw it several years ago, and took a fancy to it,' I explained. 'Marvellous luck that it came up for sale. And at a price I could afford.' *Almost* afford, I corrected myself, thinking of my plundered savings.

'Well,' Vivien shrugged, picking up a glass and polishing it with a practised motion, 'there's not much demand for houses in this area. We've only got a few farms and a half-dozen shops – it's mostly pensioners living here now. I'm afraid you'll find us deadly dull after London.'

'London is overrated,' I said, but I was sure Vivien

Wells already knew that. 'Besides, I need the quiet for my work.'

'Of course.' She took up another glass and went on polishing. 'You're an artist, aren't you? Do you paint?'

'Watercolours,' I replied. 'Actually, I'm an illustrator. I paint pictures for books.'

'Really? Anything I'd know?'

'Not unless you read children's books. I did the *Llandrah* series with Bridget Cooper a few years back.'

'*Did* you? I've a six year old niece who's in love with those stories. Well, well.' Vivien raised her eyebrows, impressed. 'You don't mind if I spread that around, do you? It'd put some of the locals at ease.' She grinned. 'They've been worried you might turn out to be one of those modern sculptors. You know, great globs of twisted metal, and things.'

I shook my head, smiling. 'No, I don't mind.'

'I don't imagine they'll . . . hang on, would you excuse me a moment?'

A summons from the lively group at the corner table diverted her, and while she attended to them I downed another mouthful of gin and tonic and wriggled into a slightly more comfortable position on the hard wooden stool.

I had not slept well the night before. While my body had been exhausted, my ears had remained alert and sensitive to every unfamiliar sound within the lonely house: every creak of the attic stairs beside my bedroom, every drip of the leaking tap in the bath down the hall, every movement of tree branch sweeping across the slate roof overhead. I had drifted in and out of a fitful sleep, and woke more in need of my morning coffee than usual.

Nonetheless, I had managed to unpack most of the boxes in my study before finally taking a break and walking the short mile into town.

The Red Lion shared Exbury's High Street with a handful of shops and offices, a string of postwar cottages, and a few lovely old homes set back from the road and shielded from prying eyes by low stone walls and wrought-iron fences. The street itself was paved, but on the west side of it the old cobbled walk had been left untouched, lending a distinct charm to the village. There was also, I had noted with some pleasure, an old-fashioned wooden gateway, with benches and roof, which I assumed led to the church whose steeple was barely visibly above a screen of budding trees.

I wondered idly how old the church was, and must have spoken the question aloud, because Vivien Wells answered me, resuming her place behind the bar. 'It's Saxon, actually, parts of it, although it wasn't properly finished until the fifteen-hundreds.' She cast a friendly eye at my empty glass. 'Would you like another?'

'Maybe just a small one,' I conceded, pushing the glass towards her. 'You really are the local historian, then.'

Vivien smiled. 'I take an interest in history,' she said, 'and I had a grandmother who loved to talk. Iain said you were looking for information on your house, is that right? Well, I'm afraid I don't know too much about it, myself. My aunt would probably know more. The Randalls have lived there as long as I can remember, and they weren't exactly an exciting lot. I'm sure I can find something out for you, though. As a matter of fact . . .'

She turned to face her co-worker, who was lounging against the far end of the bar, reading the daily paper and smoking a cigarette.

33

'Ned,' she addressed him, 'didn't your father used to do some work up at Greywethers in old Mr Randall's time?'

Ned lifted his eyes from his paper, glanced briefly at me, smiled at Vivien, and called over his shoulder, 'Hey, Dad.'

One of the old men at the corner table raised his head in reply. 'What?'

'Viv wants to talk to you.'

Ned's father tottered obligingly over to the bar and was introduced to me as Jerry Walsh, retired plumber. Yes, he told Vivien, he had done a few jobs for old Bill Randall.

'He wanted the bath done up modern,' he said. 'All new pipes and everything. You'll never need to worry about your pipes, miss,' he added proudly, tapping his chest. 'I did a proper job, I did. Not like these young lads today.'

I chose not to mention the dripping tap, nor the water that ran shockingly brown when one first turned it on.

'You don't remember who the Randalls bought the house from, do you, Jerry?' Vivien asked him.

He frowned. 'I'm not sure . . . they bought it just after the First War, I think. Seems to me it was a military chap had it before. My brother Art might remember . . . Arthur!' He called another man over from the table.

Within ten minutes I was surrounded by all seven of them, overwhelming in their friendliness and their eagerness to be helpful. Working backwards, with a great deal of argument, they determined that Eddie Randall had inherited the house from his father William, in the early nineteen-fifties, and that William had bought the house in nineteen-twenty-one from a Captain Some-body, who had reportedly had two very pretty daugh-ters. Beyond that, nobody was exactly sure, and try as they might they could not remember any interesting episodes in the history of my house.

'Except for the ghost,' one of the men ventured.

'Ghost?' I echoed.

Vivien smiled. 'I'd clean forgotten,' she said.

'She's not been seen for years,' Jerry Walsh assured me.

'Ay, it must be a good thirty years now,' his brother put in. 'The Green Lady, wasn't it?' The other men nodded, and he went on. 'I never saw her myself, but plenty of folks did. Just a young woman, in a green dress. Used to appear in the garden at dusk.'

'I saw her once,' the man who had first spoken piped up. 'Fair scared the life out of me. She just stood there, looking right through me with those sad eyes . . .'

'Wasn't a harmful ghost,' Jerry Walsh cut in, with a reproving glance at the little man. 'She didn't do anyone no harm. Just stood in the garden, sometimes.'

So even the ghosts of Greywethers were boring, I thought to myself. No clanking of chains, no mournful howls at midnight . . .'

'Not like the ghosts up at the Hall, eh lads?' Arthur Walsh grinned, displaying a row of nicotine-blackened teeth. 'Now there's a lively lot of characters for you. I've never actually seen any of them, mind, but they say that—'

'Enough,' Vivien broke in, her tone good-natured. 'You'll be giving the girl nightmares.'

'Oh, that's all right.' I smiled. 'I love a good ghost story. Where is the Hall?'

One of the men jerked a thumb over his shoulder. 'Crofton Hall,' he said, 'The old manor house just the other side of the church. Have you not been up there?'

I confessed that I had not yet ventured any further than the offices of my estate agents, just opposite the Red Lion on the High Street. Several eyebrows rose amid a chorus of disbelieving exclamations.

'Well, you must see the Hall . . .'

'. . . written up in three guidebooks, it was . . .'

'. . . sure that young Geoff would be happy to give you a tour. Most of the house is open to the public, anyway. He just keeps the north wing for his private use.'

I yielded to the protests. 'I must take a tour, then, when I've finished settling in.'

Mollified, the men settled back and launched into a lively conversation on the topic of moving house, which I found highly entertaining in spite of the fact that I could barely get a word in edgewise.

At ten-minutes-to-four, all seven of them rose as one body, politely wished me good day, and filed out the door. Vivien Wells met my questioning look with a smile.

'Teatime,' she explained. 'Time for them to get the latest instalment of gossip from their wives. Though today I think it'll be the men that do most of the talking.'

'What do you mean?'

'I mean they'll be talking about you.' She grinned. 'You've a lot to learn about village life, you know. It's impossible to sneeze here without your neighbours popping in to say "bless you".'

'I'm sure I'll adjust.'

She nodded. 'I've no doubt. Actually, you seem to have made quite a hit with that lot today. Just you watch – tomorrow you'll have a string of visitors up to the house, with plates of cakes and potted geraniums, come to see how you're getting on.'

'I'll dust off the silver tea service,' I promised. 'As a matter of fact, I could use visitors tomorrow. I'm planning to shift some of the furniture in the sitting-room around, and I could do with an extra pair of hands.'

Vivien laughed. 'Do you need help, really?' she asked me. 'Because I'm sure Iain would be happy to lend a hand.'

'Heavens, no,' I said, raising a hand in protest. 'I was only joking.' A sudden thought struck me. 'What does Iain Sumner do, anyway? Is he a gardener?'

'Farmer,' she corrected me. 'He keeps sheep. Has a small apple orchard as well, but that's mostly a hobby.'

'Oh,' I said.

'Of course, he does have green fingers,' she went on. 'He put a lot of time into helping Geoff get the gardens up at the Hall in order, before they opened to the public. Geoff's father had let the place run down a bit, and the grounds were an awful mess. There's a full-time gardener up there now, to take care of things. Lovely rose garden they have – you really must see it in the summer.'

'I'm sure I shall,' I said. 'After all, we are neighbours, aren't we? My house backs right on to the manor lands, from what I've been told.'

'So it does. You'll like Geoff. He's a genuine aristocrat – his family came over with the Conqueror – but he's very down to earth, and great fun. Come to think of it, he may be able to tell you something about Greywethers. He did a lot of rooting about in the local history books when he was writing up the guide book for Crofton Hall.' She turned to pour herself a cup of coffee from the venemous-looking pot that sat brewing on the back of the bar. 'Unfortunately, he's on holiday at the moment, in France, but when he comes back I'll be sure to introduce you. In the meantime,' she added, stirring her coffee, 'I'll see what I can find out on my own from my aunt and the local grapevine.'

'Thanks, I'd appreciate that. How much do I owe you for the drinks?'

'Not a farthing.' She waved my money aside with a shake of her honey-blond head. 'They're on the house. My way of saying welcome to Exbury, if you like.'

'But surely . . . I mean, it's very nice of you, but . . .' I glanced towards the end of the bar, where Ned was still slumped over his paper, and Vivien followed my gaze with understanding.

'Oh, Ned's not the kind to tell tales to the boss,' she assured me. 'Even if he were, he wouldn't gain much by it, since I happen to *be* the boss.'

I stammered a quick apology and flushed a brilliant crimson. Vivien graciously ignored my embarrassment.

'Is your telephone connected yet? Good. What's the number?'

I told her, and she copied it down. 'Right,' she said. 'I'll give you a ring if I find out anything of interest. Here.' She passed me a box of matches. 'My number's on the back, if you need anything. Or you can just drop by, any time you get bored with unpacking. I always have time for a chat in the afternoon.' She looked me straight in the eye and smiled her quick, frank smile.

'I'm glad you've come to live here,' she said simply.

I smiled back, feeling strangely warm inside.

'So am I,' I told her.

* * *

I was still smiling as I walked home, enjoying the fresh vibrant feel of the late April breezes and the wonderful silence of the untravelled road. My house stood waiting to welcome me home, looking already a little less neglected to my biased eyes.

'Hullo, Greywethers,' I greeted it, as I came up the drive. At least I had learned the proper name for my house. And that I had a ghost. What had the men at the Red Lion called her? The Green Lady. Somewhere in the garden.

The question was, I asked myself, just where had the garden been? There certainly wasn't any trace of one now, at least not at the front of the house. Curious, I walked round to the back yard and had a look.

Not the dovecote, I decided. That garden was new. By the kitchen, perhaps, alongside the drive? The ground there certainly looked more level, but . . .

No. Not there. I turned my attention to the other side of the yard. There, I thought with certainty. One could even see the faint rises in the ground where the flower beds had been built up by loving hands. I crossed the yard and stood on the spot in triumph.

The sun had sunk lower in the sky, and the breeze that skimmed over me was decidedly chill. Hunching further into my sweater, I hugged myself for warmth, turning to face the distant line of trees.

The man on the grey horse was there, under the sheltering oak, watching me.

I raised my chin defiantly, and could have sworn that he smiled, although he was too far away for me to see his features clearly, let alone judge his expression. After a long moment, he wheeled his horse around and headed back in the direction of Crofton Hall, his dark outline swallowed by the shadows of the ancient trees.

The Green Lady forgotten, I went inside the house, taking particular care to bolt the kitchen door behind me.

Chapter Four

By noon the following day, I found myself wishing that I'd taken my own flippant advice and polished up the tea service. In fact, I was wishing that I'd had the foresight to actually *purchase* a tea service in the first place. As it was, I had to make do with my Brown Betty teapot and an assortment of china cups that didn't quite match their saucers, to serve my guests.

And there certainly had been guests. The first arrivals, at nine o'clock, had been Mr Ridley, the house agent, and his wife, who were evidently early risers as they brought with them a plate of homemade Bath buns, still warm from the oven. Close on their heels had come Jerry Walsh and his amiable wife Eva, with two jars of Eva's blackcurrant jelly; then Arthur and Marie Walsh bearing a plate of chocolate biscuits. Several others came and departed in a kind of blur, including a soft-voiced, elderly lady named Mrs Hutherson, who brought me two dozen buttery fruit scones and her best wishes. Everyone was very nice, very friendly, and very well informed.

'Children's books, isn't it, my dear?' Mrs Hutherson asked in her gentle voice. 'How clever of you.' Her blue eyes struck a familiar chord in my memory, but she had gone before I could grasp the connection.

The quiet couple who came last with a bottle of raspberry cordial benefitted from their position by being offered the best selection of treats. The coffee-table in my sitting-room was by this time so loaded with edible offerings that anyone would have thought I'd spent hours preparing for a neighbourhood tea party.

Any lingering doubts my visitors may have had regarding my respectability were put to rest, emphatically and unexpectedly, by the arrival of my brother, wearing his clerical collar and looking eminently pious. So pious, in fact, that I doubted whether any of his own parishioners would have recognized him.

Shortly after noon, when the crowd had cleared, Tom leaned back in his chair, linked his hands behind his head, and grinned.

'I congratulate you,' he said. 'My own neighbours didn't lay seige to me until I'd been in the village a week. How long have you been here, now? Two days?'

'I moved in on Tuesday, so this is my third day here. Feet off the coffee-table, please.'

'Sorry.' He moved his shoes obediently. 'I hope you don't mind my dropping in on you like this. I suppose I could have called first.'

'You couldn't have picked a better time,' I assured him warmly. 'It'll do wonders for my image. By teatime it'll be all over town that I'm related to a vicar.'

'Mmm. Or that you're having an affair with one.' Tom grinned again. 'Village people have terribly suspicious minds, you know.'

I ignored him. 'It's your day off, I take it?'

'Yes. I left the parish in the capable hands of my new curate, young Mr Ogilvie. You'd like him, Julia. He's much less tedious than his predecessor. Of course, his views may be a little progressive for my flock, but he means well.'

'Anything would be an improvement on your last curate,' I agreed with feeling. 'Michael something, wasn't it? Very low church, never smiled, always bubbling over with hellfire and damnation?'

'That's the one.'

'Whatever happened to him?'

'I managed to have him transferred to a parish up north. I felt I'd done my penance,' Tom said, smiling. 'Anyway, back to the subject of my day off. I promised the parents I'd stop in this week and see how you were getting on. How *are* you getting on?'

'Quite well, thanks. I've got most of the downstairs rooms sorted out, I think.'

'It looks very nice.' He let his gaze roam the sun-filled, spacious room. 'It really is a lovely house. I am impressed. Are you going to give me the grand tour, or' his gaze fell on the overloaded coffee-table, 'do I have to help with the washing-up first?'

I assured him that the washing-up could wait, and began the tour in the room we were in.

'Well, this, naturally, is the sitting-room,' I said. 'I need to buy a bigger carpet to protect this floor, and the curtains of course will have to go . . .'

'I see what you mean.' Tom eyed the garish floral chintz speculatively. 'The windows themselves are nice, though. And I genuinely like the fireplace. What's through here?' He indicated a connecting door on the far wall.

'Dining-room.' I led him through.

'Julia!' My brother's tone held admiration. 'Where on earth did you get that dresser?'

'It's quite something, isn't it? It came with the house.'

The dresser was late Victorian, solid walnut, and nearly nine feet tall, its top brushing the plastered ceiling of the dining-room. I suspected it had come with the house only because it would have needed

43

a crane to budge it. The single piece of furniture so completely dominated the long room that one barely noticed the lack of table or chairs. On either side of the dresser, two tall windows looked out over the back lawn, adding to the impression of stately elegance.

From the dining-room we walked through a swinging door into the scrubbed and spartan kitchen with its old-fashioned pantry, then out through the narrow passage-way into the panelled front hall. After a brief detour into the study, where Tom might easily have settled himself for the remainder of the day had I not dragged him out again, we climbed the angled staircase to the upper floor.

'Now, I haven't done anything up here since the day I moved in,' I warned him, 'so some of the rooms may be a little messy. Just so you don't expect much.'

'Blast these ceilings.' Tom ducked too late, and stepped onto the landing rubbing the back of his head. 'Made for midgets. How many bedrooms do you have?'

'Four. But I'm only using two of them. These two,' I indicated the closed doors to our left, 'are just for storage, at present.'

'Very sensible.' Ever curious, Tom poked his head inside the first room and peered around. It was a long, narrow room, separated from my own by the attic stairs that ran behind the end wall. The light coming in the twin windows was partially blocked by the branches of a pear tree growing close against the front of the house. The other storage room occupied the front south corner, and the fact that it had only one window was compensated for by the presence of yet another fireplace.

'You'll have to learn to chop wood, love,' my brother commented, and I pulled a face.

'Come off it, Tom. You've seen me light a fire before. The whole house would go up like a roman candle.'

44

Tom grinned, and bent to examine the carved wooden mantelpiece. Leaving him there, I moved on ahead to the next door, which belonged to the small, back corner room that I'd chosen to use as my studio. I hadn't bothered to check on my supplies or equipment yet, having determined not to think about work for this first week, but it suddenly struck me that, since Tom was here, he might be coerced into helping me assemble my drawing board.

I was not normally inept when it came to routine mechanical tasks, but this particular drawing board – devised by a sadistic Swedish designer – always managed to defeat my best efforts, and left me sitting frustrated and helpless amidst a jumble of chrome poles, assorted tools, and one less bolt than the directions called for.

Come to think of it, I thought, brightening, I hadn't actually *seen* the movers carrying the table upstairs. Maybe it had been lost in the move. I pushed open the studio door, took two steps into the room, and stopped dead in confusion.

There was nothing there. Nothing of mine, anyway. Except for a low, narrow bed pushed against the back wall, and an antique clothes press in one corner, the room was completely empty.

'Well, that's odd,' I said out loud.

'What's odd?' my brother called back.

'This furniture isn't mine,' I told him, moving back across the hall to the front bedroom. 'They must have put my studio things in one of these rooms instead. There should be an easel and my drawing board and that great ugly chair. I just can't imagine where . . .'

My voice trailed off as I rummaged amid the boxes, and my brother's shadow moved past me into the hall.

'Julia,' he said, a moment later. 'Come here.'

I found him standing in the doorway of my studio, hands on hips. 'Now,' he said, as I joined him, 'what do you see?'

I looked, blinked hard, and looked again. It was all there – the easel, the studio furniture, the untidy boxes of paints and brushes and paper . . . everything, just as it should be. Moreover, there was no sign to be seen of the bed or clothes press.

'You haven't been nipping into the cooking sherry, have you?' Tom joked.

'But, Tom,' I shook my head, bewildered, 'these things weren't here a minute ago, honestly.'

My brother looked down at me, his expression concerned, and when he finally spoke his voice had lost its mocking edge. 'Listen,' he said, 'why don't we leave the rest of the tour until later? You must be exhausted after this morning.'

'I'm not crazy.'

'Of course you're not. Feel up to a pot of tea?'

I trailed unhappily after him down the stairs.

'That room was empty when I looked.'

'I'm not saying it wasn't. I'm not saying that you didn't see what you said you saw. I just think there's probably a good *reason* why you saw what you said you saw.'

'I see.' I said. 'Such as?'

Tom lifted his shoulders in a shrug. 'I don't know. You're tired, you've been pushing yourself too hard . . . when did you get to bed last night?'

'Late,' I admitted. 'But I can't believe that has anything to do with . . .'

'And what time were you up this morning?'

'Just after six. But . . .'

'There you are,' he said, raising his hands to emphasize his point. 'You're not getting enough sleep.'

I was familiar with my brother's moods. I waited until the tea was brewed and we were sitting facing each other across the kitchen table, before I dared to contradict him.

'As a matter of fact,' I told him firmly, 'I am getting plenty of sleep. And I'm not tired, honestly. I've not done any real work since I moved in here, I've only unpacked a few boxes.'

'You look tired.'

'Tom,' I smiled at his obstinacy, 'listen to me. I am very well rested. I've been sleeping like a log. And dreaming every night, come to that.'

'Really? That's rather unusual for you, isn't it? I thought you hardly ever dreamed.'

'Maybe it's the country air.'

'What sort of dreams?'

'I really can't remember most of them,' I said frowning slightly as I drank my tea. 'One of them was about a comet, I think. Yes, that was it . . . there were two comets, one right after the other, and everyone was saying how that meant something terrible was going to happen. What does Freud have to say about comet dreams?'

'Not Freud.' Tom shook his head. 'Jung. And I really haven't the foggiest idea. I didn't study psychology. Which reminds me,' he sat forward suddenly, 'Rod Denton is giving a dinner party Saturday week at his house in London.'

'How can my comet dream possible remind you of Rod Denton's dinner party?'

'Rod *did* study psychology at college,' Tom explained. 'Among other things.' Roderick Denton had come down

47

from Oxford at the same time as my brother, but had been destined for rather more worldly pursuits. He had married the daughter of an Earl, inherited a house in Belgravia, and was doing quite well for himself in the financial world.

'Anyhow,' Tom continued, 'his parties are usually rather fun. I thought you might care to come with me. Might do you good, getting out for a day.'

'You make it sound as though I'd been cooped up here for weeks.'

'I only thought,' he shot me a dark, sideways glance, 'that you could use a break from all this work.'

'Well, I could, actually,' I conceded, draining my teacup with a smile. 'Thanks. Saturday week, you said? What time?'

'Cocktails at six-thirty. You remember where he lives?'

I nodded. 'I'll meet you there, then, if you like. I'm sure my friend Cheryl would be happy to put me up for the night. I can park the car at her place, up in Islington, and take the tube down to Rod's. OK with you?'

'Fine.'

'Right. Are you ready for the rest of my guided tour?'

'Are you sure you feel up to it?'

'Of course. Besides,' I said putting an affectionate arm around my brother's shoulders, 'I want you to take a look at my drawing board.'

He frowned. 'I've already seen your drawing board.'

'A really *close* look, if you know what I mean.'

Tom caught my meaning, and sighed heavily. 'Don't bat your eyes at me, love, I know entrapment when I see it.' He led the way back up the stairs to the first floor, and I heard a shockingly irreligious oath as his dark head connected a second time with the low ceiling.

'And a good thing it is for you,' he said, turning to me with a broad grin, 'that your neighbours weren't around to hear *that*.'

Later that afternoon, I found myself once again on the narrow paved road leading into the village, walking with my face turned towards the wind and revelling in the cool, fragrant country air that blew the packing-box dust from my lungs.

Tom had been gone for nearly an hour. The remainder of his visit had passed smoothly – I had no more hallucinations, and to my great relief, every room we entered had appeared exactly as I had left it. I decided that my brother must have been right, after all. Tom, I reasoned, had an irritating habit of always being right. Perhaps I had been pushing myself too hard, trying to do too much all at once.

I had planned, after he left, to clear away the remains of the morning's impromptu tea party, do the washing-up, and try to tighten the leaking tap in the bath, but instead I decided to take Tom's advice and get away from the house for a while.

My original thought had been to drop in at the Red Lion for a light meal and a friendly chat with Vivien, but the sun was shining and the road was beckoning, and the more I walked the more I felt like walking.

I passed by the Red Lion, and the offices of Ridley and Stewart, Estate Agents, and the huddled cluster of shops. A short distance further on a massive stone portal rose up on my right, its iron gate flung invitingly wide. A narrow dirt path, tidily edged and shaded by a tightly woven canopy of closely planted trees, curved away into the cool shadows. This, I correctly assumed, must be the entrance to the famed manor house.

Resisting the temptation to trespass, I stuck to the cobbled walk of the High Street. Time enough to see the manor another day, I told myself. Besides, the man who owned the Hall was away, Vivien had said. In France. Better to wait until he returned, and have a proper inside tour. I walked on to the quaint wooden covered gate that I'd admired earlier, and pushing open the swinging half-door, entered the silent churchyard.

There are few places in England so peaceful or oddly beautiful as a country churchyard, where the ivy grows thickly in the shadowy corners and trails across the weathered stones, their carved faces almost unreadable after countless years of exposure to the sun and rain. Many of the stones here were tilted at a precarious angle, leaning to one side like drunken sentries. Some of them had toppled from their post completely and had been propped with care against the outside wall of the church.

The church itself was small and plain, a squat building of sunbleached stone topped by a square, crenellated tower. A faded, hand-lettered placard by the door proclaimed it to be the Church of St John, with services on Sundays and Wednesday evenings. One push against the thick oak door and it swung obligingly inward on its heavy iron hinges, showing me an equally plain interior that nonetheless gave the impression of soaring space. The late afternoon sunlight streamed in through narrow stained glass windows and bathed the bare stone walls in a warm, glowing light.

My footsteps sounded uncommonly loud, a modern intrusion into this peaceful, holy place, as I walked slowly into the centre of the church, reading the distinguished names on the square stone markers beneath my feet: Staynor, Alleyn, Hatch, de Mornay . . .

A violent explosion of sound brought my head up and around with a start, my heart leaping wildly against my ribcage. It was only a pigeon, trapped for a moment behind the rood screen, thrashing out in panic before it could work its way clear and beat a hasty exit through the half-open door.

My heart slowly returned to normal, leaving me feeling slightly dizzy, with a dull ringing in my ears, as though I were about to faint. The sunlit interior of the little church felt suddenly as stale and airless as a tomb, and I stumbled back outside, gulping air in deep, unsteady breaths.

In my confusion, I turned my back to the High Street and found myself in a shaded dirt lane, flanked by large, overhanging beech trees that rustled gently in the shifting breeze. My face was damp with perspiration, and a steady pounding sound rose above the ringing in my ears as I paused to rest, supporting myself with an outstretched hand upon one gnarled tree trunk. The pounding gradually became louder, more rhythmic, until it was recognizable as the sound of a horse's hooves striking the tightly packed soil. Looking up, I saw a solitary horse and rider approaching. A grey horse, carrying a tall man in dark clothing.

I blinked, my vision blurring, and the horse changed colour, no longer grey now but chestnut, with a darkly flowing mane and tail. The man astride the horse changed, too, subtly, like clay poured from one mould into another, his outline indistinct in the mottled shadows of the lane. They drew nearer still, and still I neither moved nor spoke, standing rooted to my spot and staring like the village idiot.

Closer and closer the spectre came, until the horse was pulled to a halt in front of me. I looked up. The sun was positioned directly behind the rider. Filtering through the trees, it created a blinding halo around the man's dark head, and I sensed, rather than saw, his smile.

'Hello,' he said. 'You must be my new neighbour. I'm Geoffrey de Mornay.'

I momentarily forgot the rules of proper etiquette. I raised my hand, smiled up at him, and fainted dead away at his horse's feet.

Chapter Five

It was not, I decided, as I sat on Geoffrey de Mornay's chesterfield with my head between my knees, the most auspicious of meetings. Whatever impression I had hoped to make on my illustrious neighbour, this most certainly was not it.

'I've brought you some water,' he said, re-entering the room. 'No, don't sit up just yet. How are you feeling?'

'Fine.' My voice, of necessity, was muffled.

He pressed the glass of water into my hand, and I lifted my head to take a sip, the action providing me with my first proper look at my host.

Even without – or perhaps in spite of – his cultured voice, well-cut clothes and expensive surroundings, Geoffrey de Mornay would have been classified by my former colleague Bridget as 'prime'. Bridget would have noticed his tall, athletic frame and the brilliant flash of his smile. I noticed the classic lines of his bone structure and the quiet depth of his hazel eyes, set beneath level dark brows that matched exactly the seal-brown shade of his hair.

'Thank you,' I said, giving him the brightest smile I could muster. I wasn't sure how long I had been out, but it must have been only a matter of minutes, as the sun was still pouring in through the large bay window opposite me. I had a dim recollection of being lifted and carried a short distance, and then nothing more until a few moments ago, when I had opened my eyes, tried to stand, and been unceremoniously pushed back down into my current undignified position.

'You're welcome.' He took the chair across from me, watching my face warily as if he expected me to leap suddenly to my feet. 'I'm sorry if we frightened you. Brutus is rather a big horse, and I often forget . . .'

'It wasn't your fault, honestly. I've been burning the candle at both ends the past few days, and it just caught up with me, that's all.'

'You're sure you're not ill?'

'Positive.' My tone was firm, and after studying my face for a moment, he smiled.

'Then perhaps we could try those introductions a second time,' he suggested, leaning forward in his seat and extending his hand. 'Geoffrey de Mornay, at your service.'

'Julia Beckett.' I returned the handshake. Raising myself cautiously to a sitting position, I tried to salvage the situation by making conversation. 'De Mornay . . . I've just been looking at some of your ancestors in the church, then. Yours must be one of the oldest families here.'

'That depends on your interpretation,' he replied with a shrug. 'There were de Mornays at Crofton Hall in the reign of the first Elizabeth, but they sold off a century or so later. My father waited years for the Hall to come up for sale, and when it finally did he bought it back. He was a great lover of family history.'

I looked around in appreciation, noting how the long, sunlit room with its ornate plaster ceiling and elegantly papered walls exuded all the charm and gentility of a bygone era. 'It's wonderful to preserve these old houses,' I said.

'And expensive,' he said, tempering my romance with

realism. 'Not to mention impractical. Rather a lot of room, for one person.'

'Is that why you opened the house up for tours?'

'No.' He smiled again, amused. 'No, I'm not that civic minded, I'm afraid. I applied for a government grant a few years back, to do some renovations, and one of the conditions of my being given the money was that I open up the place to the public.'

'Nice for the public,' I pointed out. 'Several people have told me that it's well worth the price of admission.'

'It is rather a lovely house. I'd give you a tour right now, for free, but you hardly look up to it.'

I *was* feeling rather weak in the knees, but I preferred not to speculate upon the reason why. I smiled. 'Another time, perhaps.'

'Certainly. Some time next weekend, maybe, when I'm a little more organized myself. I've just come back from holiday.'

'I know. France, wasn't it?'

Geoffrey de Mornay smiled, a slow, spreading smile that was unconsciously seductive, and mildly accusatory. 'You've been to the Red Lion,' he said. 'Yes, I keep a boat in the harbour at Antibes, in the south of France. I like to get down to take her out once or twice a year. Nice to get out of the rain every now and then.'

'And who takes care of the Hall for you, when you're not here?'

'I've got a terribly efficient staff to manage things for me.' He leaned back in his chair, shifting the position of his broad shoulders. 'Two tour guides, a house-keeper, a part-time cleaner, a gardener – depending on the season – and a man to take care of the horses. It's quite an operation, really.'

'Of course!' I nodded in sudden comprehension. 'That explains it.'

'Explains what?'

'Sorry. I've just solved a mystery, that's all. I've been seeing a man riding in your fields, a dark man on a grey horse. It must have been your groom.'

'Not if it was a grey horse. I only have chestnuts and bays in my stables.' He ran his thumb idly down the arm of his chair, smoothing the fabric, and his voice, when he spoke, was casual. 'You're sure it was a grey?'

'Horses may not be my forte,' I told him, 'but I do know my colours.'

He grinned. 'I forgot. You're an artist, aren't you? Well, I wouldn't worry about it. I'm not so medieval about my property rights. If someone wants to use my bridle path, they're welcome to it. What did he look like?'

I shrugged my shoulders. 'I really didn't get a good look at him, he was too far away. He was fairly tall, I think – although it's hard to tell on horseback, isn't it? He wore dark clothing, and I rather fancy his hair was long.'

'Sounds like one of the chaps from the hostel. There's a youth hostel about three miles west of here,' he explained. 'Quite a large one. Lots of tourists passing through. They hire horses out, sometimes.'

'I see.' It certainly sounded sensible to me. I finished drinking my glass of water, and Geoffrey de Mornay stirred in his chair.

'Would you like another drink?' he offered. 'Something more substantial?'

'Oh, no. I'm fine, honestly.' I set my glass down on the end table beside me and rose awkwardly to my feet, running a hand through my untidy hair. 'You've been

56

very kind, but I really ought to go. I've taken up enough of your time.'

'Not nearly. But I never argue with my neighbours.' He stood up as well, dwarfing me, and gallantly inclined his head. 'Come on, I'll show you out.'

I followed him through a narrow, dark passage to the side door, turning on the threshold to thank him once again.

'My pleasure,' he assured me, propping one shoulder against the door jamb and folding his arms across his chest. 'Rather a nice change from my normal daily routine. I don't often have comely young maidens throwing themselves at my feet.'

'Yes, well,' I said, colouring, 'that won't happen again.'

He smiled down at me, and after a final handshake I made my departure. I had almost reached the end of the neatly-edged walk when he spoke.

'What a pity,' he said, but I don't think I was meant to hear it.

'You want to watch out, my love,' my brother said sagely when I told him the story of my meeting with Geoffrey de Mornay. 'The Lord of the Manor has certain historical privileges, you know. Pick of the village virgins, and all that.'

'Don't talk rot,' was my response.

It was a week later, Saturday evening, and we were sitting in the unmistakably posh surroundings of Roderick Denton's house in London. The dinner party had been a great success, as all Rod's social ventures inevitably were, and not for the first time I had to admit that my brother's advice had been spot on.

The evening had provided me with a welcome break

from the seemingly unending cycle of unpacking and decorating, and I felt nearly human again. On top of which, I finally had an excuse to wear dressy clothes, in place of the jeans and the floppy shirts I'd been living in for the past fortnight. It gave me a deliciously sophisticated, grown-up feeling. If only I hadn't been so dreadfully bored . . .

Two weeks out of London, I thought, and already the talk flowing around this room seemed unconnected to me, and narcissistically shallow. Tom caught me yawning and nudged me playfully.

'I told you to go easy on the wine,' he reminded me.

'Sorry,' I yawned again. 'I think I've reached my limit, Tom. I have to go.'

'OK. I'll see you to the door.'

'Julia, my dear.' Roderick Denton descended upon me with outstretched arms, blocking my escape route. 'I'm so glad you came.'

I hugged him back. 'Thanks for the invitation. I've had a wonderful time. And be sure to thank Helen for me.'

'You're not leaving, already?'

'I'm afraid so. I have a friend waiting up for me.'

'Oh?' He raised a gossip's eyebrow. 'Spending the night in town, are you?'

'Yes, with my friend Cheryl. You remember Cheryl, don't you, Rod? She works at Whitehall.'

He frowned, but only for a moment. 'Red hair?' he checked. 'Quite intelligent? Lives in Camden Town?'

'Islington, now,' I corrected him. 'She's had a rise in pay.'

Rod ought to appreciate that, I reasoned, being a social mountaineer himself. It was rather underhand of me to use Cheryl as an excuse for leaving the party. She was not, in actual fact, waiting up for me. She wasn't even in London. Her boyfriend was treating her to a weekend in the Lake District, and she'd cheerfully given me the loan of her flat for the evening, along with her cat and the use of her parking space.

'If you wait a few minutes, I can find someone to give you a lift,' Rod offered, ever the considerate host.

'No, thanks.' I shook my head. 'It's just as quick to take the tube. And you,' I poked Tom in the arm 'should be leaving, too. You'll sleep through your sermon tomorrow.'

'Along with the rest of the congregation,' Rod said, and I giggled.

Tom smiled at me, indulgently. 'Laugh it up,' he invited. 'I'm not letting you take the tube in this state, you know. I'll find you a cab.'

'I don't want a cab,' I protested. 'I want to take the tube. Or walk. I fancy a bit of fresh air.'

But Tom was resolute. He saw me down to the street, hailed a cab and bundled me into it, giving the driver directions to Cheryl's flat. As soon as the cab had turned the first corner, I leaned forward and tapped the driver on the shoulder. 'I've changed my mind,' I told him. 'Embankment tube station, please.'

I should have kept the cab, after all. The entrance to the tube station was clogged with young people, and the press of bodies steeped in stale beer and Saturday night sweat made me feel distinctly claustrophobic. I had intended to take the northern line straight up to Islington, but suddenly the garishly lit tunnels of the underground held little appeal. There really was no hurry, I told myself. I could always stroll a little way along the river, and pick up the circle line at a station farther on. With a final deciding glance at the boisterous crowd, I turned my steps towards the softer streetlamps of the embankment and the myriad twinkling reflections of the slumbering Thames.

Behind me, back by Westminster Bridge, curved the impressive façade of the old County Hall building and ahead the familiar dome of St Paul's, sharply illuminated, rose like a beacon against the night sky. It was a beautiful night, surprisingly peaceful and quite mild in temperature, despite the humidity. I walked on, past Cleopatra's Needle with its watchful Sphinxes, past the looming bulk of Somerset House and the more majestic gateway leading to the Temple and the Inns of Court.

At first, I enjoyed the sense of solitude. But after several minutes my wine-fogged complacency slowly gave way to a creeping wariness. It was, after all, quite late on a Saturday evening, and as lovely as the embankment might be, it was not the wisest place for a woman to walk alone. I quickened my step, uneasy. At the very next tube station, I promised myself, I would go underground. I had walked far enough, for one night. Besides, I had drunk slightly more than I ought to, and I was feeling terribly tired. My steps swayed a little, unsteadily, and my head felt curiously light, filled with an odd, ringing sound.

A minute later I'd given up the thought of taking the tube altogether, and altered my course away from the river in search of a cab. But there didn't seem to be a single cab in sight, and the more I searched the maze of streets, the more lost I became. The streets narrowed first to lanes, and then alleys, becoming progressively darker and rougher underfoot, while the ringing in my ears grew steadily louder. After several wrong turnings, I finally came across one street that looked familiar – a crooked little street of oak-framed houses with plaster walls, their crowded overhanging top stories painted and carved. As I passed a sheltered doorway, a small, ragged boy took a step forwards, raising his lantern.

'Do you want light, mistress?' he asked me, hopefully, but I shook my head and hurried on.

A little further down the street, I stopped at one of the huddled houses and knocked urgently at the door. It seemed a long time before my summons was finally answered by a small, middle-aged woman with kindly blue eyes and a plain face. She was in her bedclothes, and wore a shawl wrapped round her head and shoulders to ward off the night chill.

Seeing me, her eyes widened in astonishment. 'My child! What are you doing abroad at this hour of the night? Come inside . . . come inside and warm yourself!'

I was practically dragged from the threshold and deposited in front of a sputtering fire. I stared at the flames, feeling a hollow cold that the fire's warmth could not touch.

'My mother is ill,' I said.

The woman's eyes met mine, and there passed between us an anguished understanding more eloquent than words.

'When?' she asked.

'She was struck suddenly.' My voice was wooden. 'At dinner. Already she is fevered and knows me not. The servants sent me from the house.'

'They did wisely. You cannot return there.' She sat down, heavily, beside me. 'Nor can you stay here. My neighbours fear the sickness too much. They would make trouble.' She was silent a long moment thinking. 'You will go to the country,' she said, at last. 'To your mother's elder brother.'

'My Uncle Jabez?' I bit my lip.

She knew the cause of my misgivings. 'He is not like your Uncle John, God rest his gentle soul. But he is highly thought of, and an honest man. I will arrange a coach in the morning. Have you brought nothing away with you?'

I shook my head, and she frowned. 'You will need clothes. My girl Ellen is very like you in size. She may have something suitable.'

She rose from her stool and bustled towards the narrow stairway. I moved in feeble protest.

'Aunt Mary . . .'

'Mariana.' Her voice was firm. 'This is the Lord's will. It is decided.'

The dancing fire flickered, dimmed and disappeared.

I blinked. I was standing in Blackfriars Lane, among the rubble of construction, in a dark and empty lot. It had begun to rain, a cold, relentless spring rain, and a passing car spat up a freezing spray that sent a chill through my entire body and set my teeth chattering. A short block above me, yellow light and laughter mixed with music poured out onto the street through the open door of the local pub, and I turned my stumbling steps in that direction.

The cab company was quick to respond to my telephone call. Settling myself in the back seat for the short ride up to Islington, I shrank into a shadowed corner, well out of the light of the swiftly passing streetlamps.

Inside the cab, out of the rain, it wasn't cold at all; but I went on shivering and shivering, as if I would never get warm.

Chapter Six

'Mariana.' Vivien Wells rolled the name around on her tongue like a wine of questionable vintage, tilting her fair head back with a frown. 'No, I don't remember hearing about anyone by that name. Do you, Ned?'

Without looking up from his newspaper, the barman shook his head, and Vivien carried on balancing the cash register.

'It's rather an unusual name, isn't it?' she said. 'Old-fashioned.'

'Funny you should put it like that.' I smiled into my glass of orange juice, and she looked up from her work with interest.

'Been finding old love letters tucked beneath the floorboards, have you?' she asked.

'Something like that. It's really not important.' I set my glass down on the bar and glanced towards the empty table in the corner.

'I see the lads aren't in today.'

Vivien followed my gaze and smiled. 'It's early yet.'

I looked at my watch and saw, with some surprise, that it was only half-twelve. Admittedly a little too early for the good people of Exbury to be heading off to the pub, especially on a Sunday. To me, though, it felt as if it were already the middle of the afternoon.

I had slept badly the night before. Slept, perhaps, was not the right word, since I had spent most of the night staring wide-eyed into the darkness, watching the glowing digital display on the bedside clock count off the minutes, one by one.

I had re-lived those strange and frightening moments in Blackfriars Lane, turning them over and over in my mind until I felt I must be going mad. It was not the sort of experience I could talk to anyone about, really. Tom might have listened, but this was Sunday, and Tom was unobtainable on a Sunday. Over the breakfast table in the lonely London flat, Cheryl's cat had stared blankly back at me.

'What do you think?' I had asked it. 'Am I losing my mind?' The cat merely went on staring. No answers to be had from that quarter, I decided. And so I had come home.

Strange, I thought, how this little sleepy village had so quickly come to feel like home. Stranger still how London, where I had spent so many years, now seemed oddly foreign and remote.

'Nice to get back to town for a bit?' Vivien was asking me, tapping into my thoughts with uncanny accuracy.

'Do you know,' I said slowly, 'I was just thinking how nice it was to be *out* of London. To be home.'

She nodded her understanding. 'Live here long enough, and London starts to seem pretty unreal. People are so tense there. I often wonder how anyone can sustain that kind of tension, day after day. What do you think, Iain?'

I started in my seat, and turned. As always, I had not heard his approach.

'Me? I've no fondness for London,' Iain Sumner said, leaning an elbow on the bar and crossing one heavily booted foot over the other.

'You move like a damned cat,' I accused him peevishly, my nerves raw from lack of sleep. He turned his head to look at me, raising an inscrutable eyebrow.

'I'm sorry,' he said evenly. 'D'ye want me to whistle, or something, to let you know I'm coming?'

'It'd be a thought.' Vivien laughed, her blue eyes dancing. I had the distinct impression that she liked Iain Sumner very much. 'You want your usual poison?'

'Aye,' he nodded, watching as she poured him a foaming dark pint of bitter. He drew a crumpled packet of cigarettes from the pocket of his shirt, shook one loose, and looked enquiringly at me. 'D'ye mind?'

'If you smoke, you mean?' I shook my head. 'Not at all.'

'Thanks.' He lit the cigarette, cupping the match in his soil-stained fingers and ignoring Vivien's disapproving look.

'I thought you gave that up,' she said.

'Aye. So does my mother.' He met her eyes innocently. 'I'm on an errand, as it happens, from the Hall. Geoff says he's found all the papers you were asking about, the ones he used to research the manor's history, and would you like to invite him over for coffee this evening, so he can show the stuff to you and Julia, here.'

'Would I like to invite him over? Of all the cheek!' Vivien grinned broadly. 'What, are peasants not allowed up to the Hall on Sundays?'

Iain raised his pint and shrugged. 'More likely the cleaner's not been in lately. You know Geoff. And he made quite a mess hunting about for those papers.'

'All right,' Vivien capitulated, 'tell him to consider himself invited. That is, if Julia's free this evening. Are you?'

I nodded.

'Good. Shall we say seven o'clock? Iain?'

His eyebrows rose again. 'Am I invited as well?'

'You're always invited,' she told him.

'You'd best be feeding me, then.'

'I'll make sandwiches,' Vivien promised solemnly. 'By the way, does the name "Mariana" mean anything to you?'

'Shakespeare,' was his instant, and unexpected, response.

'Shakespeare?' I echoed, and he nodded.

'Angelo's sneaky fiancée in *Measure for Measure*.'

'Oh.'

'Should it have meant something else?'

'It's nothing really,' I said. 'I just came across the name in a . . . letter, when I was cleaning up, and wondered if anyone knew who she was.' No-one noticed my little stumble over the lie.

'Well, I'm probably not the best person to ask about things like that,' Iain conceded, with a slight smile. 'Your Aunt Freda might know,' he told Vivien. 'Or one of the lads.' He nodded towards the empty table in the corner.

'It's really not important,' I said again. I was almost sorry that I'd asked Vivien about it in the first place. After all, my strange experience in Blackfriars Lane last night might simply have been the product of too much drink, or too much stress . . . or some latent thread of insanity that was woven into the fabric of my ancestry. Either way, the chances were slim that the young woman Mariana and her fussing Aunt Mary had ever existed. At least, I preferred to think so. Because if there really *had* been a Mariana, then that would mean that I . . .

'Right,' Iain set his empty glass down on the bar with a satisfied thump, interrupting my thoughts. 'I'm off.'

'You won't forget to deliver my message to Geoff?' Vivien asked, and Iain turned at the door.

'No, I won't forget to deliver your message to Geoff. You know,' he grinned, 'one or the other of you might learn to use the telephone, and save my aching legs.'

'The walk'll do you good,' she shot back.

'No doubt. I'll see you both tonight, then.'

'He's really a wonderful guy,' Vivien said, as the door banged shut behind him.

'And he reads Shakespeare.'

She grinned. 'That surprised you, didn't it? Iain read English at Cambridge, believe it or not. That's how he and Geoff met each other.'

'Really? And now he keeps sheep?'

'Mmm. He's a farmer at heart, is Iain. He could have done a lot of things with his life – I mean, he's fairly well set financially, and he's bloody brilliant, when he wants to be. But I think he's happiest mucking around in the dirt.'

'And what did Geoffrey de Mornay study at Cambridge?' I asked her, with what I hoped was the right degree of nonchalance.

'Politics, I think. Not that he needed to. There never was much question where Geoff's future was concerned.' She smiled. 'His grandfather started Morland Electronics.'

'I see.' It was a bit of a jolt. The blood-red Morland logo was nearly as recognizable as the silhouette of Stonehenge, and almost as awe-inspiring. From a small wartime company producing radio equipment, Morland had grown into one of the largest of Britain's multinational firms. Its annual earnings, I guessed, must amount to billions of pounds.

'You haven't met him yet, have you?' Vivien asked.

'Yes I have, as a matter of fact. Last Thursday evening. We sort of bumped into each other in the lane behind the church.'

'*Did* you, now? Funny he didn't mention it.' She eyed me curiously. 'Damn good looking, isn't he? I often think it isn't fair, one person having all that money and a face like that.'

'I imagine he's got every girl in the village chasing after him,' I said. It was a shameless fishing expedition, and Vivien smiled again.

'I chased him, myself,' she admitted, 'when I was at school. You think he's something now, you ought to have seen him then. He'd been five years in California and he had a smashing tan, even spoke with a bit of an American accent.' She half-closed her eyes, appreciatively. 'But of course, he lost that rather quickly. Cambridge knocked it out of him.'

'California?' That surprised me. 'What was he doing there?'

She shrugged. 'Geoff's parents divorced, when he was eleven. His mother went off with someone else, and Geoff went to America with his father. Morland has a big office there, I gather, near San Francisco. Anyway, Geoff was sixteen, when they finally came back. Bit of an adjustment for him, that was,' she said, with another smile. 'He still hasn't made peace with the class system here, and he was even worse back then – he'd mix with anyone. Even me,' she added, grinning. 'Mind you, we were living under the same roof, at the time, so it was only good manners, but it did raise some eyebrows. Still does, on occasion.'

I frowned a little, trying to follow. 'You lived at Crofton Hall?' I checked. 'When you were younger?'

'Yes. Sorry, I forgot you wouldn't know.' She flashed a quick, self-conscious smile. 'I do rather have to keep reminding myself, you know, that we've only just met. It sometimes seems like we've been friends for years, do you feel that? Anyway, yes, I did live at the Hall, when I was a little girl. My aunt kept house for Geoff's dad, you see, and I lived with her. My parents,' she explained, before I asked, 'died in a train crash, years ago. I barely remember them. Aunt Freda brought me up, and did a marvellous job, considering, though I'm sure I gave her every grey hair she has.' She smiled at the memories. 'One night she found out I'd been to the pictures with Geoff, and that was that. She marched me right across the road to my Gran's house, with my suitcases. No niece of *hers* was going to be a topic of village gossip. Poor Aunt Freda.'

I traced an idle pattern on the bar with my glass. 'Then you and Geoffrey de Mornay were . . .'

'Oh, heavens, no. It was nothing serious. There's never been anyone serious, with Geoff, come to that.' Vivien's smile grew broader as she met my eyes. 'Not yet.'

I coloured slightly and took a quick drink from my glass of juice.

'Are you sure you don't want something stronger than that?'

'Quite sure,' I said, turning my wrist so I could see my watch. 'In fact, I ought to be heading home. I still have to finish setting up my studio, and then if I'm lucky I can get a couple of hours' sleep before tonight. I didn't sleep well in London.'

'You do look tired,' Vivien said. 'We can always reschedule the history lesson, if you like.'

'Oh, no, I'll be fine. Seven o'clock was it?'

She nodded. 'Just come round to the back door. That's my private quarters. Ned can look after the customers by himself for one night, can't you, love?'

At the other end of the bar, Ned flipped a page of the sports section. 'Yeah, sure,' he said.

Something must have shown on my face at the thought of Ned tending bar by himself, because Vivien laughed out loud.

'You see the impression you've made on the girl, Ned?' she told him. 'She can't even picture you working.'

'She hasn't seen me in action,' Ned replied with a casual shrug.

Vivien lowered her voice and jerked her head in the direction of the co-worker. 'Ordinarily, we just keep him around because he blends so well with the decor,' she confided. 'But he actually does shift position every once in a while. It's quite exciting.'

'Keep it up,' the barman dared her calmly, 'and it'll be open taps this evening, love. Drinks on the house.'

I laughed. 'Do you want me to bring anything to-night?'

'Just yourself. You're sure you feel up to it?'

'A couple of hours' sleep and I'll be right as rain,' I assured her.

I was feeling exhausted. But for some reason, instead of going straight home when I left the Red Lion, I found myself turning to the right and wandering back up the High Street towards the church.

It had obviously been raining here the night before, as it had been in London. Apart from the tell-tale overcast sky, the pavement was still damp, and the smell of earth and wet grass and rain-soaked flowers hung heavy in the afternoon air. You could have shot a cannon up the

70

street without hitting a soul, the village was that quiet, but here and there the smear of muddy footprints on the cobbled walk provided evidence that some people at least had roused themselves early enough to attend the morning church services.

There were footprints, too, heading up the shaded lane that led to the manor house. Iain Sumner's footprints, I deduced, as there were two sets going in and only one coming out again. On impulse, I left the street and started up the lane, my shoes squelching a little in the drying mud. It was only idle curiosity, I told myself. I hadn't really taken a good look at the house on my last visit, and I doubted whether Geoffrey de Mornay would mind if I just had a peek around.

The lane was quiet and deserted. On my left, through the closely planted trees, I could just glimpse the outline of the church, its yellow stone walls flatly dull in the absence of sunshine. The path hugged the churchyard around a smoothly curved corner, straightening out again for its approach to the manor house. Ahead of me loomed the garden pedestrian gate leading to the Hall's north entrance, a freestanding doorcase carved of pale limestone, surmounted by an ornamental cornice and ball. A sign posted to one side of the gate stated politely: 'Welcome to Crofton Hall. This wing is private. The public is requested to use the East Entrance, which may be reached from the High Street.'

Rather a nice way, I thought, of telling people to get lost. Nor would anyone need to go through the bother of retracing their steps. A little swinging gate set into the low stone wall on my left led into the churchyard, offering a ready shortcut back to the High Street.

To my right, a long, low building with a stone-tiled roof stretched out level with the front of the imposing garden gate. The pleasantly pungent smell that drifted through its wide-open doorway identified it immediately as the stables for the Hall. My hesitation was only momentary. I never had been able to resist the almost magnetic lure of the presence of horses. Forgetting all about the manor house itself, I wandered towards the big boarded doors, swatting idly at a fly that buzzed about my ear.

The stables were unmistakably old, built of rough grey stone that looked identical to that used to build my house. Sarsen stone, Vivien had called it. The fly buzzed past again, louder this time, and again I brushed it away. Inside, the stables were warm, and fragrant, and I paused for a moment to let my eyes adjust to the dimmer lighting.

There were seven window bays, and most of the two-light timber windows held the original leaded glazing, with blue flies humming contentedly against the glass. Of the nine straight stalls, six contained horses, ranging in colour from a pure midnight black to a sleek golden chestnut. But it was the grey horse, in the far corner stall, that caught and held my attention.

It was a stallion, standing fully sixteen hands high, with a proudly arched neck and regal face that spoke of blistering, windswept sands and the far-off kingdoms of the infidel. As I drew closer, the grey turned his head towards me, his dark eyes mildly inquisitive, and snorted softly. I reached out a hand to rub his velvet nose, and the finely drawn nostrils quivered slightly in response, inhaling my scent.

'Hello, Navarre,' I greeted him lovingly, 'you beautiful thing.'

The stallion nuzzled my hand, searching for an illicit treat. And he might have received one, had I not at that moment heard the sound of footsteps approaching – heavy, confident footsteps accompanied by a cheerful and tuneless whistling. I spun round guiltily, and stood facing the doorway with my hands held behind me like an errant schoolgirl.

But no-one came in.

The flies sang more noisily in the window panes, drowning out the sound of my rapidly beating heart as I blinked my eyes against the suddenly bright electric lights that had not been there a moment ago. Gone were the leaded windows, replaced by energy-efficient double glazing. Gone, too, were the straight stalls, and in their place were five larger, immaculately kept box stalls. And the horse behind me, when I summoned the courage to look, was no longer a grey, but a dark cherry bay, eyeing me curiously from the safety of the far wall.

I did not take time to analyse what had just occurred. I ran. I ran out of the stables, across the lane and through the swinging gate into the silent sanctuary of the churchyard, and if I hadn't caught my foot on a snaking tree root, I would very probably have kept right on running.

As it was, I fell in a sprawling, inglorious heap amongst the tangle of weeds that grew against the churchyard wall, knocking the breath from my body so that I was forced to lie quite still for several moments. And as I lay there, gasping, hoping against hope that no-one would see me in this undignified position, my gaze fell wildly on a weathered headstone a short distance from my hand.

It was an old stone, set at an impossible angle and thickly wreathed in ivy, the vine having encircled the stone so completely that one could only read the first name of the person who lay buried beneath it:

Mariana . . .

Chapter Seven

The approach to Vivien's private rooms at the back of the Red Lion wound through one of the loveliest gardens I had ever seen – the sort of garden one comes across in the travel brochures above the caption 'An English Country Garden'. Or at least it would be that summer, in full bloom. Even now, in the middle of May, the garden was deliciously twisted and tangled, with tiny flowers clinging to every crevice of the old stone wall surrounding the yard. I stood on the back step for a moment, loitering in silent admiration.

'Coming up behind you,' Iain Sumner announced from several yards away. 'There,' he said, joining me on the steps, 'was that better?'

Laughing, I shook my head. 'I'm sorry, but no. I still jumped.'

'Ah, well,' he sighed, 'we'll think of something. I'd not want to give you a coronary.'

'Hullo!' Geoffrey de Mornay came round the corner of the house, looking oddly elegant in denim jeans and a casual shirt. His greeting was directed at Iain, but his smile, I fancied, was for me.

'Why would you be giving her a coronary?' he asked.

Iain grinned. 'I move like a damned cat.'

'I beg your pardon?'

'He keeps sneaking up on me,' I clarified.

Iain took offence at that, raising both eyebrows in

mock indignation. 'A Scotsman,' he informed me, 'never sneaks.'

'Well, whatever. I never hear him coming.'

Geoff frowned. 'You could wear heavier boots, I suppose,' he suggested, but Iain shook his head.

'Can't get much heavier than these.'

The three of us looked down at Iain's mud-splattered boots, our expressions contemplative, until the sound of a throat being ponderously cleared brought our heads up in unison.

'Hello.' Vivien smiled at us brightly from the open doorway. 'Would you three like to come inside, or should I join you out there?'

'Hullo, Viv.' Geoff leaned forward to kiss her on the cheek. 'Thanks for inviting me.'

He brushed past her into the house, with Iain and I trailing after him. Vivien closed the door behind us, shaking her head. 'What on earth were you all doing?'

'Looking at my boots,' Iain supplied, kicking off the articles in question and strolling into the little kitchen in his stockinged feet. He, too, was wearing jeans and a flannel work shirt, and I might have felt overdressed in my skirt and sweater had it not been for the fact that Vivien was wearing a dress, a nicely cut navy-blue dress that set off her fair hair to advantage.

'You have a lovely garden,' I said to her, and she smiled.

'Thanks, but I can't take the credit. Iain's done most of the planting.'

'Is there anybody's garden he *hasn't* worked on?' I wanted to know.

'Likely not,' Iain himself answered over his shoulder, rummaging in the refrigerator. 'I like gardens. Hate to see them wasted.' He straightened up with a sandwich

75

in his hand. 'There used to be a nice garden up at your house, come to that. Old Eddie let it grow over. Didn't want to be bothered with it.'

'The garden where the Green Lady appeared.'

'That's right,' Geoff spoke up, seating himself on a long sofa in the open-plan sitting-room. 'You have been digging up the local legends, haven't you?'

'I find it fascinating. I've never had a ghost before.'

'You don't necessarily have one now,' he pointed out. 'The Green Lady hasn't been seen since I was in short pants. Unless you've seen her yourself, lately?'

'No, I'm afraid not.' I shook my head, as Vivien drifted across from the dining area and handed a glass of pale amber liquid to Geoff.

'She has been finding old letters stashed about, though,' she told him. 'Was there a Mariana lived there, do you know?'

'Mariana . . .' Geoff sipped his drink thoughtfully. 'I'm not sure. Do you know what her last name was?'

'Farr,' I said. And then, in response to Vivien's questioning look, 'I found her grave in the churchyard.'

'Mariana Farr. No, I don't remember. But she may be mentioned in here.' He tapped the thick file folder he'd brought with him, that now lay on the low coffee-table at his knees, flanked by trays of carefully arranged cheese and dry biscuits.

'You'd better sit beside Geoff, Julia, so you can see better,' Vivien manoeuvred smoothly. 'Iain, did you want some Scotch as well?'

'Single malt?'

'Blended.'

'Then I'll just have one of these, thanks.' He lifted the bottle of imported beer from the refrigerator and

76

joined us in the lounge, settling himself on the love-seat that faced the sofa across the coffee-table.

'And what would you like, Julia?' Vivien asked. 'To drink, I mean.'

Every time I had been asked that question in the past, I had, without fail, managed to choose the one item that my host did not have. This time, I tried a new approach.

'You're the bartender.' I smiled. 'I'll let you choose.'

'Trusting soul,' Geoff remarked, as Vivien went to get my drink. 'So, tell me. What, specifically, are you interested in?'

'I'm sorry?'

'Historically. Just your property?'

'Mainly, yes. But I'm also quite interested in the history of your Hall.'

'Are you really?' He looked pleased.

Iain groaned audibly. 'Here we go,' he said, through a mouthful of beer and sandwich.

'Why? What did I say?'

'Nothing,' Vivien said, returning with two tall glasses filled with a pale drink. 'It's just that Geoff does tend to get stuck in a rut, sometimes, when he launches into a history of the Hall.' She set my drink in front of me and took her seat beside Iain, who shot her a sideways glance.

'That's putting it kindly,' he commented.

I looked at my drink, curious, and Vivien smiled. 'There's rum in that,' she warned me, 'but the rest of the ingredients are top secret.'

My first experimental sip was a pleasant surprise. 'It's wonderful. Thanks.'

'You're welcome. Now then, Geoff, on with the lecture. I suppose you'd better take us right back to the

Benedictine Priory, and go on from there, since Julia's interested.'

'Right,' He opened his file folder and cheerfully arranged the papers inside, just like a schoolboy exhibiting a class project. 'That was in 1173, I believe . . .'

'Seventy-four,' Iain corrected, rubbing his eyes with one hand.

'. . . when Henry II granted a plot of land to one Thomas Killingbeck, for the purpose of building a Benedictine monastery. The Benedictine order was pretty big in those days.'

'Henry II,' I mused, leaning forward. 'That's Richard the Lionheart's father isn't it? The one who had Thomas à Becket murdered?'

Geoff turned approving eyes on me. 'Yes, that's right. Not many people remember that.'

'Well, it's my brother's name, you see,' I explained. 'Thomas Beckett. I sort of paid attention to that part of the history lesson at school.'

Iain stretched his legs out in front of him, slinging one arm along the cushioned back of the love-seat. 'Your brother's name is Thomas?' His grey eyes twinkled in amusement. 'Rather appropriate naming on your parents' part, wasn't it?'

'Rather.' For the benefit of Geoff and Vivien, I explained. 'Tom's a vicar in Hampshire, not far from here.'

Geoff laughed. 'Not really? Well, if he makes Archbishop of Canterbury he'll certainly turn some heads, won't he?'

'I don't think he's that ambitious. Tom likes the country life. Anyhow, I'm getting off the subject. What happened to the Priory?'

'Well, the monks did just fine until Henry VIII decided

78

to nationalize the monasteries. The last Prior was hanged for resisting royal authority.'

'He's one of the ghosts, isn't he?' Vivien asked.

'Supposedly. Quite a few people have reported seeing a ghostly monk floating around in the hallways, but whether it's the Prior's ghost is open to speculation.' He spoke with surprising frankness, as if seeing a ghost in one's hallway were an everyday occurrence. 'At any rate,' he carried on, checking his notes, 'the property was sold in 1547 to Sir James Crofton, who started building a house on the site of the ruined monastery. The house gets its name from him. In the old maps it's referred to as "Crofton's Hall", and as time went on people just began leaving off the "s". He only lived there fourteen years, before selling the place to Nicholas Hatch, who gave it to his son Edmund as a wedding present.

'Edmund Hatch didn't have much time to enjoy the house, either, because he died in 1594. Some sort of shooting accident, apparently. He left the estate to his wife Ann, and she, bless her heart, promptly married my forefather, William de Mornay.'

'What did William do for a living?' I asked.

'He was a retired soldier. I don't know why she married him – she was barely out of mourning, and the old codger was twice her age.'

'Maybe he was rich,' Iain suggested.

'Possibly.'

I was inclined to disagree. If Geoff's charm and looks were at all inherited from his ancestors, then I thought I knew exactly why the widowed Ann Hatch had hastened to marry William de Mornay.

'Ann and William had one son, also named William, just to add to the confusion. Dad had an awful time trying to sort out which papers were talking about William the Elder and which ones were about William Junior. William Junior, any rate, was a bit of an interesting character. During the Civil War, when the country was divided between King Charles I's followers and those who supported Cromwell's Parliament, William Junior made the fatal, if noble, mistake of siding with his King.

'When the King lost his head, William Junior lost his manor, and was thrown in the Tower for his troubles. He was let out of prison in 1660, when Charles II was restored to the throne, and his lands were given back to him, but he never regained his health. He died within the year. There's quite a good portrait of him in the dining-room at the Hall – I think I've got a photograph of it, here . . . yes, here it is. That's William Junior.'

He slid the photograph across the table to me, and I leaned closer for a better look. My earlier supposition had been correct. The good looks were definitely inherited. William de Mornay cut a dashing figure in his vibrant portrait, with his curling dark hair and Van Dyke beard, and languid dark eyes that hinted at a sensual nature. In his scarlet coat and breeches, one hand upon his sword hilt and the other resting defiantly on his hip, he looked every inch the gallant Cavalier.

I handed the picture back, reluctantly. 'It's a marvellous portrait.'

'Yes. We've never been able to find a record of any of his children, but he must have had some, because the manor passed to his grandson, Arthur de Mornay. Bit of a mistake, that. Arthur seems to have been something of a compulsive gambler, and not only lost the family fortune but ended up selling off the manor itself, to pay his debts. So the de Mornays lost their land a second time. We didn't get it back until my father bought the Hall in 1964.' He turned a few more pages with an absent frown. 'I really ought to get back to this, you know, one of these days. My father had a passion for genealogy – spent days shut up in the Public Record Office, looking for wills and things. But he rather lost interest in it, towards the end, and I just never seem to have the time . . .'

Iain shifted in his seat. 'Gets a bit boring after old Arthur, don't you think, Geoff? Why don't you find us something about Julia's house?'

'What?' Geoff looked up blankly, then smiled. 'Oh, right. Just a minute, I'll have a look around a little.'

I watched his hands, fascinated, as he shuffled the papers round. He had beautiful hands, lean and strong and suntanned, and there was a certain casual elegance in the way they moved.

'Aha!' He pulled a sheet of paper from the pile. 'Here it is. Greywethers. According to the surveys, it was built in 1587 by a man named Stephen Sharington, a farmer who rented his land from our old friend Edmund Hatch. The house was inherited by Stephen's son John, who sold in 1626 to one Robert Howard, merchant. You all right?'

I nodded. 'Just a chill. Please, go on.'

'The Howards kept the house until the early 1800s, when they sold it to Lawrence Alleyn. He was kind of a fun character – fought with Wellington at the battle of Waterloo, no less, and spent a few years out in India. He only had one child, his daughter Mary, who was a little ahead of her time. Wore trousers and wrote novels.'

'Horrible novels,' Vivien elaborated with a slight shudder. 'I read one, once. Typical Victorian stuff. Full of long descriptive passages and dry as a bone.'

'Nevertheless.' Geoff smiled indulgently. 'She died in 1896, and the house was sold to Captain James Guthrie.'

'That was the "Captain Somebody" the lads were telling you about, the other day,' Vivien said. 'I asked my aunt about him. She said he was a naval officer, or something, sort of mysterious. Some people thought he was a spy. He ran the house like it was one of his ships, apparently. Had three daughters, who were hardly ever allowed to go out, poor things.'

'What happened to them?' I asked.

'Oh, eventually their father died.' She smiled. 'Poisoned, most people thought. And the girls went off and got married. That would have been in the early twenties.'

'Well, that fits,' Geoff conceded, 'because in 1921 the house was sold to William Randall, old Eddie's father. He managed to convince the man who owned Crofton Hall then – Pilkington, I think his name was – to sever off part of the property, so the Randalls were the first ones who owned their own land.'

'And after the Randalls, the next owner is you,' Vivien told me. 'No mention of a Mariana anywhere, was there?'

Iain shrugged. 'She might have been a servant.'

'Or somebody's wife,' Geoff suggested. 'These old records rarely mention the women of the household.'

I nodded. 'Either way, it's very interesting. I don't suppose you could make me a copy of that?'

'The history of your house? I'd be glad to.' His eyes smiled warmly into mine, and I suddenly felt as if I wasn't getting enough air. I turned away, breaking the contact, and reached for my drink.

'Would you like another one?' Vivien offered, looking at my glass.

'Oh, no thanks, I'm floating as it is.'

'I'll have another Scotch, though,' Geoff held up his empty glass hopefully, and Vivien rose smiling from the love-seat.

'Well, that rather goes without saying, doesn't it? Iain? Another beer?'

'Sure, why not?' He yielded up the empty bottle with a grin. He looked nearly as tired as I felt, and I remembered that, as a farmer, he was probably up at the crack of dawn each day.

Geoff leaned back in his seat, his drink replenished, and shifted a little on the sofa to face me more fully. 'So, how are you settling in up there?'

'Quite well, thanks,' I told him. 'I've got most of the important things unpacked, and the rooms cleaned, and the rest I'm just going to leave until the mood strikes me.'

Vivien settled herself back on the love-seat, curling her legs beneath her. 'I think you're wise,' she said. 'After all, the only important rooms are the kitchen and the bedroom, really.'

'And the bath,' Geoff put in.

'And my studio.' I smiled. 'I've been terrible these past two weeks, I haven't worked at all. My editor would have forty fits if she found out.'

'Julia,' Vivien announced to the room in general, 'paints illustrations for children's books.'

Iain took a long draught of his ale, his grey eyes twinkling in his impassive face. 'Aye, I think I've heard something to that effect.'

'Interesting work,' was Geoff's comment. 'It must allow you a great deal of freedom.'

'It does. But I still have to keep myself to some sort of schedule, or I'd never accomplish anything. I usually work in the mornings, and take the rest of the day off.'

'What sort of book are you illustrating now?' Vivien asked. 'Another of Bridget Cooper's?'

I shook my head. 'A collection of fairy tales, actually. It's very good. A lot of the stories are from the Orient, and the translations are marvellous.'

'Do you work from your imagination alone,' she wanted to know, 'or from photographs, or what?'

'A bit of both. Sometimes I have to draw from life, depending on the look I want.'

'Then you'll be needing models,' Geoff remarked, displaying his profile with a dramatic flourish.

Iain grinned. 'Fancy yourself as Prince Charming, do ye?'

'King,' Geoff corrected him with a look of disdain. 'Why settle for being a mere prince?'

'Prince gets the girl,' Iain pointed out, and Geoff tilted his head, considering.

'You're right. All right, then, I'll offer myself as Prince Charming. If you need me,' he qualified, with another heart-stopping smile.

I preferred not to make a response to that one, though I had to admit that Geoffrey de Mornay was certainly qualified to play the role of fairy tale prince.

Our conversation ambled on comfortably for another half hour or so, by which time I was having to struggle to keep my eyes open. Opposite me, I was aware of Iain Sumner watching me with an understanding smile, his own head sinking lower against the cushions.

'If you're wanting to be Prince Charming,' he told Geoff finally, interrupting an anecdote, 'you might think to stop talking and escort the poor girl home before she falls asleep.'

Geoff looked over at me, surprised. 'Sorry,' he said. 'I forgot you spent last night partying in London. Would you like a lift home? I can fetch the car round.'

'Take my car, if you like,' Vivien suggested. 'It's parked round the side.'

The decision had apparently been made for me, and several moments later I found myself sitting beside Geoff in Vivien's well-kept Vauxhall, having taken a somewhat sleepy leave of my hostess and of Iain, who appeared to have grown roots to the deeply cushioned love-seat.

The drive home took only a few minutes. As he brought the car to a halt in the gravel drive, Geoff turned to face me, and I was suddenly aware of the sheer physical impact of his nearness in the darkened interior of the car.

'What are you doing tomorrow?' he asked.

'I'm not sure. Why?'

'Thought you might like to take that tour of the Hall I promised you. Sort of a behind-the-scenes look, if you like. Much more interesting than what the tourists see.' His smile was very sexy, and very persuasive.

'All right.'

'Good. Just slide by sometime in the afternoon, then. I'll be at home all day.'

'I'll do that. Goodnight, Geoff.' I felt for the door handle. 'Thanks for the lift.'

'Anytime.'

It seemed natural, somehow, that he should reach across and give me a goodnight kiss. Natural, too, that I should lean a little closer to accept the gesture. It was a purely casual and friendly contact, and yet I could feel the warmth of it even after the Vauxhall's back lights had disappeared down the road leading back to the village.

With a little sigh, I turned and started across the lawn towards the house, dragging my feet a little in my sudden weariness. The wind had picked up considerably since supper time. The night air felt heavy with the threat of rain, and to my right a distant rumble of thunder could be heard above the moaning of the wind through the creaking trees.

I was still several feet from the front door when it suddenly flew open, spilling a slanting slab of yellow light across the lawn and framing the silhouetted figure of a man, who stood watching my approach with his arms folded across his chest.

'Uncle,' I said, but my voice was lost in the wind.

The thunder sounded again, and my steps faltered for a brief instant. Summoning my courage, I lifted the dripping hem of my dress clear of the grass, and forced myself to walk the final yard to the doorway.

The man lifted his head a fraction, and I could see his features more clearly – my mother's eyes, set in a hawk-like face that showed no trace of her tenderness. I raised my chin and gazed mutely up at him. I had intended to smile, but for some reason his expression did not seem to invite such familiarity. For a long moment we stared at each other, while the storm rose and swelled behind us and the wind mounted to a frenzied wail.

'So,' he said finally. 'You've come.'

Chapter Eight

It is difficult to describe the sensation of sliding backwards in time, of exchanging one reality for another that is just as real, just as tangible, just as familiar. I should not perhaps, refer to it as 'sliding', since in actual fact I was thrust – abruptly and without warning – from one time to the next, as though I had walked through some shifting, invisible portal dividing the present from the past.

When that happened, at the moment that I passed through the portal, I was blissfully unaware that anything had changed. That realization, and the full impact of its significance, would come later, when I had returned to being Julia Beckett.

But as I stood on the front steps of Greywethers that evening, staring up at the man who blocked the doorway, I was no longer Julia. Julia, and all her jumbled memories, had been stripped from me. My thoughts were someone else's thoughts, my body not my own, and as I moved I lived each new experience for the first time. I was Mariana, and it was with Mariana's eyes that I looked now at my uncle.

Jabez Howard was a tall man, with powerful shoulders and a heavy bull's neck. He needed no padding beneath his stockings to give the impression of muscles, and the woollen broadcloth of his narrow breeches and coat stretched taut at the seams, as if the clothing had been made for a much smaller man. His head, shorn close to permit the wearing of the fashionable new periwigs, looked oddly grotesque and inhuman in that strange light. But when, at last, he smiled, I saw again my mother's face and my cold misgivings were displaced by a warm sense of homecoming.

'I did not hear the coach,' he said, peering past me into the darkness.

'One of the horses went lame, and the coachman would not risk the team any further on such a night. He set me down at the village inn.'

'And you came on alone. You should have waited for morning.'

'I was eager to come to you.' The furtive, insistent voice of the leering coachman and the stench of ale, tobacco and travelling men had combined to overcome any fears I might have had of walking alone on the open road. The landlord had been kind enough to give me directions, and had promised to hold my box for me until I could collect it.

My uncle made a disapproving noise and turned away, motioning me to follow him inside. The wide hall was bright with what seemed like a hundred candles, their flames dancing in the reflecting sconces and gleaming on the darkly burnished panelling. 'Close the door,' he instructed me shortly, and I obeyed, shutting out the darkness and the coming storm and sliding the iron bolt in place.

'You spoke to the landlord of the Red Lion?' he asked.

I knew what he was asking me.

'I told him I was your sister's daughter, from Southampton, and had come to stay with you awhile. It was Aunt Mary's tale, and her advice that I should use it.'

Uncle Jabez nodded, satisfied. 'My brother John, for

all his faults, did marry well,' he said. 'Your aunt is a good woman, and a clever one. Mind you remember her advice. There is great fear of the plague here, and travellers from London are not welcome.'

'I am grateful,' I told him, remembering my manners, 'that you do offer me a home here, when you yourself must fear infection.'

His eyes were mild. 'I have no need to fear the plague. I am a righteous man. Come along.'

He led the way down the narrow passage to the back of the house, and I trailed after him, my borrowed gown dragging heavily at my weary legs. Two days of rough travel had brought me to the brink of exhaustion, my fair hair darkened with dirt and grime, my blue eyes deeply shadowed and rimmed with red. The dust from the road clung everywhere, turning my green dress an ugly grey colour and catching at the back of my throat with an irritating tenacity that even repeated coughing could not dislodge.

We emerged from the bright glare of the front hall into the quieter light of the long kitchen and the warmth of a real fire. A woman sat to one side of the hearth, nursing a round, red-faced baby. Near them, a younger woman bent over the fire, holding her skirts clear of the flames with an expert hand while she stirred the steaming contents of an iron kettle. Both women turned their heads as we entered the kitchen, their eyes flashing first to my uncle's face, and then to mine. He nodded towards the woman with the baby.

'Your Aunt Caroline,' he told me.

She had a pleasant face, firm and youthful despite the white streaks marring the dark mass of her hair. But I found her expression unsettling. It was neither friendly nor malicious; it seemed more an absence of expression, devoid of character, the eyes dull and vacant like those of a sheep. She nodded imperceptibly, acknowledging me, and went on rocking the child.

'Rachel, my wife's younger sister,' my uncle said next, as the other woman straightened from the glowing hearth. She, at least, was fully alive, and closer to my own age – a year or two younger, perhaps, than my own twenty years. Her honey-coloured hair lay in ringlets against her flushed cheeks, and her quick smile was warm and welcoming.

'I've mulled some ale,' she announced, 'and there's bread on the table if you're hungry.'

I was, in fact, ravenous, having eaten nothing since late morning. I gratefully took a seat opposite my uncle at the rough oak table, accepting the earthen mug of fragrant ale and the generous slices of heavy bread that were handed to me. The girl Rachel sat beside me, her dark eyes frankly curious.

'What news of London?' she asked. 'Is it true the King would remove to Hampton Court, for fear of the sickness?'

'I know not what the King intends,' I said honestly, 'but the common people talk much of leaving.'

Under Rachel's prodding, I told them of the panic that had gripped the City, the ceaseless whispers and muttered prayers, and of the houses I had seen shut up in Westminster, with the red warning crosses painted on the doors and the words 'Lord have mercy upon us' scrawled beneath the crosses by some frantic, hopeful hand.

My uncle shrugged.

'London is a godless, sinful place,' he said, 'and the hand of the Lord is seeking vengeance. Those who are righteous have nothing to fear.'

I lifted my chin, my eyes stinging.

'My mother did not sin,' I told him, 'and she is dead.'

My uncle finished chewing a mouthful of bread, his face impassive. His pale eyes seemed suddenly hard and remote, for all the calmness of his voice. 'She disobeyed her father. In the eyes of God, that is a sin.'

I did not need to press him further. I knew well enough that my mother had married against her father's wishes, choosing a poor scrivener over the attentions of her local suitor. Having witnessed firsthand the love of my parents, a love which had illuminated my childhood and sustained my mother through nine lonely years of widowhood, I could not bring myself to call her choice a sin. But I did bite back my words of argument, remembering in time that the independence of spirit encouraged by my parents was not to be tolerated in other households.

I lowered my eyes, and would have lowered my head had my uncle not reached across the table, grasping my chin with one large hand and tilting it to the light of the fire.

'You do not look like your mother,' he said bluntly, after a moment's study. 'Annie was a comely lass. Nor can I see your father in you, praise God.'

'I am told I am very like my father's mother.'

He grunted, losing interest, and let go my chin.

'The girl is weary, Jabez,' my aunt said unexpectedly from her seat in the corner, in a voice as lifeless as her eyes. 'Rachel can show her to her room.'

'Ay,' he conceded. 'Get you to bed, child. We rise early for prayers.'

I made to rise, but he leaned forward suddenly, his

eyes fastening on mine with a burning interest. 'Do you fear God, Mariana Farr?' he asked.

'I have been taught to do so.'

He did not touch me physically, but his eyes held me to my seat and his voice was almost frightening in its intensity. '"Blow ye the trumpet in Zion,"' he quoted softly, '"and sound an alarm in my holy mountain; let all the inhabitants of the land tremble . . ."' He paused, waiting, and I realized it was a test.

I finished the scripture for him. '". . . for the day of the Lord cometh,"' I said, '"for it is nigh at hand."'

'Good girl,' my uncle praised me, relaxing back in his chair with a satisfied smile. 'Very good. We shall do well together, you and I.'

It was a dismissal. Rising, I wished both my aunt and uncle a good night and followed the girl Rachel from the room. She walked a few paces ahead of me, holding aloft a sputtering candle to light our way up the wide staircase to the upper floor. The air was colder here, and damp, and the flame from the candle cast long slanting shadows on the bare plaster walls.

'Your room is here,' Rachel said, leading the way along the dark passage to a door at the back corner of the house.

It was a mean and spartan chamber, with a narrow bed and empty clothes-press, and I felt Rachel watching my face as I gazed about the room. 'It is a small room,' she said, 'but it's wonderfully quiet, and you've a view all the way down to the river from your window.'

She was so obviously eager to please that I forced a smile, and voiced some unfelt platitude. The girl's relief was visible, and touching in its sincerity. 'I brought one of my nightgowns for you,' she said, indicating the white ghostly shape on the bed. 'We did not know if you would have baggage.'

'Thank you.'

I picked up the gown and smoothed it while Rachel lit the candle by my bed. It must have been her very best nightgown, made of fine white lawn with tiny carved buttons. I doubted whether it had ever been worn.

'Tis no trouble,' she blushed with pleasure, hovering for a moment in the doorway with her hand on the latch. 'I'm glad you've come to live here,' she said shyly.

Before I could answer, she had closed the door between us and I heard her light footsteps retreating down the passage. I was not feeling glad myself. I felt only tired and hollow and hopeless. Stripping off my soiled green gown I laid it carefully in the clothes-press and donned the lovely nightdress, slipping beneath the coverlet of the bed and reaching out a hand to extinguish the candle flame.

There, in the dark, the full weight of my situation pressed close upon me, and misery rose like bitter gall in my throat, thick and choking. I found myself missing London, and the comfort of my own bed, and the gentle touch of my mother's lips cool against my forehead. My mother . . .

The thought of her brought a fresh dampness to my eyes. This had been her home, once, I thought, when she was my own age. Before she had met my father and followed him away. Small wonder she had fled so willingly. This was a dark and cheerless house, and no fit place for the laughing, vibrant woman of my memory. Had this once been her room, I wondered, and had she ever cried herself to sleep here as I did now, turning her face against the linens to hide the evidence of her despair?

*   *   *

I woke to silence and the cold grey light of dawn. It was the silence that most disturbed me. At this early hour of the day, the street beneath my window in the City would already have been alive with humanity – the hawkers with their pushcarts and barrows, baskets dangling from their arms as they filled the clear morning air with a cacophany of sing-song cries, while tired-eyed gallants and their wilted ladies hurried home to bed after a night of exuberant merry-making.

I was staring at the ceiling, fighting back the rising ache of homesickness and wondering what had woken me, when a knock sounded at my door and, without waiting for an answer, Rachel wafted into the room. She was neatly dressed in a plain coffee-coloured gown, her hair arranged simply and without fuss, her scrubbed face shining and composed. She carried a basin of water and a rough flannel.

'I thought you might want to wash before prayers,' she greeted me cheerily, setting the basin beside my bed. 'Did you rest well?'

'Very well, thank you,' I lied.

A cheerful whistle split the silence outside, sounding so much like my father's whistle that I was out of bed and over to the window before my mind had fully registered my actions. The window looked out over the back garden and the stables, with a view to the river that wound its way between forest and fields, and the soft green downs beyond.

A man was walking up the hill from the road, carrying my heavy box of clothing on his back as easily as if it had been a sack of feathers. He walked with long, swinging strides, and while his broad-brimmed hat hid his face from view, I caught a glimpse of a square, clean-shaven jawline and a long curl of natural brown hair.

'Rachel,' I said, motioning her to the window, 'who is that man below? He's talking to my uncle, now.'

Rachel came and looked, obediently, then turned away again, her cheeks curiously flushed. 'That is Evan Gilroy,' she told me. 'He lives at the manor in the village.'

'He has brought my box up from the inn.'

My uncle, who had come out from the kitchen to meet the man, did not appear pleased by this favour. By standing on my toes and pressing myself close against the glass, I could see both men quite clearly as they stood below me. My uncle's face was dark and unfriendly, and though I could not hear his words the tone of his voice was clipped and harsh. The stranger said something in reply, and I saw the flash of his smile as he swung the box to the ground and turned away, walking in that same jaunty, unhurried pace towards the village.

My uncle stared after him a long moment, then said something to himself and lifted my box lightly onto his shoulder, impressing me again with his great size and strength. I heard the kitchen door slam below me and lifted my eyes, intending to come away from the window, but my attention was caught by a shadow under the large oak in the hollow at the edge of the field. A shadow that shifted and became a man, a dark man on a grey horse, staring boldly up at my chamber window.

As I stood there watching, the landscape shifted subtly, becoming fluid, the colours running into one another like paints upon an artist's palette, and then the entire picture began to vibrate and I found myself clutching desperately at the window sill as the world went black.

Chapter Nine

As a child, I always kept my eyes screwed tightly shut when I woke from a nightmare, afraid that if I opened them I might find some truly terrible apparition beside my bed. The same childish instinct made me keep my eyes shut now. I lay still as the dead, curled to the wall, and the blood sang loudly in my ears as I reached out beside me with a tentative hand.

My searching fingers touched the cool, faintly textured surface of a wooden floorboard, skimmed across an abrasive wool carpet and came to rest on a reassuringly familiar bit of cold tubular steel. Either my drawing board had somehow transported itself back in time, I reasoned, or I was lying on the floor of my studio. Gambling on the latter, I cautiously opened my eyes, blinking a few times to focus.

The room quivered once, and then stood still, and with a rush of relief I saw the solid twentieth-century clutter surrounding me – packing crates and papers and paintbrushes scattered untidily across the floor. Lifting my head a fraction, I craned my neck for a better look round, then sank back onto the hardwood with a ragged sigh.

I had fallen on a clear patch of floor directly beneath the bare west window, which accounted for the cool draught I felt on my face and neck. Outside, the first faint rays of daylight illuminated a sky so pale that it appeared almost colourless. I was still wearing the same clothes I had worn to Vivien's the night before, my cotton sweater and skirt crumpled and creased as though I had slept in them.

I was alone in the room.

I pushed myself slowly to a sitting position, paused for breath, and rose carefully to my feet, leaning on the drawing board for support. I felt as dazed and disoriented as Ebenezer Scrooge must have done, when he finally awoke on that famous fictional Christmas morning. There was the corner where my bed had been, I thought, looking around; there the place where I had undressed and laid away my dusty green gown; there the doorway where the girl Rachel had stood, smiling her quick, shy smile.

Wandering into the hallway I descended the stairs on unsteady legs. The kitchen seemed smaller than I remembered, and I stood frowning a moment until the explanation struck me – the kitchen I had been in last night had had no pantry. My kitchen had probably not been divided in two until Victorian times, if the pantry's cabinets and wood trim were anything to go by.

I moved into the pantry for a closer look, and stopped to run a hand over the north wall. There were no windows here, and the plaster felt rough and uneven, as if it had been slapped on over some existing architectural feature. An open hearth, perhaps . . .

'What is happening to me?' I barely whispered the words, but they echoed in the silent space.

Feeling suddenly suffocated, I stumbled back into the kitchen and yanked open the back door, nearly falling into the yard in my rush to get out of the house. A short distance away from the building I stopped, wrapping my arms around my shivering body and taking deep, sobbing breaths of the damp morning air.

Even before the hair lifted along the nape of my neck, I knew that I was being watched. I wheeled to face the oak tree in the hollow, and the dark rider on the grey horse that I knew would be there. A sudden tide of anger, blind and furious, swelled within me.

'Go away!' I shouted at him. 'Go away and leave me alone. I don't want you here!'

Slowly, reluctantly, horse and rider retreated a few paces, and the grey morning mist rose up to fill the place where they had been. Still shaking with the force of my emotions, I hugged myself tighter and lowered my eyes.

Beneath my feet, a sprinkling of delicate blue wild-flowers, wet with dew, nestled in the long grass. The ground was level here, and firm, and it was simple enough to see the slight depression where, long ago, someone had once planted a garden . . .

The rectory at Elderwel, Hampshire, was a solid Victorian building of deep red brick, set close to the road, facing the graceful fifteenth-century church of St Stephen's. Ivy had gained a foothold on the north side of the house and the twisted tangle of vines, bursting into leaf, climbed with a steady purpose almost to the sills of the upper windows. Beyond the ivy's reach, the gabled windows in the steeply sloping roof gazed out over the village like kind, benevolent eyes.

Inside, the rectory was a rabbit warren of narrow, dark rooms, designed to accommodate the large families of the previous century. Since my brother Tom was unmarried, he contented himself with the main floor of the rambling house, and gave the upper storeys over to the use of his curate, the occasional guest or homeless parishioner. Most of the housework he did himself, but on Monday's his cleaner, Mrs Pearce, came in to do a proper job.

It was Mrs Pearce, duster in hand, who answered my knock at the door that morning and showed me through to the comfortably masculine study. Mrs Pearce, I marvelled, had a remarkable amount of tact. I looked like hell, and knew it. I'll never know how I made that drive from Exbury to Elderwel without damaging myself or the car, but when I reached the rectory it was fully an hour before breakfast time.

By now the shock was beginning to wear off, and I was shaking so badly I could scarcely control it, but if Mrs Pearce noticed she made no comment. She opened the curtains, saw me settled in Tom's favourite armchair, and withdrew in her quiet, efficient way to put the kettle on.

Tom arrived a few minutes later, still buttoning his shirt. He had, no doubt, intended to make some joke about my early morning invasion of his sanctum sanctorum, but when he first caught sight of me the mocking smile died on his lips.

'What's wrong?' he asked quickly.

My last tenuous thread of control snapped, and I burst into tears. I later wished that I'd had a camera with me, to record the expression on Tom's face – I doubt whether his look of pure, unmitigated horror had been equalled anywhere other than in silent films.

His reaction, though comic, was wholly understandable. I never cried. I rarely even whimpered. The last time Tom had seen me in tears was almost twenty years earlier, when he'd accidentally slammed the car door on my hand. Even then, the flood had been modest, nothing like the terrifying outburst of great, soul-wrenching sobs he was witnessing now.

'Julia?' His tone was uncertain. It was several minutes before I could recover myself sufficiently to answer him.

'I'm fine, really,' I told him between sniffles. 'I'm just losing my mind.'

Tom took a seat opposite me, frowning. 'What?'

'Going insane,' I elaborated. 'Cracking up. There's no other explanation for it.'

'You've lost me.'

The tears had subsided now, and I took a deep, shaky breath, wiping the dampness from my face with the heel of my hand. 'You wouldn't believe me if I told you,' I said.

'Try me.'

I gave him a long, measuring look, heaved another unsteady sigh, and started talking. I began at the beginning, from the moment I'd first seen the man on the grey horse, through the incident in Blackfriars Lane, to my discovery of Mariana Farr's headstone in the churchyard and my waking dream of last night. Mrs Pearce drifted noiselessly in and out of the room, depositing pots of tea and plates of biscuits and whisking the remains away without once interrupting the course of my narrative, while my brother sat quietly in his chair, listening. When I had finished, he leaned back and lowered his eyebrows in contemplation.

'These . . . experiences,' he said finally, 'do they come on suddenly, or do you have any warning?'

I tried hard to think back. My first inclination would have been to say that there was no warning whatsoever, but . . . 'I sometimes hear a ringing in my ears,' I told him, 'or I feel a little dizzy. Or both.'

'And you're definitely a participant in the action. It doesn't feel like you're in the audience watching a play?'

'Definitely not. I don't even feel like a cast member, come to that. Cast members have scripts, but I never have the slightest idea what's going to happen next. It's just like real life . . . just like *this*.' I spread my hands, palms upward, in a gesture that encompassed the room and the two of us. 'Even the time and space they occupy is real. I obviously move around, since I started off outside the house last night and ended up in the studio this morning.'

Tom thought about this. 'And when you have these experiences, you don't remember anything about being Julia Beckett?' I shook my head. 'But when you come out of it again, you can remember clearly being this other woman?'

'I remember everything.'

'Setting aside the insanity theory, for the moment,' he said slowly, 'what do *you* think is happening?'

I shrugged. 'I suppose . . . I suppose it could be the ghost.'

'This Green Lady that everyone talks about, you mean?'

I nodded. 'The dress I was wearing last night, when I was her . . . when I was Mariana . . . was green. I don't know. Could a ghost take possession of a living person, do you think?'

'I'm hardly an authority on the subject,' Tom admitted. 'I suppose it's possible, but in your case I wouldn't think it likely. Not unless the ghost followed you to London last weekend.' He frowned. 'There is one possibility that you haven't considered, yet.'

'Which is?'

He raised his head and looked at me. 'That everything you're seeing, everything you're experiencing, may actually come from your own memory. That you may, in fact, *be* Mariana.'

'You can't be serious.'

'Why not? Reincarnation is an accepted phenomenon in lots of cultures. There are even a few distinguished Church of England types I could name who support the theory.'

'And what do you believe?' I challenged him.

'Well,' he smiled, 'it's one of the requirements of my job that I believe in the eternal life of the human soul. And where that soul goes after death is a question that only the dead can answer.'

'So you think I may have lived in that house in some sort of past life?' It sounded ridiculous, but Tom's expression was serious.

'I think it's an idea worth exploring, yes. After all, if you feel like you've been somewhere before, the logical explanation usually is that you *have* been there before.'

I frowned. 'It could explain why I was drawn to the house, I suppose.'

'And why you knew where the old garden had been. And why you chose to make your studio in that tiny back room, instead of using one of the better rooms at the front.'

As he spoke the words an image rose swimming in front of my eyes, of the mover's young assistant holding my bedroom chair and asking, in a puzzled voice, 'Are you sure you meant the *first* room on the right . . . ?'

I shook myself back to the present. 'Good Lord,' I said flatly.

'I could try to find out more about the subject for you,' Tom offered. 'We've got a wonderfully eccentric librarian here who delights in ferreting out odd bits of information.'

'You honestly believe that past lives are possible?' I asked him, and he shrugged.

'The Lord moves in ways mysterious,' he told me, smiling.

'Oh, that reminds me,' I said, sitting upright. 'Have you ever heard a biblical passage that starts, "Blow the trumpet in Zion", or something like that? I don't recall the rest of it, something about people trembling and the day of judgement.'

Tom rolled his eyes. 'Sounds like one of the doom and gloom Old Testament chaps,' he speculated. 'Micah, maybe, or Joel.' Rising from his chair, he crossed to his desk and picked up a well-thumbed copy of the King James Bible. For several minutes he silently leafed through the pages, and I was on the verge of telling him that it wasn't that important, after all, when he suddenly jabbed one page with a triumphant finger. 'Aha! It *was* Joel. Chapter two, verse one. Here you go.'

He passed the Bible to me, open, and pointed to the place. As I read the brief, cheerless passage, Tom sat down again, scratching his forehead idly. 'My former curate used to love reading texts from Joel,' he said, grinning. 'Real hell and damnation stuff, hardly inspiring for the congregation. Though I seem to remember that old Joel was writing during a plague of locusts, so I suppose he had a right to be dismal.'

Plague . . . the word struck a sudden chord in my memory, and I lifted my eyes from the page. 'When was the Great Plague in London, do you know?'

'There were several, I think,' Tom replied. 'There was the Black Death, of course, in the 1300s.'

I half-closed my eyes, replaying the scenes in my mind,

trying to focus on the clothes that people were wearing, the style of their hair, the furniture in the house . . .

'No,' I shook my head, 'the plague I'm thinking of was later than that.'

'There was a big one in the mid-seventeenth century, then, just before the Great Fire.'

'That's the one.' I wasn't sure how or why I knew, but I knew.

'What would you like to know about it?'

'Everything.' I shrugged my shoulders expansively. 'I don't know much about the history of that period. And that's the time in which Mariana lived, I'm sure of it. Her mother died of the plague.'

'Well, I'm rather rusty on the seventeenth century myself. I remember the Civil War bit well enough, and the beheading of Charles I, and Cromwell of course, but when it comes to the Plague . . . Hang on,' he interjected, brightening, 'I've got a copy of Pepys' Diary lying about somewhere. He kept a fairly good account of the Plague year, I think. Let me see if I can find it for you.'

He rose from his seat a second time, and made a close examination of the overstuffed bookshelves on the far side of the room. After a long hunt, he extracted a wedged volume and flipped open the cover. 'Here it is. Quite a nice copy, actually. I picked it up at a book sale in Oxford.' He handed it to me, a small book that nestled comfortably in my open hand, and turning to the title page I read aloud:

'*The Diary of Samuel Pepys, Esquire, F.R.S.* What does the "F.R.S." stand for?'

' "Fellow of the Royal Society" ', Tom supplied. 'He worked in the Admiralty office, and kept a diary from 1659 to '69, when his eyesight started going. It runs to several volumes, in its original state. Mine's the edited version, I'm afraid, with all the racy bits taken out, but it's still very interesting reading.'

'Thanks.' I closed the book, holding it tightly.

Tom eyed me thoughtfully. 'You're welcome to stay a few days, you know,' he told me. 'That is, if you want—'

'Thanks. I'll wait and see how I feel.'

Mrs Pearce materialized in the doorway. 'I've made up the bed in the blue guest bedroom,' she said matter-of-factly, as though it was a normal thing for the vicar's sister to drop round before breakfast and sleep through the day. 'Do you need to use the bath, before I start in there?'

'No, thank you.' I smiled. 'Bed sounds heavenly.'

'Marvellous woman,' Tom said, as the cleaner departed. He looked at me and grinned. 'I'll bet even the lord of Exbury manor doesn't get treatment like that from his staff.'

'Oh, Lord!' I sprang to my feet. 'What time is it?'

'Just past noon. Why?'

'Can I use your telephone?'

It took several minutes for the operator to locate the telephone number for Crofton Hall, another few minutes for her to make the connection for me, and eight long rings for someone at the other end to answer the telephone.

'Hello?'

'Hello. Is that Geoff?'

There was a small pause. 'No, I'm sorry,' the voice said carefully, with an unmistakable Scottish accent. 'He's not at home right now. Can I take a message?'

'Iain,' I said, 'it's Julia Beckett. Could you please tell Geoff I won't be able to take the tour this afternoon? He'll know what I mean. There's been a . . .

minor family emergency, and I've had to come to my brother's place in Hampshire.'

'Nothing serious, I hope?'

He sounded concerned, and I felt guilty about the lie.

'Oh, no,' I responded. 'I should be home tomorrow morning.'

'Right. I'll pass the message along, then.'

'Thanks.' I rang off feeling somewhat easier in my mind, and turned to find my brother watching me.

'Everything all right?' he asked.

'Fine.'

'Then let's get you settled in,' he said. 'You look like you're about to fall over.'

In a remarkably short space of time I found myself neatly tucked between the cool, sweet-smelling sheets of the wide, brass bed in the blue guest bedroom upstairs, wearing one of my brother's roomy nightshirts with the sleeves rolled above my elbows. Mrs Pearce had drawn the blinds down to darken the room for sleeping, but there was still enough light for reading.

I sighed, comfortably drowsy, and reached with a languid hand for the small book I'd left on the bedside table. Opening the diary of Samuel Pepys to a random page, I read the entry for 6 April 1665:

Great talk of a new Comet; he had written, *and it is certain do appear as bright as the late one at the best; but I have not seen it myself.* Two comets . . .

I shifted involuntarily against the pillows, and the back of my neck tingled as though an icy hand had brushed across it. All weariness forgotten, I grasped the book more tightly and began to read.

Chapter Ten

I had expected to feel any number of emotions as I made the drive back to Exbury the next morning. Apprehension, certainly, and fear, or even excitement. But I was unprepared for the feeling of complete serenity that settled over me like a comforting blanket, almost before the spire of my brother's church had been swallowed up by the trees in my rearview mirror. It was a strong feeling, strong and calming and pervasive. And entirely illogical, given the disturbing events of the day before.

I let my eyes follow the erratic movements of my fellow motorists as they manoeuvred themselves through the rush hour shuffle, while my mind drifted idly back to the previous morning.

I had managed to read almost one whole year of the Pepys diary before my own weariness had defeated me. When I woke, it was late afternoon, and through the half-open window the air smelled gloriously clean and fresh. My clothes, newly washed and pressed by Mrs Pearce, lay spread across a nearby chair like a waiting playmate. I rose, bathed, and went downstairs in search of my brother.

I found him on the long patio at the back of the house, absently chewing the end of his pencil while he sat, lost in thought, staring with unseeing eyes out over the wide, manicured lawn. Surfacing at the sound of my approaching footsteps, he looked up with a smile, removing the pencil from his mouth and setting it on top of the open notebook on the small table beside him.

'Well, you're certainly looking better,' he greeted me. 'Maybe you ought to stay on a couple of days, get yourself rested up.'

'Thanks, but no.' I took a brightly cushioned chair, facing him. 'I have to go back tomorrow. What are you working on?'

He tilted the notebook, letting me see the heavily scribbled pages. 'Sermon. You're good with words, as I recall. What's another word for "spontaneous"?'

'Extemporaneous?'

'Perfect.' He made a few more illegible marks with the pencil and set the notebook aside a second time. 'Did you manage to read any of the Pepys?'

'Mmm.' I leaned back, crossing my leg and swinging one foot in a lazy motion. 'I read nearly all of the plague year bit. 1665, by the way. Pretty horrific stuff.'

As nearly as I had been able to make out, the Plague had started slowly, crossing over from Holland on the merchant vessels that freely sailed the waters of the English Channel, from Amsterdam to London and back again. Having once taken hold, it had caught and festered like a dripping wound, spreading through the overcrowded suburbs with deadly purpose until it reached the City itself. It was with a sadness born of twentieth-century hindsight that I read how the Londoners had, in their superstitious ignorance, quickly slaughtered all the dogs and cats that they could find, animals that might have been able to curb the rising population of plague-carrying rats. Even today, with all our modern medicine, an outbreak of bubonic plague would be a terrifying spectacle. To the people of the seventeenth century, it must have seemed like the very apocalypse.

'Find anything of interest?' Tom asked.

'Several things. Do you remember my telling you that I'd dreamed of two comets? Well, it turns out there actually were two comets seen over London, one in December of 1664 and the second in the spring of the plague year. Made quite a stir, according to Pepys. Very portentous.'

'Yes, I can imagine,' Tom nodded. 'Comets were seen as signs of impending doom, in those days. Not without cause, really. The Bayeux Tapestry shows a comet appearing when poor old Harold was crowned King, just before William the Conqueror ploughed the English army into the ground and put an arrow through Harold's eye.'

'Did not,' I contradicted him. 'You've had the wrong history teacher, love. The chap on the tapestry with the arrow through his eye isn't Harold. Harold gets hewn down with a broadsword, or something, a little further on.'

'Whatever. The point is, that comets always meant bad luck. The historical antithesis of your bloody starlings, if you like. Did anything else in the Diary sound familiar?'

'Not really.' I shook my head. 'There were a few things he mentioned, early on in the year, that rang off bells in my brain, but when he writes about the summer months, with people dropping like flies in the streets, I don't feel anything.'

My brother smiled at me, that particularly self-satisfied smile that usually meant he was about to be clever. 'Well, you wouldn't, would you?'

'What do you mean?'

'Assuming that you were, in some former lifetime, this Mariana person, then you could hardly be expected to remember what London was like at the height of the

Plague. You'd been sent out of London, by that time, hadn't you? To the country.'

'To Exbury,' I mused. I caught myself and smiled a little ruefully. 'It all sounds rather far-fetched, doesn't it? Shades of the penny-dreadful.'

'Oh, I don't know.' Tom shrugged. 'It sounds rather fascinating, to me. I've set our local librarian on the scent, by the way, so we'll have to wait and see what he manages to dig up on the subject of reincarnation.'

I smiled at him. 'He didn't think it an odd topic for the local vicar to be researching?'

'Heavens, no.' Tom brushed off the suggestion. 'I told him I needed the information for an upcoming sermon.'

Which was, I decided upon reflection, a wholly logical and plausible excuse. Tom's sermons were notoriously unorthodox, and when he stood in the pulpit he was as likely to discuss cricket as he was to quote biblical texts. No doubt his parishioners had grown used to his eccentricities, and accepted them now without question.

'I'll have to dig out some of my old textbooks on comparative religions,' my brother had continued. 'There should be some information on reincarnation in there. Both the Hindu and Buddhist faiths believe in it, I know that much.'

'Well, I'm not sure that I'm entirely convinced, myself,' I told him. 'But whatever is happening, it's definitely connected to my house.'

'And you're certain you want to go back?'

I thought of my beautiful sunlit study; of the companionable atmosphere of the Red Lion pub, with Ned perpetually reading his paper at the end of the bar; of Geoffrey de Mornay, and the way his eyes darkened when he smiled . . .

'Yes,' I said, 'quite certain. It's almost as if – and I know this is going to sound idiotic – but it's almost as if I've been drawn to Greywethers for a reason. That I somehow belong there.'

'Hardly idiotic. I believe everything happens for a reason.' That was the Vicar speaking. 'And I think you're right. You need to go back and face up to this thing, if you're ever going to have any peace. You need to find out everything you can about this Mariana person. If you can do that, then you might learn why all this is happening to you now. Some bit of unfinished business, maybe, that needs to be completed.'

'It's possible, I suppose.'

'Or,' he added with a grin, 'maybe my past life theory is all wet, and you are just going quietly insane, after all. Like Great Aunt Sarah.'

I pulled a face. 'A comforting thought.'

'What are big brothers for?' Tom asked, still grinning.

'Although,' I conceded, 'perhaps the insanity defence is the most practical one. I'm still not sure I believe in the concept of reincarnation. It does seem a little unlikely, don't you think?'

Tom flicked me a sideways glance, and shrugged. Seemingly dismissing the subject, he turned his gaze back out over the wide green lawn, where the long shadows of the early evening were spreading across the freshly-mown grass like gentle caressing fingers. '1665, you said, was the plague year? Who was on the throne then?'

I frowned. 'Charles II, I think.'

'Oh, right. Another of the ill-fated Stuart Kings, wasn't he? Did you read the bit about his coronation?'

'No. I didn't go back that far.'

'Well,' Tom leaned back, 'you want to talk about bad omens. It rained the whole day, cats and dogs.'

I shook my head, vaguely. 'It didn't rain until that evening,' I corrected him. 'After the ceremonies were over.'

'It was a Saturday, I believe.'

My answer came more slowly this time. 'No. A Tuesday.'

'And the ground was carpeted in red.'

'Blue . . .' I turned my head, stunned, to meet his knowing eyes.

'You're right,' he told me. 'There probably isn't much point in exploring the reincarnation angle.'

I had stared back at him, unable to reply at first, my mind amazed and numb. 'Bloody hell,' I had said slowly. For, after all, vicar or no vicar . . .

'Precisely,' Tom had said, and smiling, he'd returned to his sermon.

The traffic cleared ahead of me, and the sudden blare of a car horn pulled me instantly out of my reverie. Still wrapped in warm serenity, I coaxed the little Peugeot into the faster lane and depressed the accelerator, squaring my shoulders against the driver's seat with a barely audible sigh. I drove the rest of the way in silence.

As I bumped across the little bridge that marked the approach to Exbury, the blanket of contentment tightened and a small thrill of anticipation raced through my travel-weary body. *Almost home*. The words filled my brain like a spoken voice, soft and soothing.

There was that word again, I thought. Home. It sprang so easily and naturally to mind, almost as if . . .

'I don't know,' I said aloud to the spotted windscreen, 'have I lived here before, really, in some other life?'

The reply flowed back, prompt and simple, from what might have been either my imagination or the deepest recesses of my subconscious: *Yes*.

The road curved and my house rose majestically from the landscape to welcome me, beautiful in the late morning sunlight with the forsythia bursting into bloom along the north wall. It always came back to the house, I thought, as I turned up the narrow drive. I had not chosen this house, as others choose, with a free and rational mind; the house had chosen me. And if I had indeed been drawn here for a purpose, then I had better do my best to find out what that purpose was, starting today. Starting now.

'All right,' I said firmly, lifting my chin to a determined angle. 'I've come back. Now show me what it is you want me to do.'

It was a shameless bit of bravado, really. I wasn't even sure as I spoke the words whether I was addressing a ghost, the house, or myself. And I certainly wasn't expecting an answer.

But as I parked in the converted stables at the back of the house, a glimmer of movement caught my eye and turning my head, I saw the figure of a young woman standing in the dovecote garden. The still, poised figure of a young woman in green.

For a moment I panicked, my chest tightening, and then the woman turned and smiled and waved, and I saw that it wasn't a ghost at all, only Vivien wearing a shapeless old green coverall, with her fair hair tumbled anyhow around her shoulders and her face glowing with healthy colour. Relieved, I walked slowly across the long grass towards the ruined dovecote. Vivien stopped working and leaned on her rake, watching my approach with friendly eyes.

'You're home, then,' she said, unnecessarily. 'Is everything all right with your family?'

'Yes, thanks.' News travelled quickly. She looked as though she wanted to know more, but I changed the subject. I never had liked lying, much. 'I didn't know you dabbled in gardening, as well,' I said.

'I don't normally. I'm just lending Iain a hand with the weeding. Such a beautiful morning,' she explained, gesturing up at the flawless blue sky. 'I hated to be cooped up indoors.'

'You're not lending *much* of a hand, love,' Iain Sumner's voice said drily. I couldn't see him for the stone wall, but as I drew nearer the garden he stood upright and stretched. 'You've been raking that same bit of soil for the past twenty minutes,' he accused Vivien.

She shrugged good-naturedly. 'So I'm thorough.'

'Aye. I'll not argue with you there.' His eyes slid sideways away from her, and he smiled a greeting at me, pitching a handful of dirt-encrusted weeds onto the heaping mound beside him. He was looking the proper countryman this morning, in rough trousers and a faded blue flannel shirt, with the leather gauntlet gloves pulled up over his forearms. He was also looking exhausted. His grey eyes were strained and deeply shadowed in his stoic face. I thought of my cousin Ronald, in Cornwall, who rose at four every morning to milk his thirty cows, and wondered for the hundredth time why anyone would choose to be a farmer.

Iain yanked off one of the weathered gloves and wiped the sweat from his forehead with a large, sunburnt hand. 'I gave your message to Geoff,' he informed me. 'There was no problem. He's been called away himself, up north on business, for the next few days, but he said he'll give you a ring when he gets back.'

'Oh, yes?' Vivien cocked her head mischievously.

'He promised me a tour of the Hall,' I explained, hoping no-one would notice my blush in the strong sunlight. For the second time, I changed the subject. 'The garden looks lovely,' I said.

It truly did. The orderly rows of tiny green shoots were now surrounded by verdant clumps of hyacinth and primrose. He had added a climbing rose as well, perhaps a transplant from the famous rose gardens at Crofton Hall, its sleeping tendrils trailing lazily over the sun warmed stones. In a month or so, the small plot of land would be positively bursting with life and colour.

Iain followed my appreciative gaze, and shrugged his broad shoulders. 'It'll do,' he said modestly.

I glanced down at my wristwatch. It was nearly half-eleven. 'Would anyone like a cup of tea?' I offered.

'Lovely.' Vivien abandoned her rake with evident relief, and Iain gave her a look of indulgent affection before his tired grey eyes met mine and he smiled.

'I'd not say no,' was his reply.

I wouldn't have admitted it to a soul, least of all to myself, but I was glad that I was not alone when I unlocked the door of the silent grey house and, with a deep breath of determination, stepped across the waiting threshold.

Chapter Eleven

I need not have worried, after all. The remaining days of the week passed in quiet, perfect normality, dull as ditchwater. Perversely, I was disappointed. It was not a rational reaction, but I could not help myself. Patience, as my family would wholeheartedly attest, was never my strongest characteristic, and now that I was prepared – even eager – to experience another scene from Mariana Farr's life, I found it frustrating to be denied the opportunity. Even the watcher on the grey horse had deserted me, and the place beneath the old oak tree, whenever I had the courage to look, was empty.

By Friday morning I had grown restless in my impatience, and I looked to my work for diversion. It was high time I started working, anyway, I told myself in resolute tones. Seated in my familiar pose at the drawing board, with the marked page of manuscript clipped to the top bar and a fresh sheet of drawing paper spread beneath my pencil, I felt instantly more focussed and relaxed.

It had been over a month since I had last worked on the storybook illustrations. I had been too excited after buying the house, too busy during the move, and too distracted by the events since to even contemplate drawing my goblins and queens. The little characters had waited, brooding, all that time, and now they fairly ran from my mind to the tip of my pencil and onto the pristine page, bringing to life an adaptation of a Korean folk tale about a disgruntled dragon.

The story required four illustrations in all. By early afternoon I had completed the pencil sketches, with the almost fussy amount of detailing that was my trademark. The sketches would still have to be painted over in watercolours, but that could wait until tomorrow. I leaned back in the high, padded, specially-made chair, stretched my arms above my head to loosen the knots between my shoulder blades, and looked around the room with pleasure.

I could not have chosen a better spot in which to work. The room was small, and square, and low-ceilinged, but the walls were painted a pale sunrise yellow and coaxed an answering glow from the wide polished floorboards. It was a comfortable, cheerful little room.

By swivelling my chair I could command a clear view, through the window, of the dark line of trees marking the slow, winding curve of the river to the west of my property, and beyond that the clear patchwork farmlands and low rolling downs. To the southwest, just within my line of vision, the squat, crenellated tower of the village church stood sentry over the village, and the tall brick chimneys of Crofton Hall rose majestically above the green canopy of trees.

I had not yet heard from Geoffrey de Mornay, and so I assumed that he was still away on business. Up north, somewhere, Iain had said. Lancashire, maybe, I speculated, or Northumberland. Morland Electronics had factories in both places.

At any rate, I reminded myself, I wasn't holding my breath, waiting for his phone call. After all, I wasn't some lovesick adolescent, and I had plenty of other things to occupy my time. Besides, I thought, as I went downstairs to brew a long overdue cup of tea, I had only known the man a week.

Which did nothing to explain why, when the telephone finally *did* ring, I nearly vaulted over the kitchen table to answer it. Or why my voice suddenly turned sultry, conjuring up images of Greta Garbo in her prime.

'Hullo?'

'Julia?'

'Oh, it's you,' I said, my disappointment showing.

'Sorry,' Tom sounded taken aback. 'Who should I be?'

'No-one.' I recovered my normal voice. 'What's up?'

My brother paused, decided not to pursue the matter, and went on somewhat cautiously. 'I just got back from the library,' he informed me, 'and I thought you might be interested in some of the stuff my librarian has managed to scrape up for me.'

'Already? That was certainly quick of him.'

'He's a terribly industrious young chap. Anyhow,' Tom carried on, 'apart from digging up a huge list of names of famous people who believe in reincarnation – everyone from Plato to Voltaire – he also managed to find the official religious line on the matter, in both the Hindu and Buddhist faiths. Pages of information, really. The basic theory runs that the human soul is sent back to live on earth again and again until it has learned the lessons necessary to pass into a higher state of being.'

'And what lessons are those?'

'It doesn't specify. There *is* the law of karma, which says that what you do in one life affects what happens in your future lives, so if you're a real schmuck in this life, you'll have a miserable time in the next. But of course,' Tom qualified, in his usual rational way, 'that's just the religious angle. There's a lot of investigative research here that supports the phenomenon of reincarnation without delving into the religious aspects.'

'Investigative research?' I echoed. 'You're pulling my leg.'

'No, really.' I could hear the sound of shuffling papers in the background. 'Some people are dead serious on this. For example, a professor of psychiatry at the University of Virginia has collected 1,700 cases of people who have conscious memories of past lives. Mostly young children, who say out of the blue that they were so-and-so in a past life, and can identify their former homes and even their former friends and spouses. Very strange stuff. There's a fascinating case from India . . .' he coughed, and the papers rustled again. 'But I digress. The other main body of research seems to come from hypnotherapists, if you believe in that sort of thing. They've regressed literally thousands of people into the past, and found that most people were just ordinary folk living ordinary lives. Oh, here's an interesting bit. This is an article on spontaneous recall of past lives, and it says that the people in the study all reported hearing a ringing in their ears, accompanied by a sensation of dizziness, just before the incident occurred. Sound familiar?'

'It sounds like you've got quite a bit of material, there,' I commented, trying to ignore the faint shiver that swept across my skin.

'Reams of it,' Tom concurred. 'Listen, why don't I send you the whole packet and let you read it for yourself, instead of rambling on over the telephone?'

'Fine. You've got my address, have you?'

'Somewhere.'

Not trusting my brother's memory, I gave it to him again, and listened to the scratching of his pen as he wrote it down. When we resumed our conversation, he seemed as disappointed as I was that nothing had happened since my return.

'Nothing at all?' he checked. 'Not even an unusual dream?'

'I haven't had any dreams, that I remember.'

'Maybe you're trying too hard.'

'I'm not doing it on purpose, Tom.' My voice was clipped and short-tempered. 'I'm just as eager to have something happen as you are, you know.'

'I know. Sorry.' Even through the telephone line, I could sense his smile. 'Rather funny, when you come to think of it.'

'What is?'

'Well, on Tuesday you were upset because things *were* happening, and now we're both upset because they *aren't*.'

'Oh, I see. Well, it doesn't feel very funny from this end. It feels rather ominous, if you must know.'

'The calm before the storm?'

'More like . . . like I'm being watched,' I told him. 'Like somebody's standing behind me, watching me. And waiting.'

'Waiting for what, do you think?'

I shook my head, not caring that he couldn't see the gesture. 'I don't know. I don't suppose you have any useful suggestions in that bundle of information you got from the librarian?'

'Not really, no.' He flipped through the papers again. 'Oh, but there were a couple of other statements I thought you'd find interesting . . .'

'Yes?'

'There seems to be a lot of evidence that we surround ourselves with the same people in each life – that your father in one life becomes your friend in the next, and so on. They're sometimes referred to as "soul mates", those people to whom you take an instant liking without really knowing why.'

'So you could have been my brother in a past life.'

'Or your husband,' Tom teased. 'Or your son. Or your daughter, come to that. Sex doesn't appear to remain constant from one lifetime to another.'

'All right,' I accepted the information. 'And what was the other point you thought would interest me?'

'Ah,' Tom said. 'Well, the next bit is a little touchy, but . . . most of the people involved in one of the studies said that they had actually *chosen* to be reborn; that they had sort of stayed in limbo, if you like, until an opportune moment presented itself.'

'So?'

'So you said that this ghost, this Green Lady in your garden, hasn't been seen by anybody for about thirty years?'

'That's what I'm told.'

'And has it never occurred to you,' Tom said slowly, 'that it was about thirty years ago that you were born?'

Tread lightly, she is near. . . The words sprang, naturally and unbidden, to my troubled mind as I stood alone in the walled churchyard, gazing down at the overgrown grave of Mariana Farr. The poem was an old one, by Oscar Wilde. I'd had to memorize it once at school, and even now, years later, I could still remember the final, haunting line: *All my life's buried here, Heap earth upon it.*

But surely, I told myself, that was wrong? I ought to be digging to uncover the past, not heaping earth upon it to cover it up. Frowning, I thrust my hands deeper into the pockets of my jeans and stared hard at the plain little stone. *All my life's buried here . . .*

A chill breeze lifted the hair from my forehead and I turned away, lowering my head in silent contemplation as I trudged with heavy footsteps towards the church. As before, the huge wooden door opened easily to my touch. Standing in the hushed, cool interior, I marvelled once again at the exquisite stillness of the place, and the romantic, abandoned aura that permeated it. Like the ruins of Glastonbury Abbey, with the grass growing atop the high roofless walls, this little church gave one the impression that all the people had left a very long time ago.

Which was silly, I thought, since come Sunday the pews would probably all be filled with the faithful of modern-day Exbury. But the impression lingered, nonetheless. I would have sat awhile myself in one of the scarred and burnished pews, enjoying the peaceful, undemanding atmosphere, but a sound from outside the church caught my attention. It was, at first, a faint sound, filtering through the thick stone walls like the insistent tap, tap of a tree branch against a window pane, but it drew closer and grew steadily in volume, until I could clearly hear the sound of a horse's hooves pounding the tightly packed earth of the path that wound behind the church – the path that led to the manor house.

Curious, I stepped outside again and rounded the west wall of the church, walking the short distance across the grass to the low gate that led on to the manor house path. Although I could hear the horse quite plainly, I could see nothing, and I stepped out onto the path for a better view.

The dizziness came upon me rather suddenly. I barely had time to lift my fingers to my throbbing temples, closing my eyes against a blinding explosion of light, when I heard a loud explosive oath behind me and turned to see a massive pair of hooves neatly slicing the air just inches from my face. Stunned, I fell back, bruising my hip against a stone as I did so. Pinned by the tangled weight of my gown against my legs, I could only stay there, half-sitting and half-lying in the dirt, staring up at the man whose expert horsemanship had no doubt just saved my life.

I couldn't see his face – the sun was to his back, and I had only the barest glimpse of a hard profile as he worked to steady the dancing grey horse. But while I couldn't see his expression, I was certain that he wasn't smiling.

'Christ's blood, woman!' he swore again, confirming my suspicions, 'Can you not watch where you are going? D'you wish for death?'

Wide-eyed and silent, I shook my head, unsure as to which of the two questions I was answering. The outline of his jaw tightened, as if he were preparing to give a lecture, but he only exhaled a tight, exasperated sigh and looked away for a moment, letting me see that hard, finely-drawn profile in greater detail. When he looked at me again and spoke, his voice was quieter, and almost kind.

'Are you hurt?'

Again, I shook my head, and sensed his smile.

'Can you not speak, Mariana Farr?' he asked. 'I'd heard that girls from London were uncommonly good at it.'

My blood chilled nervously. 'I am not from London, sir. I come from Southampton.'

' 'Tis odd,' he said, lightly. 'I stood a drink to a man not a week ago who claimed he was a coachman come

123

from London. He told me he had brought hence but one passenger, and that a girl with hair as fair as ripened barley. He waxed poetic in his cups, this coachman did, but he did not impress me as a liar.' I said nothing, and he went on speaking, still in that light and careless tone. 'You need not look so frightened – I'll not tell. I am no peasant, mistress, to cross myself and mutter prayers when someone whispers "plague", and I would not see you driven from the town by those who have no wit to see you carry not the sickness.'

I pushed myself to my feet, brushing the dust from my gown with fingers that shook only slightly. 'You have me at a disadvantage, sir,' I told him, in as dignified a voice as I could muster, squinting up at him against the sun. 'You know my name.'

'Ay, well, we've precious few strangers in Exbury in these times,' he explained, 'and fewer still that . . . warrant my interest.' His shadowed gaze burned me where I stood, and the smile in his voice was even more in evidence. Perhaps taking pity on my eyesight, he drew the horse around so that the sun was no longer directly behind him, and lifting his hat with a flourish he bent his head in a mocking bow.

'Richard de Mornay, at your service,' he introduced himself.

'Sir.' I inclined my own head in response, partly because I could not entirely abandon my own good manners, and partly because I could not bear to look at his face any longer. It was a beautiful face, lean and darkly handsome, framed by a neatly trimmed dark beard and loose waves of natural dark hair, not one of the elaborate wigs I'd grown so used to seeing in the City.

Nor was his dress fashionably effeminate. He wore a simple black waistcoat and narrow breeches, with a long black jacket and high leather boots. The material of his clothing was very fine, and heavily embroidered, but it was not gaudy, and thus looked all the more expensive. I found myself wondering about Richard de Mornay. He seemed quite different from the plain-speaking farmers and merchants I had met since my arrival.

'You are certain you are not injured?' he asked again.

'I am certain. Thank you.' I kept my head lowered, waiting for him to move on. When he did not, I chanced another look up at him, and found him watching me.

'Then I wish you good day, mistress,' he said slowly, nodding once more before replacing the hat on his head and turning the horse towards the village once more. 'Mind you take care on this road in future.'

I had the oddest impression that he was warning me against something other than being run down by a horse, but before I had time to fully register his words he was gone, and I was left standing in the middle of the path like a fool. Pulling myself together with an effort, I left the path and walked home across the fields, not wishing to chance another meeting with Richard de Mornay on the village street.

My uncle's house, viewed from the back across the roughened fields, was a dismal and unwelcoming sight. In the few days that I had spent there since my flight from London I had learned to dread the place, as I had in my childhood dreaded the forbidding sight of the Tower of London. Both, in their way, were prisons.

There was no rational basis for my impression, nor for my growing fear of my uncle. I had not been mistreated, I had been accepted without question into the daily life of the family, and Uncle Jabez's manner towards me was invariably courteous, if somewhat distant. But I had nonetheless begun to feel uneasy, like a child roaming the hallways of a strange house in the dead of night, expecting at every turn to encounter some indescribably hideous monster. Indeed, as the days passed, I became increasingly aware of this monster's presence; I could almost feel it, lurking beneath the façade of the daily routine, like the serpent in the Garden of Eden. And although I could not yet put a face to it, I was certain of its existence.

With dragging footsteps, I entered the house through the back door, and found Rachel in the kitchen, up to her elbows in pastry. She looked up, smiling and streaked with flour.

'Did you have a good walk?' she asked, and then, as I nodded, 'I was beginning to worry for you, you were away so long.'

'I went to the churchyard, to see the grave of my grandfather,' I explained, my voice absent. 'Rachel, what do you know of a man named Richard de Mornay?'

She looked up sharply, hesitating, and her eyes slid past me, widening in sudden apprehension. I had not heard my uncle enter the room, but I felt him behind me before he spoke.

'Richard de Mornay,' he repeated, his voice lingering unpleasantly on the words. 'How do you know of him?'

'We passed on the road today,' I answered truthfully, 'and he spoke to me.'

'He . . . spoke to you. And that is all?'

'Yes.'

'And yet you ask after him.'

The interrogation was grating sorely on my nerves, but I controlled my temper with an effort and kept my voice as even as I could. 'I asked after him because I was curious,' I said, raising my chin a little. 'His clothes were uncommonly fine, and he rode a lovely horse.' I swallowed, meeting my uncle's eyes. 'I was curious,' I said again.

Jabez Howard held my gaze for a long moment before he lowered his eyes and smiled, releasing me.

'Richard de Mornay,' he said, his tone conversational, 'is the young lord of Crofton Hall. He is of a noble family, and holds the rank of Baronet from his father, who died five years ago. He is a man to be respected, but,' he caught my eyes again, 'he is not a gentleman. The devil dwells in Richard de Mornay. You will not speak to him again.'

He turned and walked into the dining-room, leaving me standing by the hearth in a sudden chill. A strange noise penetrated the oppressive silence, a shrill and persistent ringing sound, that grew steadily louder, coming in short, staccato bursts. The room wavered, shimmering like the horizon on a hot summer afternoon, and the walls and furniture reassembled themselves before coming into focus once more, clear and comfortingly solid.

I was standing in the pantry of my own house, facing the kitchen door, listening to the insistent ringing of the telephone in the front hall. I just let it go on ringing, staring dumbly at the open door, until the last vibration of sound had died away. Reality trickled back in slow, disjointed streams of conscious thought, and it seemed an eternity before I could summon the will to move from my spot by the pantry wall into the spacious, air-filled front hallway, where I stood looking down at the sleek black telephone as though it were a being from another planet.

And as I stood there, staring at it, with one hand partially outstretched, it began to ring again.

Chapter Twelve

The next day dawned fair and warm, bringing with it the first faint hint of summer's approaching heat. By early afternoon the clouds that had been in evidence that morning had dwindled to insubstantial wisps of transparent white, barely discernible against the brilliant blue sky, and the sun hung like a great yellow jewel in their midst.

In the wide, flowered borders that lined the gravel front drive of Crofton Hall, the bees were busily at work, single-mindedly unconcerned with the rather noisy and intrusive presence of the queue of tourists waiting in jostling, chatty good-humour for the start of the one-fifteen tour.

Beside me, on the lawn, Geoff stopped walking and bent to retie his shoelace, casting a quick assessing glance at the gathering crowd.

'Saturday's always our best day,' he told me. 'We'd better give this lot a quarter of an hour's start so we don't get any stragglers joining in with our tour.' He stood, smiling. 'Care for a stroll round the rose garden?'

A week had not diminished the effect of that smile. A few curious eyes followed us as we made our way across the front lawn, but it was an idle curiosity and I doubted whether any of the tourists realized that the handsome young man, casual in denim jeans and bright-red polo shirt, was in fact the owner of Crofton Hall.

But they might have wondered who the devil *I* was. Geoff had sounded so formal on the telephone yesterday that I had unconsciously ascribed that same formality to the tour itself, and had selected from my wardrobe a dignified paisley skirt, cream-coloured silk blouse and ridiculously expensive Italian shoes with foolish heels that sank into the soft lawn with every step. To keep from getting stuck, I had to adopt a slightly stilted walk that put most of my weight on the balls of my feet. I silently blessed Geoffrey de Mornay who, chivalrous to a fault, had slowed his gait to accommodate mine.

The rose garden, I learned, occupied a goodly portion of the lawn against the northern boundary wall that divided the churchyard from the manor lands. Stretched tall against the sky, the square tower of the church peered at us over the high stone wall as we walked along the tranquil pathways. The garden itself had an aura of the Renaissance about it – very neat, very precise, very orderly; yet all the geometrically laid-out beds with their neat edges could not disguise the delightfully tangled growth that they contained.

'Of course,' Geoff conceded, 'it's more impressive in the summer, when things are in bloom . . .'

'It's lovely,' I assured him. 'I don't think I've ever seen a garden design this intricate before.'

'Yes, well, we had a devil of a time restoring it until Iain figured out that it followed the pattern of the dining-room ceiling.' Geoff smiled. 'I'm told there was a maze around the west side of the house that was planted in the same design – big yew hedges, quite impressive – but one of the Victorian owners chopped it all down. Built a rather ugly fountain in its place. Italianate. Lots of statues.'

'What a shame.' I had a childish fondness for mazes. I still remembered getting lost in the maze at Hampton Court on one of our memorable family holidays. My father had led us round and round in increasingly elaborate circles until Tommy, feeling hungry and not wanting to miss his dinner, had taken charge and steered us all unerringly back to the entrance . . .

'What's so funny?' Geoff wanted to know, so I shared the memory with him.

He had an engaging laugh – a deep, resonant baritone – and I liked the way his eyes crinkled up at the corners.

'Do you only have the one brother?' he asked me.

I nodded. 'Just the two of us. I don't think my parents could have stood any more children, quite frankly. We were enough of a handful.'

'Really?' He looked down with interest. 'You don't look like someone who was a difficult child.'

'Looks are deceiving,' I assured him. 'If I wasn't in the headmistress's office I was in the hospital casualty ward being stitched up. See this?' I tilted my chin up and showed him the scar. 'I got that falling off the roof while playing Mary Poppins. And this one,' I pushed up my sleeve and exposed my left forearm, 'was from a barbed wire fence that came between me and a football. And my brother was even worse.'

'And now you're a highly respected artist,' Geoff pointed out, 'and your brother's a vicar.'

'Yes.' I grinned up at him. 'My parents are still in shock, I think.'

'Everything's all right with your family, is it? Iain said that you'd been called away to Hampshire for some sort of emergency.'

'It turned out to be nothing,' I said quickly – a little too quickly. Funny how one small lie could make you feel so damnably guilty. 'Everyone is just fine, thanks.'

'Good.'

We walked a few more paces in silence, and then I cleared my throat and tried a new tack.

'Did you enjoy your trip up north?' I asked.

He smiled at his feet. 'I'm not sure *enjoy* would be the proper word for it,' he said. 'I had to sort out a minor labour dispute at our plant in Manchester, so I've spent the past few days locked in stale boardrooms with irate people, drinking coffee by the gallon. But it all worked out in the end.'

'You came back yesterday?'

He nodded. 'Yesterday afternoon. I must have just missed you, actually.'

I looked up surprised. 'I'm sorry?'

'You didn't come to the house yesterday? No? I rather flattered myself you had.' He smiled again, his eyes warm. 'You were walking back towards your house, through the fields, when I drove up. I called out to you, but you must have been too far away to hear me. So I telephoned, instead.'

'I was at the church yesterday,' I explained, trying not to let him see how deeply his words had shaken me. I had known all along that my 'flashbacks' – for want of a better word – occupied real space and time; that when, as Mariana Farr, I crossed a room or opened a window, I was also repeating the same action as my present-day self. But I had never fully absorbed the implications of this phenomenon.

What would people think, I wondered, if I walked past them one day on the High Street, my eyes blank and staring, unresponsive? What if I walked across a road without seeing the traffic, or straight through a fence that hadn't yet been built in 1665? The possibility of causing myself injury or embarrassment was very great. If only I could find some way of controlling the process; if only I could choose the time and place . . .

'Should be safe now.'

I looked up at Geoff, my eyes startled, but he was looking back at the deserted front drive of Crofton Hall.

'The tour should be in the Servant's Hall by now, well ahead of us. Are you ready to go back?'

I nodded and, mindful of my bothersome high heels, followed awkwardly in his wake as he retraced our steps across the wide lawn.

'I ought to begin this tour properly,' Geoff said, 'by telling you that you are now approaching the south façade of Crofton Hall, constructed in 1598 by William de Mornay the Elder.' He swept one arm out in a broad gesture that encompassed the soaring, steeply-gabled building with its rows of staring mullioned windows, the ancient plaster of its walls greyed and mellowed by clinging lichen and centuries of exposure to the English climate.

'My wing of the house is older,' Geoff confided, 'and more historic, but not nearly as impressive as this.' He grinned. 'This is the view on all our postcards, of course.'

There were several postcards spread out on a small table near the door, to tempt the waiting tourist, along with a small stack of souvenir guidebooks presided over by a fresh-faced teenaged girl with corn-coloured hair and a deliberately ingenuous smile.

'How's business?' Geoff asked her.

'Seventeen in this last group,' she beamed up at him proudly. 'We've had over fifty people through today so far. Cathy hasn't even had a break yet, but she said she's going to let me take the next tour through.'

'Fine. Cathy's our regular tour guide,' he explained for my benefit. 'Sally here comes in on weekends to lend a hand with the extra crowds. Sally, this is Julia Beckett.'

'The lady who's just moved in to Greywethers? The artist lady?' The girl's eyes went round with awe, and I'd be lying if I said my ego didn't swell a little in response. 'It's a pleasure, I'm sure, miss,' Sally told me, shaking my hand with youthful fervour.

'I'll be taking Miss Beckett on a tour of the Hall,' Geoff continued, 'so keep an eye open for us, will you? We should be far enough ahead of your next tour group that we don't get in your way, but try not to hem us in, if you don't mind.'

'Yes, Mr de Mornay.'

'She's a good kid,' Geoff told me, as we passed under the great stone porch and through the open front door. 'Her mother is the local chemist, quite a formidable woman.' He grinned. 'She's determined that I'm going to marry one of her daughters, so I thought the least I could do was employ one of them.'

'How very noble of you.'

'Well, it's all part of the "lord of the manor" bit. I'm young, I'm well off, and I'm not married. That makes me fair game in a place like this.'

I glanced over at him, eyebrows raised. He was either incredibly modest or incredibly thick. He wasn't simply young and well off – he was downright gorgeous and a millionaire into the bargain. Small wonder that the mothers of Exbury were manoeuvring on behalf of their daughters.

We emerged from the entrance into a room that rendered me momentarily speechless.

Walls hung with exquisitely cut velvet soared upwards to meet an elaborately plastered ceiling, at least twenty feet above the gleaming oak floor with its covering of priceless Persian carpets. It was a room designed to impress, and it achieved its objective with relative ease; but what clinched it for me was the fireplace.

I had never seen a fireplace like that before, not even in films. It was large enough for two tall men to stand in with their arms outstretched, fashioned of a glorious white stone. Richly carved, fanciful figures twined their way up the sides of the fireplace and across the heavy mantelpiece, and above the mantel, crowning it, was a beautifully carved and painted coat of arms.

'The Great Hall,' Geoff said, beside me. 'Quite something, isn't it? That's a Genoa cut velvet on the walls, late Elizabethan and rather rare, I'm told. We had a conservator come in and patch it up for us – it's amazing the whole thing didn't fall to shreds centuries ago.'

I lifted my hand involuntarily, then let it fall to my side again. I knew better than to touch it. One of my neighbours in London had worked as a guide for the British Museum, and had frequently bemoaned the irreparable damage done by ignorant hands and flash photography. Clasping my hands behind my back, I looked round in awestruck, appreciative silence.

'The fireplace, of course, is absolutely unique,' Geoff continued his commentary. 'The white stone comes from Compton Basset, just a few miles from here, and the carving was done by a local mason.'

'Is that your coat of arms, above it?' I asked.

'Yes. Well, my family's, anyway. The arms were granted to William de Mornay, the younger, in the seventeenth century. As a direct male descendant, I've a right to use them if I want – put them on my stationery, that sort of thing. But it always seemed to me a little snobbish. Besides, there's the matter of differencing to think of.' To my blank look, he explained: 'Arthur de Mornay – that's my ancestor – was, by his own account, William's grandson, but without proper records we've no way of knowing whether Arthur's father was a first or second son, or even a third or fourth. They'd all have had to use different marks on their coats of arms – roses and crosses and crescents and such – depending on order of birth. Cadency marks, they're called. Only the head of a family is entitled to use the full coat of arms.'

'I didn't know that,' I confessed, moving closer for a better look. 'I'm afraid I'm a little rusty on armorial bearings. I had a teacher at Art School who did work for the College of Arms, so I learned a little about the design and terminology . . .'

'Well, let's see how you do, then,' Geoff grinned, stepping up behind me. 'What can you tell me about the shield?'

It was a direct challenge, and I had never been able to resist a direct challenge. I clasped my hands harder and gazed thoughtfully up at the painted carving. I knew enough to know that the shield was only part of the coat of arms, and that the two terms were not synonymous.

'Well,' I began, 'it's been split along the middle horizontally, which in heraldic language is party per something, isn't it?'

'Party per fess,' he nodded.

'And the bottom colour is gold, but I don't recognize the top colour.'

'Sanguine,' Geoff supplied. 'Blood-red. It's not common.'

'So the bottom part would be "or a rose gules, barbed and seeded proper"', I told him, looking up at the red rose with its green thorns and gold centre, bright against the gold background. 'How am I doing?'

'Wonderfully well,' he admitted. 'What about the top half?'

I frowned, studying the two hooded hawks gleaming gold against the deep blood red, their hoods a shining silver, their wings and talons outstretched. 'Sanguine, you said? Then it would be "sanguine two hawks or displayed . . . hooded argent"?'

I was less sure of that one, but his approving smile gave me confidence.

'I am impressed,' he said softly. 'The rose symbolizes the family's patriotism and loyalty to the crown, and the hawks our blind faith and tenacity. Hoods and talons. Try a little more,' he urged. 'What does the helmet on top of the shield tell you?'

That one I knew.

'That the owner of the arms is a knight or a baronet,' I said with certainty.

'And how do you know that?'

'Because the helmet is facing forward and the visor is up, with no bars on it.'

'And the helmet's steel,' he added, 'not gold or silver. Well done. And the crest?'

'It's that thing on top of the helmet, isn't it? The hawk's head on the twisted wreath.'

This hawk was also hooded, and very fierce-looking.

'Now,' Geoff folded his arms across his chest, 'tell me what the scrolled bit framing the shield is called, and I promise I'll fall over backwards in astonishment.'

'Sorry,' I grinned. 'I don't remember what it's called, but I do know that it's supposed to represent the mantle of cloth that knights wore to keep the heat of the sun off their armour.'

'It's called the lambrequin,' he told me with a triumphant smile. 'At least there's one thing I know that you don't. "I'm a little rusty on my armorial bearings",' he mimicked me, his smile broadening. 'Are you angling for a job as a tour guide?'

I blushed a little, shaking my head. 'No. I just have a good memory for details. I see things, or read them, and I remember them.'

'I didn't mean to embarrass you,' he frowned. 'I was just teasing. You shouldn't be embarrassed about having brains.'

'I'm not, really, I—'

'I like smart women,' he told me with a good-natured wink. 'Intelligence is very sexy.'

I blushed deeper and concentrated fiercely on the coat of arms above my head. 'What does the motto mean?' I asked him.

'You're a little rusty on your Latin, as well?' He grinned, moving closer until I felt the warmth of him through the thin fabric of my blouse. His voice was a low, pleasant rumble beside my ear.

'*Everti non potest*,' he read the words aloud, slowly, reverently, solemnly. 'It means "Indestructible".'

The word hung in the air between us for several seconds before the excited murmur of voices approaching jolted us out of our contemplation. We had lingered too long in the Great Hall, and the next tour was about to begin.

'Bloody hell,' Geoff swore without violence, looking round for an escape route. 'Come on,' he said, and grabbing my hand fairly hauled me through a doorway to the left of the fireplace and into the narrow passage beyond.

Chapter Thirteen

'And this is the west passage,' Geoff said. Pulling the door shut behind him he leaned back against it with a wolfish grin. 'I couldn't wait to show it to you.'

'It's lovely,' I said laughing. 'Are all your tours like this?'

'Usually,' he admitted. 'I don't much like crowds. You ought to count yourself lucky – when I took Vivien round to show her the restored rooms, a couple of years ago, we had to hide in a cupboard for twenty minutes.'

'Lucky Vivien,' I almost said, but I caught myself in time. Instead I asked him, tongue in cheek, 'There's a name for that, isn't there? A pathological fear of crowds?'

He nodded. 'Privacy.' He gestured to the door directly opposite. 'That's the servant's hall across there, but since the tour will be going there next I think we'll skip ahead to the kitchens, if you don't mind.'

I trailed after him down the long passage with its sloping flagstone floor. 'Does it bother you,' I asked him, 'having all those people tramping about your home?'

'Not really,' he shrugged, his tone amiable. 'As I said, I kept the best part of the house for myself, and that's my home – those are the rooms I grew up in. All this is just . . . superfluous, I suppose. It's too much for one family to live in, let alone one person. Most of these rooms would probably never see the light of day if it weren't for the tourists. Besides, it's all a bit much, don't you think? I mean, can you honestly see me whipping up a midnight snack in *this*?'

He stopped walking and raised a hand to indicate a kitchen of truly baronial proportions, all brick and polished copper, with a monstrous hearth. The turn-of-the-century stove planted in one corner looked as if it could hold twenty roasting turkeys with room to spare.

'I see your point,' I told him, raising my eyebrows.

We toured at leisure through the kitchens, the brewhouse, the dairy, the buttery, the larder, and finally the scullery, built round an unusual indoor well. From the scullery a small, heavy door gave onto a square courtyard, open to the sky and surrounded on three sides by the house itself. The fourth side of the square was closed by a high stone wall, overgrown with trailing ivy and surmounted by imposing iron spikes.

Rather like having a private park in the middle of one's house, I thought. Except that it was dreadfully overgrown. You couldn't see the ground at all, in some places, and a tangled mass of weeds and wildflowers had choked off the stone walkway that angled across the courtyard. I was surprised that Iain hadn't done anything with the place, and said as much.

'Make it into a sort of secret garden, you mean? Yes, well, I suggested it to him, once, but he wasn't keen on the idea. He doesn't like the courtyard,' Geoff said. 'Says it feels like a tomb.'

It did, rather, come to that. The air within the walls was still and lifeless, the silence palpable, and though the sun beamed brightly down upon us, beneath my feet the grasses sighed from sadness and neglect.

'But if it's gardens you're after, come take a look at

this,' Geoff offered. He led me back along the pathway to the main body of the house, and drew me once again into the west passage. Opposite the kitchen wing a short flight of steps led down into the conservatory, a wonderfully formal Victorian room filled with glass and light and painted wicker, and the smell of lilies hanging over everything.

For a second time, the sound of approaching footsteps sent us scuttling for cover. Geoff shepherded me across another passage and into a darkened stairwell that was saturated with the cool dank scent of stone. Halfway up the stairs he held me back with a hand on my arm, and pointed to a spot near our feet.

'See that? That bit of carved stonework below the panelling? That's twelfth century. It dates from the time of the Benedictine priory. Apart from a few ghosts and some Gothic arches in the west wall, that's all the monks left us.'

I stooped low for a closer look, tracing the carving with my fingers. 'Left you a lot of ghosts, did they?'

'Oh, one or two. I think they're the only respectable ones I have. The ghosts of Crofton Hall are a rowdy lot,' he grinned.

'So you believe in them.'

'I admit the possibility,' he clarified. 'After all, when a dozen or more people, who don't know each other or the house, claim to have seen the same thing, you have to concede that there's something there. They can't all be crazy.'

'And are there any ghosts upstairs?' I asked, gazing up the staircase with blatant curiosity.

Geoff laughed. 'A baker's dozen,' he informed me. 'That's where the bedrooms are, you see, and ghosts seem to like bedrooms. My ghosts do, at any rate.

There's one in particular – not so much a ghost, really as a *feeling* – that seems to get a lot of people . . . but I'll let you find if for yourself.'

'Oh, thank you very much,' I said drily. 'This isn't an axe-murdering sort of ghost, is it?'

'No, nothing like that,' he shook his head smiling. 'It's rather difficult to explain, especially since I've never felt it myself. Here we are,' he paused on the top step to push open the solid oak door. 'After you.'

The upstairs chambers were lovely, and richly furnished with an eye to detail. Heavy embroidered curtains and spreads made the massive four-poster beds look even more stately and luxurious, like miniature rooms unto themselves, and the fifteen-foot ceilings made me feel very small and plebeian.

I particularly liked the huge King Charles bedroom, where the ill-fated King himself reputedly passed a few nights while mustering his troops against Cromwell. The bedroom was directly over the Great Hall, and had the same massive proportions, with a beautiful ceiling plastered in curvilinear ribs that gave the room an almost continental gracefulness.

'And this is the cavalier bedroom,' Geoff went on, leading me through the final doorway. 'It used to be called the crimson bedroom, but "cavalier" sounded much more romantic for the guidebooks, and seemed to tie in with the King Charles room next door.'

The original name was the more logical, I decided, letting my gaze roam the faded red fabric-covered walls and the deeper crimson colour of the heavy draperies hanging from the imposing Jacobean bed. And then I felt the cold.

Geoff continued on with his narrative, but I was no longer listening. Some force, some irresistible, unexplainable force, was drawing me towards the room's only window, a large mullioned and transomed window that looked out over the wide front lawn and the walled churchyard.

He stopped talking, watching me, and then I think he said, 'So you feel it, too,' or something like that, and my body was suddenly invaded by a tidal surge of powerful emotions that I was powerless to control. First a longing, so deep and wistful that it tore at my soul, and then a kind of frantic praying, a desperate litany that raced round and round in my fevered brain, and finally a stab of sorrow as deep as a twisted knife. I sagged against the window-ledge, my eyes brimming with sudden tears.

'Are you all right?' Geoff clasped my shoulder with a warm, strong hand, his voice concerned.

I blinked back the tears and showed him a reassuring smile that only wobbled a little. 'I'm fine,' I said. 'So that's the ghost, is it?'

'Yes. Look, I really am sorry,' he gazed earnestly down at me. 'I should have given you some warning – told you what to expect – instead of being so damned secretive about it.'

'No harm done.' I moved away from the window, smoothing the folds of my skirt with an absent gesture. 'Like you said, it's only a feeling . . . nothing more.'

'A sort of deep sadness, was it?'

'Yes.' I held back a shiver of remembrance. 'Do you know the cause of it?'

Geoff shook his dark head, frowning. 'No. It's a woman's sadness, I should think. Only women seem able to sense it, and it's always in that same spot – just there in front of the window. But I've never been able to pin down the source of it. Nothing in the family history to account for it. No-one died in this room, that we know of, or flung themselves out the window, or anything like that.'

'I don't think it's really connected with the room,' I said slowly. He gave me an odd look, and I flushed a little, lowering my head self-consciously. 'Sorry,' I said, 'it's just an impression I got. It seemed to me that she – if it was a she – saw something through this window. Something out there . . .' I nodded towards the smooth, level expanse of freshly green lawn that stretched out to meet the high churchyard wall with its overhanging trees. Everything was pristine and still and innocent – even the shadows lay quiet and unmoving on the grass. 'She saw something terrible. Something that broke her heart. And it's left an imprint, here in this room.'

'It's possible, I suppose.' Geoff was still looking at me strangely, with that odd blend of concern and wariness. 'Look, maybe we should finish the tour another day.'

'Heavens, no. I'm fine,' I assured him again, smiling up at him. It was a genuine smile this time. Silly to let one incident darken my entire day. 'What's next on the agenda?'

'The library,' he replied, relaxing. 'Or is that too boring for you?'

'Not at all. I love libraries. I shall probably want to steal some of your books, though, so be forewarned. You don't have any first editions of Dickens, do you?'

'Not *Dickens*, no,' he grinned.

'Oh, Lord,' I rolled my eyes heavenwards, 'I knew it. It's going to be one of those disgustingly marvellous collections of rare works of literature, all hand-bound in matching leather covers, isn't it?'

'Something like that,' he said, smiling at my groan, 'but if it makes you feel any better, all the truly rare and valuable volumes have been moved over to my side of the house. Can't trust the tourists with them, can I?'

'It's the only thing I begrudge the rich,' I said, as I followed him back down the damp-smelling staircase to the ground floor.

'What's that?'

'Their ability to buy books that the rest of us can never hope to own.'

Geoff grinned in understanding. 'Well, if you want to borrow any of mine, just let me know.'

I sighed. 'It's not the same.'

We had come to a stop in the wide front passage, with the Great Hall behind us, and my worst fears were confirmed as Geoff swung open the door to reveal floor-to-ceiling mahogany shelves filled with books of every possible size and shape and age. The shelves covered all four walls of the square room, broken in three places by tall narrow windows with stained glass inserts above and upholstered seats below, liberally adorned with loose cushions – the sort of window seats that every book-lover dreams of, visualizes, yearns for . . .

I stepped forward into the room, wonder-struck, inhaling the rich smell of oiled leather bindings and ancient paper and polished wood.

'How absolutely lovely,' I said.

'Yes,' Geoff agreed. 'You have my father to thank for this. He loved books – spent his whole life collecting them, having them restored. The original library for the house was a cramped little room off the south passage, near the old kitchen. Too small for my father. He built this one from the walls out, you know. The former owners used it as a sort of games room – billiards, and all that – and before that I think it was a storage room. Dad thought it was perfect for the library.'

'He was right. Wherever did he find those shelves?'

'Country house in West Sussex. The place was being torn down, and the builders agreed to sell the shelving to Dad for a modest fortune.'

'Worth every penny,' I justified his father's action. 'They're just beautiful. All you're missing is the sliding ladder on the brass rail.'

'Aha,' Geoff smiled, 'you haven't looked closely enough.' He pointed to the far corner. 'Dad always believed in doing things down to the last detail.'

There, in truth, was the ladder, reaching up to the top shelf and fixed to glide on casters round a polished brass rail. It was too much like a film set to be true, really, and I was just about to voice my delight when another object in the corner caught my attention, and I froze, my throat working convulsively.

'Richard,' I whispered, my voice oddly slurred and indistinct.

'I beg your pardon?' Geoff moved forward, into my line of vision, but I went on staring up and over his shoulder at the great dark portrait hanging on the wall opposite. A portrait of a tall man with knowing eyes and an arrogant smile, a dark man dressed in black with a cape flung over one shoulder while in the other hand he clasped a gleaming sword . . .

I licked my lips and tried again, forming the words more carefully. 'That picture . . .' I began, nodding my head towards it.

He turned and looked. 'Oh, that. We've dubbed him "The Playboy". He came with the house. That might be old Arthur de Mornay himself, or perhaps even his father. The resemblance is really quite remarkable, don't you think?'

I didn't have to ask which resemblance he was

referring to. It might have been a portrait of himself hanging there. I looked from the portrait to Geoff, and back again, my eyes wide.

'It's by Lely,' he went on, as if it were all part of the tour. 'Quite a distinctive style he had.'

A gentle, apologetic tap on the door behind us broke the contemplative silence and made us both spin around like a couple of guilty schoolchildren. A tall, elderly woman was standing in the open doorway. The neatly-pressed apron covering her demure, dark blue dress and the classic arrangement of her softly white hair presented a picture of calm, well-ordered efficiency, and her face, with its smiling blue eyes and gentle expression, seemed oddly familiar to me.

But she wasn't looking at me – she was looking at Geoff.

'You have a phone call,' she told him, her voice pleasantly melodic. 'I wouldn't have bothered you with it, but it's Mr McCandless from the Manchester plant, and he sounded rather urgent.'

'Right,' Geoff grimaced. 'I'll take the call. Thanks, Freda. Oh,' he said, as an afterthought, 'have you met? Julia Beckett, Alfreda Hutherson, my housekeeper.'

We smiled and shook hands, and then I remembered.

'We have met,' I said. 'You came round to the house to welcome me.'

'That's right,' the older woman replied. 'Settling in all right, are you?'

'Yes, thank you.'

Geoff touched my shoulder, brushing past us. 'Look, I'll just go take that phone call, shall I? Won't be a minute.'

Mrs Hutherson moved aside to let him pass, then stepped forward again, tilting her head to one side as she looked first at me, then at the dark portrait in the corner.

'Quite a nice painting, isn't it?' she remarked, and I nodded.

'Very nice.'

'A very handsome man.'

'Yes.'

She brought her eyes back to mine, and for a moment I felt a curious sensation of nakedness, as though she were looking straight into my soul. Only a moment, and then there was only an old woman with friendly blue eyes, looking at me.

'It's a pity no-one knows who he is,' she said. 'Handsome man like that, and such a dashing figure. Somebody must have loved him, once.'

She looked at me again, and smiled.

'You'll have to excuse me, I've the upstairs windows to do yet. I hope you enjoy the rest of your tour.'

I had to clear my throat before speaking. 'Thank you.'

She nodded graciously and departed, her footsteps ringing in even measure on the polished hardwood floor of the long passage. Odd that neither Geoff nor I had heard her approach, I thought. Alone in the lovely, quiet room, I lifted my eyes once more to the portrait.

Richard de Mornay smiled down at me.

It was Richard de Mornay – I was certain of that. There was no mistaking that proud, handsome arrogance, nor the gentle cynicism of his dark, hooded gaze. *Someone must have loved him*, Mrs Hutherson had said, and again that little, knowing voice inside me made reply.

Yes, it said, with painful clarity . . . *I did.*

But then, I already knew that. Had known it, it seemed, for some time. And I had the strangest feeling – based on intuition rather than on any rational fact – that Alfreda Hutherson had known it, too.

Chapter Fourteen

The Red Lion was the busiest I'd ever seen it, several tables swarming with Saturday afternoon patrons, and it was a long while before Vivien could work her way back to the bar to serve us. Even Ned had been moved to action, and had ambled by us at least twice bearing plates of sandwiches and chips from the back kitchen.

'Right,' Vivien swung herself into position behind the bar, her fair hair swirled around her flushed face, 'let me get this straight.' She looked across at Geoff. 'You gave Julia a tour of the Hall today.'

Geoff nodded.

'And as payment for this enormous privilege,' Vivien went on, 'Julia has agreed to let you buy her a drink.'

'Correct.'

Vivien shrugged, grinning.

'Sounds like a rare fair deal, my girl,' she said to me. 'What can I get you?'

'Gin and tonic, please,' I smiled back.

Two stools away, beside Geoff, Iain Sumner leaned forward with a disapproving frown.

'What kind of a drink d'ye call that?' he asked me, his own hand cupped around a sweating pint of dark bitter.

'Ignore him,' Vivien instructed me. 'He's in one of his difficult moods.'

Iain raised an eyebrow at that. 'I am not.'

'You see what I mean,' Vivien winked, sliding my drink across the bar.

Geoff turned in his seat to face his friend.

'You do seem a little out of sorts today, Iain. Everything all right?'

'Everything's bloody fine,' Iain retorted, 'and I'm in a bloody wonderful mood, thanks.' He drew a cigarette from the packet in front of him and lit it, the very angle of his jaw an open challenge.

Geoff and Vivien exchanged significant glances. Vivien turned her attention back to me, resting her elbows on the bar and leaning forward to shift some of the weight from her tired feet.

'So,' she said brightly, 'how did you enjoy the tour?'

'It was lovely,' I told her. 'Someone's done a wonderful job of restoring the old rooms – it's just like coming face to face with the past.'

'Quite literally, at that,' Geoff chimed in. 'Julia had an encounter with our ghost in the cavalier bedroom.'

Vivien's eyes flashed excitedly. '*Did* you really? And what did it feel like to you?'

'Shock,' I replied, thinking back, 'and pain, and . . . a sort of praying, if that makes any sense.'

'That's it, exactly,' Vivien nodded. 'It's really something, isn't it? Rather creepy, but exciting all the same.'

Iain leaned forward again, fixing me with a curious stare. 'You believe in them, then. Ghosts, I mean.'

'Yes, I do,' I decided, lifting my chin a little. 'I think there are definitely some things in this world that we can't explain in scientific terms – not yet, at any rate – but that doesn't make them any less real. Hamlet said it best.'

'"More things in heaven and earth, Horatio"?' he quoted. 'Aye, well. Hamlet was a bit of a fruitcake.'

'Don't you think they exist?' Geoff asked him.

'Please,' Iain's grey eyes smiled derisively. 'I am a Scotsman, after all. You can't walk half a mile in Scotland without treading on the coat-tails of a ghost or two. But I've not yet seen one up at the Hall.'

'You need to talk to Aunt Freda,' Vivien advised him. 'She sees them all the time. She even says she's seen the woman in the cavalier bedroom.'

'Sees a lot of things, does your Aunt Freda,' Iain replied, dragging at his cigarette. 'Five hundred years ago they'd have built a bonfire under her.'

Vivien leaned across the bar and slapped him laughingly on the sleeve. 'That's a terrible thing to say,' she admonished him. 'You mind your tongue, or I'll tell her!'

'No need,' Iain shrugged. 'She knows perfectly well what I think. Besides, I've never said that there's anything wrong with being a witch . . .'

Geoff laughed, 'She is rather remarkable,' he agreed. 'You have to admit, Viv, that her ability to keep me organized denotes some sort of supernatural power . . .'

'Oh, go on!' Vivien dismissed them both with a wave of her hand. Turning to me, she asked, 'Have you met Aunt Freda, yet?'

I wasn't entirely sure, until Geoff stepped in and answered for me. 'Yes, she met her today, as a matter of fact. Freda is my housekeeper,' he told me, by way of clarification.

'Oh.' I thought a moment. 'Mrs Hutherson, you mean? Yes, I've met her. Twice, actually. She came by the house a couple of weeks ago with the town welcoming committee. Brought me some smashing fruit scones. She seems very nice.'

'There, you see?' Vivien challenged the men. 'Julia thinks she's nice.'

'Of course she's nice,' Iain shot back.

'A nice witch,' Geoff confirmed, trying without much success to suppress a grin.

I ignored them both. 'So she's seen the ghost in the upstairs room, has she?'

'Yes,' Vivien said. 'Some years ago, when she first went to work up at the manor house. Apparently, it's a young woman, just like everyone thought. Quite a pretty young woman, Aunt Freda says, with long fair hair.'

'Not wearing a green dress, by any chance?' I tried to make it sound like a joke.

'No, I don't think so. I'm pretty certain she said the dress was dark. But then, she said the whole ghost looked sort of grey and indistinct.'

Geoff looked down at me, smiling. 'You think your Green Lady is hiding out in my bedroom?' he asked.

'Rather a dull spot for her,' Vivien teased him.

Even Iain smiled at that, his mood improving. He lit a second cigarette and settled back in his seat.

'Speaking of the Green Lady,' he said to me, 'I'd be happy to dig that old garden back up for you, if you'd like.'

'Oh, no, thank you,' I raised an appealing hand, 'I couldn't keep a garden to save my life. I kill plants just by looking at them.'

'Julia thinks you ought to do something with the courtyard at the Hall,' Geoff told him. 'She was quite surprised you hadn't already planted it over.'

'What, the crypt, you mean?' Iain narrowed his eyes in contemplation. 'I may get round to it, yet,' he said. 'You never know.'

'And just when would you find time for that, I'd like to know.' Vivien eyed him indulgently. 'Seems to me you've enough work on your plate.'

'Gardening's not work,' Iain corrected her. 'It's recreation. And you're always telling me I need more of that.'

'And fewer of *those*,' she nodded at his cigarette. 'Not that you ever listen to me.'

Geoff leapt to his friend's rescue by switching the subject. 'I hear there's to be a big estate sale near Calne next weekend. Lord Ashburn's place, I believe. Anyone fancy a trip down there?'

'Are they auctioning any books?' I asked him.

'Only a few hundred.'

I smiled. 'Then you can count me in.'

'Wonderful. Vivien?'

'I'd love to,' Vivien said, 'but the sale's on Saturday and I promised Ned the day off so that he could watch his boy play rugby.'

I'm not sure which surprised me more – the revelation that Ned the barman was married, or the knowledge that his offspring had the energy to play at sports.

'That's too bad.' Geoff looked at Iain. 'What about you?'

'Can't,' was the Scotsman's response. 'The shearers come on Saturday.'

'Shearers?' I asked him.

'Aye. For the sheep. They have to cover all the farms in the district so they're on a tight schedule.'

'You don't shear the sheep yourself, then?'

'Lord, no,' he grinned. 'I've no skill with a pair of shears – the sheep would look bloody awful if I did them. No, my shearers come from the north. Young lads. Professionals. They can do my flock in an afternoon.'

'So Saturday's out for you as well,' Geoff concluded. It struck me that he didn't look particularly upset by the news. 'Well,' he said, 'what a shame. I suppose that just leaves Julia and myself.'

'Aye.' Iain gave me a brotherly look. 'You want to watch him, Julia,' he told me. 'He may look harmless enough, but appearances can be deceiving.'

Geoff grinned. 'That's slander, that is. You know I always behave like a perfect gentleman.'

'Right then, Sir Galahad,' Iain said drily, 'd'ye think you can spare a moment to help me mend that fencing at the west end of the orchard, like you promised?'

'Damn, I'd forgotten all about that. I suppose I did promise, didn't I?'

'Aye. And the sheep will be all out on the road and halfway to Beckhampton if I don't get it mended by nightfall.' He nodded at Geoff's glass, trying not to smile at his friend's crestfallen expression. 'Drink up,' he advised solemnly.

Geoff finished his pint reluctantly and rose to his feet, stretching to his full height of six-foot-something. 'Ladies,' he said theatrically, 'I take my leave of you.' Turning to me, he added, 'Thanks for the company today.'

'Thank you for the tour,' I smiled back at him. 'I enjoyed it.'

'Anytime.' The warmth of his look was tangible. 'I'll give you a ring this week sometime and we'll get the arrangements for next Saturday sorted out, all right?'

'Fine.'

'Well,' Vivien said, heaving a sigh of relief as the men departed, 'at least he was smiling when he left. Iain, I mean. Honestly,' she told me, grinning, 'that man and his moods. He was parked on that stool there for the better part of the afternoon, drinking and smoking and looking blacker than the devil. I was hoping Geoff would come in, to shake him out of it.'

'They're very good friends, aren't they?' I mused. I was thinking, oddly enough, not of Geoff and Iain, but of a dark man on a grey horse, watching another man striding across the fields with an easy step, carrying a heavy travelling trunk on his shoulder as if it were a child's toy. *That's Evan Gilroy*, I heard Rachel's clear voice saying, *he lives at the manor* . . .

'The best of friends,' Vivien answered me, her tone emphatic. 'You'd think they'd known each other all their lives, to hear them talk.'

I frowned a little, tracing a pattern in the moisture on the side of my glass with one finger. 'Your Aunt Freda,' I said, choosing my words carefully. 'Why did Geoff and Iain call her . . . I mean, why do they both think that she's . . .'

'A witch?' Vivien finished for me, flashing a smile. 'I don't know. Perhaps she is one, after all. She's always been something of a psychic, has my Aunt. Always knew when I'd fallen out of a tree, or when I'd been up to something I shouldn't have. She just seems to know things, somehow. Besides which,' she leaned on the bar again, tilting her head to one side, 'she's just a remarkable sort of woman. Earthy, if you know what I mean. She can heal wounded animals and birth a baby and talk to songbirds, *and*,' again the smile flashed, 'she grows bigger tomatoes in her garden than anyone else in the village. For all I know, that's what witchcraft is. Would you like another?'

I looked blankly down at my glass, and shook my head.

'No thanks. I ought to be heading home, myself. I have some sketches to finish off, and my publisher will have a fit if I don't send her something this week to prove that I'm still hard at it. It's the country life,' I protested, stretching my shoulders. 'It saps all my energy.'

'It's like I told you,' she nodded. 'There's no stress here to worry about. Not like London. Nothing ever happens in a place like Exbury.'

I wouldn't have said that, exactly, I thought to myself several minutes later, as I plodded slowly back up the road towards my house, past thickening hedges and earth-scented fields. No, I thought, smiling a little to myself, I wouldn't have said that nothing ever happened here . . .

A sheep, perhaps a truant member of Iain's flock, had wandered onto the road and was busily devouring a young flowering shrub. It raised its head as I drew near, and stared at me with placid, uninterested eyes. It made the perfect advertisement for Vivien's picture of the pastoral village life – lethargic and simple and deadly dull.

'You don't fool me,' I told it.

So much had happened to me in the past month that, had the animal stood upright and spoken back to me, I doubt I would have batted an eyelid. But it didn't. It just stood there and went on munching, staring at me with that blankly supercilious gaze that sheep have, looking for all the world as if it thought I was daft.

It rained all the next day – a steady, depressing rain that pelted tirelessly against the window of my little studio. I was grateful, at least, that there was nothing to distract me from my work – no gently beckoning breezes laden with the scent of spring flowers, nor twittering birds to lure me out of doors with song. There was only the rain, and a dark grey sky, and a wicked wind that rattled the window panes and set the trees to shuddering.

By suppertime I had finished painting my sketches for the Korean folk tale, the thick pages boasting a kaleidoscope of watercolour tints. I rinsed out my brushes with cramped and aching hands, tidied my paints away and went downstairs to the kitchen for a meal of cold meat and cheese. Carrying my tea into the library, I selected a favourite murder mystery and settled myself in the leather armchair for a relaxing evening read. I was asleep before the detective had even discovered the body.

I woke before dawn, to a stiff neck and the almost painfully cold feeling that precedes the rising of the sun. The sky was still dark, and the east-facing window reflected my own image back at me, an eerie outline in the light of the small reading lamp beside my chair. My cup sat empty on the table beside me. Lifting it, I rose jerkily to my feet and made my way back into the kitchen, craving the comforting warmth of a whistling kettle and a fresh pot of tea.

It was while I was sitting there, listening to the silence of the house with my cold hands wrapped around the steaming cup, that the idea first came to me. Since Saturday I had been worried by the fact that I could not control what was happening to me – that I could, in short, regress at any time, in any place, wandering around the village in full view of everyone but oblivious to all. The problem seemed to be that the 'flashbacks' came at random, without warning, giving me no chance to prepare myself for the experience.

But what if I *could* prepare myself? What if I could find some way of triggering the flashbacks myself, when I wanted them, and suppressing them when I did not want them? If I was in fact dealing with memories – with scenes generated by my own mind – then I ought to be able to find some way of 'remembering' upon demand.

It was as least worth a try, I told myself. And now was the perfect time for such an experiment. I was safely installed in my own house, bolstered by the false bravado that comes from being not fully awake, and in the event that I did wander out of the house I was at least fully dressed in the faded blue-jeans and rumpled T-shirt that I used for painting. I was respectable. Besides, it would be hours before anyone in the village woke up.

Having convinced myself of the practicality of my plan, I spent the next several minutes rummaging through my disorganized cupboards in search of a candle. I had read somewhere that candles were essential to self-hypnosis. I finally found the stump of one buried in the cutlery tray, and set it to stand in a shallow saucer. Taking my seat at the scrubbed table, I set the candle before me and lit it, holding my breath.

The flame flickered expectantly, dipping and dancing in the currents of air that played round the silent room. My entire world seemed reduced to that single point of light, that tiny, wavering, mesmerizing flame, radiant in the near-darkness. I kept my eyes fixed upon it, staring and concentrating, while in my mind I kept repeating a single thought: *I want to remember. I want to remember.* Over and over again, like a movement from Handel's Messiah, insistently, monotonously purposeful. *I want to remember. I want to go back . . .*

The air swept singing past my ears, and the candle flame dipped sharply in response.

'Have you not finished your draught yet?' Rachel asked in amazement. 'The market has started already, and we'll be missing the best buys.'

I drained my cup guiltily, nearly choking on the strong wine. 'I am sorry,' I apologized. 'I was thinking.'

'You do too much thinking. In this house, that can only lead you into trouble,' she said, smiling at me from the doorway while she adjusted her heavy cloak, drawing the hood over her bright hair. 'The rain has stopped, at least, and the sky is clearing. It promises to be a fair day.'

I left my own hood down. I liked the feel of the wind in my hair, especially the clean wind that followed a late spring rain. My dark blue cloak was worn, and mended in places, but the dress beneath it was new, and I was looking forward to a morning away from the house and my uncle's influence. Unbolting the kitchen door was like unlocking a prison cell, and my smile was wide as I followed Rachel across the back garden towards the road that would lead us away from the house, away from the village, to a marketplace full of people and laughter and life.

Chapter Fifteen

The market town of Wexley Basset lay four miles to the east of Exbury, on the Marlborough road. We were not the only travellers on that road – three times we were passed by carts bearing people and produce to market, and a little further on we ourselves passed a young lad leading a gentle brown cow and her soft-eyed calf. The temptation to speak to people was great after my weeks of solitude, but I followed Rachel's example and kept well to the side of the road, my eyes demurely downcast.

That was the hardest part, waiting until the strangers had moved on, or fallen behind so that I could once again lift my head and drink in the scenery that surrounded us. Freedom was a new and heady wine to me, and the fresh scent of rain-soaked wildflowers blew the bitter smell of despair from my nostrils and made me forget for a moment the hopeless uncertainty of my situation.

The road was straight as an arrow's flight, straight as a Roman road, with deep ruts washed smooth by yesterday's rains. To the right of us lay level fields of new-planted wheat and fenced enclosures dotted with sheep; to the left the broad green sweep of Wexley Down and the rolling chase beyond. In my grandfather's time, Rachel told me, the first King Charles had himself hunted there, cantering after his hawks with his nobles at his heels and half the village tumbling after.

It made a romantic and colourful picture, and I was so busy re-creating it in my imagination that Rachel had to speak twice in order to get my attention.

'Not long now,' she told me. 'You'll be able to see it when we get to the top of this hill.' And then the sun came out from behind the blanket of clouds as we crested the hill, and I got my first glimpse of Wexley Basset.

The markets of my memory were city markets, London markets, crammed into narrow streets or cobbled squares, with hoarse-voiced vendors hawking their wares and all around me the relentless press of people, people everywhere. It was a pleasant change to see the bright striped awnings gaily ringing round the weathered market cross, and the sunlight beating cheerfully down upon the market square. There were crowds here, too, to be sure, but these were friendly country folk, their voices clear and plain, with honest faces scrubbed red by the wind and weather.

'What do you think?' Rachel asked me.

I could only gape, wide-eyed, like an entranced child, and she laughed her lovely musical laugh, grabbing my hand to lead me down into the thick of the crowd. We were jostled and bumped, but I found I did not mind it, and to my own amazement I heard myself laughing as the final shreds of oppression fell away from me. The breeze lifted my hair and the sun warmed my face, and I felt suddenly, gloriously alive.

'It's wonderful!' I cried to Rachel, but my voice was swallowed by a sea of voices, and she did not hear me. She led me on a little further, then turned back towards me, her face flushed with excitement.

'Come, you must see the players,' she said.

A large cluster of people had gathered in one corner

of the square, and she pulled me towards them. When we reached the spot, Rachel smiled sweetly at one of the taller men, who moved aside to let us slip in front of him, where we could view the goings on with ease. The players were eight in number, dressed in weird and fanciful clothing of every conceivable rainbow hue. One of them, a young lad of about fourteen, was speaking a Prologue in a high, ringing voice.

'I'd hoped they would be here,' Rachel confided in an elated whisper. 'They often come on market day, to entertain.'

The young Prologue had finished, and an anticipatory hush fell on the watchers. It was a short play, only several minutes long, but it was acted wonderfully well.

One of the men came forward draped in sombre black, with a Puritan's hat upon his head, and the word 'Parliament' painted on a banner across his chest. He spoke at length about the ruinous morals of the English nation, with such droll turns of phrase and twists of meaning that he merely mocked himself, and made those watching laugh aloud at his foolishness. By and by came Oliver Cromwell himself, and a Roundhead soldier, and a leering preacher, and all three joined in the general lamentation, and made such evil and sinister plans that the crowd made a mighty protest with shouts and hissing noises.

In came an angel, who listened sadly and unseen, then crossed to the 'Parliament' and touched him, whereupon the dark Puritan clothes were cast away to reveal a new Parliament, gleaming white and gold. A player representing the people, clothed in red and brandishing a sword of fire, joined this new and holy Parliament, and together the two challenged and defeated the diabolical conspirators. And such a cheer rose from the assembled crowd when a fair facsimile of good King Charles appeared to claim his crown, that it rivalled the very din of the coronation day itself.

There were many 'Hurrahs!' and a good many coins thrown when the players had finished.

'It was a good play,' I said to Rachel as we drew away.

'Ay,' she agreed, 'but your uncle would not have thought so.'

'Why would he not?'

She looked at me, and seemed to be considering something, then suddenly thought the better of it.

'Look,' she said, instead, 'there is the orange-seller. Shall we share an orange? I have money to spare.'

I had money of my own – a few hoarded pennies safely tucked within the lining of my dress, but I let Rachel buy the orange that we split carefully between us, savouring the sweet juicy flesh and the exotic fragrance of the zest, a fragrance that clung to our fingers long after we had finished eating.

'Now,' said Rachel, remembering our instructions, 'I am to get a goose, and a joint of beef for Caroline. The butchers be over there, across the way.'

I hung back, hesitating. 'If you don't mind,' I told her, 'I'd like to look about a bit on my own.'

The truth was, I dreaded the stench of the butcher's stalls, and I had never been able to bear the sight of animals doomed for slaughter. Rachel did not seem to begrudge my reluctance.

'Do as you will,' she invited with a small shrug. 'I'll come to find you when I've finished with the shopping.'

I felt a tiny twinge of guilt. 'D'you not need my help? To carry the meat, perhaps?'

'Not at all. Don't trouble yourself so,' she laughed. 'I usually come to market by myself. Be off with you, and amuse yourself. You can carry your share of the load on the walk home.'

It was not difficult to amuse myself, surrounded as I was by such an array of wonders and trinkets and marvellous things: tonics to improve the health, imported French silks and Flemish laces, apples and lemons spilling from their carts onto the cobblestones, dried fish and tin horns and wooden buckets and delicate jewellery. Entranced, I wandered from stall to stall, pausing on the fringe of the gathered crowds to hear one seller crying up his wares, or to watch another remove tallow stains from white linen with a liquid strong as magic.

At one of the stalls, a beautifully worked bracelet caught my fancy, and I paused to admire it. It was daintily made of gleaming gilt, a linked procession of fanciful birds of paradise with eyes of blue glass that glittered like royal jewels. I lingered over it wistfully, tracing the delicate creatures with my fingers. My pennies seemed to shift impatiently in their hiding place and the merchant, sensing my weakness, sidled cautiously closer.

'That's real quality, mistress,' he told me, accompanying his words with an ingratiating smile. 'Just like the ones the fine ladies wear at court nowadays. Only ten shillings.'

Ten shillings! I drew my hand back reluctantly. I had only sixpence in my pocket, and I could never hope to bargain him down as low as that. My disappointment lasted only a moment, though, for as I turned away from the stall my eyes fell upon a bookseller's cart tucked into a shadowed corner on the fringe of the marketplace, and my heart leapt up joyfully. How wonderful it would be, I thought, to hold a book again, to feel the smooth, crisp pages and smell the rich, intoxicating smell of oiled leather and paper.

Our house in London had been full of books. They had been crammed into cupboards and every shelf had groaned with the weight of them. But in my uncle's house, there was only a heavy, stately volume of King James's Bible, and nothing more.

So happy was I to see such a quantity of books that I scarcely paid attention to the bookseller himself, a lean and quiet man who leaned against the cart, lit his pipe, and watched in indulgent silence as I pored over his collection of titles. There were several that I would have wished to buy, but I settled finally on *Nature's Pictures drawn by Fancy's Pencil to the Life*, by Margaret Cavendish, the celebrated Duchess of Newcastle. It was not a new book – in fact it was some ten years old, having been written during the lady's exile from the Commonwealth – but my father had read it, and had remarked upon it with approval. Best of all, it was only fourpence.

'A good choice,' the bookseller commended me with a smile, 'providing you don't let all her romantic fancies turn your head. The lady is unique, and deserving of admiration, but she is not, I think, to be imitated.'

I smiled back at him. 'I shall keep your counsel in mind, sir,' I promised, quite certain that I would never be tempted to emulate the Duchess of Newcastle's extravagant dress and lifestyle.

I made to hand my pennies over to him, but he shook his head slightly, pushing a small dish of liquid towards me. The strong, acrid smell of vinegar assailed my nostrils.

'A caution against this cursed plague,' he explained.

'You may not be from London, child, but there's no saying where your coins have been.'

I tossed the four pennies into the vinegar with trembling fingers, certain that he could read the guilty knowledge in my downcast eyes. Grasping my purchase, I backed hastily away from the cart, and did not slow my pace until I had lost myself in the anonymity of the milling crowd.

My sense of direction having quite left me, I found myself wandering in aimless circles, unable to find either Rachel or the row of butchers' stalls. After making what seemed an endless circuit round the market square, I paused in the shelter of a lane to rest a moment, and found myself facing an enormous grey stallion that seemed curiously familiar.

The beast was tethered to an iron ring in the wall, and stood quite calmly, staring down at me with great liquid eyes that betrayed only mild curiosity.

'Oh,' I said softly.

I had always had a weakness for horses. Even as a small child I had displayed no fear of the animals, and had developed a worrisome habit of running into the road to try to pet the carthorses and hackneys that crowded the London streets. I felt no fear now, as I stepped closer to the towering stallion and stretched out a questioning hand.

'Oh,' I said again, 'you beautiful thing. It's all right, I won't hurt you.'

The wide nostrils flared, testing my scent.

'There, my love,' I went on, speaking in that foolish tone that one reserves for babes and animals, 'don't be afraid. I only want to touch you. There.'

I curved my hand over the horse's nose, stroking lightly, and after a moment I felt the stallion relax, pressing its face against my caressing hand. I laughed in triumph and leaned forward to kiss the stallion's questing nose, running my hand along his beautifully arched neck.

The man's voice, coming from directly behind me, was a startling intrusion.

'You hold your life cheaply, mistress,' the voice said drily. 'He's a bad-tempered devil, and his affections are often false.'

'Nonsense,' I said. 'He's a lovely brute.' And I turned my head to look Richard de Mornay squarely in the eye.

I had to look quite a long way up, in fact. He seemed no smaller standing than he had on horseback, and the top of my head was barely level with his shoulder.

He swept the hat from his head with a gallant gesture and bowed low before me, his eyes laughing.

'We meet again.'

'My lord,' I acknowledged him, nodding my head in response.

He had beautiful hair, I thought idly. As he stood and shook it back it caught the sun like gleaming sealskin, and I was sorry to see it once again covered by the broad-brimmed hat. Viewed at this close range, he also seemed to me much younger than I had originally judged him to be. Surely he was no more than fifteen years my senior, and not above thirty-five years of age.

'I congratulate you on winning Navarre's confidence,' he said, nodding at his horse.

'Navarre? Is that his name?' I stroked the animal's muscled jaw. 'It is a lovely name.'

Richard de Mornay shrugged and moved past me to tuck a parcel into one of his leather saddlebags.

'I've no ear for names. I called him Navarre because

that is where I bought him. Have you lost Rachel, or did you simply tire of the market?'

I blinked warily. 'How did you know I was with Rachel?'

'I saw you earlier. 'Tis difficult not to notice two fair-haired beauties in a place such as this.' He did an extraordinary thing, then. He reached across and touched my arm, just above the wrist, his fingers warm upon the plain fabric of my sleeve.

'You should have bought the bracelet, you know,' he told me, in a contemplative tone. 'The stones would match your eyes.'

Pride kept me from saying that the trinket had been too expensive for my purse. I took a small step backwards and he let his hand fall, his expression unconcerned.

'I bought this, instead,' I held up my book to show him.

'You can read, then.'

'My father was a scrivener. He viewed illiteracy as an unpardonable sin.'

'You were fortunate. I cannot imagine you would find much to read in your uncle's house.'

I smiled, in spite of myself. 'Very little.'

'Then you must come visit me at the Hall. I have a good library. You would be welcome to borrow anything you wanted.' His eyes went past me for a moment and swept the marketplace behind us. 'There is Rachel.'

I turned and looked, my eyes widening a little as I spotted Rachel in the company of a man. The man was tall, with broad shoulders and large, capable hands and a strong and compelling face. I looked again at those shoulders, and suddenly remembered where I'd seen him before.

'Is that Evan Gilroy?' I asked.

'Ay.' Richard de Mornay eyed me strangely. 'I wasn't aware that you'd met.'

'We have not. I saw him when he brought my box up from the village. Rachel told me his name. He is a friend of yours.'

It wasn't really a question, but he answered it anyway.

'Ay, we are friends. Your Rachel is in good hands.'

There was little doubt about that, I thought wryly, watching as Evan Gilroy handed several parcels over to Rachel and bent down to speak to her. Whatever he said brought a flush of colour to her pale cheeks, and as he turned away to walk in our direction she watched him leave with eyes that did not bother to hide their longing. She did not see me, standing in the shadowed corner beside the tall grey horse, and I sighed in unconscious relief.

'Evan,' Richard de Mornay hailed his friend, 'this is Mistress Farr, lately come to Greywethers.'

Evan Gilroy lifted his hat as he drew level with us. The frank, intelligent appraisal of his grey eyes was not unpleasant, and I smiled easily at him.

'I believe you have already done me a service, sir,' I told him, 'for which I owe you thanks.'

'The delivery of your box, you mean? 'Twas no great matter, I assure you. And it is Richard you should thank, since it was he that asked—'

'We must be going,' Richard de Mornay cut in, casting a black look at Evan Gilroy that was easily deflected by the latter's guileless smile. 'You should find your horse, my friend.'

''Tis in the next lane,' the big man said, nodding at me once more before moving off. 'A pleasure, mistress.'

Richard de Mornay swung himself into the saddle and reined his horse tightly, turning so that his polished boot in the stirrup was only inches from my face.

'You will remember,' he said, 'to come and view my library.'

I strained my neck to look up at him. 'I am sorry,' I told him, 'but I cannot.'

'May I ask the reason?'

'My uncle,' I said plainly, 'has forbidden me to speak to you.'

He stared down at me for a long moment, his eyes narrowed in thought.

''Tis odd,' he said slowly. 'I'd not have thought you a coward.'

Before I had a chance to reply, he touched the stallion's neck with the reins and was gone, leaving me for the second time to stare after him in foolish confusion.

'Mariana!' Rachel called me from the street, and I went slowly out to join her.

'I thought you were lost,' she said to me, handing me a wrapped joint of beef to carry and shifting her own parcels into a manageable load. 'Did you find what you were looking for?'

'I bought a book,' I nodded, showing her.

Rachel raised her eyebrows.

'You will have to hide that from Jabez,' she said, matter-of-factly. 'He takes a dim view of women reading for pleasure.'

I was beginning to think that my uncle took a dim view of anyone doing anything for pleasure, but I merely bit my lip and hugged my book more tightly. We began our four mile walk home in silence, both occupied with our own private thoughts. With each step I took, the heavy joint of meat seemed to grow heavier yet, and more unwieldy. When we had gone but a mile on the road I nearly dropped it altogether.

''Tis a pity that Evan Gilroy was not chivalrous enough to carry this wretched thing home for us,' I told Rachel ruefully, struggling to recover my burden.

Her head snapped round with a start, her eyes wide and alarmed. 'You saw us?'

I nodded, touched by her embarrassment. 'He is a handsome man, Rachel.'

She lowered her head, not meeting my eyes.

'I am betrothed,' she said, her voice slow and steady, 'to Elias Webb, the bailiff of Exbury.'

I had seen the bailiff. He was a stern, unyielding man with a dour, humourless mouth and a perpetually black expression that matched his sombre clothing.

'Oh, Rachel.' I could not contain my dismay.

She went on stoically.

'He is a friend of your uncle's, and an honest man. We are to be married at the summer's end.'

I said nothing, and after a minute she lifted her eyes to mine once more, her expression almost pleading.

'So you see,' she told me, 'it would not be seemly for me to be seen speaking to Evan Gilroy. Of course, I would never do such a thing.'

I reached to give her hand a small squeeze of reassurance. 'I saw nothing,' I said.

Her taut face relaxed into a smile, and as I watched I saw the twinkle return to her forget-me-not eyes.

'No more did I,' was her cryptic reply.

We spoke nothing more until we came to Exbury and the lonely grey house. Aunt Caroline was in the kitchen when we arrived, feeding baby John beside the hearth. She looked incredibly grey and weary, and her eyes were red.

'Jabez is gone to Salisbury for a time,' she informed us dully. 'He has some business there.'

It was not unwelcome news. Caroline was colourless and weak, but she had a reasonably pleasant disposition and I could not help feeling that, given time, we might become friends. She was close to my own age, although she looked years older, her hair already whitening with the strain of her miserable existence.

I smiled at her, but she did not respond.

'A man came to the house,' she said to me. There was no interest in her voice. 'A servant from the manor. He left a parcel for you. Said you dropped it in the market-place. It's there, on the table.' She shrugged her shoulder, careful not to disturb the nursing baby.

I looked. It was a small, flat parcel, tied up with coloured string in bright paper. I was, frankly, astonished by its presence, but I had no wish to let Rachel or her older sister view my reaction.

'How wonderful,' I exclaimed brightly. 'I thought I had lost it. Thank you, Caroline.'

My aunt eyed the package with a flicker of curiosity, glanced at the book in my other hand, and raised a pale eyebrow, but she said nothing. Nor, to my relief, did Rachel.

A short time later, alone in my upstairs room, I set the parcel on my bed and carefully unwrapped it, my blood racing with anticipation. I could feel the hard outline of the contents through the paper before I had removed even half the wrapping.

Still, I was unprepared for the actual sight of the beautiful bracelet, ringed with the blue-eyed birds of paradise, spilling out across the plain, homespun coverlet.

Chapter Sixteen

'Julia.'

I was shaking all over, or at least I felt as if I were. Perhaps it was the room itself. Certainly the walls seemed something less than solid; they shimmered and danced as if the subtly shifting daylight was being reflected through a thousand swaying prisms.

'Julia.' Again the voice spoke, and I turned my head slowly, with a great effort, towards it.

At first, I could see nothing but the open doorway of my bedroom and a curious grey, shapeless thing that blocked my view into the hall. A grey, shapeless thing that swelled and drifted, cloud-like, towards me, addressing me in a male voice that was growing decidedly sharper in tone.

'Julia.'

My first thought was, *that's not my name*, and then I thought, *but I know that voice*, and then I thought, *Oh, it's Tommy*, and sure enough, there was my brother standing over me, wearing on his face the same expression our father had assumed whenever one of us had fallen ill. It was an expression of dismay and concern mingled with a sort of piteous helplessness, and my response to it was automatic.

'I'm all right, Tom. Honestly.' Then, as reality took a stronger hold, 'What in heaven's name are you doing here?'

He ignored my question, and went on staring down

at me with eyes that now seemed more fascinated than concerned. 'You weren't here,' he stated in a tense voice, 'were you? You were somewhere else. Someone else.'

I was still kneeling on the floor. I pushed myself stiffly to a standing position, feeling my joints creak a protest. Mutely, I nodded my head.

There was certainly no doubt in my mind as to what had just happened. My hair, when I pushed it away from my face, was wet, and there was mud on my shoes and on the hardwood, smeared where I had walked across the floor of the studio. My hands were stiff and reddened with cold, and I looked down at them stupidly, as if surprised to find that they belonged to my body.

'My God,' Tom breathed, his eyes still fixed on me.

It was the first time I had heard him say that since he had come down from Oxford. He tilted his head and narrowed his eyes. 'Do you have any brandy in the house?'

'What?' Puzzled, I glanced down at my wristwatch. 'Tom, it's barely half-ten. Don't you think it's a little early yet? Especially for a man of the cloth.'

My brother grinned irreverently. 'I'm certain God would forgive me if I drank an entire keg of brandy, given the circumstances. But it isn't for me. It's you that needs the brandy, my love. You look bloody awful.'

'Vicars can't say "bloody",' I reminded him wood-enly.

'Then it's a good thing the bishop isn't here to hear me,' Tom retorted, steering me by the arm across the room and into the upstairs hallway, where he turned me towards the stairs.

'I don't have any brandy in the house,' I told him, caving in, 'but I think there's some Grand Marnier in the cupboard over the stove.'

'Capital,' said Tom. 'That'll do.'

I had some trouble negotiating the stairs because of a curious stiffness in my legs, a condition that baffled me until I realized that, as Mariana Farr, I must have walked over eight miles that morning.

Tom seated me unceremoniously at the kitchen table, located the Grand Marnier, and poured a generous measure into a tumbler for me. Under his stern, insistent gaze, I drank. The liqueur prickled warmly through my insides, bringing a sharp flush to my skin and driving the numbness from my fingertips. I drank again, pushed the damply curling hair out of my eyes and raised my head to face my brother.

'You still haven't told me what you're doing here,' I reminded him.

'Visiting you,' was the simple reply. 'I didn't have any pressing business to attend to today, so I left my curate in charge and drove out here. Thought I'd see how you were getting along – make sure everything was all right. And I wanted to deliver these,' he added, looking down at a thick sheaf of papers on the table between us. The title of the article on top showed plainly that this was the information that Tom's librarian friend had unearthed for us. Tom was looking at it now as if it had lost some of its importance, as if it had been somehow made redundant by what he'd just witnessed.

'Anyhow,' he went on, 'when I arrived I found the back door wide open and the house deserted. I called out but no-one answered, so I went upstairs to check your room and saw that your bed was made, which meant either you'd got up early and made it,' his eyes told me plainly how unlikely he thought this idea, 'or that you hadn't slept in it at all. At that point, I began to worry, and I had just come down here to try to decide what to do next, when you came waltzing in through the back door, staring like a sheep and dripping water all over the floor.'

'Did I say anything?'

'No,' he shook his head. 'No, you just stood there a moment, by the door, then you went right past me and up the stairs to your studio. I suppose I could have waited for you to come out of it naturally, but I'm afraid I rather panicked. Did I interrupt something important?'

I thought of that lovely bracelet, half-felt it again trickling through my hand, and heard Richard de Mornay's voice saying 'you should have bought the bracelet' while he held my wrist in the market-place. My wrist. Mariana's wrist. I lifted one hand to my forehead and closed my eyes.

'No,' I said, 'it was nothing important.' But I could hear the regret in my own voice, and wondered if Tommy could, too.

'You're lucky you were dressed when it happened,' he commented, eyeing my damp, wrinkled shirt and jeans. 'It would be a bit awkward to be seen roaming the countryside in your dressing gown and slippers.'

I smiled. 'Oh, I made certain that I was dressed. I just didn't allow for my being able to unlatch doors, that's all.'

'I'm not sure I follow.'

'I planned it, Tommy,' I said, unable to prevent a small trace of pride from showing in my tone. 'This was a sort of experiment, you see. I wanted to know if I could trigger a regression myself, in a time and place of my own choosing.'

'And?'

'And it worked, obviously, though it didn't go off

177

exactly the way I'd hoped. I had thought to contain the regression within this house.'

Tom glanced over his shoulder at the kitchen door, which still stood ajar, letting in the invigoratingly damp scent of a late May morning.

'And Mariana opened the door,' he guessed. 'I see. That can't be the same lock that was on in the seventeenth century, surely.'

I looked at the heavy latch, curious. 'No, but it's in the same place, and the design is similar. You just have to lift it, you see, and the door opens.'

'I do see.' He frowned. 'That's an antique, that is. No protection at all. What you need is a good deadbolt. In fact, we can buy a couple this afternoon, and I'll install them for you myself.'

'You sound like my mover,' I told him, wrinkling my nose. 'He said I needed new locks, as well.'

'Sensible man.'

'You worry too much, Tom. No-one locks doors around here, it's very safe. Besides, what if I go back into the past again, and try to open the door when it's locked? I might hurt myself.'

'I don't see how. It would just stop the flashback, then and there, I'd think. Mariana, in the past, would open the door and sail off outside somewhere, but you'd be stuck behind.' He looked again at my damply dishevelled figure, curious. 'Where did she take you this morning, anyway?'

I finished my drink and set the glass down firmly on the table. 'Come on,' I said, rising. 'I'll show you.'

'What, now?' He shot a startled glance towards the kitchen window. 'In that?'

It was raining again, lightly but steadily, and I could hear the water gurgling through the downspout from the

178

gutters overhead, collecting in a muddy pond outside the back door.

'I had thought, perhaps, we might use the car,' I explained, with exaggerated patience. 'I've already gone for one walk in the rain this morning.' And I held out the tails of my sodden shirt as evidence.

Tom smiled. 'Right. Sorry, I wasn't thinking. Are you going to change your clothes, first?'

'I suppose I'd better.' I looked down at myself. 'Hang on, I won't be a minute.'

It did, in fact, take me less than five minutes to change into a pair of dry jeans and a bright red jumper, shrug on my weathered anorak and join my brother in my stables-cum-garage.

'Which direction do we go in?' Tom asked me, as he slipped the car into reverse.

'Turn left at the end of the drive, then take the right fork in the road once we cross the river.'

Tom followed my instructions in obedient silence, bumping the sporty Ford over the little bridge and turning off the main road to follow the narrower, less-travelled route.

'"Old Marlborough Road",' he read the signpost. 'This is the way you came?'

I nodded. 'I think so.'

In another few minutes I was sure of it, as the trees thinned and dwindled and the rolling green sweep of Wexley Chase fell away to the left of us. The road was paved and washed with rain – if I had walked this way, I had left no mark – but the richly pastoral scenery had burned a vivid imprint upon my memory.

It had changed in the hour or so since I'd seen it last. Modern houses crowded the road and grew in the fields where sheep had once grazed. There were trees where none had been before, and level flat land where the forest had stood. And yet the road was as familiar as the streets of my childhood, and as we crested the hill and began the descent into Wexley Basset I could not suppress a tiny homely thrill of recognition.

It was a plain little town, for all that – nothing more than a cluster of shops around a square market-place, restored half-timbered façades vying with Victorian red brick and the ugly utility of more modern buildings. Like many English towns, it was a curious blending of architectural styles and fancies, of progress tempered by tradition, the whole effect being, in the end, one of rather comfortable compromise.

The medieval market cross that I remembered as being in the centre of the square was gone, perhaps a victim of fire or development or simply the wear and tear of time. In its place was a pleasant enough statue of a stern-faced man in Regency clothing, doubtless one of the sober town fathers of the past century.

Tommy parked the car in the shadow of the statue, and turned in his seat to look at me.

'That's quite a walk,' he commented. 'Almost four miles. It must have taken you well over an hour each way.'

'I suppose so. Of course, it didn't seem that long, because I had company.'

'What sort of company?'

'Rachel.'

'Who?'

'Rachel,' I repeated, before I realized that, as familiar as all these people of the past were to me, to Tom they meant nothing. They were strangers from a foreign land, without substance or meaning.

And so I proceeded to tell my brother all I knew

about Greywethers – how it had belonged to Mariana's grandfather, and subsequently passed to his eldest son, the ubiquitous, unyielding Jabez Howard. I told him of hollow-eyed Aunt Caroline, and of Rachel, who had lived with her sister and brother-in-law since their marriage. I sort of skimmed over the inhabitants of the manor house, but by then Tom wasn't paying much attention. He was more interested in my trip to the market that morning.

'So you and Rachel came into this square,' he said, 'and . . . then what? What did you do?'

'We stood over there,' I waved a hand towards a newsagent's on the far side of the statue, 'and watched a bit of a play going on, and then we both went our separate ways and I just sort of wandered around, if you know what I mean. Stopped to look at a few of the stalls, but mostly I just wandered. I ended up in that lane there, between the teashop and the bank.'

Hardly a lane anymore, I corrected myself. It had been widened to accommodate motor traffic, although it was still on the narrow side, and the cobbles lay buried beneath smooth black pavement.

Tom looked.

'What did you do there?'

'I patted a horse.'

'And then you left?'

'Yes. Rachel came and found me, and we went off home, back the same way we'd come.'

'I see.'

I looked at him suspiciously. 'You think I've snapped, don't you?'

'I do not! I've never said—'

'Oh, leave it,' I told him, raising a weary hand to my head. 'I'm sorry. It's not you, Tom. It's just that

181

'. . . I don't know, it's just that everything seems so damned real when it's actually happening, and then when it's over I feel so . . . so lost. Like maybe I dreamed it all, I don't know . . .'

My voice trailed away miserably, and Tom subjected me to a hard, brotherly stare before pushing open the driver's side door.

'Well,' he said brightly, 'there's one way of finding out whether you were really here this morning.'

'How's that?'

He flashed me a patronizing smile. 'My dear woman, you were puddling about the market square in the pouring rain. Surely someone must have noticed you.'

'But the shops wouldn't have been open yet.'

'I'll lay you odds at least one of them was,' was my brother's determined reply, and I watched him walk across the square and disappear into the newsagent's. When he emerged some ten minutes later, he was carrying two polystyrene cups and looking terribly pleased with himself.

'Coffee?' he offered, handing me a cup as he slid back into the car seat and pulled the door shut behind him. It was still raining lightly, and he brought the dampness with him, drops of moisture glistening on his black hair and dark blue overcoat.

'I can't drink this stuff,' I complained, looking down at the cup in my hands. 'It isn't real coffee, Tom.'

'Suit yourself.' He took a great swallow from his own cup before speaking again. 'You *were* here this morning, as it happens. The lady in the shop saw you. Or at least she saw a "wee little dark lady with short curly hair", standing in the square at around seven-thirty. At first she thought you were looking in the window of her shop, but when she went to speak to you, you had gone. She saw you a few times, walking around the square. Figured you were waiting for someone to come and get you.'

'And how did you get her to tell you all this?' I asked him politely. 'Or do I want to know?'

'Nothing to it,' Tom shrugged. 'I told her I was a doctor from the psychiatric hospital, and we were missing one of our patients. She was properly sympathetic.'

'Tom!' I was scandalized. 'You're not serious! This is a small community, you know – word gets around. I won't be able to set foot outside my house!'

'It's still too easy, love.' His smile was indulgent. 'To get a rise out of you, I mean. You can calm yourself, I only told her that I was supposed to meet you here earlier, and that I'd had car trouble so I arrived late. I asked if she'd seen you, she said yes, and then I pretended an enormous amount of guilt and bought my coffee. She probably thinks you got tired of waiting for me and went home, and that I'm now on my way to try to placate you. All right?'

'Yes.'

'Good. Then just duck your head down a little as we drive by, will you? I don't want the woman to think I'm a philanderer as well as a thoughtless cad who leaves his girlfriends waiting in the rain.'

I ducked my head obediently, and we rounded the market-place statue, heading back along the Old Marlborough Road towards Exbury.

'So,' I said, straightening up now that we were safely out of range, 'what would you like to do for the rest of your visit? All this melodrama must be terribly boring for you.'

'On the contrary, I haven't had this much excitement in ages.' Tom grinned broadly. 'But I have to admit my plans for the day were more mundane. I had thought we could have lunch at that pub of yours . . .'

'What, the Red Lion?'

He nodded. 'I think it's time I met some of your new friends. For curiosity's sake, if nothing else. And then, after I've put new locks on your doors, I thought I might take you up to Swindon for the rest of the day. We could poke around the shops, if you like, have a classy dinner somewhere, maybe even go to the pictures afterwards. Remember going to the pictures?'

'No.'

'Neither do I,' he sighed. 'So, what do you think?'

'I think it sounds heavenly,' I admitted.

'Good. Then that's what we'll do.'

We drove in silence for a moment, and then Tom frowned suddenly and looked at me.

'Julia, I've been thinking.'

'Yes?'

'This past life business. I don't think you ought to be playing around with it, trying to make things happen.'

I stared at him. 'But last week you said—'

'I know. But that was before I'd seen . . . what it was like. What you're like when it's happening. And now that I've seen it, I've changed my mind. Just think about it, for a minute,' he implored me. 'You could get mown down by a car on the road, or something. And the past might be just as dangerous. How do you know this Mariana person didn't hang herself, or drown herself in the river, or throw herself off a cliff?'

'There aren't any cliffs near Exbury.'

'You know what I mean. We simply don't know enough about the whole phenomenon, yet, and I don't think it's safe for you to be playing around with experiments, that's all. Bad enough it happens spontaneously, sometimes.'

I turned my head to look out the window at the passing landscape, not answering him, and Tom went on in a cautious tone.

'Julia? I want you to promise me that you won't try anything like this again until we learn a little more about what's happening. Will you promise me that?'

Beyond the rain-soaked swells of Wexley Chase, a flock of birds rose in a beating shifting cloud, wheeling in tight formation above the softly smudged green fields. I looked away from the window and smiled sweetly at my brother.

'Yes, Tom, of course,' I said. 'I promise.'

Chapter Seventeen

'I think your brother is rather wonderful,' Vivien commented. 'Not at all like a real vicar.'

It was half-past-nine in the morning on the following Saturday, and I was taking advantage of the brilliant sunshine and mild temperature by attempting, in my amateurish way, to weed the dovecote garden behind my house, while Vivien sat perched on the tumbled stone wall, drinking tea from one of my cracked cups and keeping me company in my labours.

'Yes, well,' I straightened my back, tossing a handful of what I hoped were weeds to one side, 'I'm afraid the Church tends to agree with you. Nothing like a real vicar, although the people of his parish think the world of him. And he can be serious, when he wants to be. Is that a flower, do you think?'

I looked dubiously at a small, delicate plant with fern-like leaves, tilting my head to one side.

'I honestly can't say,' Vivien told me. 'I'm hopeless with gardens. Look, are you sure you want to be doing this? Iain'll have your hide if you pull up one of his prize South African whatchama-whoosits by mistake.'

I left the questionable plant alone and ripped out what looked like a clump of grass, instead, setting my jaw in what my brother would have instantly recognized as defiance.

'I'm not afraid of Iain Sumner. Besides, he can't possibly do everything. He can't help out up at the manor and keep this garden going *and* take care of his sheep all at the same time.'

'He's got an orchard, as well.'

'There you are, then.' I pulled another clump to emphasize my point. 'I'm saving him from a nervous collapse.'

Vivien grinned. 'Well, don't say I didn't warn you. You've never been on the receiving end of one of his tirades.'

'They can't possibly be any worse than my brother's.'

'What, that lovely sweet man who sat at my bar telling funny stories all the afternoon? Don't tell me he has a temper?'

'Fire and brimstone,' I affirmed. 'In biblical proportions.'

'Well,' Vivien smiled, swinging her legs, 'at least when Iain starts yelling his accent gets thicker, so you usually can't understand a word he's . . . no, don't pull that one,' she stopped me suddenly. 'That one I do recognize. It's some sort of a daisy, or something.'

I withdrew my hand obediently and sat back on my heels, surveying my handiwork with satisfaction. The garden *did* look neater, I told myself, and happier, free of the creeping green tendrils that had been choking out beautiful flowering mounds of columbine and peonies and purple iris.

'It really is a pretty garden,' I said aloud, and Vivien nodded.

'Built on several centuries of pigeon droppings,' she rationalized. 'There must be heaps of nitrogen in this soil.'

'I hadn't thought of that.' I rose to my feet, gathering my stock of weeds into a neat pile for disposal. 'When did this stop being used as a dovecote?'

'I don't know. I'll have to ask Aunt Freda. Probably sometime in the last century. Not many people eat pigeons anymore, do they?'

'I don't. I suppose those little niches are where the birds nested.'

Vivien leaned forward to look, slipping her hand into one of the narrow holes between the stones. 'Yes. You can hardly see them anymore, can you, the stone has been worn down so much. The holes get bigger behind the opening, you see, and the birds could—' she broke off abruptly, her expression changing. 'Well, I never!'

'What is it?'

'There's something in here,' she frowned. 'I can't reach it from this position, I'm afraid. Do you want to try? It's something metal, I'm sure of it, right at the back of the nesting hole.'

She drew her hand out and I stepped forward, sliding my fingers across the damp, weathered stone. The narrow entrance of the hole executed a sharp right-angled turn and opened up into a cave-like space, presumably designed to give the nesting pigeons an illusion of privacy.

My fingers brushed across a gritty layer of dirt, and a small tuft of what felt like moss or lichen, before touching metal. My hands were small, but my fingers were conveniently long, and by scraping my wrist slightly against the constricting walls of the opening I could just grasp the object between my searching fingertips.

I withdrew my hand, and stared down at the small object on my palm with unbridled curiosity.

'It's a key,' Vivien said, unnecessarily. 'What an odd place for it.'

I heard a faint humming sound in my ears, felt the first faint twinge of dizziness, and closed my eyes resolutely, clenching my teeth with determination. *Not now*, I told myself firmly, *It can't happen now*.

The ground rocked and then steadied, and I opened my eyes again to find Vivien bending down to look at our find, unperturbed. I was still riding a rush of relief when she asked, in an offhand manner:

'Is that Geoff coming?'

I looked up and towards the back of my house, and saw a familiar dark figure striding across the grass towards us. How she could possibly have been aware of his approach, with the turf absorbing his footsteps and her back turned to him, I did not know. Either Vivien Wells had very sensitive hearing, I ruminated, or else her Aunt Freda wasn't the only witch in the family.

'Yes,' I said simply, 'it is.'

He was wearing a black sweater over dark jeans, and his hair had been trimmed since I'd seen him last. He drew level with the ruined wall and leaned his elbows on it, squinting into the sun.

'Good morning,' he said. 'And what are you . . .' His face fell suddenly as he took in my rough, dirt-stained clothing and the pile of weeds at my feet. 'You're not messing about in Iain's garden, are you?'

I felt irrationally guilty.

'I just pulled a few weeds.'

'I warned her,' Vivien said, in self-defence, 'but she didn't listen.'

'Well,' Geoff gave me a faintly pitying look, 'what's done is done. We'll make sure you have a proper funeral, at any rate.'

I was opening my mouth to respond when he caught sight of the tarnished bit of metal in my hand.

'What on earth is that?' He arched an eyebrow.

'It's a key.'

'We found it in one of the nesting holes in the wall, here,' Vivien supplied, when I failed to offer any further information. 'Quite intriguing, don't you think?'

He held out a hand, 'May I see it?'

It looked even smaller in his hand than it had in mine. He turned it over once or twice and scraped at the metal with his fingernail, frowning. 'It's brass, I think. It could be a door key, I suppose, though it doesn't seem big enough. How interesting.' He studied it a moment longer, then handed it back to me. 'I didn't know that pigeons collected keys.'

'Someone could have put it there,' Vivien suggested.

'But why would they bother?' Geoff asked.

I pocketed the key and shrugged. 'I guess we'll never know.'

We were all three silent for a minute or so, reflecting on the possibilities, and then Vivien swung her head back and smiled brightly.

'So, you two are off to that estate sale near Calne, are you?'

'Yes,' I nodded. I turned to Geoff. 'I'm not late, am I?'

He shook his head. 'I think I'm early.'

'I've got to change, anyway,' I told him, looking down at my gardening clothes. 'Do you mind waiting a few minutes?'

Vivien waved me off. 'Take your time,' she said, 'I'll keep him amused for you. I don't have to open up the Lion for another half hour, yet.'

'Thanks.'

I scurried across the yard and into the house, pausing just inside the back door to kick off my tattered shoes, my heart racing. I was more excited by the fact that I had been able to stave off an impending 'experience' by the force of my own willpower, than I was by my discovery of the mysterious key.

That the key held some connection to Mariana Farr, I had no doubt, but I knew I would have to wait for that connection to be revealed to me. In the meantime, I could revel in the knowledge that I was capable not only of triggering my own flashbacks, but of preventing them as well. For the moment at least, I was in control, and it was an exhilarating sensation.

No less exhilarating, I thought, than the thought of spending the rest of the day in the company of a handsome young man, basking in the sunshine of a glorious English spring afternoon. Upstairs, I placed the key carefully on my bedroom dresser and smiled into the mirror.

A short while later, having bathed and changed into clothes that were in keeping with Geoff's casual wardrobe, I found myself standing on the neatly mown lawn of a sprawling Victorian mansion to the north of Calne, caught up in the cheerful whirl and bluster of a genuine country estate sale.

Massive cupboards and chests of drawers and elegant sideboards were lined up beside the gravel drive, like troops awaiting review. Countless smaller items littered the tops of trestle tables and blanket chests, and spilled out of boxes tucked beneath the tables for want of space. I accompanied Geoff through the wildly intoxicating display, pausing to examine a mantel clock here, or a musical box there, or to stroke a particularly appealing piece of satinwood furniture.

My father had loved sales such as this one. Even when I was very young he had often taken me with him, teaching me how to spot quality in an old chair, and how to recognize an antique dealer hidden among the crowd of common countryfolk. Once, I remember, there had been a small statue of a hunting dog that I wanted very badly. It was nothing special, just painted celluloid over a plaster form, a cheap Victorian thing – but I wanted it. I would have been about seven years old at the time.

I had stood guard over my treasure until the auctioneer worked his way round to it, by which time everyone in the crowd could see I had staked my claim. The opening bid – of fifty pence – was mine, and I was so eager and so determined that when the auctioneer asked if anyone would give him seventy-five, my hand shot into the air again, making me the first person in our county to outbid herself at auction. Had the auctioneer been a less scrupulous man, he could probably have worked me up to two pounds, the amount I was carrying in my pocket, but instead he only laughed and gave me the garish piece for my original fifty-pence bid.

Afterwards, he leaned down and warned me never to let anyone know how badly I wanted to own something. 'You're young now, child,' he'd said, 'and chances are that no-one will bid against you. But when you get older, it will cost you dearly.'

I had long since forgotten what happened to that plaster hunting dog, but I never forgot the auctioneer's advice. I remembered it now as I passed a box of books, and what appeared to be a first edition of J.R.R. Tolkien's *The Hobbit* peeked out at me from amidst a jumble of cheap hardcover mysteries. Casually – oh, so casually – without letting my expression change, I opened the covers of a few of the books in that box, leafing idly through the yellowed pages.

'All this belonged to just one man, you said?' I asked Geoff, striving for a normal tone of voice.

'That's right. Lord Ashburn. He died last month, I believe. Old fellow was in his nineties, at any rate. I hadn't seen him in years, but he used to play golf with my dad when I was a kid.'

I opened the Tolkien book, flipped a page to check the date, then turned to the back flap of the dust cover to read the jacket copy, my excitement mounting as I spotted a misspelled word that had been corrected by hand, another detail that marked the book as a first edition. Closing the book, I looked at Geoff and smiled.

'Lord Ashburn certainly had eclectic tastes,' I commented.

'And heaps of money,' he nodded. 'He was a bit of an eccentric, actually, almost a hermit. Didn't even live in the main house. He lived in that cottage over there,' he pointed out the roof among the trees at the back of the property. 'Made the house into a sort of museum, for his own private use.'

'I guess we should be thankful for that,' I said, letting my eyes roam the cluttered lawn and milling crowd of browsers and buyers. 'Do you see anything that interests you?'

He shrugged. 'A few things. Those globes, for instance.' He nodded towards a pair of standing library globes, terrestrial and celestial, a few yards to the left of us. 'They're dated eighteen twenty-eight, and in rather good condition. Rosewood stands, I think, which makes them fairly high quality. I'm always on the lookout for something that will add more character to the house.'

I was smiling at the thought of anyone referring to Crofton Hall as a mere 'house', as though it were nothing grander than a three-bedroom bungalow, when the auctioneer tentatively cleared his throat over the microphone and called the crowd to order. Geoff slung his arm around my shoulder, quite naturally, and guided me to a good vantage point at the outward edge of the tightly massed group. Bending his head, he spoke low into my ear.

'Are you going to bid on it?'

'Bid on what?'

'The Tolkien,' he said, smiling. I could feel that smile against my hair, and tried stoically to ignore the sensation. 'It *is* a first edition, isn't it?'

'Yes.' I smiled back, in spite of myself. 'And yes, I do intend to bid on it.'

As it happened, when the box of books finally came up, I didn't bid very high. I took one look at the man who was bidding against me, pulled my hand down, and refused to go any further. Geoff nudged my shoulder.

'Why aren't you bidding?' he asked.

'Because that man is a dealer,' I told him. 'He knows full well what the book is worth, and I can't afford to pay that much.'

Geoff followed my gaze to the deceptively languid fellow standing in the middle of the crowd, his hands in his pockets, a well-used briar pipe clenched between his teeth, looking every inch the common farmer.

'You're sure?'

'I'm sure.'

He thought a moment. 'Do you want me to buy it for you?'

'No.' It came out too hastily, and a bit too harshly, but I did not want Geoffrey de Mornay to think I was at all interested in his money. 'No,' I said again, more softly this time, 'thanks very much, but it isn't that important to me.'

I bit my lip and looked on as the bidding escalated into the hundreds, until it seemed certain that the dealer would win it, then watched with delight as the smug expression was wiped from his face by a last-minute entrant who stole the box of books with an unheard-of bid of five hundred pounds. A ripple of excitement swelled through the crowd as the elderly, grey-bearded man came forward to collect his purchase. The dealer, anxious but not *that* anxious, rocked back on his heels, folded his arms and puffed furiously at his pipe, sending a succession of small, blue-tinged clouds floating upwards into the bright, clear air.

For my part, I consoled myself by entering in the bidding on the next item, a plain little oak lap-desk that I eventually bought for rather more than it was worth. I hugged it close, triumphantly, while the auctioneer moved on.

'Here we have,' he said enticingly, 'a pair of Cary's library globes, dated 1828, of rosewood and painted beech with boxwood stringing all round. Who'll give me £5,000 to start?'

The dealers leapt at that one, and beside me Geoff nodded at the auctioneer, with whom he was obviously well-acquainted. When the bidding stopped at twenty-one thousand, the entire crowd – myself included – seemed to exhale its collective breath, and not a few heads turned to stare at the handsome, unassuming young man who had made the final bid.

Geoff drew out his chequebook and went to pay, and I stood frowning for a moment, watching him and thinking of the yawning social gulf that separated us. He was lord of the manor, for heaven's sake, I reminded myself. And medieval as that might sound, there was nothing medieval about the fact that his bank balance would make my own earnings look like mere pocket change. I had to be out of my mind.

But when he returned I had only to look at his face and my middle-class misgivings were forgotten. At that moment, Geoffrey de Mornay looked nothing like a lord. He looked, I thought, exactly like a small boy – happy and carefree and terribly pleased with himself.

'Anything happen while I was gone?' he asked.

'Nothing much. A few of the older ladies fainted when they saw you writing that cheque, but other than that it's been pretty dull.'

He laughed, throwing back his dark head and regarding me warmly. He had told me once not to apologize for being clever, and he didn't apologize to me now for being rich. I liked him for that. Instead, he put his arm around my shoulder again and directed my attention to a nearby sideboard. 'The sideboard itself is nothing,' he said, 'but I'll wager that pair of urns sitting on it will go for at least £6,000.'

I looked. 'You're on,' I accepted the wager. 'I'll bet you fifty pence.'

We stayed for another hour or so – long enough for me to lose my fifty pence and spend another twenty-five pounds on a totally unnecessary painting for my hallway – then, reluctantly, we made our way to the end of the drive, somewhat hampered by our cumbersome purchases.

The grey-bearded gentleman who had nabbed my box of books was leaning on the bonnet of Geoff's car, smoking a cigarette and gazing vaguely back at the continuing sale with a peaceful expression. He shifted as we approached.

'Sorry,' he apologized to Geoff. 'I'm just waiting for my son to come and collect me. Didn't fancy lugging *those*,' he nodded to the box, 'any further than I had to.'

'I don't blame you,' Geoff said, trying to wrestle his coveted library globes into the boot without damaging them.

I smiled at the old man. 'That's quite a good buy you made back there.'

'I know,' he nodded sagely. 'My father wrote most of those mysteries. Can't put a price on that, can you?'

Geoff stopped struggling and sent me an apprehensive, sideways look, but I had already spotted my opening.

'Oh, look!' I bent down and dislodged the Tolkien from the toppled books, pretending surprise. '*The Hobbit!* Look, darling, isn't that little Jimmy's favourite book?'

Geoff just grinned at me, refusing to play, and I turned a hopeful, enquiring face up to the gentle old man, hoping that I had retained at least some of the childish appeal I'd had as a seven-year-old.

'I don't suppose,' I said, faltering a little, 'I don't suppose that you'd . . .'

'You can have it,' he said generously. 'It's the mysteries I want. You take that book, for your little boy.'

To my credit, I felt a tiny twinge of guilt.

'Let me pay you for it,' I offered, handing him a ten-pound note which, to my great relief, he accepted. 'After all,' I smiled broadly, 'it must be worth something.'

Geoff slammed the boot shut with a curious cough and opened the passenger door for me. 'Come along, *darling*,' he said. 'We have to get going.'

In the car, he gave me another long look before we both burst out laughing at my good fortune.

'You are shameless,' he accused me. 'Shockingly good, but shameless.'

'I had a wonderful teacher,' I explained, and for the next few miles I regaled him with stories of my father's auction-house exploits and the conniving duplicity that ran strong in my family's blood.

'I'd enjoy meeting your father, from the sounds of it,' said Geoff.

My reply was little more than a noncommittal mumble. It was just as well for Geoff, I thought, that my father was still out of the country. My previous boyfriends had run for cover at the sight of him, as a rule. Daddy could be rather difficult, at times, and he hadn't yet found any young man who measured up to his exacting standards. The best thing, I'd found, was simply not to introduce them to him. It saved a lot of bother, all round.

The drive back to Exbury was far too short, and all too soon we were pulling up to the side of my house. Geoff reached into the back seat and handed me my lap-desk and the small framed painting I had foolishly bought. For the first time that day, our speech became stilted.

'That was a lot of fun,' I said. 'I really enjoyed myself.'

'So did I.' He looked at his hands on the steering wheel. 'Look,' he said, 'I have to go up north again for a few days, maybe even a week, but when I get back I'd like to see you again.' He turned his head to face me. 'I'd like to take you to dinner.'

'I'd like that,' I said, and he smiled, the full force of his charm making me momentarily dizzy.

It was a better kiss than the first. For one thing, I reasoned, we had known each other nearly two weeks longer, and we had just shared an absolutely perfect day in each other's company. When the kiss had ended I sent him a happy smile and reached for the door handle.

'Bye.'

He leaned across the seat, helping me with the door.

'You're sure you'll be all right with that?'

'Yes, thanks.' I nodded, clutching my purchases more tightly.

'Right, then.' Again the smile. 'I'll give you a ring when I get back.'

I watched him drive away, feeling ridiculously happy, and all but danced around the house to the back door. In stubborn contrast to my own mood, the key refused to turn in my new lock, and in the process of wrestling with it the oak lap-desk slipped from my grasp and fell with a thud and a clatter to the ground, missing the stone step my inches.

'Blast!' I cursed my brother and the lock, and knelt in the grass to recover the lap-desk. It had sprung open when it fell, and the loose, velvet-covered writing surface lay skewed on its hinges. I closed the box, and with my finger wiped a smear of mud from the elaborate letter 'H' on the lid's brass nameplate.

When I picked the lap-desk up, something rattled inside, and I groaned mentally, attacking the back door with renewed vigour. This time, the lock co-operated, stiffly. I pushed the door open with my shoulder, kicking it shut behind me for good measure.

Setting my purchases down on the kitchen table, I opened the lap-desk once more and examined the hollow cavity beneath the writing surface. Nothing appeared to have broken, but a narrow secret drawer had been sprung by the fall. With curious fingers I pried it fully open.

Inside the drawer lay a daintily worked bracelet of chipped and tarnished gilt, a linked procession of fanciful birds of paradise with eyes of blue glass that glittered like royal jewels.

Chapter Eighteen

With fingers that trembled slightly, I lifted the bracelet from the shallow drawer where it had lain concealed for . . . how long? Centuries? It *was* the same bracelet, I knew it with a certainty that surpassed logic. The sight of it, the feel of it, the weight of it against my palm were so familiar to me, there was no question that the bracelet had once been mine.

But how had it found its way into a wooden lap-desk that – if the maker's label was to be believed – had not even been crafted until the mid-1700s, seventy years or more after Mariana Farr had come to Exbury? Still clutching the bracelet, I closed the lid of the lap desk and looked again at the swirled letter 'H' on the nameplate, frowning. Was it possible, I wondered, that the 'H' stood for 'Howard'? Had this plain little box once belonged to one of the Howards of Greywethers?

I shook my head, bewildered. It all seemed so incredibly fantastic to me, beyond the realm of probability. Too much of a coincidence to be true, I thought. Or . . . was it? I ran the bracelet through my fingers like the beads of a rosary, and the birds of paradise seemed to wink at me as their glass eyes caught the light. Maybe, I speculated, just maybe, if everything was truly happening for a reason, and if there really was a mystical force that drove us on to fate or destiny, then my finding the bracelet was not much of a coincidence, after all. Maybe, in fact, it was *necessary* . . .

A sharp, imperious knocking at my back door startled me out of my ponderings, and I thrust the bracelet back into the lap-desk before moving to answer the summons. My mind had not yet fully abandoned its train of thought, and the distraction must have shown plainly on my features when I pulled open the door to face the man who stood on the step outside.

Iain Sumner filled the door frame, blocking out most of the sunlight, his expression accusing.

'You've been weeding,' he said flatly, 'haven't you?'

He was undoubtedly preparing to launch into one of the animated lectures that Vivien had warned me about, but I was saved at the last moment by a quite extraordinary occurrence – for the second time in as many weeks, I began to cry.

It was, I admit, not nearly as spectacular as my outburst at Tom's house in Hampshire, but nonetheless my eyes grew misty and my mouth trembled a little, and Iain abruptly stopped frowning to stare at me in concerned contrition. It was almost comical to see the self-possessed Scotsman so completely at a loss for words, and I couldn't stop my lips from curving into a small smile.

'I'm sorry,' I said, wiping my eyes, 'it's not you. It's just that . . .' I hesitated, searching for an explanation, before deciding that there simply was no easy way to explain my over-emotional state. 'Well, anyway,' I sniffed, 'yes, I have been weeding in your garden. Did I make an awful mess of it?'

Iain looked silently down at a limp, withered bit of greenery he held in one hand, considering, then seemed to think the better of it. Putting his hand behind his back he let the plant fall to his feet, and met my eyes levelly.

'No, it's not too bad, really,' he said.

He was a charming liar, and I told him so. Laughing, he put his head on one side and, satisfied that I had regained my composure, said, 'Look, I tell you what. If you're bent on helping me with my work, why don't you come on out for a minute and let me show you what everything is?'

'I thought you didn't like people mucking about in your gardens.'

'It's an ugly rumour, that,' he grinned. 'Come on, it won't take a moment.'

As I stepped across the threshold, following him, I bent to pick up the mangled plant that he had so gallantly discarded. 'This wasn't a South African something, was it?' I asked cautiously.

He looked at me with eyes that twinkled only slightly.

'It was not,' he assured me emphatically. 'If you'd pulled up one of those, you'd have heard about it, tears or no.'

It was, I realized afterwards, exactly what I had needed – a half hour of messing about in the dirt, feeling the dry, dusty feel of earth against my fingertips and smelling the pungent sweet scent of leaves and flowers warmed by the sun. It comforted me, reassured me, grounded me once again in reality. Iain proved to be quite a good teacher, actually. With painstaking thoroughness he identified each flower and plant in the garden, pointing out the almost invisible shoots of flowers that would not be seen until late summer. He told me what needed to be done, and showed me how to do it, so that when he had finished I felt quite confident in my ability to at least weed the garden without destroying it.

'You'll get the hang of it,' he promised. 'It just takes practice.'

'You're sure you won't mind?' I wrinkled my forehead sceptically, and he turned an impassive face towards me.

'D'ye not trust me?'

'Well, Vivien and Geoff seemed to think that I was taking some sort of mortal risk . . .'

He grinned, and reached to snap a dead blossom off a nearby stalk of iris. 'I won't mind,' he said. 'Besides, it'll do you good to get out here once in a while. Keeps you healthy, gardening does.' He checked his wristwatch and stood up, stretching. 'I'll leave you to it, then. Time I was getting home.'

I had no idea myself what time it was, but the sun was lying low in the sky and it must have been close on seven o'clock. I stood up with him.

'Thank you,' I said. I was thanking him for a number of things, really. For not being angry with me, for understanding my mood, for being so damnably *nice* . . .

He just shrugged, and smiled.

'It's no trouble.'

He took his leave of me and strode away across the field, while I turned to face the dying sun, fitting my back to the smooth, crumbled stone wall behind me, half closing my eyes dreamily. It was a perfect, fairy-tale sunset, golden red with cotton-wool clouds whose gilded edges gave them an almost artificial appearance, as though they belonged in one of my own illustrations. To complete the picture, all that was missing was the rider under the oak, a romantic dark knight on his noble charger, watching the distant hills for dragons. I turned my head to look towards the hollow with eyes that were almost hopeful, but there was nothing there.

Above the oak, a hawk drifted lazily in an aimless circle, and his voice was a lonely cry.

*   *   *

The days passed, quickly and quietly, and I applied myself to my illustrations with a diligence that was completely foreign to my character. I was procrastinating, and I knew it. In a strange way, learning that I had the power to transport myself into the seventeenth century at will had made me reluctant to do so. All that week, while I sketched and painted and carried on with my normal routine, I think I was secretly hoping that something would just *happen* in a nice spontaneous way, so I wouldn't be consciously responsible for what might follow.

But of course, nothing did happen, although by the end of the week I was completely surrounded by watercolours in various stages of the drying process, which made me feel – if nothing else – terribly productive. On Friday, Geoff telephoned to let me know that his week up north had been stretched to two weeks, and did I mind waiting a little longer for that dinner? I told him of course not.

To be perfectly truthful, dinner was the furthest thing from my mind at that moment. My preoccupation with my work was, as usual, making me anti-social in my habits. For several days I slept and worked and saw no-one, eating my meals from tins and crawling off to bed in the small hours of the morning. When Vivien rang me up shortly before lunch on the following Tuesday, she couldn't resist commenting on the rusty quality of my voice. My explanation – that I hadn't spoken in three days – only made her more curious.

'Don't you even talk to yourself?' she wanted to know.

'No.' I grinned against the receiver. 'I have a cousin

who does that, and I'd rather not be bracketed with her, thanks all the same.'

'I see. Well, do you fancy getting out for a bit this afternoon? Or is the creative flow flowing at the moment?'

'Oh, I'm sure I could be persuaded to tear myself away for a few hours,' I told her. 'What did you have in mind?'

'Tea at Crofton Hall.'

I frowned. 'Geoff's not back yet, surely?'

'No, no, he's still up north. Actually the invitation comes from my Aunt Freda. She's been after me for several days now to bring you round for a chat, but this is the first day I've been able to take the time off. Ned's been down with the flu, you see.'

So the White Witch of Exbury was inviting me round to tea. It sounded a thoroughly delightful prospect.

'I'd love to come,' I said.

'Wonderful. Is three o'clock all right with you? You can drop by here if you like, on your way, and collect me.'

'Fine. Shall I bring anything?'

'Just yourself. And a healthy appetite,' she advised me. 'Aunt Freda's teas could sustain a hard-working family of four, and we'll be expected to eat what we're served.'

At three o'clock that afternoon, I was glad that I had taken Vivien's advice and skipped lunch, as I doubted whether I'd have had room to put everything otherwise. The table in front of me groaned beneath the weight of heaping plates of cakes and sandwiches and pickled relishes and cold ham pie.

'You don't have to eat it all, child,' Mrs Hutherson assured me. She topped up the teapot with freshly boiled water and sat down facing me. 'No matter what Vivien's told you, I'm not quite as nasty as all that.'

We were sitting in the kitchen of Crofton Hall. Not the great, echoing kitchen that I'd seen during my tour of the manor house, but a smaller, more functional room in the private north-east wing, with scrubbed pine floors and lace curtains and plants spilling from every window-sill. Alfreda Hutherson obviously spent a great deal of time in this kitchen, and the room had absorbed much of her personal energy, radiating warmth and friendliness and comfort.

I found her quite fascinating – a tall, spare woman in a plain dark dress, with laughing blue eyes that were so like Vivien's that I wondered how I could have missed the resemblance before. She moved with a regal, wholly natural grace, and though her hair was nearly pure white I found it impossible to guess at her age. Like her niece, she was a wonderful conversationalist, intelligent and well-read, with a deliciously sly, quiet wit that surfaced from time to time.

'I must say,' she said now, passing the sandwiches round for the third time, 'it is nice to have company in the house. I always feel at a loose end when Geoffrey is away.'

'You've been feeding Iain instead, this week – he told me so.' Vivien grinned accusingly. 'He'll be putting on weight.'

'He works hard,' her aunt rationalized. 'He'll keep it off. And it's nice to see someone who appreciates good food.'

'You still live, here, then?' I took a sandwich. 'In the manor house?'

She smiled. 'Oh, no. No, I have a small house of my own in the village. I just work days here, do the cleaning and watch over the younger girls, then before I leave I put Geoffrey's supper in the oven for him and he does the washing-up. It's a very informal arrangement.'

'Aunt Freda's house is just the other side of the old Vicarage,' Vivien put in. 'It was my Gran's house, when she was alive. Little stone house with green shutters. Is that the phone?' She cocked her head suddenly, listening. 'Yes, it is. No, stay where you are, I'll get it,' she told her aunt, pushing her chair back and disappearing down the long dark passageway. She returned a moment later, shaking her head.

'Crisis,' she pronounced. 'That was Ned. The taps have apparently stopped working and the lads are getting sober. I'd better run over and see what I can do. I'll be back as soon as I can.'

'No hurry, dear,' Alfreda Hutherson told her with a wink. 'Plenty of food to go round. We'll save some biscuits for you.'

Vivien laughed. 'I'll bet you will.'

The door closed behind her, and the woman across from me raised her teacup, her eyes suddenly thoughtful as they watched me over the brim.

'You look very tired,' she said, unexpectedly. 'Has it all been too much for you?'

I hesitated a minute before answering, not sure how to interpret the question, and struggling with a question of my own. I met her eyes uncertainly and she smiled, setting her teacup down in its saucer.

'You want to ask me whether I know, and what I know, and how I know it,' she said calmly, 'but you're afraid I'll think you're mad if you speak first. So I'll save you the trouble. Yes, I do know. I'm well aware of what's been happening to you since you moved here. I've been quite concerned about you, as a matter of fact,' she told me frankly. 'That's why I had Vivien bring you round to see me. I wanted to see for myself how you were getting on.'

After which remarkable speech, she lifted her teacup once more and waited for my response. She didn't have to wait long. I had been sitting bolt upright in my chair, staring, but now I blinked at her and smiled, raising my eyebrows.

'They said you were a witch.'

She laughed, but did not deny it. She poured me a fresh cup of tea and leaned back, folding her arms expectantly. 'You have questions.'

'Dozens of them,' I admitted. 'But I'm not entirely sure I want to know the answers.'

She nodded, just once, but with emphasis. 'Nor should you. It's a kind of journey that you've begun, Julia, and no-one can show you the way of it. You must find your own direction.'

'But, surely *you* could . . .'

'I could tell you certain things, yes. But my interference might be more of a hindrance than a help to you.'

'Oh.' I was disappointed, and she smiled at my expression.

'Don't look so crestfallen, child,' she said. 'You've come this far, without me, and you've done very well. You know something about Mariana, and you've accepted a reality that many people would be unable or unwilling to accept. And more importantly, you're beginning, I think, to understand that you have more control over the situation than you realize, are you not?'

I nodded.

'Well, then,' she spread her hands in an expressive gesture. 'It seems to me you're doing fine all on your own. You must be patient, Julia, and trust the process. You will have your answers soon enough, and without my help.'

'I bought something last weekend,' I told her, running a finger along the rim of my cup. 'A sort of box.'

'The lap-desk. Yes.'

I raised my head. 'It was inscribed with a letter "H".'

She tilted her head, bird-like, and studied me. 'The "H", of course, is for Howard. You knew that, didn't you?'

'Yes. But . . .'

'Which one? Well, I don't suppose I can do any harm by telling you that much.' Her eyes slid away from mine. 'It belonged to John Howard.'

'John?' I turned the name over in my head. 'John? Caroline's baby, John?' I thought of the tiny, red-faced baby, and then of the faded bracelet set carefully away in the lap-desk's secret drawer. 'But how did he . . .?'

She cut me off with a shake of her head. 'That is for you to find out,' she told me. 'And you will. Would you like another biscuit?'

She passed me the plate and I took a chocolate wafer, feeling a little dazed. It was strange, I thought, to be sitting here in a perfectly ordinary, cosy kitchen, discussing reincarnation with a witch. In these normal, plain, everyday surroundings our conversation seemed oddly surreal, like people discussing dress patterns at a funeral. And yet, here I was, placidly munching my biscuit and sitting not three feet away from a woman who could read my thoughts as easily as I might read a printed page. She was reading me now, I could tell by the way her eyes met mine . . .

'I'm sorry if it disturbs you,' she said quietly. 'My

knowing things that you don't. But I'm not an old woman for nothing. I've seen a good deal of time, and I've watched it passing, and if I've learned nothing else I've learned that fate works to a schedule of its own making.' She sat back in her chair and faced me, philosophically. 'It's all rather like a circle, you know,' she went on, 'life is. You start off in one place, and choose your path, and when you finish up you find you're right back where you started from. And that's what you're doing now, with Mariana's life. When you've gone all the way round, when you've closed the circle, then and only then will the purpose of your journey become clear to you.'

'And you're absolutely sure,' I asked her, 'that I'm her . . . I mean, that she's . . . that Mariana Farr and I are the same person?'

'Oh, yes.' Her eyes were gentle. 'I recognized you at once.'

'Recognized me?'

'I'd seen you before,' she explained. 'Not you as you are now, of course, but you, all the same.'

'Of course,' I said, remembering. 'The Green Lady.'

'And the woman in the Cavalier bedroom upstairs,' she added. 'Mariana haunted both places, for a long time.'

I frowned. 'But I thought that the ghost upstairs was still in residence. It's impossible, isn't it, for a soul to be in two places at once?'

Alfreda Hutherson shook her head patiently. 'There is no ghost upstairs,' she told me. 'Not anymore. What you felt up there was simply the aura of what had been. She left that in the room, you see, much as a person casts a shadow on a wall.'

I was silent for a moment thinking.

'I see a man, sometimes,' I said slowly. 'A man on a grey horse . . .'

'Richard.' She nodded. 'He is a kind of shadow, too, when you see him like that. Under the old oak tree in the hollow, isn't it? Yes, he spent a good deal of time there. It's natural that something of him should linger. Part of it, you must understand, is a projection of your own mind. When you stare at the sun too long, you see it everywhere.'

Then my instincts were correct, I thought. If Richard de Mornay was not a ghost, then he, like Mariana, could be alive and well and living in Exbury. He could even, I postulated, be living at Crofton Hall. What was it that Tom had told me before? That people who chose to be born into new lives tended to surround themselves with people from their previous lives. We were all of us connected, somehow. Vivien and Iain and Geoff and me . . . and perhaps even . . .

'Have you and I ever met?' I asked Mrs Hutherson, suddenly curious. 'Before, I mean. Were you someone I knew?'

She smiled at that, but it seemed to me a sad little smile, and her eyes, when they met mine, had a far-away look in them. 'Ah, well,' she said, turning her gaze away towards the window, 'we were all somebody, once.' She cocked her head, listening. 'That'll be Vivien,' she said, in a decided tone. 'I'd best put the kettle on for a fresh pot of tea.'

I myself could hear nothing but the wind and a faint twittering of birds, but I wasn't in the least surprised a moment later to see Vivien come bounding through the kitchen door as the kettle came shrieking to the boil on the stove.

Chapter Nineteen

That night I dreamed of my mother. I dreamed I was a small child again, with skinned knees and pigtails, playing in the yard of our home in Oxford, while my mother sat on the lawn beside me, reading. In my dream, my mother's eyes were blue. She is very dark, like me, and I remember thinking how very odd that was, that her eyes should have suddenly turned blue in place of their normal brown, but when I asked her about it she merely smiled, and kissed me, and sent me off to play.

Our backyard was actually quite small, but as I walked towards the fence the boundary seemed to recede before me, until I found myself walking in a field of waving flowers, with the sunshine warm upon my shoulders and the air alive with the humming of contented insects. If I reached out a hand and brushed the tops of the flowers, I could smell the sweet and sudden release of their fragrance.

I was quite far from the house now. When I turned to look behind me, it was nothing more than a small speck in the distance. As lovely and beckoning as the field of flowers was, I knew that my mother would be worried if I strayed too far. Reluctantly, I started back. It seemed an even longer walk this time, and I had to scramble over the fence to get back into the yard. When I finally arrived back the sunshine had faded, and the air was cool and damp. My mother was no longer sitting on the lawn.

I went into the house, but there was no-one there, either. It was quite empty, and desolate, the silence itself more disturbing than any eerie sound I could have imagined. Confused and terrified, I ran, half-stumbling, up the street to a friend's house and pounded urgently on the door. My friend answered the summons, but she was no longer a child like me – she was a grown woman, and she stood on the doorstep gazing down at me with pitying eyes.

'I'm so sorry,' she said. 'Hasn't anyone told you? Your mother died years ago . . .'

The tears were still on my face when the dream ended. I could taste them as I lay there in the darkness, listening to the dripping of my bathroom taps and watching the shadow of the poplar dance across my blankets while I tried to calm the frantic beating of my heart against my ribs. When I could breathe normally again, I reached to switch on the reading-lamp on my bedside table and sat up, pushing both hands through my damp, tangled hair and drawing them down to cover my eyes.

It was only a dream, I told myself. *You're not a child anymore, you're nearly thirty years old, and your mother isn't dead.* I picked up my dressing-gown from the floor, where I'd discarded it before going to bed, and shrugged my arms into the sleeves, wrapping the belt around my waist as I shuffled out into the hallway. I would not sleep, I knew from experience, until I had shaken off the clinging memory of that dream. At times like these I often wished I had a television, like normal people, but I had given away my own set years ago. It had been too tempting a distraction from my work.

Instead, I settled now for a late night talk programme on my portable radio and a soothing cup of cocoa. When that failed to work, I tried reading. A full hour later, still unable to shake my vague uneasiness and the dull, cold, unnamed fear that had wrapped its tight fingers round my heart, I gave in and picked up the phone, dialling the New Zealand number with an unsteady hand.

My mother answered after eight rings, her voice distracted but carefully precise. Seconds later she was fully alert.

'Julia? Is everything all right?'

I had to admit, rather sheepishly, that it was, and explain that I was only calling to say hello, and to see how they both were.

'At four o'clock in the morning?' My mother made the time calculation, sounding unconvinced.

I sighed. 'I had a nightmare, actually. I dreamed that you were dead.'

'Oh, darling . . .' Her voice was like a hug over the telephone line. 'How terrible. Well, I'm not dead, as it happens, and I've no intention of dying in the foresee-able future, so you can stop worrying.' I heard a faint rustling sound and knew that she was settling herself in her chair, propping pillows to cushion her back. 'How are you enjoying life in your village?' she asked me. 'Tommy tells us that your house is absolutely lovely, though he has his doubts about the plumbing . . .'

Without waiting for a response, my mother plunged easily into a rather one-sided conversation that dealt mainly with the goings-on among our various relatives in Auckland, punctuated with periodic mumblings of an incoherent nature from my father, who was no doubt trying to read or nap beside her.

'What's that, Edward, darling?' she would ask him brightly. 'Oh, yes, I mustn't forget that. And then, Julia, she showed up wearing the most incredible *hat* . . .' And off my mother would go again, spinning out another gossip-laden anecdote, cleverly designed to make me forget the terror of my nightmare.

My parents were really quite wonderful, I thought to myself, when I finally replaced the telephone receiver nearly an hour later. Stretching my arms above my head, I looked around the hallway with idle interest. My mother's ploy had definitely worked. I was no longer afraid, nor apprehensive. I was also, unfortunately, no longer sleepy.

Well, I told myself stoutly, if I was going to be up and awake, I might as well get properly dressed. I trudged back up the stairs and exchanged my dressing gown for a pair of jeans and a loose T-shirt, in honour of our recent spell of warm weather. As I brushed my hair in front of the mirror, my eyes fell on the small blackened key that still sat on the dressing-table before me. Slowly, my forehead creasing in a studious frown, I set the hairbrush down and picked up the little key, weighing it thoughtfully in my palm.

What hidden secrets was it waiting to unlock for me, I wondered? I remembered Mrs Hutherson's gentle, knowing face smiling at me yesterday across the kitchen table at Crofton Hall. *It's a kind of a journey that you've begun*, she had said. Closing my fingers around the key for a moment I looked up at the resolute face in the mirror. There was no point in delaying the inevitable, I thought. It was time for me to take the next step on my journey. It was time to go back.

Downstairs, I lit the candle I had used during my last experimental session and placed it squarely in the centre of my table. It was beginning to grow faintly light outside, and the candle flame was less mesmerizing as a result, but I focussed on it with an effort and concentrated, half-closing my eyes. Time stopped, and wavered. The sound of my breathing was very loud in the quiet room.

'Mariana!' Caroline's voice was sharp, and I snapped my head up, instantly alert. My aunt smiled a little at my reaction, her voice softening. 'You'll be doing yourself an injury,' she warned me, 'dreaming away like that. Did we wake you too early?'

'I slept badly,' I excused myself with a minor lie, not caring to confess that my inattentiveness had been caused by thoughts of a certain dark-haired neighbour. I took a firmer hold on my knife and went on cutting vegetables for the soup that Rachel was simmering on the hearth.

'It is uncommonly warm,' Rachel said, in my defence. ''Twould make anyone sluggish.' She stood up, away from the fire, her face flushed and moist, and cast a sly sidelong glance at Caroline. 'I even saw you nodding at your prayers this morning, sister.'

'I do not nod at prayer,' Caroline responded primly, but her eyes twinkled merrily and she looked almost young as she returned Rachel's teasing. 'I was only being devout.'

Rachel would have made comment on that, but before she could speak the words the kitchen door opened and my uncle came into the room. In an instant the life disappeared from Caroline's eyes, as though some unseen hand had passed across her face. My uncle did not notice the transformation. He was red-faced and uncomfortable from the heat, and his expression was sour.

'This is the hottest day I have ever known,' he complained, wiping the beads of perspiration from his chin. 'It is the heat of the devil himself. Mariana, fetch me a drink of water, girl, and make haste with it.'

I complied without saying a word, handing the cup to him and returning to my work. He drank the water as an animal drinks, with a great noise, and set the cup down again on the table with satisfaction. His hard, gleaming eyes turned towards me.

'You look tired, Mariana.'

Caroline stirred in her corner by the hearth. 'She slept ill, Jabez. 'Tis no great concern.'

His eyes narrowed. 'She wants exercise. A walk in the open air will cure her ills.' He addressed me in a tone that was almost kind. 'When your work here is finished,' he told me, 'you may spend the rest of the morning out of doors. Walk down by the river, it will be cooler there.'

I tried to hide my surprise at his words. It seemed such an odd and unlikely turnabout, for this man who had rarely permitted me out of his sight to suggest that I spend time away from the house, that I could scarce believe it. Even Caroline raised her eyebrows, though she wisely said nothing.

Uncle Jabez turned to Rachel. 'There will be guests for the midday meal,' he informed her. 'Four others besides myself. For the meal I want a pigeon pie, with no fewer than two birds for each person, and a jug of the good cider from the cellar. Mariana can fetch the birds for you, before she leaves.'

I made a small sound of protest, my eyes stricken, and Rachel looked up from her kettle of soup. 'I will get the birds,' she told him. 'Mariana is too soft-hearted. She does not like to wring their necks.'

My uncle shrugged. 'I do not care who kills the wretched things, so long as they are on my table at dinner.' He flicked a glance at his wife. 'I trust you will tend to the child,' he said, 'and keep it silent. I do not wish a squealing brat to ruin the appetite of my guests.'

Caroline murmured something in reply, her head lowered submissively. I knew his unkind comment had wounded her deeply. Rachel had told me of her sister's yearning to conceive a child, her years of barren unhappiness and her joy when she had finally given birth to John. That Jabez did not share her pride in the child was a constant source of pain to her.

'Johnnie is a fine child,' I heard myself saying. 'I doubt that he would disturb anyone.'

My uncle rested his cold blue eyes on my face once more. 'You may go whenever you are ready,' he told me, his voice even. 'And see that you promenade yourself well. I do not wish to see you back here before mid-afternoon.'

He turned abruptly and left the room, with Caroline trailing like a pale shadow in his wake. Rachel looked at me with wondering eyes, and chided me softly; 'You should not have spoken to him so. It is of no use to speak on my sister's behalf, Mariana. She goes like a lamb to the slaughter.'

'I know,' I said. 'But I could not stop the words from coming.'

'Well,' Rachel crossed the room to stand by the table, ''tis no great harm done. And you will have an entire morning to cool your temper, from the sound of it. That ought to be a pleasant prospect for you.'

I *was* pleased by the thought of a few hours out of doors, but my pleasure was tempered by irritation. My uncle did not want me to be in the house when his visitors arrived, that much was plain, and I was hard pressed to contain my curiosity.

'Rachel,' I asked casually, 'who are the guests my uncle spoke of? Do you know them?'

I had learned that Rachel could not lie easily. When she was unable to give a truthful answer, she would seek to deflect the question. She sought to deflect mine now, lowering her head so that the fall of bright hair hid her face from me. She chose her words slowly, and with care.

'It is sometimes better,' she advised me, 'to cover your eyes and stop up your ears, instead of asking questions.'

I knew she would say no more about the matter, so I let the subject drop, taking my bowlful of vegetables over to the hearth and emptying it into the boiling pot.

'Shall I go now?' I asked, rubbing my damp hands on my skirt.

Rachel shrugged. 'Unless you want to fetch the pigeons from the dovecote,' she said, then laughed at my expression. 'Be off with you,' she ordered, in a brave imitation of my uncle, 'and see that you promenade yourself well.'

I was only too happy to comply. The sky was wide and inviting, and the grass was cool and sweetly refreshing under my bare feet as I walked across the undulating field towards the river. It was a short walk, only a mile or so, but I did not hurry it, letting my soul soak up the glorious sensation of freedom and lightness.

Even the heat could not diminish me. The scorching heat of the sun had a cauterizing effect, burning away the sick and dying parts of my being so that the healthy parts of me could grow back, fuller and more vital than before. Closer to the river there was shade, a rich, deep shade provided by the flanking groves of thickly clustered trees that grew beside the idly flowing water.

Here, the only sounds were those of nature – birds chattering in the highest branches, the gentle rustle of an unseen creature of the forest and the sudden splash of a fish breaking the surface of the shallow river. It was, I mused, like entering the gardens of paradise after sojourning in the underworld. The plague and London seemed a long way off, and the dark halls of Greywethers even further.

I gathered the folds of my skirts in my hands and waded into the river, lifting the hem of my dress clear of the water. The rippling coolness washed my skin above the ankles, and I went no further, turning instead to push my way upstream, enjoying the feel of the smoothly washed pebbles beneath my tired feet.

I walked a goodly distance, splashing a little as I went and humming happily to myself, a tuneless ditty of my own invention. Coming to a place where the river bent in its course, and the trees grew still more thickly, I paused and ventured even deeper, raising my skirts accordingly.

The birds startled me, rising from the trees without warning in a panicked, beating cloud that dipped and shifted in perfect unison against the burning sky, and then was gone. The noise was like a blast of cannon fire in that still place, and in alarm I lost my footing, falling backwards into the water with a loud splash and an unladylike oath. Pushing the wet hair from my eyes, I looked to see what had so frighted the birds, my own heart pounding an echo of their flight.

At first, I could see only shadows. Until one of the shadows moved, and became real, and the greenwood parted to reveal a tall dark rider on a grey horse, moving with leisured grace along the riverbank towards me.

Chapter Twenty

Richard de Mornay reined Navarre to a smooth halt a few feet from the lazily flowing water and leaned an elbow on the horn of his saddle, regarding me with interest over the horse's broad neck.

'Good morrow, Mistress Farr.' He swept the wide-brimmed hat from his dark head and presented me with a fair imitation of a bow. 'I did not know that you numbered swimming among your many accomplishments.'

To return a proper curtsey from my position would have appeared ridiculous. Besides, he was laughing at me, and I resented it. I rose swiftly to my feet and tossed my head proudly. 'I have a multitude of talents, my lord,' I told him curtly, spreading my skirts to survey the damage.

'Of that I have no doubt.' A thoughtful expression replaced the laughter in his eyes, and he swung himself from the saddle, gathering the reins in one large hand. 'You have wetted your dress,' he said, as though it were a revelation. 'You must walk in the sun to dry it.'

I stubbornly held my ground. 'I do not wish to walk in the sun, my lord. I find the coolness of the woods refreshing.'

'You must walk in the woods, then. Come, let me help you.'

He extended his free hand towards me, his eyes challenging mine. After a moment's consideration, I placed my hand in his and let him assist me in stepping out of the water onto the riverbank. It was welcome assistance, I was bound to admit, since the wet fabric of my dress weighed heavily against my legs and threatened to drag me back into the river. When at last I stood upright, I released his hand as though it were a snake, breaking the warm contact.

'Thank you, sir,' I told him sweetly. 'You are most kind.' Taking my leave of him, I began once more to walk upstream, on land this time, feeling less than graceful in my dripping gown but keeping my head held high.

''Tis no trouble.' Richard de Mornay fell easily into step beside me, leading the horse behind us. 'You will not mind, surely, if I walk with you. I would be less than a true soldier if I let a lady walk through the woods unattended.'

I attempted a casual demeanour. 'I did not know you were a soldier.'

'I come from a family of soldiers.' He smiled, but it was a smile without humour. 'Brave knights and gallant cavaliers, and me the only one remaining to champion the family's honour.'

'Then I need not fear to lose my virtue in your company.' It was a bold statement, and I knew it. He turned amazed eyes in my direction and laughed outright, a pleasant sound that echoed in the secluded wood.

'You are a brazen wench,' he grinned. 'No, you need not worry. I'll not demand the lordly privileges of my estate. I've never yet had cause to force a woman to my will.'

I looked up at his handsome, laughing face and did not doubt that he spoke the truth. Perhaps it was my own intentions that worried me, and not his . . .

'Tell me,' he went on, changing the subject, 'how fares your uncle? He must be ill indeed to let you venture forth like this. In truth, 'tis but the second time I have seen you walking on your own. Come, tell me, why did he let you off the lead this morning?'

I smiled at the expression. 'He sent me from the house by his own order,' I explained. 'He fears, he told me, for my health.'

'Ay,' he said drily, 'he is a most compassionate man. 'Tis why he uses his household so civilly.'

I glanced at him. 'You do not like my uncle, I perceive.'

'I find him cruel and callous,' he said, with a shrug of his broad shoulders, 'and there is little love lost between us.'

I nodded understanding. 'He told me once that the devil dwells in you.'

He grinned again. 'No doubt he does believe it. And what do you think, Mariana Farr?'

He did look faintly devilish, smiling down at me with his dark clothes and his dark hair and those glinting eyes the colour of the forest that surrounded us, shutting us off together from the wider world. I studied him closely, and shrugged in my turn.

'I am no simple chit in hanging sleeves, my lord. I have eyes of my own to judge with, and I see no horns.'

He looked down at me soberly as we walked. 'It must be difficult for you,' he said quietly, 'to live in that house.'

I drew myself up stiffly, not welcoming his pity. 'I am but an orphan, my lord, dependent upon the charity of my relations. I do not question my position.'

His eyes doubted my sincerity, but he let my comment pass, and we walked on a ways in silence. When we came to another slight bend in the river, the grey stallion behind us flung his head back and tugged sharply at the reins, bringing my companion to a standstill.

'I believe Navarre is thirsty,' he interpreted the action for me. 'Come, sit with me while he drinks. This is a pleasant spot to pass the time.'

I let myself be led to a grassy clearing several yards from the water's edge, and seated myself on the trunk of a fallen tree, brushing off the small twinge of guilt that nagged at my conscience. My uncle would never learn of this, I reminded myself, and even if he did, what shame was there in it? After all, I had not invited Richard de Mornay's company, and one could not simply dismiss the lord of the manor from one's presence as if he were a common farm lad. The fact that I did not particularly want to dismiss him from my presence was, to my mind, inconsequential.

He seated himself at my feet, his back against the rough bark of the tree trunk, one booted leg drawn up to support his outstretched arm. With lazy eyes he watched the grey horse drinking.

'You said you were the last of your family,' I reminded him, attempting to make conversation. 'Have you no brothers?'

'I have five brothers,' he said, 'but they are in their graves. They died in service to the first Charles.'

I looked down solemnly. 'Your father stood for the King, then, against the Parliament.'

'Ay.' The word was bitter. 'And for their trouble they lost their lives, their lands, and all they owned and ever loved.'

'You did not die,' I pointed out.

'No, I did not die.' He shifted his shoulders against the fallen trunk and half-smiled at me. 'The youngest of us was eighteen, and newly wed, when he did fall, and then the King himself was put to death. I was myself but twenty. After the execution, I fled to France and joined my mother's family at the French King's court. I had no stomach left for fighting, and with my father in the Tower I could be of little help to him in England.'

I stared at him. 'Your father was in the Tower?'

'He was captured at the defence of Exeter, in 'forty-six. Fourteen years they kept him within the Tower walls, without a lawful trial. He grew old in that dismal place. He lived to see freedom, and his lands restored, but not my return from France.' He pulled a blade of grass and passed it between his fingers, the shadow of an old pain crossing his stoic features.

'I am sorry.' I leaned forward a little in my sympathy. 'I know what it is, to lose a father. So you have no-one left?'

'Not quite no-one. I have a nephew, Arthur, the son of my younger brother. He lives in Holland with his mother. He is fifteen and a leaping gallant, but he is my nephew nonetheless. And I have Evan. That is family enough.'

Evan Gilroy, he told me, had been a friend in the old days, before the fires of war swept across the countryside and left a sovereign dead. When Richard de Mornay had followed Charles Stuart home to England five years ago, Evan Gilroy had offered his services to the new lord of Crofton Hall, taking charge of the stables and the tenant farms.

The man at my feet smiled at the memory. ''Tis no great welcome for a man to come home to an empty house and a barren land,' he told me. 'Were it not for Evan, I doubt I would have stayed.'

I silently acknowledged my debt to Evan Gilroy. I was feeling very much at ease, in spite of my wet clothes, sitting here in the dappled sunlight of the little clearing and talking to a man who stood several notches above my station in life. My father would have liked this man, I thought, for all that Uncle Jabez did not approve.

I leaned back and clasped my hands around my knees, lacing my fingers together. 'Have you met the King, then?'

'Officially? Only once.' He glanced at me over his shoulder. 'Although I have seen him quite often, and even gamed with him once or twice. He was very much in evidence at the French court, during his exile.'

'I saw him only once, myself. At the coronation.' He had made a great impression on me at the time, I recalled, a regal and vivacious figure with his long curling hair, sensuous mouth and languid dark eyes. 'He seemed a kind man,' I commented.

'He is kind enough,' Richard de Mornay agreed, 'and fairer than most. He has a large heart, but he is not a great king. The time for great kings is past.'

I furrowed my brow, thinking. 'They say he is, at heart, a Catholic.'

The man beside me shrugged his powerful shoulders. 'My mother was a Catholic,' he said. ''Tis no great sin, I think.'

I feigned nonchalance. I had never met a Catholic before. 'And you?' I asked him. 'What is your faith?'

Richard de Mornay bent his head, his features darkening. 'I have no use for God,' he told me flatly. 'Nor He for me.'

He cast aside the mangled blade of grass and idly reached to capture both my hands in one of his, drawing them forward so that he could see my wrists. 'You're not wearing the bracelet,' he observed.

I flushed crimson, pulling ineffectually against his grasp. 'I cannot wear it,' I protested. 'Faith, I cannot accept it, it would not be seemly. I meant to return it to you.'

'I will not have it returned.' He looked seriously offended. 'I bought it for you as a present, and I would have you wear it.'

'My uncle would doubtless not approve, my lord,' I reminded him gently, but he merely shrugged, releasing my hands and rising to collect the grazing horse, gathering the trailing reins in his fist.

'I care not,' he told me. 'What business has your uncle in my affairs?'

'None, my lord,' I had to admit, 'but he takes a great interest in mine, and I would not wish to rouse his ire.'

He turned at that, looming tall against the grey stallion, his expression serious. 'If Jabez Howard dares to mark you in any way, I will hear of it.'

I stood up, too, and faced him squarely. 'I am flattered, my lord, but it is none of your concern. I am not your responsibility.'

'You are wrong, mistress,' he informed me in a voice as smooth as honey. 'You are very much my responsibility. I have made it so.' He advanced on me, one hand steadying the horse's saddle. 'Come, I'll ride you back.'

I looked up at him nervously. 'I do not ride pillion behind any man, my lord.'

'Ride alone, then,' he invited, smiling at my discomfort.

I glanced up at the heavens for assistance, and noted with vague relief that the sun was yet low in the eastern sky. 'It is too early for me to return,' I apologized. 'My uncle gave instructions that I was to walk until mid-afternoon.'

Richard de Mornay narrowed his eyes in disbelief. 'It is a pretty household you've fallen into, and no mistake. No matter,' he shrugged off my objection, 'you may ride with me to Crofton Hall, and pass the afternoon as my guest.'

I was sorely tempted by the offer, but in the end I shook my head, taking a small step backwards and nearly tripping over the fallen tree trunk in so doing.

'I am grateful for your kindness, my lord,' I told him weakly, 'but I think I had better not.'

''Tis your decision,' he assured me, swinging himself into the saddle with fluid grace. He brought the horse closer, reining in sharply so his muscled thigh was scarcely a handsbreadth from my face, knowing that the heavy log at my heels prevented any retreat. 'I've told you once I would not force you to my will,' he reminded me, drawing one finger along my upturned jawline. 'When we become lovers, it will be because you desire it as much as I.' His finger brushed my lips, the fleeting phantom of a kiss, before he raised his hand to his hat and bid me a polite good day.

The grey horse, for all its size, moved with great speed and agility. I watched the trees swallow them up and then stood listening for some minutes to the sound of the receding hoofbeats. I suppose I could have moved, had I wanted to, but I really did not want to. I just stood there in the dappled shadows, trying to hold the moment for as long as I could, all the while feeling it slipping away like sand through my open fingers . . . slipping . . . slipping . . .

My vision blurred, and the moment vanished.

I was standing alone by the edge of the lazy river, where only a scattering of knee-high shrubs and the occasional willow remained to hint at the grandness of the forest that once followed the river's shores. The river was set now in a kind of hollow, steeply banked on either side, and I could see nothing but the water and grass and the blue sky above me. I had no idea where I was.

Scrambling up the sloping bank, I looked out over the fields and attempted to get my bearings. Far off to my left, I could see the fenced pastures and crooked roofs of a small village that might be Exbury. It was difficult to tell from this unfamiliar angle. There was a stone fence in front of me, too, not three feet away, and some distance beyond that a small whitewashed cottage, neatly kept, with gaily blooming flower boxes at every window. A miniature forest of crooked, gnarled apple trees stretched away in orderly fashion on the far side of the house, and several newly shorn sheep stared placidly back at me from their side of the stone fence.

I knew whose property it was even before Iain Sumner came whistling round the side of the cottage and paused outside the leaning back shed, fiddling with something mechanical that I couldn't identify at that distance. His back was to me, muscles taut against the fabric of his cotton T-shirt, his red hair washed almost fair by the strong light of the morning sun.

I must admit, when I jumped the fence and began wending by way through the incurious sheep, my only intention was to walk over to Iain and beg a cup of coffee, but as I drew closer to the cottage, with him remaining unaware of my presence, a tiny niggling devil stirred inside me.

Here was my chance, I thought, to pay him back for all the times he had startled me out of my wits by sneaking up on me. I would never have a better opportunity. I slowed my steps to deaden the sound of my approach.

When I was still a few yards away, I saw the reason for his inattention. He was busy working on a heavy wooden block and tackle, the kind that I had often seen strung up in barns. Blue smoke from a cigarette curled above his head as he bent forward, using both hands to make an adjustment to the unwieldy contraption.

I was less than four feet away, now. One more step, and I could stretch out my hand and touch his shoulder. My hand was actually half-raised when Iain lifted his head and angled it slightly, plucking the cigarette from his lips with capable, grease-stained fingers.

'Good morning, Julia,' he said.

Chapter Twenty-One

To his credit, he could not hold the innocent expression long. Grinning, he took another pull from his cigarette and straightened away from his work, turning to face me fully. 'My kingdom for a camera,' he said, his grey eyes crinkling in amusement. 'You ought to see your face.'

I closed my gaping mouth and shook my head, amazed.

'How on earth did you know I was there?' I asked him.

Iain braced both fists in the small of his back and stretched, his grin widening. 'I'm no clairvoyant,' he assured me. 'I saw you hopping the fence. Thought you were taking a devil of a time getting here. Besides,' he added, pointing at the clear outline of our shadows on the shed wall, 'if you've a mind to sneak up on a Scotsman, you'd best do it when the sun's not at your back.' He narrowed his eyes a little and looked me up and down. 'You've had a ducking,' he remarked.

I was surprised that I had not noticed the fact myself. Perhaps I had grown accustomed to the feel of Mariana's dripping wet gown against my skin, to the point where my mind no longer registered discomfort. Faintly curious, I looked down at myself, suddenly aware of the clinging dampness of my heavy denim jeans and oversized shirt. I ran an experimental hand through my hair and was relieved to find it dry, if slightly windblown and unruly. I must have looked a sight.

'I fell in the river,' I told him. 'I'm nearly dry, I think.'

Iain looked at my bare feet and scrubbed face, and raised a russet eyebrow. 'You'll catch cold if you stay like that,' he warned me. 'Come inside and dry off, you can have the loan of some of my clothes if you like.'

'Well,' I wavered, 'if it wouldn't be any trouble . . .'

'No trouble at all,' he said. 'I'm glad of the company at breakfast time.'

Good heavens, I thought, was it only time for breakfast? It seemed incredible, before I reminded myself that I *had* left the house at five o'clock that morning. A wall clock in Iain's kitchen chimed eight times as we came into the cottage through the back door, confirming the earliness of the hour.

'I'll have to wash,' he said, holding up his hands in evidence, 'but you can go on ahead and change out of those wet things. You'll find the bedroom down the hall on your right, and there's plenty to wear in the closet.'

It was odd, I thought as I stood barefoot in Iain Sumner's bedroom a few minutes later, how a man's wardrobe somehow defined him. Iain's closet boasted hanger after hanger of smartly pressed shirts, plain cotton and flannel plaid, flanked by several pairs of trousers and an oddly incongruous dinner jacket. I peeled the wet clothes from my body – leaving my underthings on for the sake of decency – and selected a pair of jeans and a blue plaid shirt from the assortment before me.

The jeans were ridiculously long on me, and stood up stiffly round my waist like a clown suit, but by rolling up the legs several times and leaving the shirt tails hanging loose I managed to produce a rather fashionably frumpy effect that might have graced the cover of a teenage magazine.

Iain, ever the gentleman, made no comment on my appearance when I rejoined him in the kitchen. The cottage had a very simple and practical design, one large room split evenly into kitchen and lounge, divided along the line of the narrow hallway that led to the bedrooms and bath. You could have shot an arrow in the front door and out the back again without hitting so much as a stick of furniture, so open and free of clutter was the room's decor.

'Where shall I hang these?' I asked him, holding aloft my bundle of sodden clothes.

'I've a clothes drier in the back shed,' he said, jerking his head towards the back door. 'It's a bit of a relic, but it works all right if you let it know who's boss. You have to be forceful.'

I found out what he meant when I located the drier beneath a pile of tools in the brightly lit shed. It took four tries and a swift kick to start the machine running, but I returned to the kitchen with a feeling of decided accomplishment.

'Everything OK?' Iain looked up enquiringly, and when I nodded he returned his attention to a sizzling pan on the stove. I noticed he was automatically cooking for two, and a steaming cup of coffee waited for me on the table beside him. 'It's liable to be a bit stewed,' he warned me, when I reached to pick up the coffee mug. 'I made it a few hours ago. You like eggs and sausage?'

I took a cautious sip of coffee. 'Yes, I do.'

'Academic, really,' he said, lifting the pan from the stove and dividing its contents between two plates. 'It's all I can cook. Toast?'

'Yes, please.'

He placed a thick slice of buttered toast on the edge of my plate and set it on the table in front of me, slinging himself into the seat opposite.

'So.' He sent me a questioning look. 'What brings you out this way at this time of the morning?'

I shrugged. 'I just felt like a walk, that's all. I hadn't been down to the river before, and I wanted to see where it went.'

'So now you know.'

'Yes.' I smiled back at him, scooping up another forkful of the hearty breakfast.

'You've walked about three miles, you know, if you've come the whole way along the river. It's less than a mile to your place from here by the road. Shorter still if you cut across the fields.'

'Then that is Exbury I saw, over there?' I indicated the general direction, and he nodded.

'Aye. Did you think you were lost?'

'Don't laugh,' I told him, 'it's been known to happen. I have a terrible sense of direction.'

'You can't be a patch on my mother,' he said. 'She takes a tour of the highlands every time she heads out to visit the market, I think.'

I laughed at the image. 'Are your parents farmers, as well?'

'Christ, no.' He took a swig of coffee to wash down a mouthful of toast. 'Neither of them could tell the work end of a hoe from the handle. No, my dad's an accountant, in Balloch. My mother was a lawyer, before she retired.'

Which explained, in part, why their son had gone to Cambridge, I thought. I looked around the large room with a more discerning eye, and saw the scattered evidence of a comfortable lifestyle – a piece of really good quality furniture, a lovely pair of prints hanging on the wall, a glass-fronted bookcase crammed full of leather-bound volumes . . .

'I'm not a burglar, in my spare time,' he said, reading my thoughts with uncanny ease. 'Some of it comes from my family, and the rest I bought when I was working for Geoff's dad, in Paris.'

'You worked for Morland, then?'

'Aye, for a few years. It all but drove me mad,' he confessed, grinning. 'I'd rather have my hands in the dirt, thanks all the same. So I chucked Morland, and bought this place just after my thirtieth birthday, five years ago. Close to Geoff, it was, and it suits my pace of life.'

I tried to imagine him sitting behind a desk in some modern office, and failed. 'You met Geoff at Cambridge, Vivien tells me.'

'Aye, and a wicked day that was.' He grinned into his cup. 'My grades went straight downhill after that. I'm surprised we weren't both sent down.'

'You read English?'

He nodded. 'More for interest than anything else. You can't make a living writing poems.'

Somehow, I couldn't picture Iain Sumner writing poetry, either. He was, come to think of it, rather difficult to define. Not handsome, exactly – his jaw was too stubborn and his eyes too shrewd – but still, there was something . . . He was solid, I thought. Solid and warm and dependable, and I felt an odd, seductive comfort in his company. He leaned back in his chair and pushed his empty plate to one side.

'Do you mind if I smoke?'

I set my fork down and shook my head. 'Not at all.'

He lit a cigarette and shook the match out, setting it neatly on the side of his plate. 'You were up to the manor for tea yesterday, I hear.'

'It was more like a five course meal,' I corrected him. 'Vivien's aunt is a wonderful cook.'

'She is that,' he agreed. 'I've been doing some work in the rose garden the past week, so Freda's been cooking my dinners. I'll not fit my trousers if my work lasts much longer.'

'She says you ought to be able to work it all off.'

'Does she, now?' He puffed at the cigarette, smiling. 'Well, I expect she knows best. She usually does. That's what the name Alfreda means, you know – "supernaturally wise", or something to that effect. Vivien looked it up in a name book, once.'

'It doesn't surprise me.' I picked the plates up from the table and carried them over to the sink. 'Names are funny things, aren't they?'

'I suppose.' His voice was absent. 'I got stuck with a boring one, though.'

'What, Iain? I think that's a nice name.'

'Boring,' he maintained. 'Just a Scottish form of John, for all that. No imagination involved. Iain, Evan, Sean, Hans – they're all variations on a theme.'

The plates went clattering into the sink with an ugly splintering sound, and Iain turned in his chair to look at me.

'Sorry,' I said, 'I think I've broken one.' I looked down at the wreckage, my heart pounding. *Evan* . . .

'You didn't hurt yourself?'

I surfaced from my daydreaming, and shook my head. 'No. Just the plate, I'm afraid.'

'No harm done,' he assured me. 'That's one less I have to wash. D'ye want some more coffee?'

'I wouldn't mind.'

He rose from his seat and filled both our cups. 'Fancy a tour of the estate?' he offered grandly. 'It's not as impressive as the Hall, I'll admit, but there is a lot of it.'

I pushed myself away from the counter. 'I'd like that.'

'You'd best not go barefoot,' he advised, sweeping me with a glance, 'or you'll be stepping in something you'll wish you hadn't. There's a spare pair of wellies behind the kitchen door, I think.'

I found the boots and slipped my feet into them, feeling more like a dressed-up clown than ever. Iain looked at me and grinned.

'A bit large, aren't they?' was his comment. 'Don't worry, I'll walk slowly.'

I grinned back at him. 'Never mind that. Just don't let anyone else see me looking like this.'

'Only the sheep,' he promised, 'and I'll warrant they've seen odder sights.'

I shifted to let him move past me, and one of my ludicrous boots knocked a ceramic dish sliding.

'I didn't know you had a dog,' I said, looking down.

'I don't.' His smile was self-conscious. 'She died a few months back. I just haven't had the heart to move her things, yet.'

'You ought to get another one.'

'I'll have to, eventually. It's no small task herding sheep without a dog. I've a neighbour that gives me the loan of his collie, when I need it, for the time being.'

He held the back door open for me, and we went out into the sunlight, Iain walking ahead with his easy, athletic stride, and me squelching after him in the oversized boots. It took us well over an hour to circumnavigate the property, and by the time we made our way back to the cottage there was a faintly scorched smell in the vicinity of the back shed, and my clothes were completely dry.

'If you want to get changed, I can give you a lift into town.' Iain offered. 'It's quicker by car, and you shouldn't be walking on the road in your bare feet.'

'I don't want to be a bother,' I began, but he brushed my protestations aside.

'It's no bother. I have to stop by the Lion for a few minutes, anyway. I can run you home afterwards.'

It took Iain a few tries to get his aged car started up, and I accurately guessed that he hardly used the vehicle, since every time I saw him he seemed to be on foot. It was, as he said, a very short run to Exbury, scarcely worth the bother of starting the car. The fields and hedges flew by us, and before I had time to really register them they had been replaced by houses and gardens, and we were pulling into the parking lot of the Red Lion.

Vivien was outside washing windows, and she came over to greet us, folding her arms across her chest as we climbed out of the car.

'I've just had your brother on the phone,' she informed me.

'Tommy?' I raised my eyebrows in surprise. 'What was he doing calling you?'

'He was trying to hunt you down, from the sound of it,' she said, smiling brightly. 'He's up at your house, eating his way through your refrigerator and waiting for you to come home.'

'This would be your brother the Vicar, I take it?' Iain checked, and I nodded.

'You didn't meet him last time he was here, did you, Iain?' Vivien looked at him. 'You were in Marlborough that day, I think. He's quite a lark. I say,' she turned to me with a sudden thought, 'why don't you ring him up and tell him to come and meet you here?' I don't have to open up for two hours yet; we can sit in the bar and make a party of it.'

Iain looked over at her. 'It's a little early for drinking, don't you think?'

'You don't know Julia's brother,' was her reply. 'Come on around to the back, Julia, you can ring him from there.'

My brother restrained his curiosity admirably when I talked to him on the telephone, showing no surprise when I rather cryptically asked him to fetch a pair of shoes from my closet and drive in to meet us at the Red Lion.

'Dress or casual?' was his only question.

'I beg your pardon?'

'The shoes,' he elaborated. 'Dress or casual?'

'Oh.' I grinned against the receiver. 'Casual.'

'Right. I'll be there in five minutes.'

I relayed the message to Vivien, who smiled like a child getting a present. 'Wonderful,' she said. 'Come on through to the bar, you two, and I'll open a bottle of wine.'

Iain followed us through the connecting door from Vivien's rooms to the front of the pub, his eyebrows lifting. 'A Vicar who drinks wine at ten o'clock in the morning,' he mused, speculatively. 'This I have to see.'

He got his opportunity when, true to his word, Tom pulled into the car park five minutes later. When Vivien opened the door to him he was standing on the step balancing one of my tennis shoes on his upraised fingertips as though it were the glass slipper.

'I have brought you a tennis shoe,' he said dramatically. 'Does that qualify me to enter these premises?'

'Idiot,' I greeted him. 'Come on in.' I took the shoe from his hand. 'What, you only brought the one?'

'I could only find the one,' he responded drily. 'Your cupboard is a disaster.'

'You can borrow a pair of my shoes,' Vivien assured me, laughing. 'I've got dozens.'

She found me a pair of well-worn loafers and we spent a mirthful couple of hours sitting at the bar, watching the level of the wine bottle sink. I was pleased to see how well Tom and Iain got on together, after they had been introduced. One stray comment about politics, and the two men were soon deep in animated conversation, moving from subject to subject at the speed of light, while Vivien and I sat back on our stools and drank our wine at a leisured pace.

'I quite like Iain Sumner,' Tom told me later, when we had tottered out of the Red Lion and strapped ourselves into the car.

'I'm glad,' I said. 'Should you be driving?'

My brother sent me a superior glance. 'I only had one glass. Unlike some people.'

I attempted a dignified expression. 'Are you implying I'm drunk, or something?'

'Plastered.' He nodded. 'And before noon, at that.' He clucked his tongue reprovingly. 'I'm shocked.'

'Get over it,' I retorted good-naturedly, rolling my head sideways against the seat to look at him. 'It's good to see you, Tom. I don't think you ever visited me this much when I lived in London. You'll be wearing grooves in the motorway.'

He smiled. 'It's just a flying visit, this one. I'm on my way to a conference in Bristol. I just thought I'd stop and say hello, while I was in the neighbourhood.'

I studied his face. 'Mother sent you to check up on me, didn't she?'

'Bingo.'

'Well, you can tell her I'm fine,' I said, looking back at the windscreen. We were on the road now, just leaving the village, the hedgerows closing in on either side of us.

'You can't really blame her for worrying,' Tom commented. 'That's what mothers are supposed to do. You had me rather worried myself, this morning, when I turned up and found you missing.'

'I couldn't get back to sleep after I got off the phone with Mum,' I explained. 'So I went for a walk.'

My brother slowed the car to let a hedgehog scramble across the road. 'You didn't lock the door when you left.'

'I'm not overly fond of that new lock,' I told him. 'It's very stiff, and I can't always turn it. So unless I'm going to be miles away from home, I just don't bother. Besides,' I added in a practical tone, 'Iain does work in that back garden, sometimes, and he might need to get a drink of water, or use the lav.'

'The village life, indeed.' My brother smiled, faintly. 'If I were a less trusting person,' he said, 'I might think that you'd gone on one of your little excursions into the middle ages.'

'The seventeenth century,' I corrected him.

If he asked me directly, I thought, I would have to tell him. I had never been any good at telling lies to Tom, he could always find me out. But he didn't ask.

'Whatever.' He shrugged, and gathered speed again, and we drove the rest of the way in silence.

Chapter Twenty-Two

The month of June was a glorious one, long sun-filled days and warm, scented nights, when the summer breeze came drifting across the greening fields while a nightingale sang to its mate in the darkness, down by the murmuring river. Even the rains fell more softly, and the little dovecote garden crept shyly into bloom. The columbine and iris bowed down to make way for bolder sprays of red valerian, and a mingled profusion of clustered Canterbury bells and Sweet William, pale blues and pinks intertwined, danced at the feet of more stately spears of deep purple foxglove and monkshood.

The changing nature of the garden fascinated me. By borrowing books from Iain I learned the name of each and every new flower, and soon the flowers themselves were working their way into my drawings, lending joyful colour and variety to the dark medieval forests of my fairy tales. My editor was thrilled with the samples I sent her, and if she noticed that all my princes bore a peculiar resemblance to one another, she made no comment.

I, too, was blossoming, basking in the sweet exhilaration that heralds the beginning of a new romance.

Geoff had returned home two days after my walk by the river, and on the Saturday evening, as promised, he treated me to dinner and dancing at an elegant restaurant this side of Swindon.

It was an incredibly magical night, like something out of one of the fairy tales that I'd been so diligently illustrating. The restaurant itself might have been a set from a film – all candles and flowers and linen and waiters who never hurried. By the time we had finished our after-dinner cognac, I think I had fallen halfway in love with Geoffrey de Mornay. I'd have had to be superhuman not to.

We didn't really change towards one another, but as the month waned it became apparent that something had been added to our relationship, a hint of potential yet to be realized that lurked beneath the friendly smiles and easy conversation. I was being wooed.

With my days divided equally between work and play, I had little time for further experimental trips into the past. Whenever I felt the warning dizziness begin to rise, I quickly forced it back, closing my eyes tightly and resisting the whirling darkness with every ounce of my being. Plenty of time for that later, I reasoned. But every morning, when I paused to finger Mariana's bracelet, the jewelled eyes of the birds of paradise stared up at me in mute accusation. 'I haven't forgotten,' I argued, speaking as much to the face in the mirror as to the gilt birds. 'I only want a little bit of fun, that's all.'

It was rather like being on holiday. Geoff and I walked the long paths that snaked through field and countryside, spent afternoons poking about antique shops and evenings playing darts and sharing stories at the Red Lion, under Vivien's indulgent eye. I celebrated my thirtieth birthday at the Lion, and the taps flowed freely, each of the old men at the corner table insisting on standing me a birthday drink. I had forbidden anyone to buy me a gift, but still Geoff gave me roses, and Vivien produced a pair of earrings, and even Iain gave me a present – a shining garden trowel with a bow tied round it. 'So you'll stop losing mine,' he told me drily. 'There must be ten trowels rusting in the field as it is.'

At the month's end my parents finally flew back from Auckland, and Tom and I drove together down to Heathrow to collect them. True to form, they insisted upon seeing my house straight away, before going home to Oxford. Their reactions were much as I'd expected. My mother, her mind full of plans for wallpapers and curtains, wandered round the rooms in a pleasantly preoccupied state, while my father bounced one or twice on the floorboards to check the soundness of the structure. Hands in his pockets, he lowered his chin to his chest and nodded, faintly. 'Very nice,' he said. It was the highest praise I could have hoped for, and my spirit swelled.

I grew reckless in my happiness. On one memorable afternoon in the first week of July, Geoff coaxed me into going riding with him, despite the fact that I hadn't been on horseback since my schooldays. Fortunately, only the horse seemed aware of my lack of skill, and I put on a brave show by keeping my back ramrod-straight and my expression calm.

'You see?' Geoff turned an encouraging smile in my direction when we paused to rest the horses. 'You needn't have worried. You ride perfectly well.'

Leaning forward in my saddle I patted my mare's neck, silently thanking her for graciously allowing me to stay on her back. 'Yes, well,' I affected a casual tone, 'I suppose there are some things one never forgets.' The mare's ears twitched, catching the lie, but Geoff was already looking the other way.

'Well, this is it,' he told me. 'The end of the property.'

'Where?' I looked for a fence, and found none.

'Just beyond that row of trees. It used to go much farther, of course, but most of the land's been sold off over the years. It would be foolish to own that much land these days, I think. And selfish.'

It all depended, I thought, upon one's sense of proportion. After all, the manor lands stretched practically to my back door, and it had just taken us half an hour to ride from the Hall to the westernmost boundary of the property.

After a moment Geoff turned his horse to follow the line of trees, and with a graceful step my mare fell in behind, moving as cautiously as a thoughtful pony balancing a small child. I let the reins lie loose upon her neck, and enjoyed the scenery.

'It's so lovely, Geoff,' I said, watching a hawk trace lazy circles high over our heads. 'How can you bear to leave it as often as you do?'

He shrugged, and half-turned in his saddle to speak over his shoulder. 'I don't know. I like variety, I guess. My home in France is just as beautiful. I don't think I could stand being tied to one place my whole life. Besides, this has always been more my father's house than mine.'

I was silent, thinking over something he'd said. 'Why France?' I asked him.

He turned again. 'I beg your pardon?'

'Why did you buy a house in France? Do you have family connections there?'

'Not really,' he replied. 'Though I suppose if I carried the family history across the channel I'd find a whole army of de Mornay cousins populating the countryside. The first de Mornay was a Norman, after all. No, I bought the house because I liked it. It has a gorgeous view of the Mediterranean, and there's a harbour close by where I can keep my boat. And the sun shines all the time,' he added, grinning, 'which puts it a notch above Exbury, in my book.'

'I thought you said you liked variety,' I reminded him with a smile, and he shook his head staunchly.

'Not when it comes to weather.'

From the corner of my eye I caught the glimmer of a shadow moving among the trees to the right of us. Excited, I called Geoff's attention to it a split second before a stag – a majestic, powerful stag with branching antlers – broke clear of its cover and went bounding across the field in front of us. When it had disappeared into another cluster of trees I turned to Geoff, my eyes still shining, and found him watching me with a quizzical expression.

'Who's Richard?' he asked me calmly.

'What?'

'You called me Richard just now.'

My smile was not quite natural. 'Did I? I can't imagine why. Sorry.'

'Old flame, is he?' He clung to it, persistent.

'Something like that,' I nodded, trying to turn it into a joke. 'Why, are you jealous?'

Instead of smiling back, as I had expected, he kept his eyes hard on my face for a long moment before answering.

'I'm not sure,' he said slowly. After another moment the smile came, the one I had been waiting to see. 'Come on,' he invited, turning his horse towards the tall chimneys of Crofton Hall, 'I'll race you back to the stables.'

The heavens took pity on me, and by some miracle I managed to remain upright for the thundering gallop back. In the stableyard I dismounted with dignity, my knees still shaking at the thought of how nearly I had escaped sailing over the mare's head into the manure pile when we'd finally stopped running.

'Stiff?' Geoff eyed me assessingly as the groom led our horses away.

'A little.' Which was an understatement. I was hobbling like a bandy-legged cowboy, and I knew it. 'It has been a while since I've ridden.'

He smiled knowingly. 'You did fine. Better than fine, actually.' He took hold of my elbow and steered me towards the house. 'Come on, let's see what we can find in Freda's kitchen.'

What we found, quite unexpectedly, was Iain, rocking back on a kitchen chair with his boots propped against the table rail underneath, smoking a cigarette in an attitude of wholly masculine satisfaction.

'What was that?' Geoff asked, pointing at the suspiciously empty plate on the table in front of his friend.

Iain grinned. 'Steak and kidney pudding,' he said, 'with home-made chips, a salad and blackberry crumble.'

'You bastard,' Geoff said with a slow smile. 'How do you do it?'

Iain tilted his jaw indignantly. 'I've been working hard all day, my lad, not cantering about the countryside like the bleeding gentry. How was your ride, by the way?'

'I stayed on top of the horse,' I answered. 'It was a success.'

We didn't see much of Iain these days, it seemed. Now that the truly warm weather had arrived, he was too busy working his farm and the orchard to make it into town on a regular basis. I found I missed him, and his undemanding presence.

'How are the sheep?' I asked him, in my turn.

'Stupid as ever. I thought I'd take a break from them today and get some work done on the rose garden, here.'

Geoff sent him a fatherly look. 'We have a gardener to do all the slogging, Iain. You don't need to worry about it, you'll only wear yourself out.'

'When your gardener learns to do the job properly, I'll stop worrying,' Iain promised drily. 'Besides, I thought I'd try something a little different this year. I'll be wanting your opinion on it, if you can spare the time.'

'When?'

Iain shrugged his broad shoulders. 'How about now? It shouldn't take long.'

Geoff checked his wristwatch, looked at me, and waited for my nod before answering. 'OK,' he said. 'If you think you can still move after that meal you've eaten. Where is Freda, by the way?'

'She went to dust the library.' Iain took his feet off the table rail and brought his chair forward with a crash. 'That was about fifteen minutes ago.'

'Right.' Geoff turned to me. 'I don't suppose you could track her down for me?'

I looked at him dubiously. 'What, in the public side of the house, d'you mean?'

'Sure. You'll have no trouble,' he assured me. 'We don't take many tours through this late in the afternoon. You know which door to use? Good. See if you can't persuade Freda to whip us up some reasonable facsimile of Iain's feast, here.'

'I'll see what I can do,' I promised.

He sent me a wink and a winning smile before following Iain out the back door. The low hum of conversation and laughter rattled the window panes as the two men passed by on their way to the rose garden.

When they had gone I went back down the dim, uneven passageway and pushed open the heavy door at the end, the door that divided Geoff's private domain from the public portion of the manor house. Passing through another door I found myself standing in the Great Hall, staring up at the colossal fireplace and the carved and painted coat of arms that crowned it. The hooded hawks upon the blood-red shield looked fiercer than I remembered them, their golden talons grasping at air. *Indestructible*. That was the translation Geoff had given of the family's Latin motto. I looked at those talons again and shivered.

The great house was quiet, as Geoff had said it would be. No footsteps but my own echoed through the cavernous room as I moved from shadowed dimness into sunlight beneath the tall east-facing windows. I didn't really expect to find Mrs Hutherson still in the library, but there was no harm in looking there first. And if I happened to waste a few minutes looking at the books, well, that could hardly be helped, could it? Especially since there were no tour guides or other visitors to spoil my enjoyment of the lovely room.

I had forgotten, of course, about the portrait. *His* portrait. From the moment I entered the studious silence of the library, I felt Richard de Mornay's eyes upon me, as surely as if the painted image had been a living man. I stared hard at a shelf of books, even read the titles of some of the more beautiful volumes, but always my gaze kept returning to the black and towering figure, watching me steadily from his corner of the room.

Finally I gave up altogether and walked over to stand before the portrait, aware that the cleverly painted eyes had followed my approach. Clasping my hands behind my back, I tilted my head upwards to get a better look, marvelling at the skill of an artist who could so perfectly capture the arrogant set of a jaw, the placement of hand on hip, the barely discernible half-smile that lingered knowingly on those lips . . .

What had become of this man, I wondered, that future generations had forgotten his name. 'We've dubbed him "The Playboy",' Geoff had said to me when I'd first commented on the portrait. An inglorious legacy, certainly, for any man. I had looked for Richard de Mornay's name in the weighty registers of baptisms, marriages and deaths that the Vicar of St John's Church kept locked in the vestry. The Vicar himself had helped me, peering with failing eyes at the neatly handwritten entries, row upon row. 'My eyesight's not what it used to be,' the kindly old man had apologized. 'I used to do this sort of thing by the hour, you know, searching out names for Americans tracing their ancestry. No,' he had said finally, 'there doesn't appear to be a Richard. Of course,' he had added, by way of consolation, 'we don't have all the registers. Some were lost, you understand, during the Interregnum, when Cromwell was in power. It was not a pleasant time for the Church, I'm afraid.' He smiled gently. 'The Roundheads often destroyed records, and all things sacred to our Church, and even when they did keep up the registers the entries were sadly incomplete. This register here, you see, ends in the year 1626, and the next does not begin until 1653, nearly thirty years later. But you may perhaps find a later reference . . .'

I ought to have known, really, that it would be a wasted effort. Geoff's father, with his love of family history, would already have searched those parish registers for William de Mornay's offspring and found nothing.

The death of Mariana Farr, on 3 October 1728 had been duly recorded in a flowing, unemotional hand. But Richard's fate remained a mystery.

I stared up at the portrait, now, with an absent frown. Lifting one hand, I let my fingers trail across the flowing sweep of painted cloak that fell in artful folds from the lifeless Richard's shoulders. It was a mistake. Even as my fingertips left the canvas, the walls began to waver, the colours of the painting running as if the artist's hand had brushed carelessly across it, smearing the outline of that handsome, taunting face. Taking a hasty step backwards, I squeezed my eyes shut.

I can't, I pleaded silently, urgently. *Don't you see that I can't? There isn't time . . .*

As if in answer to my thoughts the dizziness subsided and the shifting, vibrating walls righted themselves, appearing placidly innocent when I dared to open my eyes. My breath was coming in short, nervous gasps that hurt my lungs. Quickly I turned my back to the portrait and stumbled out of the room, steadying myself against the comforting solidity of the massive door jamb. A peal of girlish laughter drifted into the dim hallway through the partly open front door, and I turned my steps towards it, like a prisoner seeking fresh air and the warmth of sunlight.

I didn't reach the door. I had only gone a few paces before the sensation was upon me once again with a violent, almost punishing force that brought beads of icy sweat to my forehead and made my fingers clutch at the panelled walls in an effort to stay upright. I tried to fight it back, but failed. This time the high-pitched ringing rose deafeningly in my ears, and I spiralled downwards into darkness. It seemed an eternity before the storm passed, leaving me standing alone in the silent hallway, my hands shaking in anticipation.

A footfall sounded in the main passage behind me, and I spun round, my skirts sweeping the polished floor. Richard de Mornay halted his approach when he was still several feet away, and I waited for his reaction.

It was shockingly bold behaviour, for me to come calling on him like this, and I wasn't sure why I had done it. Perhaps it was because my uncle and aunt had gone down to Salisbury, and I had grown wild in my unaccustomed freedom. Or perhaps it was because of what Richard himself had said to me that day at the market, about my not seeming a coward. I had read the laughing challenge in his eyes that day, and I saw it again now as he took a step forward into the light, gallantly bowing his head.

'Welcome to Crofton Hall,' said Richard de Mornay.

Chapter Twenty-Three

He advanced on me with a gracious smile. 'So you are not a coward, after all,' he said, and I fancied his tone was faintly pleased. 'You would face the devil on his own footing.'

He looked less like the devil this day. In place of his usual black clothing he wore a fine hanging coat of pale dove grey, and his plain cravat spilled over a yellow silk waistcoat that was tied to his body with a wide sash. I was pleased to see that he did not follow the foppish fashion of London gentlemen. His grey breeches were not loose and beribboned; they fitted smoothly over his muscled thighs and disappeared into the high practical boots of a countryman. No high-heeled shoes with buckles and bows for the lord of Exbury manor.

I smoothed my hands over my own plain skirt and faced him bravely. 'I am but accepting the invitation of a gentleman, my lord,' I corrected him smoothly, 'to have the loan of some of his books.'

''Tis well for you I am a gentleman,' his eyes laughed back at me, 'for you do take a risk in coming thus un-chaperoned. No doubt my servants are at this moment fainting from the impropriety of it.'

I smiled, recalling the expression on the face of the man who had opened the door to me, and his stammering discomposure as he'd left me to find his master. A sudden thought struck me, and I glanced up, sobering.

'They will not tell?' I said quickly. 'That is, my uncle . . .'

'. . . shall never hear of your adventure,' Richard de Mornay finished the sentence for me. 'My servants may be Puritan in their morals, but they are a loyal lot. Your uncle is not at home, I take it.'

I shook my head. 'He has gone down to Salisbury, with Aunt Caroline.'

'Has he, now?' I thought his eyes hardened for a moment, but it was a fleeting impression and soon forgotten. 'Well, then you need not hurry your visit,' he decided. 'Would you like to see the library first, or view the house as a whole?'

That was a simple question to resolve. 'The library, please.'

'As you wish.' He inclined his head, not surprised. 'Follow me, if you will.'

He led me along the dark passage and out into a cloistered walk that gave onto a tranquil courtyard, cool and green and peaceful. No flowers bloomed here save a handful of tender blossoms that trailed lovingly across a flat square of white stone set into the turf.

'My mother's grave,' Richard said, when I asked him what it was. 'Being Catholic, she was refused burial in the churchyard.'

I frowned thoughtfully. 'Is that why you do not attend the services yourself?'

He shrugged. 'I had rather pay the fines and pray according to my conscience,' he replied. 'I could not hold with any church that would so judge a pious woman.'

He pushed open a heavy, creaking door and led me into another passage, where the air was heavy with the glorious scent of leather. I had often dreamed of rooms filled with nothing but books, but I had never actually seen one, and so the first sight of Richard de Mornay's library left me momentarily speechless.

'These are all yours?' I asked in wonder, my eyes raking row upon row of the handsomely bound volumes, and he laughed at the unbridled envy on my face.

'Ay. One day I will build a larger room for them, but for now this must suffice. You may borrow whatever you like.'

It would have taken me a month to read all the titles. I stepped forward and quickly selected a small, fat book from one of the lower shelves. 'May I borrow this one?' I asked him.

'Shakespeare?' He checked my choice, raising one eyebrow curiously. 'Take it, if you will. That is the Second Folio, and contains a curious verse by Milton, the old sinner, in the form of an Epitaph.'

I brushed my fingers across the book's cover lightly, reverently. 'My father spoke highly of Milton's poetry,' I said, 'though he did not applaud his politics.'

'He is an odious man,' Richard agreed, 'but a brave poet. He has just finished an epic on the fall of man, I am told, but cannot find the wherewithal to see it printed.'

Since the Restoration the once fiery Milton had fallen from favour, and the man who had penned such venomous defences of the killing of Kings now lived in blind and bitter solitude. I, for one, did not mourn his downfall. Fanaticism such as his had always frightened me.

My selection made, we left the library and skirted the courtyard once more, entering the main part of the house through a different door this time. I followed my host down a long gallery, where the dark portraits stared down at me from their vantage points on the pannelled walls. All the eyes held disapproval. All the eyes, that is, but the pair belonging to a defiant young man in the last portrait but one.

'Your portrait, my lord?' I stopped to have a look. 'It is an admirable likeness.'

''Twas done by Lely,' he told me, giving his image an assessing glance, 'soon after I returned from France. A minor vanity, on my part.'

'And this?' I moved on to the next portrait, and frowned a little into the face of a smug, self-satisfied boy with curling blond hair and idle eyes.

Richard looked. 'My nephew, Arthur,' he identified the boy. 'He has the look of my brother, but not, I fear, the character.'

I would have lingered in the gallery but he pressed me onwards, through yet another doorway into a great soaring room with glittering glass windows and a ceiling that seemed as high as the arches of a cathedral.

'Oh,' I breathed, my eyes drifting upwards. Here was a room, I marvelled, fit for the use of princes. The walls were hung with cut velvet and tapestries woven in scarlet and blue, showing dark-eyed satyrs and pale white nymphs, Vulcan and Venus and a host of ancient heroes. All round the room hung silver sconces set with candles, ready to illuminate the room with a hundred points of light and banish darkness forever. There would be light from the fireplace as well, I thought, that huge stone fireplace that could shelter burning logs the length and breadth of a man . . .

'It is a handsome room,' Richard said, beside me. 'I regret the furnishings are so poor, but much of the furniture was sold off during my father's imprisonment.'

There was, in truth, but a handful of chairs and small tables, clustered near the cold fireplace, but it scarcely seemed to matter. I took a step forwards, stretching my neck to look up at the heraldic carvings above the mantel.

'The arms of my family,' he supplied. 'The hawks wear hoods to remind us not to trust our eyes in battle, but to follow our sovereign blindly. We lead with our hearts,' he explained, 'and not our heads. And much it has cost us.'

'But you cannot be destroyed,' I pointed out. 'So says your motto. At least that lends some comfort.'

'You read Latin?' His tone was incredulous, and I lowered my eyes, embarrassed.

'My father taught me,' I said, in a small, defensive voice. 'He said that if a queen could read Latin, then so should I.'

'He must have been a remarkable man, your father. Did he die recently?'

I shook my head. 'Nine years ago. He fell into a fever, and did not recover. I was eleven years old.'

'Did you keep none of his books for yourself?'

'They were burned,' I said flatly. 'Everything in our house was burned, upon my mother's death, for fear of the plague.'

He stared down at me. 'Your mother died of the plague?'

I nodded, unable to speak, and he shook his head sympathetically. 'It is a dreadful thing,' he said. 'I have heard that some five hundred people have died of it in London this past week alone, and it is far from over.'

'The Lord's vengeance on a wicked people,' I mused, slowly, then glanced up in apology. 'That is what my uncle calls it.'

His face hardened. 'Your uncle is a fool. The vengeance is in his own mind, and nowhere else. His side has lost the battle, and he would see the victors suffer.'

I stared at him, uncomprehending, and he smiled suddenly, the blackness lifting from his features. 'But our talk had grown dreary,' he complained. 'I apologize. Come, let me show you round the house before we dine.'

'I cannot dine with you, my lord,' I protested, shaking my head.

'I insist. I am not often graced by visitors.'

I held my ground. 'I cannot,' I repeated. 'Rachel would worry if I were late in returning home.'

He smiled slyly. 'I could send Evan round to Greywethers, to inform her of your delay,' he suggested. 'She would not be so eager for your return, then.'

I flashed him a quick look of alarm. 'You would not send Evan to her, surely!'

'He may be there already, for all I know.'

'But Rachel is betrothed,' I told him, 'to Elias Webb.'

'What of it?' He shrugged again. ''Tis plain to see that she does not love that corrupt old man. And I'll wager Evan will not cheerfully step aside for our black-hearted bailiff.'

'She cannot go against my uncle,' I said quietly.

'Then she is not worthy of the love of my friend. Christ's blood, I despise a weak and mincing woman!' He was challenging me, and I knew it. He took a step closer, crowding me against the fireplace. 'Will you dine with me, or no?'

I shook my head again, not trusting my voice.

'A dance, then,' he suggested unexpectedly, with a laughing gleam in his eyes. 'I must have some recompense for my hospitality.'

'I do not dance.'

'I'll keep the step simple,' he promised, and I shook my head helplessly. It was unheard of, I thought, to dance in private with a man, and that man not your husband. It would be improper, wanton, and yet the thought of it set my blood racing with unladylike excitement.

'There is no music,' I remarked, retreating another step.

Richard de Mornay smiled. 'Would you like me to call for my stableboy? He is unequalled on the lute, and I'm sure he would favour us with a danceable tune.'

'No,' I said hastily. I had no desire for a witness to my folly.

'Then you must make do without. Or I could sing, if you wish it.' He held out his hand. 'Come, you are no coward. One dance, a simple step, and the debt is paid.'

Trapped, I took his hand.

He did sing, after all, softly and in French. He had a deep and pleasant voice, and his warm breath fanned my cheek as he twirled me round and round the deserted, echoing room. It was a sinful feeling.

I coughed a little to clear my throat. 'What is that air you sing?'

'*Aux plaisirs, aux delices bergères,*' he replied. 'My mother used to sing it when I was a boy.'

'It sounds a happy song.'

'It is. It tells us to pass our lives in loving, for time is lost, hour by hour, until only regret remains.' He whirled me wide beneath the long windows. '*A l'amour, aux plaisir, aux boccage,*' he quoted softly, then turned the words to English: 'In love, in pleasure, in the woods, spend your beautiful days . . .'

I stared up at him, dumbly, my heart rising in my throat. I was not aware of the precise moment when we stopped dancing, when he turned those deep, forest-coloured eyes on mine and traced the outline of my face with a delicate touch.

'These are your beautiful days, Mariana Farr,' he said gently, and then his shoulders blocked the sunlight as he lowered his head to mine and kissed me.

He must have known that it was the first time I had been kissed by a man. I had no idea what to do, no idea how to respond to the flood of strange and new sensations. His touch was sweetly, exquisitely, achingly wonderful, and when it ended I felt robbed.

He looked down at me and laughed, and took my face in his hands and said something, low and in French, some phrase I couldn't catch, and his face blurred before my eyes as he bent to kiss me again . . .

My vision cleared. I was standing, quite alone, by the tall windows of the Great Hall, gazing out over the lawn where the gathering shadows of late afternoon were growing longer. I could see Geoff and Iain, still standing in the rose garden by the churchyard wall, the dark head bent to the russet one, listening, while Iain leaned on his spade and talked.

I saw them only for an instant, really, and then my vision blurred a second time, this time with tears. As quickly as I could blink them back, they rose again from some seemingly endless spring inside me, welling hotly in my anguished eyes. It was foolish to cry, I told myself firmly. Utterly foolish. It was only a kiss, after all, and it had happened so long ago . . . so very long ago . . .

I heard a small tentative footstep on the floor behind me, followed by an uncertain cough. 'Excuse me, miss, but . . . may I help you?' It was a girl's voice, and I suddenly remembered the tour guides.

I turned, and saw the girl's face relax as she recognized me. 'Oh, it's you, Miss Beckett. I couldn't think who it . . . I say,' she said, frowning, 'are you feeling all right?'

I raised my hands to my burning face and felt the tears come spilling over onto my cheeks, horrified that I could do nothing to stop them. It was a relief to hear the calm, crisp voice of Mrs Hutherson speaking from the doorway of the room.

'Nothing to worry at, Sally,' she said evenly, dismissing the young girl. 'Miss Beckett's just had a bit of a shock, that's all. You can get on with the locking up, now.'

She might have been my mother, taking me firmly by the arm and leading me out of the Great Hall and down the long corridor to the kitchen, all the while keeping up a steady stream of cheerful talk. I didn't really hear anything that she said to me, but the quiet strength of her voice calmed me, and by the time she deposited me in one of the kitchen chairs my tears had subsided into small, hiccuping sniffles.

'There now,' she patted my shoulder reassuringly. 'What you need is a nice strong cup of tea.'

A nice strong cup of tea would, I felt certain, be Alfreda Hutherson's first reaction to any crisis.

She put the kettle on the stove and looked at me, her eyes sympathetic. 'Bit of a jolt for you, I expect, having it happen like that.'

'He kissed me,' I said, as if that explained everything.

'Yes, dear, I know. Now give your face a wipe with that,' she instructed, handing me a damp cloth. 'The men will be in from the garden any minute.'

I wiped my face and dried it, pulling myself together with an effort. I suddenly remembered something, and looked up sharply, troubled by the thought. 'I couldn't stop it from happening,' I told her. 'I've been able to stop it before, but this time I just couldn't stop it from happening.'

'Well, now,' her blue eyes were very wise, 'you've learned a valuable lesson from this, then, haven't you? You can't cheat fate, Julia. If you don't go looking for the lessons of the past, then the past will come looking for you.'

Chapter Twenty-Four

I remembered those words often over the next few days, and thought long about their meaning. Not that I had any idea, then, what the lessons of the past might be. I knew only that the past – my past – would not be ignored, and that the longer I delayed the journey the more difficult the trip back would be, both physically and emotionally. And after my most recent experience, I wasn't sure I wanted to delay the journey any longer. However disturbing it might be, I had to admit that the memory of a man long dead had a more powerful influence over me than anything I could touch in the modern day.

If the thought disturbed me, it horrified Tom. I could feel the force of his disapproval over the telephone line.

'It's too dangerous,' was his judgement.

'Well, it's hardly my decision any more, is it?' I challenged him bluntly. 'It's going to happen whether I like it or not.'

'I thought you said you could control it. You said you'd found some way of blocking it out, making it go away.'

'It doesn't always work,' I admitted. 'Look, Tom, I promise I'll be careful. I'll lock all the doors and hide the keys, if you like. I'll stay inside the house. And I'll only do it once a week, I pro—'

'No, don't promise.' He was smiling, finally. I could hear it, and I felt myself relaxing in response. When he spoke next his voice was less uncompromising. 'I don't like the idea,' he told me. 'I still think you're taking too great a risk. But if you're cautious and sensible, and try to keep things in perspective, then I guess I can't really object, can I? I mean, like you say, there don't seem to be a lot of alternatives.'

It was my turn to smile. 'Exorcisms don't apply in this sort of situation, do they?'

'No.' He laughed. 'You're all right otherwise, are you?'

'Perfectly,' I assured him. 'My work is coming along wonderfully, and I've no complaints with the house so far.'

'You're still going around with that Geoff fellow, I take it?'

I replied in the affirmative, and was grateful when he dropped the subject. I had not yet confided in Tom my suspicion that Geoffrey was really Richard. Nor had I told him about Mrs Hutherson. I suppose I was afraid that, by telling him I was in effect consulting a psychic and chumming with the reincarnation of Mariana's lover, I might stretch the bounds of my brother's credulity. And I very badly needed him to believe in me.

So far, it appeared that he did. 'Take care of yourself,' was the only advice that he gave me before I hung up the phone. I kept it in mind.

I selected a convenient hour of the morning, when few other people were yet awake. I slid all the furniture in my studio into one corner, so that there was nothing to impede Mariana's progress from the doorway to her bed and from there to the window. I locked the deadbolts on both doors, from the inside, and buried the keys among the bills and letters in my desk drawer. Then, and only then, did I settle myself at the kitchen table and light the candle.

My first journey back lasted less than half an hour, which, after such elaborate preparations, was something of a disappointment to me. It was also, I conceded, deadly dull. For nearly all that time, Mariana was simply peeling vegetables at the kitchen table, while Caroline nursed the baby John by the fire. Neither woman spoke. When I returned to the present I felt utterly discouraged.

But my next few attempts were more fruitful. Curious, I tried my candle process in the lounge instead of the kitchen, and found myself sitting over an embroidery frame, listening to Caroline and Rachel discuss wedding plans. It was rather a one-sided conversation, actually. Caroline talked of flowers and gowns and guests in an animated voice, while Rachel bent low over her needlework and mumbled inaudible responses. She kept her expression hidden from her sister, but behind the fall of flaxen hair her face was flushed and miserable.

The wedding feast was to be held at Greywethers, the home of the bridegroom being too small to hold all the guests – and from Caroline's talk I gathered every soul in the village had been invited. Bride and groom would spend their first night beneath my uncle's roof, before removing to the bailiff's house in the village. It was difficult to picture Rachel living with Elias Webb in that narrow, bleak little house with its dark chimneys and cheerless windows; more difficult still to imagine wedding guests dancing in my uncle's parlour. I was trying to conjure the image when my aunt's voice broke my thoughts.

'. . . and of course we must have my lord de Mornay, for courtesy's sake, although Jabez will not brook the man's presence on any other day. And I do not doubt but that my lord will bring that Gilroy fellow with him, for all he is not invited. 'Tis the trouble with the gentry,' she complained. 'They may do what they will, and we bear the consequences.'

Beside me Rachel caught her breath as the needle bit painfully into her finger, and I saw a tiny drop of blood fall onto the linen she was working . . .

That particular excursion into the past ended there, and I waited a few days before trying again. By restricting myself to the inside of my own house, and repeating the process in various rooms, I found I was gaining a fairly complete picture of Mariana's daily life, and the lives of those around her. The pity that I felt for Caroline deepened as the days passed. Rachel told me that Caroline had once been as lively and spirited as herself. That the spirit had gradually been beaten out of her by Jabez was a realization that dawned on me gradually, a suspicion strengthened by the sometime appearance of a bruise on Caroline's pale face, or a newfound temerity in her gaze, as she held and rocked the squalling babe. The babe I pitied, also. There was no love in Jabez Howard's eyes, no hint of tenderness when he looked upon his son, only a cold and distant form of loathing. I thought of my own father, and what he'd taught me, and my heart wept for baby John.

To me, Jabez Howard remained brusquely courteous, frequently indifferent, and irritatingly enigmatic. There were days when he was absent on business, and other days when a knock would sound at the front door and I would be summarily ordered to my room, to spend hours in pious silence. I did not mind overmuch, for it was then that I read the Shakespeare, drawing the precious borrowed book from its hiding place beneath my bed.

Once, though, filled with reckless bravado and a burning curiosity, I left my room and stole to the top of the stairs as my uncle's guests arrived. Peering through the balusters, I could see only the back of my uncle's head and the face of the black-eyed bailiff Elias Webb, Rachel's betrothed, although the voices of other unseen men filtered up to me. After exchanging greetings, they moved into the parlour and closed the door, and their voices were lost. Defeated, I slunk back to my room, none the wiser about my uncle's strange activities.

Of course, because I never left the house during these backward trips in time, I never encountered Richard de Mornay, although I did see him several times riding in the fields behind the house. I also knew that Mariana had, on at least one occasion, returned to Crofton Hall. I knew this because the book I was reading changed from Shakespeare to Fletcher, and because I held in my mind the memory of Richard's company on my last visit, when we'd walked to the centre of the great maze, thick with the smell of rain-washed yew, then lost our bearings on the way out again so that we turned laughingly this way and that, seeking in vain the elusive opening.

He had kissed me then, too, as he had that day in the Great Hall, and the memory of that kiss brought a burning flush to my cheeks. I had run the whole way home in the rain, and Rachel had taken one look at my dripping gown and shining eyes and deduced instantly where I'd been. She smiled at me, a sad, forgiving little smile, and I knew she would not tell. 'One of us, at least, should have some happiness,' she had said.

But while Richard de Mornay had undoubtedly kissed Mariana Farr, and on more than one occasion, they were not yet lovers. I was so certain in my own mind that they were destined to *become* lovers, that I found myself increasing the frequency of my trips backwards. What had started as a weekly ritual became a daily one, and by the last week of July I was spending two or three hours each morning lost in the seventeenth century.

I explained my morning seclusion to everyone by saying that I was working on my drawings, but nobody seemed to take much notice, anyway. Geoff rarely rose more than an hour before midday – his excuse being that he stayed up late at night reading – while Tom was kept unusually busy with his parish and Iain applied himself so diligently to his farming that I hardly saw him. Vivien, too, had begun to disappear some mornings, although no-one was entirely sure where she went. On occasion, her disappearances extended into the afternoons, and when Geoff and I stopped in at the Lion on the last Saturday of July, we found Ned tending the bar by himself.

'No good asking me,' Ned told us, pulling our pints with a disgruntled air, 'I haven't a clue where she is. No-one ever bothers to tell me anything.' He returned to his newspaper and, since there was plainly no more conversation to be had at the bar, Geoff and I retired to a table by the window.

Jerry Walsh did not share his son's taciturn nature. He hailed me cheerfully from the crowded corner table. 'Hullo, love! How's life been treating you?' he asked me, in a voice robust with drink.

I smiled back and assured him that life had been treating me fine.

'Hooked up with this troublemaker, have you?' He jerked a thumb at Geoff, and shook his head in mock sympathy. 'You want to watch out for him, darling, he's a real heartbreaker, he is.'

Geoff grinned. 'You mind your words, Jerry,' he warned the older man good-naturedly, 'or I'll tell the girl the stories I've heard about you.'

'Fair enough,' Jerry said. He winked broadly at me, and turned back to his rollicking table-mates, several of whom glanced with interest in our direction as they drank their pints, no doubt speculating on the potential of this latest piece of gossip. 'I saw young de Mornay with that artist girl in the pub today . . .' would, I wagered, be the opening line to many a tea-time conversation that afternoon.

'So,' I said to Geoff, continuing the conversation we'd begun on our way to the pub, 'you'll be off to France again in September.'

'For six weeks,' he nodded. 'Some of that will be business, unfortunately, with our office in Paris, but then I'll be headed down to Antibes, and the boat. And my mother might be in Spain, in September, or so she says. I may nip down and visit her for a few days. I don't know.' He hadn't often mentioned his mother, in the months I'd known him.

'Does she have a house in Spain, then?' I probed, in my best casual tone.

'No.' Geoff shook his head. 'She lives in Italy, mostly, these days. But she mentioned something about Spain last time she rang – Pamplona, I think it was.'

'Where the bulls are?'

'Yes.' His mouth twisted wryly. 'Rather an ordeal, visiting my mother, most of the time. She's always trying to fix me up with her friends' daughters, trying to get me married off. I expect she means well, but it's bloody tiring.' He grinned then, and changed the subject. 'What would you like me to bring you back, for a present?'

'I don't need anything.'

'Rubbish, Now, what would you like?'

I thought about it. 'Well,' I told him, 'you might bring me back a couple of those huge coffee cups that they use over there. You know, the breakfast cups, that hold gallons of coffee. I've always wanted some of those.'

'Then,' Geoff promised grandly, 'you shall have some. How would an even dozen suit you?'

I laughed. 'Two would be plenty, thanks. Besides, they'd never let you back on the plane with a dozen of the things.'

'I don't fly commercial airlines, my dear,' he reminded me, his eyes forgiving my ignorance. 'I can carry whatever I like. Besides, you've got that huge dresser in your dining room, and no dishes to fill it with, so it's a dozen coffee cups whether you like it or not. Any other requests?'

I grinned wickedly at him. 'Somehow, I have a feeling this would be the perfect time to ask for that Louis Vuitton luggage I've always coveted, but I won't push my luck.'

'Why ever not?'

'I'm afraid God might strike me dead for being greedy,' I explained, and Geoff laughed.

'It's not always a sin, you know,' he said, 'being greedy.'

I sent him a long, motherly look. 'You need to have a talk with my brother,' I advised him. 'Your soul's in mortal peril.'

Vivien sailed into the pub on a wave of energy and radiant good health, her fair hair whipped by the wind into a tangled mass of gold. 'Who's in mortal peril?' she asked, pausing beside our table with interest.

'I am,' Geoff informed her. 'Or at least, my soul is, according to Julia, here.'

Vivien nodded agreement. 'Past redemption, I should think,' she told him.

'Then another drink won't spoil it.' He drained his glass and held it up hopefully. 'That is, if you're serving.'

'You might give a girl a chance to get her coat off,' Vivien laughed, snatching the glass away from him. 'Have you missed me that much? I'd have thought Ned would be keeping you entertained,' she teased, and the barman glanced idly up from the pages of his newspaper, not missing a beat.

'You missed seeing me tap-dance, earlier,' he said drily.

'Give over,' Vivien told him, slapping him on the arm as she passed. 'You'd have a coronary if you tried, and we both know it.' She pulled another pint for Geoff and came back around to join us at our window table.

'You're in a good mood, today,' I commented, and she grinned broadly, her eyes secretive.

'I have reason to be,' was all she would say, and no matter how hard we pressed her, we could not make her tell us where she'd been.

'She's probably out meeting some married man,' Geoff joked, as we made our way back up the road towards my house an hour or so later.

I looked at him, horrified, thinking more of Iain Sumner than of the moral implications. 'Oh, I hope not.'

'I'm joking,' Geoff explained, hugging my shoulders with a laugh. 'She'll tell us her secret, when she's ready to. What are your plans for the rest of the afternoon? You working?'

I nodded. 'I have to get the next batch of illustrations ready to send to my editor, or else she'll have my head. What about you?'

'I think I'll take a walk over and see what Iain's up to,' he said, looking off towards the river. 'I'll ring you later, OK?' He bent and kissed me swiftly and we parted, Geoff taking the smaller turning that led off to the right while I continued on up the main road to my house.

The wind had been dropping steadily all afternoon, and by the time I reached my drive the air was almost still, and the heavy clouds hung overhead, unmoving, blotting out the sun. Despite the warmth, I shivered as I went round to the back door and fitted the key in the lock.

The kitchen was dark and deserted and cool, and I left the door partly open to let in the warmer outside air. Somewhere, a baby was crying, and the sound filtered into the room, faint but persistent. Dumping my keys on the table, I raised my hand to my forehead as another shiver struck me, bringing beads of perspiration to my skin.

The child's cry became a scream, behind me, and I lowered my hand to find Rachel watching me with concern.

'Does your head ache?' she asked.

It had a right to, I reasoned. Johnnie had been fussing steadily for the past hour, despite all Caroline's attempts to quiet him. But the truth was that my head did not ache, I had only been trying to clear my thoughts. I was about to tell Rachel so, when the kitchen door opened and my uncle came into the room, his expression black as a thunderstorm.

He had been out of humour these past few days, and we had all borne the brunt of it. Now, he turned the force of his displeasure upon his wife. 'Are you not accomplished enough, woman, to keep your own child from crying?'

Without thinking, I came to Caroline's defence. 'He is breaking a tooth,' I informed my uncle evenly. 'He cannot help the crying.'

I might have been invisible. Jabez Howard leaned closer to his wife, his expression calm. 'Shut the babe's mouth,' he advised her pleasantly, 'or I swear I'll shut it for you.'

Terrified, Caroline smothered the child against her breast, rocking back and forth in an agitated motion. As if he could sense the danger, John stopped crying. Satisfied, my uncle straightened and turned to look at me, his eyes frightening with the depth of their cruelty.

'Mariana,' he said, 'I would have squab for dinner. Go you to the dovecote and fetch me a bird.'

I looked at Rachel, and she rose cheerfully from her work, brushing her hands against her skirt. 'I'll go,' she offered, but my uncle stopped her with an upraised hand.

'I did not speak to you,' he told her, in a voice as smooth as honey, 'I spoke to Mariana. I would have her fetch me a bird, and I will wait here for her to deliver it dead into my hands. 'Tis time she learned how to take a life.'

My hands trembled and I placed them behind my back so he would not see my weakness. There was no help to be had from any quarter. Rachel's eyes held sympathy but she could not act, and Caroline was all but sobbing over her child in the corner by the hearth. Under my uncle's insistent gaze, I turned and went out into the sunlit yard, my heart a heavy weight within my chest.

Chapter Twenty-Five

The dovecote stood to the back of the garden, a stout, square building of rough stone with a roof of wooden shingles, crowned with an open cupola. The pigeons entered and left through that cupola, always returning with unerring exactness to the dovecote, to raise generation upon generation of young in the dim and crowded nesting-boxes. It was a highly efficient structure – a comfortable, cunning, and deadly trap.

One sharp tug on a rope that hung from the ceiling and a trapdoor fell to block the opening to the cupola. Unable to escape to the shelter of the skies, the birds could only flutter in panic while their nests were ravaged and their number culled. Why they chose to stay on in the dovecote afterwards I would never know. Why didn't they fly away, when the trap was opened again? Why did they linger on and wait for death, like rabbits raised in a warren beside the kitchen door? Did they lack the sense to foresee their fate, I wondered, or was it simply that the horror of living had deadened their brains; that having grown accustomed to the security of their prison, they no longer knew where else to go?

I could become like that, I thought suddenly. If I did not guard against it, I too could become like the doomed birds in the dovecote. Like lovely, dead-eyed Caroline, with her hair turning white from worry at twenty-five. For if the dovecote was a trap, then so was Greywethers, and my uncle's hand held the rope that could pull shut the door and bar my flight.

I could feel his eyes upon me now, watching me from the house, and I squared my shoulders defiantly before pushing open the low wooden door and taking a determined step inside the little building. At first, I could hear nothing, only the sharp creak of the door behind me as I leaned upon it to close it. Then subtly, pervasively, the sound began to permeate my senses – the gentle cooing of a hundred softly vibrating throats, a hundred pigeons nestled plump and warm within their niches.

The place had the look of a tomb, dim and neglected. The shadows lay thick in the corners, and from where I stood I could make out only the suggestion of walls. What little light there was fell in a circular, spreading shaft from the open cupola overhead, caught the dust in the air and set it idly dancing against the darkness.

I searched low on the wall for an occupied nesting hole, and found a likely squab perched upon a ledge. The bird came easily into my hands, without fear, and lay there looking up at me with a round and vaguely interested eye. I could feel the insubstantial weight of the creature, the small heart racing against its fragile breast.

'Jesus, help me,' I pleaded in a whisper, closing my eyes. 'I cannot.'

The deep voice that spoke in reply from the darkness behind me was so unexpected it sent me spinning round in sudden fear, clutching the startled pigeon to my bodice.

'There is a penalty to be paid for the theft of one of my birds,' the voice said.

Before the words had died away I recognized the speaker, and my own heartbeat slowly resumed its normal pace. Richard de Mornay took a step forwards, nearer the light, but his smiling face remained half in shadow.

'How came you here?' I asked him rudely, my voice little more than a whisper.

'By the back door,' he replied, pointing out the little-used entrance on the west wall. 'Your uncle did not see me, if that is what worries you.'

'And how can you be sure of that?'

'Because I saw him. He was well occupied within the stables at the time, I can assure you. I was a soldier, Mariana,' he chided me gently. 'I know the art of ambush.'

'And is this then an ambush?'

'In truth, 'twas merely hunger brought me here.' He stretched one hand forward into the light to show me the two dead birds he held, but I was not entirely convinced.

'You have servants, surely,' I said, 'who could fetch the pigeons for you.'

'Ay.' A faint gleam from the darkness. 'But then I should have missed the pleasure of your company.'

I looked quickly away from the drooping dead pigeons, cradling my live one more closely. 'You flatter me, my lord.'

'Ay. 'Tis time someone did.' For a moment he was silent, and I felt his scrutiny. 'Are you enjoying your latest book?' he asked me finally.

'Very much,' I nodded. 'I shall need another, soon, I have almost finished with it.'

He smiled. 'You will have to wait a few days, I'm afraid. I must go away for a short time.'

'For how long?' I looked up sharply, surprised at how much the thought of his leaving disturbed me.

'A week, perhaps. No longer. I go to Portsmouth to ride with the King back to Salisbury.'

My eyes rounded childishly. 'The King would remove to Salisbury?'

'He fears to remain in London. The weekly Bill there lists more than one thousand who died from the plague this past week alone. The King's counsellors have persuaded him that it would be more prudent to seek the country air.'

'But why must you ride with him?'

He shrugged. 'It is my duty, and the duty of my family, to protect the King. These are still unsettled times, Mariana. The Roundhead legacy yet taints the countryside, and there are many who would see this Charles lose his head like his father before him.

'And you hold it your responsibility to stop them?'

'My sword is as sharp as any man's.'

'Ay, and your flesh as thin.' There was bitterness in my voice, and he came forward, stooping down to look into my face.

'You fear for me?' He touched my cheek with a gentle finger. 'There is no need.'

I was embarrassed at my transparency. 'I fear nothing, my lord,' I told him, 'but my boredom in your absence.'

'A diplomat's reply,' he praised me, grinning. 'Well, then, I leave you the run of my library, while I am away. So that you will not be bored.' Reaching in the pocket of his coat, he produced a key which he held out to show me. 'This will open the door to the courtyard, on the west side of the house. From there you may access the library when you wish.'

'I cannot take your key,' I protested.

'Why not?'

I searched for an excuse. 'I have no place to keep it,' I said, 'where it would not be discovered.'

'Then keep it here,' he said, solving the problem easily. Leaning forward so that his arm brushed mine, he reached past me and slid the key into one of the empty nesting holes. 'It is in the box with the cracked ledge, you see? You shall have no trouble finding it again, when you need it.' He straightened, but did not draw away. The air grew thick between us. 'Which leaves but the matter of your forfeit,' he said, in a low and languid voice.

'My forfeit?'

'For stealing one of my pigeons,' he reminded me.

'I do not steal this bird, my lord,' I said evenly, 'and 'twas my understanding that the dovecote belonged to my uncle.'

'Your uncle makes use of it, to be sure, but it was built by my ancestors, and it lies on my land. My ownership is indisputable.'

I tried to voice a protest, but he merely pressed closer, shaking his head. ''Tis no use denying the crime,' he told me, 'with the evidence there in your hands. 'Tis plainly theft; and I have the right to exact a penalty.'

He held me still beneath his kiss with his free hand, his fingers sliding beneath the weight of my hair, supporting the curve of my jawline and the backward arch of my neck. When he lifted his head, my heart was racing in tempo with that of the bird that I still held to my breast. I had half a mind to select a dozen more pigeons, if he could promise the same penalty for each of them, but I dared not tell him so.

He read my thoughts, anyway. 'Would you wish another bird?' he asked me, grinning.

'I cannot kill the one I have,' I said, shaking my head. 'My uncle sent me here as punishment. He knew I could not do it.'

The grin vanished. 'And what have you done to deserve punishment?'

'I defended his wife,' I replied bluntly. 'He did not care for my interference.'

'A grievous offence, indeed,' Richard said, in a satirical tone. He looked at me, his expression serious. 'Your soft heart does you justice, Mariana. There is no shame in hesitating to kill something. We'll let this fellow live, then, shall we?' Gently, he detached the placid bird from my grasp and replaced it in its nesting hole. 'Here, you may take these, in its place.' He handed me the birds that he had killed earlier.

I looked down at the stiff and lifeless bodies, reluctant even to hold them. 'But what of your dinner?' I asked him.

Richard de Mornay smiled mirthlessly. 'My heart is harder than yours. I have no difficulty taking life.' He closed my fingers round the dead pigeons. 'Take these to your uncle,' he said. 'I have more than I need.'

I would have left him, then, but rather than step aside to let me pass, he caught my face again with both hands and kissed me a second time. It was a long, breathless minute before I was released, my ragged breathing nearly drowning the cacophany of contentedly cooing birds.

'After all,' he excused himself, his own voice not quite steady, 'you are availing yourself of two more of my best birds.'

The warbling birds grew louder still, the circle of light at our feet growing suddenly, blindingly, bright, and then there was only silence, and sunlight, and I found myself standing alone beside the low, crumbling wall, with bruised and broken flowers waving at my feet.

* * *

280

By walking directly across the fields and making a wide arc around the stables, I could approach the west side of Crofton Hall without being observed, finding myself at last in a rutted, little-used lane, deep with shade, that closely hugged the towering stone walls. It was a simple matter to locate the section of wall that hid the courtyard. Shorter than its neighbouring sections it had no roof, and the ivy had grown clean over the top of the wall – a solid curtain of massed green leaves and twisted stems, impenetrable, that hung heavily to the ground beneath.

In spite of the ivy, I found the door on my first try. It was a low door, set flush with the wall, old oak weathered to the same dun colour as the stones that surrounded it. The grasping ivy came clear with a tearing sound as I worked my hands around the edges of the door, searching for the handle and lock.

Having located it, I felt in my pocket for the little key and held my breath in anticipation. The key fitted smoothly into the lock . . . but it would not turn. Decades, perhaps centuries, of neglect and dampness had rusted the lock into immobility.

I let the ivy fall again, obscuring the door, and releasing my disappointment in a small sigh I turned back, retracing my steps across the empty fields. I had not really expected the key to still work, I reminded myself. And I wasn't even sure what opening the door would have accomplished, at any rate. At least now I knew what the key was for, and why it had been left in the dovecote for me to find.

It gave me a queer feeling to come out of the hollow and see the tumbled, L-shaped wall that was all that was left of the dovecote, when in my mind's eye I could still see clearly the squat, square building standing there. The queer feeling was replaced by a sinking sense of dismay as I drew closer to the garden.

It was blooming wildly and more colourfully than ever. Scarlet flax burst forth in loose sprays of vivid flowers, while campion and phlox crowded in among the pinks, and tall spiky blades of larkspur joined the dwindling, nodding heads of monkshood. Even the rose, the lovely, old country climbing rose that Iain had planted along the one wall, was thriving and covered with fat round buds. But the perfect beauty of the little plot had been spoiled. My own feet had cut a swath through the centre of the garden, from edge to wall, and the flowers there were crushed and trampled beyond repair.

Stepping gingerly amid the survivors, I walked to the low wall and stood looking down at the rows of long-abandoned nesting holes. The one with the cracked ledge was still clearly identifiable, and I smiled slightly, tracing the ledge with my fingers. No need for me to keep the key any longer, I thought. It might as well go back where Richard had placed it, those many years ago. I took it from my pocket again and slid it back into its resting place within the niche. The rasp of metal on the worn stone sounded decidedly final.

I was still standing there, lost in thought, when Geoff came round the side of my house a few minutes later, walking slowly and carefully, as though his feet hurt.

'Finding more treasures?' he asked me, and I shook my head, summoning up a smile.

'Nothing new, I'm afraid. How was your visit to Iain?'

'Fine. I managed to persuade him to stop working for a while,' he said, leaning on the wall and grinning across at me. He looked terribly cheerful, if slightly vague. 'I even got him to open up a bottle of his twelve-year-old Scotch. We had a grand afternoon.'

'I can see that,' I said. 'It's a good thing you were walking.'

'Not necessarily in a straight line,' Geoff admitted, 'but I managed. Good God!' He suddenly noticed the state of the garden, and focussed his eyes with difficulty. 'What's got into your bleeding hearts?'

I followed his gaze. 'Is that what they were?' I murmured vaguely. Bleeding hearts. And quite appropriate, I thought.

'Some animal's made a right mess of that, haven't they?' he commented, shaking his head. 'Iain will have a fit.'

'He will not,' I countered, with certainty. 'He hasn't thrown a single fit about this garden, not even when I've pulled up something I shouldn't have. He's a lot more even-tempered than you and Vivien give him credit for.'

'Maybe.' He shrugged his shoulders noncommittally. 'Anyway, I didn't come up here to talk about Iain, or the garden.'

'You had a more interesting reason?'

'Two reasons, actually.' He sagged a little on the stone wall, but quickly drew himself erect. 'Firstly, to tell you that I'm not going to be able to make our dinner date on Saturday. I have to go to London for a few days. Sorry.'

'Business again, is it?' I asked, and he nodded. 'Well,' I said, 'that's no trouble. We'll go another time.'

'You're not disappointed?'

'Heavens, no.' I stared at him. 'Why should I be? You can't help having to work. No such thing as the idle rich, is there?'

Geoff grinned. 'Don't you believe it. This is the first

283

real work I've had to do all month, and I'll be idle again in August.'

'And what was the second reason?' I asked him.

'The what?'

'Your second reason for dropping by to see me,' I prompted, and his face cleared.

'Oh. I wanted to ask if you would make me a cup of coffee.' He smiled happily. 'Iain's Scotch is terribly strong, you know, and he's generous in the pouring of it, and I was far too proud to tell him when I'd had enough. He has a habit of reminding me how Englishmen can't hold their liquor. But I don't think I'd be able to walk home right now,' he confessed, 'without falling into a ditch along the way.'

'Well, we can't have that,' I agreed. 'With your luck Jerry Walsh would fish you out, and you'd be the talk of the town for sure. Come along, then,' I said, cautiously negotiating my way out of the garden, 'I'll make you some coffee.'

He was definitely looking a little worse for wear, listing to one side like a waterlogged ship as he crossed the lawn ahead of me. He managed to reach the back door without incident, but misjudged the size of the opening and ricocheted slightly off the door jamb before swinging himself rather stiffly into the kitchen. I was following him, one foot across the threshold, when from the corner of my eye I saw a dark shadow hovering in the hollow, beneath the old oak tree.

I turned my head quickly, but not quickly enough. The place beneath the oak was innocently vacant, and there was no sound but the whispering voice of the wind in the empty dovecote garden.

Chapter Twenty-Six

The rain lasted four solid days and nights. It fell steadily, drearily, without respite, raising a melancholy mist that settled over the landscape like a shroud and made the world as viewed from my studio window appear uniformly grey and colourless.

Ordinarily, I liked rain. I liked to watch it, walk hatless in it, listen to its random rhythm on the window panes while I sat curled into a cosy chair, reading. But after four days even my nerves were beginning to twitch.

My forays into the past were no help. Three times I managed to transport myself, and three times I found myself sitting alone, working to finish Rachel's trousseau, with no-one around me to break the solitude. When I returned to the present I was invariably more depressed than before. I hated sewing.

It was boredom, in the end, that drove me from the house in search of the Red Lion's more sociable atmosphere. Apparently I wasn't the only one with that idea. Every table in the bar was jammed with people, all of them talking at once. From a corner came the jovial sound of a darts match in progress, and the atmosphere was thick with cigarette smoke and the smell of damp and drying clothes.

Iain had obviously come straight from the fields. He smelled like a sheep wearing aftershave. He shifted to make room for me at the bar, and lit a cigarette.

'I haven't seen you for a while,' I told him.

'You shouldn't be seeing me now. I've a heap of work waiting for me, but this rain's been driving me round the bloody bend, so I thought I'd come in for a pint or two. I had to pick up the post, any rate.'

I crooked my neck to examine the flat, narrow package on the bar beside his elbow. 'Is that my brother's writing?' I asked.

Iain nodded. 'Aye. When he was here last we got talking about the poet Robert Herrick, and Tom promised to send me his copy of Herrick's works, so I could refresh my memory. I expect that's it.'

'You mean you haven't opened it, yet?' Vivien leaned across the bar towards us, frankly incredulous. 'Honestly, Iain, you've got no proper sense of curiosity. It could be *anything* . . .'

'Go on, then,' he invited, nodding towards the parcel. 'Open it, if you're so eager.'

'All right, I will.' She tore at the brown paper, lifting the small book away from its wrapping with a lopsided smile. '*The Poems of Robert Herrick*,' she read the cover aloud.

Iain said nothing, but his eyes were faintly smug as he exhaled a thin stream of smoke.

'I don't think I've read any Robert Herrick,' I said.

Vivien had flipped to the table of contents. 'Well, you ought to,' she told me. 'He wrote an awful lot of poems about you.'

'About me?'

'Well, to Julia. Heaps of them. He's even got one here about Julia's clothes.'

'How fascinating,' I said drily, leaning forward to look. Vivien turned the pages, slowly, scanning the lines.

'That's probably why your brother bought the book in the first place,' she speculated. 'He is rather fond of you, isn't he? Oh, look, here's one for you: "Then, Julia, let me woo thee, Thus, thus to come unto me; And when I shall meet Thy silv'ry feet, My soul I'll pour unto thee."' She read the sentiment with appropriate drama, frowning a little at the end. 'What do you suppose he meant by "silv'ry feet"?'

Iain sent her a lazy look. 'Would the fact that they're meeting by moonlight give you a clue?' he asked.

'Oh. I get it.'

'It's lovely stuff, most of it,' he commented, stretching out a hand to repossess the book. 'I haven't read Herrick since Cambridge. Nice of your brother to loan it to me.'

I didn't answer immediately. The poet's call for his lover to come to him still echoed in my brain like a spoken voice, deep and familiar. I shook my head a little to clear it, and smiled up at Iain. 'You must have made quite an impression,' I said. 'Tom's usually very jealous of his books. Probably my fault, come to that – I've still got volumes on my own shelves that I borrowed from him when we were kids, and never gave back.'

'And one or two of my gardening books, as well.'

'Mm, I know.' I took a hasty swallow of gin and tonic and smiled apologetically. 'It's a bad habit of mine, hoarding books. Libraries all over the country shudder at the sound of my name. I promise I'll get your garden guides back to you soon.'

'No panic.' He shrugged. 'I don't use them much, anymore, and you seem to be getting something from them. The garden looks good.'

'You've seen it recently?' My voice was a casual probe.

'Couple of days ago.'

'Oh. I'm sorry the bleeding hearts got ruined.' I said, but Iain's response was philosophic.

'Not your fault,' he absolved me. 'It's not as if you mowed them down yourself. These things happen. Could I get another, love?' he asked Vivien, lifting his empty glass a few inches off the bar.

'Certainly. Julia?' She looked a question at me, but I shook my head. My restlessness had reasserted itself, and I wanted to be on the move.

'Actually,' I said, 'I think I'll drop in and see your aunt for a few minutes. Is she likely to still be at the Hall?'

Vivien checked her watch. 'At three-fifteen? I should think so. Even with Geoff away, she usually keeps at it until supper time. It's a lot of house to clean.'

'Should I telephone her first, do you think?'

'Who, Freda?' Iain's mouth quirked, amused. 'There's no need. She'll have a pot of tea waiting for you when you get there, you just see if she doesn't.'

He was, as it turned out, quite right. It was wonderful to walk into that warm, bright kitchen, where the teapot huddled under its checked cosy on the table while the kettle whined a dying whistle on the stove and the sweet smell of indefinable baking permeated everything.

'What a lovely surprise,' Alfreda Hutherson said, filling my teacup and setting a plate of warm scones on the table between us. 'I was hoping for an afternoon visit.'

'It's a visit with a purpose, actually,' I told her, biting into a crumbling scone that dripped with butter. 'Are there any tours going on in the house today?'

'Not on Wednesdays, no.' She tilted her head and looked at me, her eyes shrewd and knowing. 'You want to use one of the rooms.' It was not a question.

'Yes.' I gathered my courage and looked up. 'I want to know what it was that Mariana saw through the window in the Cavalier bedroom. All my flashbacks are tied to a physical place, you see, and I have to be standing on that exact spot if I want to go back there.'

'Yes, I know. But are you sure that you want to go back to that moment just yet? You felt the pain yourself.'

I was silent a moment, remembering. 'I have to know,' I said, finally. 'You should understand that. These people, they're all so *real* to me . . . I have to know.'

'Would you like me to go with you?'

'No, thanks,' I said hastily, smiling to soften the rudeness. 'I'd be embarrassed to have someone watching me.'

'Well, then,' she said, setting her teacup on its saucer, 'you just go on up whenever you're ready. I don't suppose you can come to any harm up there. The furniture is all in the same place, I think.'

'I'll let you know,' I told her, grinning. I would know soon enough, I thought, if I tried to walk through that huge four-poster bed. A sudden thought hit me and I frowned. 'These . . . experiences of mine,' I said, slowly, 'they sometimes last a few hours. If I'm not finished when you want to leave, then . . .'

'. . . then I shall leave the lights on for you and lock the doors,' she promised. 'You know how to unlatch the side door, don't you? Good. I'd rather not interrupt you, once you get going. If you just leave the side door latch turned to the right, it will lock itself behind you when you leave.'

I smiled at her gratefully. 'Thank you. Well,' I pushed myself to my feet, a little nervous, 'wish me luck.'

The great, echoing rooms of the manor house felt even more cavernous than usual, empty and yet not empty. I could feel the press of unseen bodies crowding me as I climbed the staircase, and anticipation hung like cobwebs from every corner. Expectantly, silently, the spirits of Crofton Hall waited, watching me approach the doorway of the Cavalier bedroom.

It was a darker room without the sunlight. Raindrops chased each other down the windowpanes and clung to the casement before falling to the lawn below. The church tower was little more than a dark, square shadow rising above the paler shadow of the churchyard wall, before which lawn and rose garden blended into a watery blur, green and mauve and dull, dull brown. Keeping my eyes fixed on that view, I stepped further into the room, clenching my fists without thinking.

The feeling, when it came, hit me with the force of a tidal wave and brought my chin up with a jerk. Anxiety, and pain, and panic, emotions tumbling one over the other with a soul-searing urgency. *No*, my mind pleaded of its own accord, racing madly, *no, no, no . . .*

The ringing in my ears increased to an unbearable pitch, my every nerve vibrating with the feel of it, and then suddenly, as suddenly as if a door had been slammed upon it, the noise stopped, and I was left in peaceful silence. I opened my eyes.

The lawn stretched out before me in the sunlight, distorted slightly by the panes of window glass, green and lush and level, broken only by the sweep of dusty drive to the right and the intricate meanderings of the rose garden to the left. Not far from the house, in one of the high spreading oak trees, a bird was singing the same sweet, wavering notes, over and over, nature's plainsong.

Behind me, Richard shifted his position on the bed. I could feel him watching me.

'What are you thinking?' His voice was low, tinged with sleep. The voice of a lover. I gathered the rough folds of the shawl more closely round my naked shoulders and shrugged, a tiny gesture.

'Everything.' I told him, 'and nothing.'

'And which am I?'

Everything, I could have told him, but the words caught in my throat. I turned from the window to look at him, lying there with his shoulders propped against the bolster, his chest wide and brown above the white linen, his hands laced neatly across his flat stomach. It was an attitude of masculine self-satisfaction, and yet his eyes looked oddly vulnerable, uncertain.

I misinterpreted that look. 'Is it your wish that I should leave you now?'

'Why would you think that of me?' His eyebrows rose, the vulnerability gone. 'You are not a servant, Mariana, to be thus ordered from my sight.'

'No,' I admitted, looking down at my feet, 'I am not a servant. I am a mistress. A minor difference, I'll grant you.'

His eyes were steady on my face. 'You are my love,' he corrected me, softly, 'and there is no shame in that. Do you wish this afternoon undone?'

I raised my head. 'No,' I told him honestly.

'I will not force you to my bed,' he said. 'I do not want a frightened woman, nor a coy one, but one who gives me love because she wills it so. If I make no promises, it is because the world is an uncertain place, and words matter little. But if you doubt the honour of my love, come,' he stretched his hand towards me, palm upward, 'let me renew my pledge.'

I went to him, as blindly as a flower seeking sunlight, and the shawl fell forgotten from my shoulders as he drew me down to his embrace. It was a tender lovemaking, with none of the urgent passion of before, and when it was over he held me close, my head against his heart, his hand tangled in my hair.

'And what think you now?' he asked me, lazily.

I smiled. 'I think my uncle's absences may not be frequent enough.'

He laughed, twisting a strand of my hair round his fingers. 'Your uncle returns tomorrow, you said?'

I nodded. 'He left soon after you did. I have forgotten to ask you, how was your journey? How is the King?'

'He was well when I left him yesterday,' Richard replied. 'He kindly recalled my father's service, and bid me sup with him, but I was tired and eager to return home and besides, the Court is no place for a gentleman.' I sensed his smile. 'Faith, you worry about the propriety of having one lover. At Court you would be considered uncommonly prim.'

'One lover is all I need,' I said, snuggling deeper into his chest.

''Tis all you'll have.'

'And when my uncle promises in marriage me to some merchant?' I shifted my head, curious. 'What will happen then?'

'I'd not allow it. I'd marry you myself.' His arm tightened. 'I will not lose you.'

It was all fantasy, I told myself. Of course he could not marry me, the difference in our stations was too great. But it was a pleasant fantasy, and for a glorious, aching moment, my heart was full.

I curled my hand against his chest and he covered it with his own, smoothing the hair back from my forehead.

'Sleep,' he told me. 'There are a few more hours of daylight yet, that we may call our own.'

I was not tired at first, and for some minutes I simply lay there, listening to the tenor of his even breathing, feeling the strong heartbeat beneath my cheek, wanting to commit the whole sensation to memory lest I lose it altogether. But finally sleep came to claim me as well, settling over me with the comforting warmth of a blanket.

When I woke, the room was deep in shadow and the moon was full above the lawn. I was lying alone on the bed, on top of the dark crimson coverlet, my hand outstretched towards an absent lover.

Alone on the bed, but not alone in the room. Someone was standing in the corner, a tall grey shadow with faintly gleaming eyes. As I lifted my head from the mattress the shadow stepped forward, and a sliver of moonlight touched the hard, elegant contours of the man's face. I couldn't see Geoffrey de Mornay's expression as he stood there with his back to the window, staring down at me, but I felt his tension.

'I think we need to talk,' he said.

Chapter Twenty-Seven

In the end, it was left to me to do most of the talking. Geoff sat facing me in the richly decorated parlour where we'd first spoken on the day we met. His face looked tired in the lamplight, showing clearly the strain of his long drive from London, but his eyes were unwavering and attentive. He interrupted my rambling narrative now and then to ask a question, or clarify a point, but he didn't move from his chair except to refill our wineglasses from the bottle on the table between us. By the time I had finished telling my story the morning sun had risen, a lark trilled brightly in a tree outside the window, and the bottle of wine was empty.

Geoff didn't pass judgement immediately. He made a steeple with his fingers and looked down at his shoes, frowning.

'You think I'm mad,' I guessed.

'Of course I don't.'

'It's all right,' I said, rubbing my forehead with a weary hand. 'Sometimes I think I'm mad, myself.'

'It's not that I doubt what's been happening to you. Well,' he smiled, 'maybe I doubt it just a little bit, but I don't doubt that you believe, honestly believe, the truth of what you've seen. I'm just not sure how to take this.' He leaned back in his chair and frowned again. 'Richard,' he mused aloud. 'If only we had some record of a Richard de Mornay . . .'

'There's nothing in your father's files?'

'I'm sure there isn't. I can check again, if you like, but I'm certain I would have remembered . . .' He rose and fetched a sheaf of papers from a nearby writing-desk. When he spread them on the table at our knees, I recognized them as the same papers he'd shown me that night at Vivien's. He flipped through them silently for a few minutes, then closed the file and repeated his verdict: 'Nothing. You're sure it was Richard?'

I nodded emphatically. 'Positive. William de Mornay was his father.'

'Well, that doesn't help much. My father didn't find anything on William's children, only some portraits that look to be the right age. There might be papers somewhere, but I'm afraid I don't have them.'

'Can't you check their father's will, or something?'

'He didn't leave one.' Geoff's mouth quirked. 'Most inconsiderate, from a genealogical point of view. I only know that after William's death the next recorded owner of Crofton Hall is his grandson, Arthur.'

'Arthur . . .' I clutched at the name. 'Richard showed me Arthur's portrait, in the gallery. Unpleasant looking child. He lived in Holland, I think, with his mother. Oh, what was his father's name?' I asked, pressing my fingers to my eyes. 'Richard mentioned it once . . . it started with an "R" as well . . . Robert? Robert,' I said, more firmly. 'Robert was Richard's younger brother.'

Geoff checked his notes again and shrugged. 'Sorry. You may be right, you're probably right, but there's no way I can confirm it without some sort of record.'

'There must be something,' I said. 'What about the portrait in the library? Would there be any clues there?'

He shrugged again. 'It's worth a try.'

I chattered nervously while we crossed the Great Hall,

trying to make conversation. 'How did you know I was upstairs?'

'I found your raincoat in the kitchen. Knew you had to be around somewhere. Freda must have let you in, did she?'

'Yes.' I nodded. I hadn't mentioned Mrs Hutherson earlier. For some reason, I wasn't ready to share the confidences that had passed between us. Instead I said simply: 'She and I had tea together, and then I went off to look around upstairs. She must have thought I'd gone home, if she locked up when she left.'

He made a vaguely noncommittal sound and nudged open the library door. 'After you,' he invited, following me across the wide carpet to stand beneath the towering portrait. 'What sort of clues were you hoping to find?' he asked me, looking up.

'I don't know. Anything that might help me prove to you that this is Richard.'

'Are these the same clothes he's wearing when you . . . see him?'

'No.' I peered more closely. 'They're black, of course, but the style is different. Older, I suppose. After all, the portrait was painted nearly five years before I met him.

I felt his quick, assessing glance. 'I see.'

'He wears a ring on the little finger of his left hand,' I said. 'A fairly heavy ring. Silver. It's got the family crest on it, that hooded hawk's head on the braided wreath. You can sort of see it, in this picture.'

I pointed, and Geoff looked.

'Not that it really matters,' I went on, 'since it only shows that he's head of the family. It doesn't prove his name was Richard.'

'No,' Geoff admitted, cocking his head, 'but it might prove that someone owned the Hall in between

William's death and Arthur's inheritance. Unless, of course, this is Arthur we're looking at.'

I shook my head emphatically, my curls bouncing. 'Not a chance. Arthur has a weaselly sort of face, and looks a proper brat.'

'Watch it,' Geoff warned, grinning. 'I'm a direct descendant of that weaselly-faced brat.'

'Sorry.'

He leaned closer, until his nose was just inches from the brushstrokes. 'It's a pity the poor chap's mother didn't sew a nametag onto his jacket,' he quipped.

'That's it!'

'What's it?' He brought his head round, curious.

'Richard's mother,' I told him, my excitement mounting. 'Look, suppose I could prove to you that I knew something, something I couldn't have learned any other way than by seeing it, and suppose I could back that up with evidence, physical evidence. Would you believe in Richard then?'

'I believe in him now.'

'No you don't. Not really. But if I can show you that one part of my story is factual, then maybe you'll accept the rest of it as fact, too.'

'The law of logical deduction, you mean.' He smiled faintly. 'All right, Sherlock. What did you have in mind?'

'We'll need a shovel,' I told him, and the smile faded.

'A shovel?'

'Something to dig with.'

The sun was creeping overhead, and there were scarcely any shadows in the sleeping courtyard. I stood knee-deep in a tangle of weeds and briars and looked at the tools in Geoff's hands.

'I'm not sure those will be enough,' I voiced my doubts, and he looked down himself, frowning over the slightly rusted ice pick and trowel.

'Well, they'll have to do,' he replied. 'It's not my fault Iain hides all the tools. He's got all sorts of spades and shovels stashed away somewhere, but I haven't the faintest idea where he keeps them.'

'All right.' I shrugged, taking another step forwards and shifting the matted growth with an experimental foot. 'I think it was around here, somewhere.'

'What was?'

'The tombstone,' I told him plainly. 'Richard's mother's tombstone. They wouldn't bury her in the church-yard because she was a Catholic, so William de Mornay had her buried here.

'You're joking.'

'Not at all. It's a white slab, about this wide,' I spread my hands two feet apart, 'and her name is carved on it.'

His eyes caught a gleam of my own excitement. 'Right here, you say?'

'I think so. It might be underneath a lot of soil,' I qualified, looking around us. 'The ground seems higher against the wall than it looked back then, but that could just be my imagination.'

'What about using that door as a reference point?' he suggested, nodding back over his shoulder towards the house. 'Where did the ground level used to be relative to that door?'

'The door wasn't there, then. The whole west passage used to be open on this side, like the cloisters in a monastery.'

Geoff accepted my statement philosophically. 'Well, we'll just have to hope for the best, then. The ice pick has a seven-inch blade, that ought to be enough.'

I felt an urge to cross my fingers as I watched him crouch down on his heels and begin to probe the overgrown earth with the ice pick, his movements cautious, half-believing. I suppose I had been secretly hoping, all along, that Geoff knew that he had once been Richard. I had envisioned in my waking fantasies a sort of euphoric moment of revelation, with both of us running into each other's arms like those hackneyed couples on television, glorying in the fact that we had found each other again after more than three centuries of waiting . . .

Of course, it hadn't happened quite like that. Reality rarely conformed to fantasy, in my experience. But perhaps, I thought, if I could convince him at least that I wasn't mad, that Richard de Mornay had in fact existed, then in time he might come to realize who he was. What we were.

His voice drifted over my thoughts. 'You think I'm Richard, don't you?'

'What makes you say that?'

'Deductive reasoning, again,' he said, slanting a smile in my direction. 'If you were Mariana, then . . .' He shrugged, significantly.

'I can't say the thought hasn't crossed my mind,' I admitted, choosing my words with care. 'We did hit it off rather well, you and I, and your last name is de Mornay, and you love France nearly as much as he did.'

'How do you know he didn't come back as a Frenchman, then?'

I gazed down at that dark head, bent low over his work so that I couldn't see his expression. 'And you look exactly like him,' I finished in a quiet voice.

He let that one pass, moving his exploration a little further from the house. 'It may not be here, anymore,' he warned. 'The tombstone, I mean. It may have been broken, or someone may have dug it up in later years and got rid of it, sacrilegious as that sounds. Or it may be down deeper than seven inches.' He glanced at my face and grinned. 'But you're going to keep me out here until I find the blasted thing, aren't you?'

My eyes implored him to be serious. 'It's important.'

'Well, then,' he said, 'I guess I'd better find it, hadn't I?'

He took an energetic stab at the soil by his knee, setting loose a shower of tiny wildflowers that scattered to the wind, and we both heard the sharper, ringing sound as the ice pick's blade struck stone.

For a full minute neither of us spoke, and then I was on my knees beside him, both of us tearing into the earth with pick and hands and trowel, ripping away the turf to expose the smooth white stone beneath. When Geoff reached past me to brush the clinging dirt from the worn inscription, his fingers were not altogether steady.

'Louise de Mornay,' he read the words out loud. He brushed more dirt from the surface, and sat back on his heels, turning his head to meet my eyes. 'My God,' he said.

'I know. Join the club.' I brushed the hair from my eyes. 'You ought to try it from my angle.'

He squinted up at the sun for a moment, then rubbed his dirt-stained hands against his jeans and rose slowly to his feet. 'How be we take a bit of a breather?' His voice was deliberately light. 'Have some lunch. It'll give me time to absorb all this.'

'All right.'

Back in the west passage, I headed automatically towards the kitchen and Geoff caught me by the elbow.

'Not here,' he said. 'I'd rather get out of here for an hour or so, if you don't mind. Let's go to the Lion.'

It was a short walk, and a silent one. I was so lost in thought that I nearly walked straight past my own brother seated on one of the bar stools, and probably would have done if Vivien hadn't said something to me.

'Look who's here!' was what she said. 'He couldn't get an answer up at the house, so he came down here to keep us company.'

'I figured you'd turn up sooner or later,' Tom said. His kiss smelt of Scotch, and as we drew apart I turned to cast a faintly accusatory glance at Iain, sitting in his usual place at the bar, one stool over.

'Have you been getting my brother drunk?' I asked him.

'Have a heart,' he told me, with a slow wink. 'I'm trying to keep up with him.'

'Hmmm. Another day off?' I asked Tom, and he smiled.

'Yes. Aren't curates wonderful.' His gaze slid past me. 'It's Geoff, isn't it?' he said, holding out his hand in greeting. 'Nice to see you again. Can I buy you a drink?'

How like my brother, I thought warmly, to dip into his own shallow pockets to treat a millionaire to a pint of beer. Geoff accepted the offer graciously, and within minutes we were all four settled in a row along the bar, with Vivien leaning on her elbows facing us. Iain lifted his drink, nudging Tom's arm.

'What's that you were saying about Morrisey?' he asked my brother.

'He'll never stand up to Conner.'

Geoff looked enquiringly at Vivien, and she rolled her eyes back at us. 'Chess match,' she explained, 'if you can believe it. We've run the gamut of conversation topics this past hour.'

Tom wan't listening. 'Ned,' he called along the bar, 'what does it say in there about Morrisey's chances?'

Ned flipped a page of his newspaper and answered without lifting his head. 'Doesn't have a snowball's chance,' was his summation, and Tom looked vindicated.

'See?'

'You're way off beam,' Iain shook his head. 'Morrisey is a Scotsman, after all.'

'Precisely.' My brother smiled into his beer, and a sly look entered Iain's grey eyes.

'Would you care to make a wee wager on it, then?'

Geoff intervened, raising a warning hand. 'Be careful, Tom,' he advised my brother. 'I've lost more money to this man than I'd care to mention.'

Tom wavered, but only for a moment. He had never been able to resist a 'wee wager'. 'Five pounds,' he offered.

'Done.'

Iain sealed the bet with a handshake, let his eyes twinkle briefly at Geoff and lit a cigarette. 'You look bloody awful,' he told his friend bluntly. 'What the devil have you been up to?'

'It's Julia's fault, really,' Geoff replied, passing on the blame. 'I haven't slept since I got back from London.'

I cringed mentally at his choice of words. Three pairs of eyes swung speculatively in our direction. Even Ned glanced over at us before turning to the next page of his paper. Geoff caught his mistake and grinned broadly.

'Get your minds out of the gutter, you lot. As a matter of fact, we've been sitting up going over some of the old history of the Hall.'

Not exactly a lie, I thought, congratulating him silently on his truth-twisting abilities. Beside me, Tom lifted a dark eyebrow in an unspoken question, and I nodded imperceptibly. The message flashed clearly between us: *Yes, I've told him*, and Tom shifted his gaze from me to Geoff with new and sudden interest.

'We found something interesting, actually,' Geoff was saying, toying casually with his glass of beer. He looked at Iain. 'Remember how you always said that my courtyard felt like a tomb?'

'Aye.'

'Well, it is. We found a headstone buried in the weeds. William de Mornay's wife.'

'First or second?' Vivien asked, and Geoff frowned. 'What, wife?'

'No, William. First or second?'

'Oh.' Geoff's face cleared. 'Second. The Cavalier chap who got sent to the Tower.'

Vivien raised her eyebrows. 'Why would they have buried her in the courtyard? Wasn't the church the usual place?'

'Don't know,' Geoff replied. 'Maybe she was a Catholic. Her first name was Louise, a French name.'

Bravo, I applauded him secretly. He was even better at this than I was.

Iain didn't appear at all surprised by our discovery. 'Either way,' he said, 'we'd best get it cleaned up a little, if there's someone at rest in there. I'll drop round tomorrow with the scythe and see what I can do.'

Vivien sighed in mingled amusement and impatience. 'What's that on your job list?' she asked him. 'Number one hundred and one?'

'I like to keep busy,' he defended himself.

'I'll help him,' Geoff promised, and Vivien let it go with a toss of her fair head.

Tom was still stuck on an earlier thought. 'It's rather sad, isn't it, to think of someone being denied burial in consecrated ground.' He took a thoughtful sip of Scotch. 'The Church certainly has a lot to answer for, in history.'

'Keep talking like that,' I teased him, 'and you'll be unfrocked by Christmas.'

My brother grinned. 'Not a chance. The archbishop and I get on rather well together. Besides, there's my name to consider. I was destined to become a man of the cloth, and you know how strongly I feel about the path of destiny.'

I glanced at Geoff and our eyes met in a flash of silent shared communication. As Tom and Iain launched into an esoteric discussion of Christian ethics, Geoff leaned across me to order another drink, resting a warm hand on my back between my shoulder blades. It was a touch of reassurance, of promise, of gentle apology, and my heart swelled in response.

I could wait a little longer, I told myself. For Richard, I could wait.

Chapter Twenty-Eight

'Yes, Mum, I know.' I cradled the telephone receiver against my shoulder and reached to straighten a tilted picture frame on the wall beside the stairs. 'Tom told me all about it this afternoon. Quite a nice surprise for you and Dad, I expect.'

'Mmm.' My mother's voice was absent, and not entirely convincing. 'Your father *will* keep entering these crossword contests, you know, so I suppose it was only to be expected. Although I'm not sure that a week's holiday in Brighton would be my idea of a truly grand prize. Still,' she said, adopting a positive attitude, 'your father is pleased as punch. You'd think we'd never been on holiday to hear him talk, and here we are barely home a month.'

She couldn't hide the smile in her voice, though. We both knew my father well enough to know it was the winning, and not the prize, that excited him – the thought of having something for nothing.

'Is Dad at home?'

'No, he's gone off shopping for swimming trunks. Imagine,' she said, chuckling, 'with his legs! I shall have to walk ten steps behind him and wear dark glasses so no-one will think we're together.'

I grinned. 'They have naked bathing in Brighton, don't they?'

'Are you trying to cheer me up, or put me off going?'

'Oh, you'll have fun, Mum. And it is only a week. When do you leave?'

'Next Saturday. We'll be stopping the night at Tom's place in Elderwel, and we thought if you weren't doing anything that evening you might want to drive down for dinner, make a family gathering of it.'

'Sorry,' I shook my head, 'I couldn't possibly. Not next Saturday. Rachel's getting married that day, and she'd be disappointed if I wasn't there.'

'Rachel?' My mother's puzzled voice halted me in my tracks, and my hand tightened around the receiver as I realized the significance of what I'd just said.

'Rachel Evers,' I elaborated, keeping my voice steady. 'An old school chum.'

'Oh.'

From the silence that followed I knew that my mother was systematically searching her memory for a face to match the name, and I hastened to switch the subject. 'Tom said that Dad had been having problems with his shoulder again,' I prompted, and relaxed when my mother sailed off on a new tack. She was always happy to discuss my father's health problems – brought on mainly, in her opinion, by too many evenings of wine and snooker at his Club.

For the rest of the conversation I was only half-listening, filling the occasional pauses in my mother's narrative with appropriate noises of agreement or sympathy.

'Are you sure you're all right?' she asked me, at the end of a particularly long anecdote.

'Of course I am. Why?'

'You haven't said two words in the past ten minutes.'

'Haven't I? Sorry. I was up rather early this morning, and it's starting to catch up with me.'

'Well, see that you get your rest,' my mother advised me, in a tone I remembered all too well. 'And eat properly. And make sure your vitamins have iron added. You are still taking vitamins? Good. You wouldn't want to be taken ill, now, would you?'

'I feel fine,' I said again, for what seemed like the hundredth time that day. It was a lie, I admitted to myself as I hung up the telephone. I had told it to Geoff that morning, and to Tom that afternoon, and just now to my mother, but it was a lie. I didn't feel fine, at all. In actual fact, I was feeling rather depressed, and I knew there was only one person in the village who would fully understand the reason why.

Mrs Hutherson's house was the second house past the old red-brick vicarage on the High Street. It was more of a cottage, really, small and square and sagging beneath the weight of its ancient tile roof. The walk was edged with lavender and flowers dripped from the window ledges between freshly-painted green shutters. Even if Alfreda Hutherson herself had not been crouching by the side fence, tending a bed of gargantuan tomatoes, I would have known that the house was hers.

She straightened as I came through the low, swinging gate, greeting me with a smile of welcome and understanding.

'I'd expected you sooner,' she said, 'but I suppose you've been having a busy day. You're disappointed, naturally.'

How wonderful not to have to explain. 'Yes, I am.'

'You wanted more.'

'I wanted the fairy tale,' I admitted with a rueful smile. 'Foolish of me.'

'Not at all,' she replied stoutly. 'But even fairy tale lovers have some difficult moments, before the happily

307

ever afters. Give it time. Trust the process, and it will all work out in the end. You'll see. Have you had your supper yet?'

'No.' I shook my head. 'I wasn't hungry.'

'Well, come inside. You'll feel better when you've had something to eat.'

The cottage was as cosy inside as out, cheerful with overstuffed chintz in bright florals, white walls, and lace curtains letting the last of the day's sunlight pour through the square casement windows. I was not surprised to see a cat fluffed up on the window-sill; what surprised me, in a childish way, was that the cat was pure ginger, and not black. And then, upon reflection, I realized that maybe it wasn't so surprising, after all . . .

'I believe I saw your cat once,' I remarked, 'walking across the road by my house.'

'It wouldn't surprise me. He's a regular gadabout, that one. His mother was more the stay-at-home type, but he takes after his grandfather, I'm afraid.'

Leading me into the small kitchen, Mrs Hutherson busied herself loading the table with sandwiches and savouries, and brewing the ever-present pot of tea. If she could not give me answers, she seemed at least determined to give me comfort and to lessen the sharpness of my disappointment.

'Was that your brother I saw up at the stables with Geoff and Iain?' she asked me, unexpectedly.

I nodded. 'They gave him the grand tour, I think.'

'He's quite like you to look at. Vivien tells me he's a Vicar.'

'He has a living in Hampshire. I'll introduce you next time he comes,' I promised. 'He drops in to check up on me every few weeks.'

'He worries about you, I think.' She tilted her head, studying my face carefully. 'Perhaps he has reason to?'

I brushed aside the suggestion. 'No, no . . . I'm fine, really.' Under the gentle challenge of her eyes, I softened my stance. 'Well, I have been having a little problem with control, if you must know. I can't always choose the times of my regressions, sometimes I just slide backwards without meaning to.'

'You're going back every day now, aren't you?'

'Nearly.' I nodded. 'It's so difficult not to. I care about them, you see. I care about what happens to them, and they're all so *real* . . .'

'More real, perhaps, than the rest of us?' My expression answered for me, and she nodded. 'Yes, I understand. Time enough for the present, once the past has been settled. But you mustn't lose touch with the present, Julia,' she warned me. 'The past can teach us, nurture us, but it cannot sustain us. The essence of life is change, and we must move ever forward or the soul will wither and die.'

I spent the next few days quietly, working alone in the garden where the climbing rose was creeping shyly into bloom along the ruined wall. When the first pink bud unfolded, I snipped it lovingly from the vine and placed it in a vase beside my drawing board. Carefully I copied each delicate whorl onto paper and shaded the drawing with precise attention to detail. In my illustrations it would become Beauty's perfect, single rose, stolen from the Beast's garden. On paper, the flower was immortal. In the stale confines of my studio, it dropped its petals within three days.

I took advantage of my semi-seclusion to finally read the reams of information Tom had gathered from his librarian friend, on the subject of reincarnation. The writings ranged from New Age nebulous to bone-dry academic, but the whole package was nonetheless interesting. I was especially intrigued by the different ways in which people remembered their past lives.

To some, like myself, it happened quite unexpectedly, out of the blue. Others as young children had a vivid awareness of their former lives, only to lose the memory as they grew older. Occasionally, it took a major trauma or hypnotic trance before the memories surfaced. And some people . . . some people never remembered . . .

'I don't feel anything,' Geoff said bleakly, as the week drew to a close. We were standing in the courtyard, staring down at the neatly swept white stone, pristinely edged all round. The tangle of weeds had fallen beneath Iain's expert scythe, revealing tender patches of fragile green grass and a few low-growing wildflowers that hugged the ground for protection. Geoff dug his hands in his trouser pockets and stared harder, his brow furrowing. 'Surely I would feel *something* . . .'

We spoke very little of what had happened the week before. Geoff seemed to be turning the whole thing over in his mind, exploring his own thoughts and feelings at leisure. Outwardly, we went on just the same as before. Our days were as full and his touch as warm and his eyes still smiled at mine, but somehow a part of him had withdrawn from me. I let it go, both because I was sure it would return, and because my growing obsession with Mariana Farr's life overshadowed my own petty problems.

When the day of Rachel's wedding arrived, there was no question of my being sociable. Before the first faint light of dawn came stealing over the downs, I up and dressed, took my telephone off the hook and settled myself in comfort to await the inevitable.

The inevitable was a long time coming. The day began fairly enough, a glorious late-summer Saturday spread beneath a rare blue sky, but as the hours ticked past the clouds began to gather and the sun was gradually extinguished by a veil of cheerless grey. The darkness that followed in mid-afternoon was almost prophetic, and the gentle wind swept past my windows with the low voice of a weeping woman.

I found Rachel in the cramped front bedchamber which had so lately been her own. The narrow bed was stripped and bare, no mark of her occupation remaining. She would spend her wedding night in the comparative luxury of the corner chamber, in the great four-poster bed that had been my grandfather's. It would be the last night she slept in this house.

How I would survive the days without her I did not know, and the thought weighed heavy on my heart. Her thoughts, I knew, were heavier still than mine, yet she did not share them. She touched the window with a steady hand, staring with unseeing eyes towards the road.

'It will be rain by nightfall,' she said, aware of me standing in the doorway. 'Our guests will get a wetting.'

'They'll scarcely notice, like as not.' I stepped into the room, closing the door behind me to shut out the sounds of music and merrymaking below. 'In spite of Uncle's disapproval, they've already drunk two barrels of the ale he set by.'

She smiled faintly at the news. She still wore her best gown of pale pink silk, ruched and embroidered, in gay contrast to her husband's sombre attire. Elias Webb had proved a dour bridegroom, and in the church that morning the minister himself had hesitated over the words of the service, as though it troubled him to join a young and vibrant girl to such a man.

'My husband does not drink, I'll warrant,' Rachel said. 'He is Puritan in his habits. Know you what the hour is?'

I shook my head. ''Tis approaching supper time, but I do not know the exact hour. Will you be coming down, soon?'

'Presently. I—' She broke off suddenly, flattening her palm against the window glass. I was standing close behind her, close enough to see what she saw approaching by the road. The huge grey horse and rider were unmistakable. Beside them, Evan Gilroy sat tall and determined on his own bay steed, leading behind him a spirited black mare that seemed to dance above the rutted road.

'He came,' Rachel breathed, on a kind of ragged sigh. 'He actually came.' She turned to face me, her eyes shining with a wildness I could not understand. 'Grab you your happiness with both hands, Mariana,' she advised, her lip trembling, 'and hold it tightly, for you cannot tell when you might lose it.'

I wanted to hold her, comfort her, but before my arms could move she brushed quickly past me with downcast eyes, and I heard but the echo of her footsteps descending the staircase. Below me in the yard, Navarre gave a toss of his grey head as Richard dismounted. Evan led all three horses to the crooked pear tree by the south wall, and tethered them there. Downstairs, the sound of revelry swelled and dipped and swelled again, unaffected by the arrival of the new guests.

Richard's voice floated upwards through the

floorboards beneath my feet, bringing me away from the window and down the stairs to rejoin the general company.

'My lord,' Rachel's voice cut clearly across the din of babble, her smile wide as she crossed the floor to greet them. 'You do us honour with your company.'

Richard doffed his hat and bent gallantly over her outstretched hand. 'Your company, madam, would do honour to any man,' he countered smoothly.

Her smile did not falter as she turned her attention to the man beside him. 'Mr Gilroy,' she acknowledged, offering her hand again.

His kiss was brief, but his eyes lingered on hers. 'I wish you happiness,' he told her quietly.

My uncle came forward as well, his cold eyes betraying his mask of hospitality. 'You are welcome, gentlemen. Come and partake of some refreshment.'

Richard nodded absently, his eyes searching the room. 'Where is the good Mr Webb?' he asked. 'I would speak with him a moment.'

Uncle Jabez beckoned to the bridegroom, and Elias Webb approached the men, a black scowl on his wizened features. Richard appeared not to notice the coldness of their greeting.

'May I offer you my congratulations, sir,' he said pleasantly, 'on your most excellent marriage.'

'I thank you, your lordship.' It was a grudging reply.

Richard smiled. 'I wish to make you a present, in honour of the occasion. In the yard, you will see a black Barbary mare. It is a lady's mount, and a fitting accessory to your wife's beauty. I pray you do me the honour of accepting this small gift.'

Elias Webb glanced back at a blushing Rachel before

making reply. 'On behalf of my wife, I do accept your wedding present with thanks,' he said. But it was plain he was not pleased.

The musicians, on lute and pipe and tambourine, struck up a rollicking air, and Richard tilted his head, listening.

'That is a pleasant tune,' he commented. 'Tell me, sir, would you think it bold of me to claim a dance with your lovely wife?'

The bridegroom's ugly face froze over. 'I regret, my lord, that I cannot permit dancing at my wedding. Music and drink I can endure, in moderation, but dancing is the devil's pastime.'

Richard had not once glanced at me since I had come downstairs, and I had thought him unaware of my presence, but now his eyes found mine unerringly. I pressed back against the panelled wall, praying that he would not dare to challenge me to dance, with my uncle standing there at his shoulder.

From his smile I knew that the thought had also crossed his mind, but he looked away politely and, excusing himself from Rachel and her husband, moved on to mingle with the other guests, trailing Evan Gilroy in his wake.

Several minutes later, when I passed among the guests to fill their empty cups with wine, I found him standing at my shoulder.

'You'll wound my pride,' he warned me softly, 'ignoring me so.'

I flicked him a look that was only half impatient. 'I must not speak with you, by my uncle's own instruction.'

'And when have you obeyed instructions?' He held out his own cup to be filled, his mouth curved in amusement. 'Besides, your uncle is engaged at present, with a most serious gentleman. If he should look this way, I've only to duck my head.'

'You are impossible, my lord.'

'Ay. And your good humour is lacking, madam. What is it that has so offended you?'

I bent my head, frowning. 'I am sorry, my lord, but this day has soured my stomach. How could you have brought Evan here?'

His voice was calm. 'We were invited.'

'Rachel is desolate enough, without being reminded of the happiness she once knew, and it does not help that he seems scarcely inconvenienced by her marriage.'

Richard's eyes followed mine to the tall, silent figure of Evan Gilroy, lounging against the wall by the fireplace, one boot propped insolently on the cold hearth.

''Tis no marriage at all,' Richard objected with a faintly wicked smile, 'until it be consummated.'

My uncle turned at that moment, and saw us, and despite his earlier promise Richard de Mornay did not duck his head. Instead he lifted his cup and his rich voice boomed from the rafters as he called upon the company for a toast.

'To his Royal Majesty, King Charles!'

'The King!' All assembled raised their cups in reply, draining the contents in a single draught. My uncle joined the toast, but his eyes were narrow and hard when he lowered his drink.

'To the bride and groom!' someone shouted, from the back of the room, and again the great refrain rang out and the cups were lifted.

'To love,' Evan Gilroy proposed in a crisp, level voice, not stirring from his position by the mantelpiece. For a third time, the voices echoed the sentiment and the toast was drunk. Richard kept his eyes on mine while he drained his cup, then set it down again with a wink.

'Mark you remember how I drank that toast,' he told me, before moving away.

The sack posset was brought out shortly afterwards, a warmly intoxicating blend of curdled milk and Spanish wine and spices, and when it had been merrily consumed the lamps were lit and a fire kindled in the upstairs chamber, where the great bed lay prepared to receive the bridal couple.

Caroline and I accompanied Rachel to the bed-chamber, to help her undress. In a few moments the entire company of guests would follow, as custom demanded, to fling the bride's stocking and see the newly married couple into bed. Rachel clearly did not relish the prospect, but she sat stoically beneath our ministrations.

'You must look cheerful,' Caroline chided her younger sister, pinching Rachel's cheeks to raise the colour in them. ''Tis not a wake. Jabez has wedded you to a rich and respectable man, and you should show your gratitude more plainly.'

'I am exceeding grateful,' said Rachel dully.

Caroline fussed with Rachel's hair, clucking her tongue reprovingly. 'You do not appear so. You must smile, and say—'

'Oh, leave her be, Caroline!' I snapped, my patience strained, and the fussing stopped. I met Rachel's eyes in the looking-glass. 'Would you have us stay with you?'

She shook her head, slowly. 'I think I would like a moment alone, if neither of you mind. 'Twill give me time to collect my thoughts, and . . .' she paused, smiling at her sister, 'to pray that God see fit to make me a good and obedient wife.'

She rose and hugged us both, pale and lovely in her

flowing nightdress. 'I shall miss you,' she whispered beside my ear, clinging to me with the desperation of a frightened child.

'I will visit you often,' I promised, my voice unsteady. 'You will have no cause to miss me.'

She merely shook her head, her eyes bright with tears, and hugged me again. I withdrew with a troubled mind. Downstairs, the celebration had grown boisterous with toasts and song, and the guests were all high-flown as they gathered to escort the bridegroom to his marriage bed. I had not the heart to join them, and when they finally mounted the stairs I lingered in the hallway miserably, hoping I would not be missed.

I was only vaguely aware of the hum of voices breaking, then changing, growing more discordant. The people seemed to be returning, pouring down the narrow staircase in an excited, trembling stream that spilled to every corner of the hall, and in the midst of it all my uncle stood, looking blacker and more dangerous than I had ever seen him.

'Take horse!' he ordered those around him, 'they shall not get away with this. By God,' he thundered, standing very tall, 'they shall not get away with this!'

The air around me filled with agitated, eager whisperings, 'Gone . . . did you ever hear . . .? . . . through the window, of course . . . Gilroy, my dear, from the manor house . . . never suspected anything . . .'

Elias Webb, shaking with rage, ploughed through the press of bodies towards me. 'Open the door!' he ordered, and I obeyed automatically, then flattened myself against its surface to let him pass. Several men followed him out onto the lawn, spreading purposefully in all directions. Instinctively, I looked past them to the spot where Evan had tethered the horses. Navarre stood alone in the moonlight, a ghostly grey shape with his head turned in the direction of the distant hills.

I pulled my gaze away and looked behind me. Richard de Mornay was standing halfway down the stairs, one shoulder propped against the wall behind, his arms folded casually across his chest. Above the sea of wondering faces his eyes met mine, and he smiled.

Chapter Twenty-Nine

Mrs Hutherson smiled at me above the rim of her flowered tea-cup. 'What do *you* think happened to them?' she asked.

'I don't know,' I answered, chewing my lower lip. 'I suppose I want to think they got away, lived happily ever after and all that.' I smiled faintly. 'The fairy tale again.'

It was becoming a familiar scene, the two of us facing each other across the scrubbed table in the kitchen of Crofton Hall, with the sunlight streaming in the windows and the kettle still steaming on the stove.

'I went to the church this morning,' I continued, 'and checked the registers again. There's no record of a burial of either Rachel or Evan, or of any marriage between them. The marriage record of Rachel and Elias Webb still stands,' I pointed out. 'No-one put a line through it, or anything.'

'They probably saw no need to,' Mrs Hutherson explained. 'Elias died soon afterward. But there,' she caught herself, smiling. 'I've gone and told you, and after I promised myself I wouldn't.'

'You wouldn't care to tell me what became of Evan and Rachel, then?'

'I would not.'

'It was quite a serious thing, in those days, wasn't it? Running away with another man. I expect they would have been hanged, if they'd been caught.'

She lifted the teapot, refusing to rise to the bait. 'Would you like another cup?'

'No, thank you.' I held a hand to my stomach. 'I'll be swimming as it is.'

'Have you told Geoffrey about this, yet?'

'No. I only saw him for a moment, just before noon, as he was heading out for his ride. He still doesn't remember anything. About Richard, I mean.'

It was an unnecessary comment on my part, but she nodded anyway. 'I know.'

'Will he ever remember?'

'Have another biscuit.' She passed me the plate.

'You're not going to answer that, are you? Right, then let's try this angle. Is there anything I can say or do that might help Geoff to remember?'

'Nothing.' She shook her head with regal certainty. 'You cannot force the pace of destiny, Julia.'

My smile was tight. 'No harm trying.'

'On the contrary, you might do a great deal of harm.' She put her head to one side and studied me closely. 'Do you mind if I make a suggestion?'

'Not at all.'

'You said before that you couldn't always control your experiences. That you sometimes went back without meaning to.'

'That's right.'

'Then I think it would be wise if you left your house for the next few days, went on holiday. Not that you're in any danger, mind, but Mariana's uncle was a brutal man, and Rachel's running away did not improve his temper. It might be painful – physically painful – for you to relive any episodes just now. You understand?'

I thought of Caroline's bruises, and her hollow, defeated eyes. 'Yes,' I said. 'I think I do.'

'You don't need to stay away long. Till Thursday, perhaps. Things ought to have settled down by then. Jabez Howard's rages never lasted long.'

I looked at her, curious. 'You seem to know a good deal about him.'

'As well I should,' she replied, calmly levelling her gaze on mine. 'Jabez Howard was my—'

The outside door swung open suddenly and Vivien stuck her head around the door jamb. 'Sorry to interrupt,' she said, without sounding in the least apologetic, 'but I've been looking everywhere for you, Julia. I desperately need your opinion on my outfit for this evening.'

Alfreda Hutherson smiled indulgently at her niece. 'What's on for this evening?'

'Never you mind,' Vivien told her, grinning. 'I just need to borrow Julia for a few minutes, that's all.'

'Won't my opinion do?'

'No, thanks,' Vivien's grin widened. 'I've seen your wardrobe. Besides, Julia's an artist. She has an eye for colours and lines and things.' She looked at me hopefully. 'Have you got a minute, or am I really interrupting something?'

'Nothing that won't keep,' Mrs Hutherson answered for me, waving a dismissive hand. 'You'd better go with her, Julia. We can't have Vivien looking out of fashion, or clashing with the table linens. And don't let her wear anything black, it fades her out completely.'

'I don't own anything in black,' Vivien confided to me as we wended our way down the back lane to the Red Lion. 'Not anymore. I do occasionally listen to my Aunt Freda, you know.' Smiling, she pushed open the gate that led to her private rooms at the rear of the pub.

Inside, Vivien dropped her keys on the kitchen

counter and shook her head. 'Will you look at that, then,' she said, with a sweep of her hand. I looked. Iain lay stretched full length on the carpet in her lounge, one arm crooked behind his head, ankles crossed, eyes closed. 'That's the problem with tradesmen these days,' she told me, amused. 'You turn your back for half a minute and they fall asleep on you.'

He looked quite different, in his sleep. Gone were the strong, impassive lines and angles of his face, and the stoic self-control that held them there. He looked younger, somehow. That was the dreamer's face, I told myself, the poet's face, and not the farmer's. But then he half-opened one eye and looked back at us, and the impression vanished. 'I'm not sleeping,' he said. 'I'm just resting my eyes.'

'You're supposed to be fixing my sink, as I recall.'

'Yes, madam. Right away, madam.' He grinned, and the one grey eye slid from Vivien to me. 'Christ, you'd think I was getting paid for the job.'

'I didn't know you were a plumber, Iain.' I said.

'I'm not, but I can manage the basics.' He sat up, rubbing the back of his neck. 'Viv made the mistake of mentioning her leaking pipes in the bar yesterday, and Ned's father offered to fix them for her. So Viv called me round in a panic to sort the problem out before he got to it.'

'If there's one thing you don't want,' Vivien put in, 'it's Jerry Walsh tinkering with your pipes.'

I laughed. 'I know. I've a tap in my bath that I think has been dripping for thirty years.'

'You're lucky,' she said. 'He flooded my kitchen first time I had him do a job for me. Safer to have the work done by an amateur.'

'Oh, thank you very much,' Iain said drily, rolling to his feet. 'Your confidence is heart-warming.'

'You know what I mean.'

'Aye. Do you mind it I take a beer with me while I bash your pipes around? Or is drinking on the job not allowed?'

'Help yourself.' She moved aside to give him access to the refrigerator. With the daylight full on his face, the lines of exhaustion were clearly visible, and Vivien told him as much. 'You need to get more sleep, you do.'

He slid her a look of quiet amusement. 'You might have thought of that, love, before you woke me up. And what are you two up to, then?'

'Julia's going to help me pick my outfit for tonight.'

Iain shrugged. 'I told you which one I like,' he said, closing the refrigerator door and forcing the top off a bottle of lager. 'The green dress, with the buttons.'

'I just want an expert opinion, that's all.'

A half hour later, having seen a parade of all the potential outfits, I had to admit that Iain was quite right.

'The green one,' I told her, 'definitely. It's got a lovely cut, and it suits you.'

'Suitable for a slightly stuffy gathering of rather proper and dignified people?'

'I think so. Where *are* you off to, anyway?'

'London,' she supplied, twisting to study her reflection in the long mirror. 'I've been invited to a dinner party in Belgravia.'

'With Iain?'

'Heavens, no. Iain can't stand London.' She eyed the hemline of the dress critically. 'You don't think it's too short? No? Well, I suppose if you both hit on this one, then I ought to take your advice and wear it.' She glanced at her watch and grimaced. 'Lord, is that the time? I promised Ned I'd let him have a break before I went.'

Personally, I'd never seen Ned expend enough energy to warrant a break, but I kept my opinion to myself. Vivien kicked off her high heels and changed hurriedly back into her everyday clothes, combing her fingers through her hair to tidy it.

'I won't be long,' she said. 'You can come through to the bar, if you like, or hang about here.'

'I'll wait here. Someone should probably keep an eye on your plumber, anyway.'

She smiled. 'Too right. Call me when the water reaches your knees.'

Iain was actually, from what I could tell, doing an expert job. I perched myself on the rim of the bath and watched him working. Again, as always, the quiet comfort of his being there flowed round me like a cleansing tide. Vivien, I decided, was a very lucky woman.

'We decided on the green dress,' I informed him.

'Eh, well,' he said, smiling, 'there wasn't much question, was there? It looks great on her, that dress.'

I looked down at the top of his bent head. 'You really do look tired, you know.'

'You should talk.' He lifted his eyes briefly. 'Have you seen a mirror lately? You look as though you need a holiday.'

I smiled. 'I'm taking one, as a matter of fact. Starting tomorrow.'

'Oh? Whereabouts?'

'Brighton.'

He looked up again, grinning. 'Brighton? Of the naughty postcards, and all that? It hardly seems your style.'

'It isn't, really. But my parents are there for the week, and I thought I'd join them for a few days.'

'Oh, right. I remember your brother saying something about that. Some sort of a contest your father won, wasn't it?'

'Crossword.' I nodded. 'Mum's not overly thrilled, but my being there might cheer her up. Besides, it's been years since I went to the seaside.'

'Well, you go and enjoy yourself. We'll keep an eye on the house for you, if you like. There,' he gave the pipe a final wrench with the spanner and sat back, surveying his work. 'I think that deserves a free pint, at least. Why don't we go and see what Vivien's doing out front?'

Brighton was as gaudy as my childhood memory of it, but the weather proved exceptionally fine and my parents were delighted to see me. I frittered away four days in their undemanding company, walking on the beach and taking snaps of the Royal Pavillion and laughing at the spectacle of it all.

I returned home on Thursday afternoon in a wholly refreshed state of mind, dropped my luggage in the hallway and went in search of Geoff. I found him in the bar of the Red Lion, nursing a pint of ale and talking rugby with Ned.

Ned was, for once, almost animated. 'Pewsey'll take Calne by ten points this Saturday, you see if they don't.'

'Care to back that opinion, my lad?'

'A tenner says you're wrong.'

'Done.' The two men shook hands, and Geoff turned with a smile as I hoisted myself on to the stool beside him. 'A lad who works for me is right-winger for Calne,' he explained. 'I'm only being loyal.'

Ned grinned. 'Like taking candy from a baby,' he said.

I sent Geoff my best motherly look. 'Is this what you get up to when I'm not around?' I asked him. 'Drinking and gambling?'

'I've been bored stiff,' was his defence. 'No-one to play with. Iain's been too busy this week, and Vivien ...' He looked at Ned, frowning. 'Where exactly is Vivien, anyway?'

The taciturn barman raised one hand and shook his head. 'No use asking me. My lips are sealed on pain of death.'

'Well,' Geoff went on, 'Vivien is somewhere. I had to make my own amusement.'

'Well, I'm back now. What would you like to do?'

He tilted his head, considering the offer. 'Why don't I take you to dinner, for starters, and then you can come back to the Hall with me and help me pack.'

'Pack for what?'

'I leave for France on Saturday,' he said. 'Or had you forgotten?'

'*This* Saturday? But I thought you weren't going until the end of August?'

Geoff smiled. 'This is the end of August, or very nearly. Don't look like that. I'll only be gone for six weeks.'

Six weeks! It seemed a minor eternity. I was still frowning as we left the pub and turned to walk along the shaded laneway leading up to the Hall. Geoff kept close beside me, his shoulder brushing mine. After a few moments' silence he turned his head and looked down at me, his eyes unreadable.

'Why don't you come with me?'

I looked up swiftly. 'What?'

'To France, I mean. Why don't you come with me? There's plenty of room on the plane, lots of space at the house, it'd be no trouble. And I'd enjoy your company.'

'Oh, Geoff, I couldn't.' My eyes pleaded with him to understand. 'I just couldn't.'

He understood. 'Because of Mariana.'

'Something important is about to happen, Geoff, I can feel it. Something that might help explain why this is happening to me. And it's going to happen soon. But I have to be here, in Exbury, if I want to find out how the story ends. I couldn't possibly leave now.'

We were nearing the bend in the path where it rounded the churchyard. Beyond the church loomed the stone gates of Crofton Hall, but before I could take another step towards them I was suddenly seized by the shoulders and hauled unceremoniously into the cover of the trees. There, in the cool green shadows, Geoff took my face in his hands and kissed me, and his kiss was almost rough in its urgency.

'What was that in aid of?' I asked him, when I could finally breathe again.

'I'm not sure. Maybe I just wanted to make certain you were paying attention.'

'I'm paying attention.'

He smiled, and kissed me again, more gently this time, then lifted his head and reached to tame a wayward curl by my cheekbone. 'Will you miss me, while I'm in France?'

'Of course I will.'

'I wonder.' The smile disappeared, and his face grew very serious in the dancing shadows of the leaves.

I stared up at him. 'What's that supposed to mean?'

'Who do you see, when you look at me?' he asked. 'Geoff? Or Richard?'

It should have been easy to give him an answer, but I couldn't. I couldn't say anything, I just went on looking at him, trapped by the dark intensity of his eyes. He stopped toying with my hair, brushing my chin with one finger before dropping his hand from my face altogether.

'Which one of us it it, Julia?' he asked, softly. 'You'd do well to think on that, while I'm gone.'

Chapter Thirty

September was a grey and lonely month, soggy with rain and tediously uneventful. The rose garden at the Hall never really reached its full glory, blighted petals hanging limply above blackened vines and leaves spotted with the damp. In my own little dovecote garden, a scattering of wine-red anemones made a brave showing against a sea of Michaelmas daisies, but the rains soon finished them, too. There was little colour anywhere, only a drowned and tired green and the dull, dun grey of sky and stone.

The bright postcards Geoff sent from the south of France were a welcome bit of cheer, and I propped them in a row along my window ledge so I could look at them while I worked on my illustrations. I was in another of my anti-social moods, but nobody seemed to mind.

Iain was kept busy harvesting his apples for shipment to some cider-maker in Somerset. From time-to-time I noticed a neatly cleared patch in the garden and knew that he had been there, but I never saw him. He must have worked in the dark. Vivien rang me occasionally to chat, and Mrs Hutherson dropped in one morning to check up on me, but most days I was able to bury myself in my work without interruption.

After three weeks, I was no closer to answering Geoff's question whether I cared more for him or for Richard – I found myself missing both of them. Mariana's days were as dreary as my own, and since I took care to confine my flashbacks to my own house, Richard de Mornay did not enter into them. I was tempted to experiment a second time in the manor house, but for some reason I hung back, perhaps because some inner instinct kept telling me that it wasn't necessary. *Whatever is going to happen*, the niggling voice said, *it will begin at Greywethers*. And so I waited.

The twenty-third of September began much as any other Saturday. I woke early, to the sound of the ever-present rain gurgling down my gutters. It seemed almost overkill to run the bath as well, with all that water outside, but I bathed nonetheless and went downstairs to breakfast.

The morning post brought another card from Geoff, a spectacular snowy view of the Pyrenees, with a caption that said simply: 'Basque Country'. *Am bored with the beaches*, his message read, *and so off to Mother and Pamplona for a few days. Might even try to find Roncevalles, where good old Roland of the 'Chanson' died trying to capture Navarre for Charlemagne. My history tutor would be proud. Love, Geoff*.

Navarre . . .

An image rose unbidden to my mind, of the great grey horse with the gentle liquid eyes, and of his darkly handsome rider. I touched the postcard with wistful fingers and set it aside to be placed with the others later, cheering myself with the thought that I could use that view of the snow-capped mountains for my next illustration of a Swiss folk tale.

My immediate plan for the morning, however, was to clean out the dining-room. I hadn't actually used it since I'd moved in, and it had become a handy dumping ground for unpacked boxes, furnishings that hadn't yet been assigned to a room, and reams of papers that I fully intended to sort through 'later'. Really, the only time I opened the dining-room door was when I wanted to toss something else into storage. Working on my mother's principle that a tidy house begets an ordered life, I descended on the room with determination.

The dizziness came on just before lunchtime. At first I thought it might be simple lack of food, but then the clamorous ringing started in my ears and my hands began to blur before my face. The ringing rose, and swelled, and stopped, as if a door had shut upon it.

I lifted a hand to my forehead, pushed the hair away from my heated face and went on polishing the floor, my legs tangling in the rough fustian skirts as I slid across the thick oak boards. As I drew near the door to the parlour, the sound of a stranger's voice from within stilled my hand and brought my head up sharply.

'It is to be tonight, then,' the voice said.

'Ay.' The second voice was my uncle's. They were standing not an arm's length from me, so near that their shadows blocked the light beneath the door. I held my breath, not daring to move, and was relieved when my uncle continued speaking.

'He will remove this night to Oxford. One of our number rides with him, in confidence, and will find cause to delay the party at the place of our choosing.'

'How many will they be?'

'Himself, and but five others, including our confederate.'

'And we are seven.'

'Ay. We are not likely to fail.' I recognized the tone of my uncle's voice, and shrank from it. The two men moved a step away from the door, but still their voices carried clearly.

'What news from Holland?' the stranger asked.

'Richard Cromwell rejects our plan, but methinks 'tis only caution on his part. When he finds the way clear for his return, he'll judge our cause more fair.'

'I've heard he is grown weak, and shiftless.'

My uncle made an impatient sound. 'A weak protector is yet worth more than a hundred kings, who whore and play at cards and take the name of God in vain. No,' he said, 'the people of Sodom must tremble, for the day of the Lord cometh.' He paused, and his voice when he next spoke held a faint smile. 'My niece is wondrous versed in the Bible, did I tell you?'

'You did. Mayhap you should offer her to poor Elias, as recompense.'

'I would it were possible. He would have been her father, had not my sister stole away, and Rachel now has shamed the both of us, and damned her own soul forever. Elias is a man much wronged, and will not claim a wife of me again, I think.'

'He knows the meeting place tonight?'

'Elias? Ay, he knows it well, and carries a sword well for his years. Get you the others in readiness, and gather at the crossroads in three hours' time.'

'I will pray for our success,' the stranger offered, but my uncle brushed the offer aside.

'There is no need. The Lord has already declared himself for us by delivering the Devil into our hands, and come tomorrow we shall all toast the restoration of the Commonwealth.'

They moved away from the door then and I shrank back against the table leg, my blood chilling, the forgotten polishing-cloth clutched tightly in my trembling hand. This was no dream, I told myself, nor yet some idle fancy of my own imagination. They meant to kill the King. They actually meant to kill the King, and put another Cromwell in his place. It seemed incredible, and yet . . .

I touched my cheek with searching fingers, and felt the faint tenderness of bruises still remaining.

My uncle was capable of killing.

I must warn the King, I thought . . . then realized the foolishness of that thought. I, warn the King? Not only foolish, but impossible. Yet a warning was called for. Richard, I decided. I would tell Richard, and he would find some way to send word to the King. I rose to my feet and was halfway to the kitchen door when a clattering of dishes reminded me that Caroline still stood between me and the back door. My uncle and his visitor were no longer in the parlour, but I could hear the echo of their voices from the front hall. There was no escape to be had there, either.

Panicked, I turned and my desperate gaze fell upon the windows looking over the garden. One of the windows stood open a crack, and by applying my weight to it I managed to inch it upwards by degrees, silently, until the opening was wide enough for me to slip my body over the sill. I dropped carefully to the soft ground beneath, and pulled the window sash down again behind me, lest someone look into the room while I was gone. With luck, I told myself, no-one would notice my absence. It had been a bitterly quiet household since Rachel's leaving of it, and my aunt and uncle paid me little heed.

I prayed fervently that they would not think to seek me now, as I inched my way around to the blind south wall of the house and ran lightly through the long grass to the hollow, where I lost myself in the welcome cover of the forest. I ran blindly, as a frighted hare runs, mindless of my bare feet and rough clothing. I did not stop running until I was brought up short against the great oak door of Crofton Hall, and raising my fist I pounded upon it with all my remaining strength.

The door swung inward, revealing Richard's steward. The merest flicker of his eyes betrayed his surprise at seeing me, although he kept his expression carefully schooled.

'I must speak with my lord de Mornay,' I begged, nearly breathless. ''Tis a matter of great urgency.'

The steward nodded politely and stepped aside to let me pass. 'His lordship is in the Little Parlour, Mistress Farr. I believe you know the way.'

'Yes.' I smiled gratefully. 'Thank you.'

Richard was seated alone at his desk by the window, frowning over the papers spread before him. He turned his head as I entered, and lacking his steward's calm reserve he showed his surprise plainly. 'Mariana! How came you here?' His first reaction was one of pleasure that I should so visit him, but as his eyes roved my wild face and coarse dishevelled clothing his smile vanished. 'What is it? What has happened?'

'Treason, Richard.' I took a stumbling step towards him, swaying a little on my unsteady legs. 'They mean to kill the King. I heard them talking . . .'

'Heard who talking? Your uncle?' I nodded, and Richard's features hardened. 'To whom did he speak?'

I shook my head. 'I know not. I could not see them, and the voice was unfamiliar. But they number seven, all in all, and Elias Webb is one of them. They mean to kill the King, and restore Richard Cromwell.'

'Richard Cromwell wants no part of politics.'

'They think to change his mind.' I took another step forwards but my legs were shaking too badly and they nearly collapsed beneath me. Before I could move again, Richard was there beside me, his warmth and strength

334

reassuring as he led me to a deeply cushioned chair by the window and settled me in comfort there.

I tried to smile at him, ashamed of my weakness, but he was not paying attention. His eyes were locked in anger on the curve of my cheek, where the sunlight warmed my skin through the open window, and he raised an oddly gentle hand to touch the faint marks. 'Who has done this?'

'Richard,' I said, refusing to be drawn out, 'you must warn the King. He is in mortal danger, and one of his own guards is in league with the traitors.'

His hand fell from my face, and the forest-green eyes slid to meet mine. 'When do they plan to set upon him?'

'Tonight. They said the King will travel from Salisbury to Oxford tonight, with only four guards to accompany him, and one of them a false fiend who would lead him to his death.'

'Christ.' Richard brushed a hand across his eyes, looking away from me to where the rolling hills stretched peacefully towards the south.

I watched his face. 'You will warn him?'

'Ay, I will do my best to reach him, count on that. The blood of a murdered King has stained this country once, and I will not live to see it happen a second time. Besides,' he added with a tight smile, 'Charles Stuart is a kind man, and a generous one, and I would not wish his death.'

'Then you must take horse,' I urged him. 'My uncle will meet his companions in but a few hours, and then I know not where they go.'

'I would have you wait here, for my return,' he said firmly. 'My servants will take care of you.'

Again I shook my head. 'Richard, I cannot. If I am

discovered missing 'twill only warn my uncle and set him on his guard. And I cannot leave Caroline and the baby alone in that house. He is much worse since Rachel left, I know not what harm he might do them. I must go back.'

'I will see you free of Jabez Howard before this week is out,' he told me, touching my cheek again with that disturbingly gentle touch. 'Do not smile at me, so – I mean to do it, and I shall. Or do you find the prospect of marrying me so amusing?'

The smile died on my lips. 'You cannot marry me.'

'Oh, can I not?' He grinned boldly. 'I have a reputation, my love, for doing the impossible. In one week's time I warrant you'll not doubt my word.'

He kissed me then, and offered a hand to help me to my feet. 'Come,' he said, 'I will see you safely home.'

'There is no time,' I protested. 'The King . . .'

'. . . will wait until I see you home,' he finished smoothly, with an insistence that I knew better than to oppose. 'Faith, your safety is of more concern to me than that of Charles Stuart. His life has hung in the hedge so long a moment more is of no consequence. But we shall ride, if the time worries you. Navarre can carry the both of us.'

It was too brief a contact, I thought later – a short ten minutes cradled in Richard's arms, before him on the saddle, my hands clasping his coat for balance while the hilt of his sword pressed cold against my hip.

'You said you would not ride pillion,' he reminded me, teasing, 'so this will have to do.'

I bit my lip. 'If anyone sees us . . .'

'Then we are seen,' he said, bending to brush my hair with a kiss. 'You must learn not to care so what others think.'

But he stopped the horse in the hollow to the south of Greywethers, beneath the spreading shelter of a rustling oak, and helped me to the ground.

'How will you enter the house again?' he asked me.

'The same way I left it, by the dining-room window. 'Tis an easy scramble.'

'Which window is that?'

'There,' I pointed, 'second from the door, above the garden.'

He found the place, and fixed his eyes upon it. 'When you are in, and sure of safety, close the window behind you, but not before,' he instructed. 'If the window remains open, I will know you are discovered, and will come to remove you.'

I rested my hand on his boot a moment, frowning. 'Richard.'

'Yes?'

'You will be careful?'

The quick grin was intended, no doubt, to reassure me. 'Mark you well my family's motto,' he said. 'I am indestructible, and your fears are wasted on such as me. Be off now, and look to your own welfare. I will wait until I know you safe.'

I skirted wide through the trees and raced back across the open grass with all the speed that I could muster. I felt as though a hundred eyes were upon me, and prayed they were but eyes of my imagination. It was a more difficult manoeuvre to hoist myself over the window-sill from the outside in, but after several tries I found myself back in the silent dining-room, with the smell of polish my only company. I straightened my skirts and moved away from the window, but before I could resume my place the kitchen door swung open and Caroline peered around with curious eyes.

337

'You have been quiet in here,' she said, attempting a smile. 'I thought you might have slept.'

I smiled back, hoping that she would not see my shaking hands. 'I have opened the window,' I said, unnecessarily. 'The smell of the polish is strong, and makes my head ache.'

She made no comment, merely looked at my handiwork and seemed to find it to her satisfaction. 'Would you come watch Johnnie for a minute?' was her next request. 'I must attend your uncle.'

'Of course. 'Twill take me but a moment to clear this away.'

She nodded and withdrew to the kitchen, and I released my pent-up breath on a long and trembling sigh. It was clear from Caroline's behaviour that I had not been missed, but I had escaped disaster by little more than a hair's breadth, and the knowledge left me quaking like a leaf in the autumn breeze.

Pulling myself erect, I crossed back to the open window and stood before it, turning my eyes in the direction of the hollow. He was still there, as he had promised, a tall dark shadow on the towering grey horse, standing impassively beneath the canopy of oak. Slowly, deliberately, I pulled the window down until the sash rested firmly on the sill, and watched as Richard raised his hand to acknowledge the action.

My own hand lifted in reply, but he had already reined the grey horse round to follow the line of trees along the river, and as I lowered my hand, forgotten, to press against the cool glass of the window, I saw the horse and rider break into a rolling gallop, turning their faces southward, towards Salisbury.

Chapter Thirty-One

The evening settled over us like the shadow of death. Johnnie fussed and fretted with his painful teeth, and would not go to sleep, but I was glad of the distraction as I rocked him in my arms, close beside the kitchen fire. If Caroline knew where her husband had gone, and what his purpose was, she gave no sign of it. We spoke of idle things, when we spoke at all, but the tension was there and tangible, and we were all three restless because of it.

It was approaching midnight when we heard the horses stop outside the house in a confused tossing of harness and dancing hooves and the shouts of men across the yard. And then the sounds retreated. The front door slammed and my uncle's footstep sounded in the hall. Caroline and I sat straight and still, our eyes upon the door, and I fancied that we both held our breaths.

The kitchen door rushed inwards on its hinges and crashed against the wall behind. Framed in the opening, my uncle glowered at us both, his expression blacker than the depths of Hell. Johnnie, in my arms, began to cry.

'Elias Webb is dead,' he said, his quiet voice more dangerous than any raging shout. 'And good Bill Pogue, and Edmund Harrap. All dead.'

We were not expected to make reply. Nor was there time for one. Immediately he spoke the words he turned and sent the table toppling to the floor with a great splintering of wood and crockery.

'The Devil take that rogue de Mornay!' he exploded, his face flooding with angry colour. 'I will not stand to suffer this from him!'

Johnnie bawled more loudly, burrowing his tiny face in my breast and clinging to my dress with frightened hands. I gathered him close and rocked him, trying not to let my own fear get the better of me.

'What injury has my lord de Mornay done you, Uncle?' I asked him, calmly, but he was past the point of hearing me. His eyes were fiery wells of hatred, glowing blackly in the flickering light cast up from the hearth.

'The others would accept defeat,' he muttered, speaking only to himself, 'and let the Devil triumph. But I have seen the Devil's blood, and know he is a man.' He clasped a gloved hand round his sword, then frowned, and looked at me. 'Can you not silence that child?' he barked roughly, and I clasped the infant more tightly, shielding him.

'Uncle Jabez,' I said, wetting my dry lips, 'what do you intend?'

His smile was a thing unholy. 'I intend to await your lord de Mornay's return from his evening ride, and give him a welcome he'll not soon forget.'

I kept my voice calm. 'You mean to harm his lordship, Uncle?'

'I mean to see him dead.'

Caroline blanched in her corner by the door.

'But Jabez, surely—'

'Do you defy me?' He turned his wrath on her instead, looming very large and threatening above my chair. 'By God! Do you think to defy me?' I saw the terrible intent in his eyes an instant before he moved, but I was powerless to stop him. Before I could protect the child he was torn from my arms and, with a cruel gesture, dashed against the stone hearth where he fell like a discarded plaything, twisted and broken. 'I am the master of my house,' my uncle thundered, 'and by heaven, you'll not question it again!'

Shock kept me silent, a screaming protest trapped within my tightly constricted throat. My uncle stood motionless for a moment, glaring down upon us like the ruler of the damned, then turning sharply on his heel he left our presence, and the front door banged to in the hall behind him. A heartbeat later I heard the sound of a single horse heading in the direction of the village, and Crofton Hall.

It was that sound, and the accompanying thought, that roused me from my stupor. Dazed, I lifted my head and turned to look at Caroline, who had flung herself with a wild cry across the room and crumpled on the flaming hearth, her arms wrapped tenderly around the lifeless body of her son. Her body rocked convulsively, her lips moving in a mumbled song of comfort, but he was far beyond her touch. I looked once into her eyes and could not bring myself to look again. They were dead eyes, dead and flat and inhuman. It was as though the horror of what she'd just seen had pushed her anguished mind past all sufferance, leaving but an empty shell where once there had lived a human soul. It was a painful thing to see.

'Caroline.' I spoke softly, imploringly. 'Caroline, we cannot stay here.'

She did not answer me, yet I pressed onward, resolute.

'Jabez has lost his reason, Caroline. 'Tis dangerous to wait for his return. We must seek help.'

The hollow eyes stared through me, unresponsive.

'Wait here for me,' I said to her, 'I will but be a moment.' I did not wait to mark whether she had heard my instruction, but swung my cloak down from its nail behind the back door and, wresting back the latch, stumbled out into the night.

The dovecote was dark as a tomb inside, the thrumming of the birds a weird accompaniment to the frantic beating of my own heart. The trapdoor was closed. I pulled on the rope to open it, grateful for the rush of clean night air and the ethereal shaft of moonlight that pierced the living darkness, giving me light enough at least to see the faint suggestion of walls surrounding me.

Groping my way along the wall, I nearly sobbed my relief as my fingers touched the broken ledge of an empty nesting-box. If there was a God, I thought feverishly, the key would still be there. The key that Richard had placed there for my use some two months earlier. The key that would admit me to the courtyard of the manor house. There would be safety there, I knew – safety at least for Caroline, Richard's servants would see to that. For my part, there could be no sanctuary until Richard was delivered from my uncle.

I have seen the Devil's blood, my uncle had said, and the words ran like ice through my veins. Was Richard wounded, then? No, of course, he wasn't, I told myself staunchly. Had he been wounded, my uncle would surely have gloated over the fact. Perhaps Richard had ridden the whole way to Oxford with the King. Oh, please, I prayed, let him have the sense to stay with the King. Do not let him return home tonight . . .

My knuckles scraped raw against the jagged stone as my fingers closed around the key, and I drew it forth hurriedly, gripping it tightly as I ran back across the yard to the house.

Caroline was sitting primly in a chair, waiting for me, her cloak neatly fastened about her shoulders. With careful hands she wrapped a shawl around the lifeless baby in her lap. 'He might take cold,' she explained, speaking low as if she feared to wake him.

My heart wrenched painfully in my chest, but I made no protest. Now was not the time to break her fantasy. 'Come, then,' I beckoned to her, and together we went out of the sombre house, closing the door behind us.

Not once did Caroline ask where I was taking her, nor show the slightest interest in her surroundings. She followed behind me blindly, silently, clutching her dead child tightly to her breast. The night was cool, and fair, spread bright beneath a pale and shining moon. It was the kind of night that the hunted things fear, a night when your own shadow chased you across the fields and even the forest could not shield you from the waiting, watching eyes.

We passed swiftly through the trees towards the Hall, skirting wide around both Church and stables to approach the house by the western wall. At the edge of the stableyard another shadow scurried past us, and I gasped in terror before I saw it for what it was – only a prowling, timid dog, its tail between its legs. I fancied I heard another indrawn breath besides my own, but Caroline had made no sound and I put it down to a strained imagination and the echo of the wind.

It was a simple matter to find the low door nestled in the courtyard wall, but my trembling fingers took three passes to fit the key to the lock. Once fitted it turned easily, and as the door swung inward on its oiled hinges I ushered Caroline in before me, hastily locking the door again behind us. Pressing Caroline back against the wall, where the shadows lay deepest, I raised a finger to my lips and warned her not to speak.

'Wait here,' I whispered. She hugged her baby and nodded dumbly, her eyes dull and uninterested.

A yellow stream of light spilled into the courtyard from the library, and I made my way cautiously in that direction, lifting my skirts so they would not rustle against the grass. My heart pounded in my throat as I neared the open doorway, then stopped altogether when strong arms grabbed me from behind in a grip of iron, hauling me into the light.

I would have screamed had I been able to breathe, but both actions were made impossible by the large hand clamped around my nose and mouth, stifling me. My eyes widened first in fear, and then in recognition, and the choking hand dropped from my face as suddenly as it had come.

'Mistress Farr!' the steward's face, for once, betrayed his astonishment. 'I pray your pardon! I took you for a thief.'

I rubbed my neck, and smiled wanly. 'I do but seek asylum,' I corrected him, 'in the chamber of his lordship. Tell me, has my uncle come before me?'

The steward shook his head. 'He has not. No-one has called here since yourself this morning.'

'Good sir, I beg you,' I placed a hand upon his sleeve, 'on no account admit my uncle to this house. He means to do your lordship mischief, and there is one with me who can attest the evil of his nature.' Turning, I called out to Caroline, who still clung to the shadows of the far wall. 'Come, Caroline, this man is a friend. You will be safe.'

Slowly she came, in that stiff and painful shuffle, clasping the pitiful bundle to her breast protectively. As she drew level with us the light from the library fell full upon the child's waxen, lifeless face, and showed the trail of drying blood that stained the blue-tinged skin.

The steward looked, and lifted horror-stricken eyes to mine. 'Where is your uncle now, Mistress?' he asked me.

'I fear he waits in hiding outside this very house,' I answered him plainly. 'Have you a man that you can trust?'

'I have three men as able as myself,' was his loyal response, 'and a young lad who would not shrink from duty, were he called. Do you wish me to send for the bailiff?'

I shook my head, my heart sinking. 'The bailiff would be of no use, sir, for he is dead and a traitor besides. I confess, I know not who to trust in this affair. The wolves are well disguised among the lambs.'

The steward squared his shoulders proudly. 'Then it is left to us,' he said. 'I will send my men to watch the road for his lordship's return, that we might warn him of this danger.'

I smiled at him in relief. 'I thank you, sir. Where may I take my aunt, that she may be more comfortable?'

'There is a fire in the Great Hall, Mistress, where you both might warm yourselves. I'll send a maid to attend to you, and to the . . . child.' He looked with pity at Caroline, but she only stared back at him with wooden eyes, and followed us when she was bidden to.

I waited until the maid arrived and saw Caroline settled in a chair before the fire, where she rocked Johnnie back and forth, humming contentedly. Unable to remain, I took my leave of both women and went upstairs, taking the steps two at a time in my haste.

The crimson bedchamber felt cold and lonely without Richard there to fill the room. The moonlight made ghosts of the bed-hangings, and cast a spectral pool about my feet, but I dared not light a candle for fear of my uncle's eyes. He was out there, I knew, concealed somewhere behind a tree or hedge or garden wall, driven by a cruel and single purpose. The lawn spread pale and peaceful beneath my window, but I could sense the evil presence of the serpent.

I stared out over the lawn, towards the road, hoping that one of Richard's servants had already intercepted him, and turned him back. I went on watching, hoping, until my vision blurred with weariness, and still I did not look away. I do not know what hour it was when the first small flicker of movement caught my eye, and jolted me awake.

At first I could see nothing clearly, only a flash of white between the trees that marked the curving road from the south, and then I saw it was Navarre, cantering innocently homewards with Richard on his back. Ghost-like, silently, they moved against the darkness, the rising scream of the wind stealing the sound of the stallion's thundering hooves.

They must have seen him, surely – one of the servants must have seen him, and spoken to him; yet still he came on.

He had come back for me, I thought painfully. He knew that Jabez Howard lived, and that my uncle in his anger would return to seek revenge. It had been fool of me to think that Richard would choose to turn from danger, and yet his reckless bravery saddened me, I knew not why.

346

It was not until the horse drew nearer that I saw the reason Richard had not turned on the road, and why his servants' warnings had not reached his ears. The stallion ran with a single purpose and would not be stopped, his rider sprawled senseless across the broad grey neck. Navarre eased finally to a slow walk, and then stopped altogether, his heaving sides bathed in foam. In horror I watched as Richard pitched forward, sliding heavily from the saddle to land full length upon the ground. He did not move.

I remembered my uncle's leering smile, and the sound of his rasping words . . . *But I have seen the Devil's blood, and know he is a man.*

For the second time that night, my mind filled with screams of terror, and for the second time I was powerless to give them voice. I saw a shadow running across the lawn towards the fallen man, and an urgent litany ran through my agonized brain. Get up, I begged the dark and crumpled figure. Oh please, get up. Please . . . please . . . please . . .

The running shadow was much closer now, and spurred to action I dragged my leaden feet from the spot before the window, flying with a speed unnatural down the stairs and through the darkened passage.

The silence in the Great Hall should have warned me. The wind wailed still against the tall windows, but there was no other sound, and my running feet had carried me well into the room before I perceived my error.

Caroline and the maid still sat before the fire. They sat like pokers, stiffly wary, eyes fixed upon the man who stood upon the hearthrug with his hands outstretched towards the blaze. Beyond him lay the door to the outside, and beyond that lay Richard – helpless, perhaps

347

dying, on the lawn. But my uncle blocked my way to both.

He turned his head, still with his back to me, and addressed me over one shoulder. 'Well, Mariana. This is a pretty welcome. And what have you to say for yourself?'

I said nothing in reply. From somewhere in my stunned and reeling mind, I noted that my uncle had removed his belt and gloves, though he yet wore his sword. My flailing gaze lit upon the belt where he had thrown it across a chair, and dimly I registered that his dagger yet rested in its scabbard. It was a lethal enough weapon for my purpose.

Jabez Howard followed my gaze, his brows lowering ominously, and I moved. My lunge was quick, but not quick enough. I had but crossed the floor and closed my fingers round the dagger's handle when he was upon me, grabbing the blade from my hand and sending it clattering to the floor, his eyes contemptuous.

'Would you play me for a fool?' he demanded, his hand closing painfully round my wrist. 'Did you think I would not learn of your sins? You are the Devil's harlot, Mariana Farr, deny it not.'

I set my jaw and met his eyes. 'I am no harlot,' I denied the charge. 'And Richard de Mornay is no devil. He is to be my husband.'

Again I saw that evil, twisted smile, and hated it.

'You cannot marry a corpse, I think,' my uncle said.

'He is not dead!'

'What matter? If he is not now, he soon will be.' The smile faded beneath those mad and piercing eyes. 'And you may wish yourself so, when I have finished with you. You are a wanton sinner, Mariana, like your mother before you, and the Lord will shower vengeance upon your head.'

I saw the blow coming and flinched from it, but his hand against my jaw had none of its original force. Instead I felt him shudder, felt the convulsive tightening of his hand around the fragile bones of my wrist, and even as I cried out from the pain his fingers loosened and fell away. He reeled sideways, his eyes rolling backwards in their sockets, and fell without a sound.

I stared a moment at the creeping stain between his shoulder blades, where the handle of the dagger still protruded, then raised my eyes to look at Caroline. She stood close by the body of my uncle, her hands held stiffly in front of her body, fingers half-clenched. Her features yet showed no trace of expression, but in her eyes there gleamed a faint glimmer of triumph.

I heard the running footsteps approaching, and turned in a daze to face the returning steward.

'The stable lad thought he saw a man enter by the scullery door,' he warned us breathlessly, then halted at the sight of the tableau before him.

I cleared my throat. 'My uncle has met with an accident, sir.'

The steward's eyes met mine above Caroline's shoulder, and a flash of understanding passed between us. He nodded tactfully. 'It shall be attended to, Mistress.' Then, almost as an afterthought: 'His lordship has returned.'

I swallowed painfully. 'Is he . . . is he . . .?'

'We carried him into the church, not knowing whether the house was safe, you understand.' His eyes were guarded. 'I am sent to ride to Marlborough, to fetch the surgeon there.'

'Then he is . . .?'

'He is alive, and asks for you.'

It was all that I needed to hear. I forgot about the body slumped at my feet, about Caroline, about everything. I thought only of Richard, and his need for me, and my feet scarce touched the ground as I raced over lawn and garden towards the church, its tower looming tall and black against the dawning sky.

Chapter Thirty-Two

'You are not to grieve.'

He was awake, and watching me. I lifted my chin and met his eyes squarely. 'I've no intention of grieving,' I said, with a calmness I did not feel. 'You're going to get well. The surgeon will be here presently.'

'Mariana.' It was a gentle admonition, rumbling low in his shattered chest. His eyes slid away from mine and focussed on a dimly lit corner of the church, where the torchlight could not reach.

He had heard the talk, of course, as well as I – the vaguely conspiratorial whispers of the servants who had carried him here, and who now stood watch outside the door. It was a mortal wound, they had told me, if ever they had seen one, and they had seen some wounds in their time . . . not safe to move him, best let him lie in peace . . . and they had shaken their heads sadly, their faces lined with the grief of old men who must watch a young man die.

I found I could not take my eyes from his face. Each nuance of expression, each flutter of an eyelid, seemed more precious to me now than life itself. There had been several long moments when he had scarce seemed to breathe at all, but I fancied he looked stronger now.

It had been a terrible shock to see him stretched long and grey upon his cloak, on the cold stone floor of the narrow alcove beneath the tower; his head resting against the base of the ancient baptismal font, his chin lolling awkwardly against his shoulder. I hadn't seen the blood at first – it did not show upon the black cloth of his coat – but his shirt was stiff with it, and the smell of it clung sickly to my nostrils.

His were brave wounds, and bravely won. The King, I'd heard, had been warned in time, and with Richard had faced and scattered the traitors in my uncle's charge. Four men lay dead upon the downs, the King was safely on his way to Oxford, and Richard . . . I dared not finish the thought. Some might have called it a fair exchange, for a King's life. I did not.

Above our heads, glass saints gazed down impassively upon us from the arched stone tracery of the window. The church felt somehow different in the dead of night, and it was not the cold alone that made me shiver. Richard felt it too, and smiled faintly in the flickering light.

'When I was a lad,' he mused, 'I feared this place after sunset. I thought the tombs might open up beneath my feet, if I did step upon them. And the chancel seemed alive with the ghosts of monks and priests long dead. If I screw my eyes up I can see them still, come to visit with me. Perhaps they would have me join them.'

'Don't talk foolish,' I said. His voice was coming from very far away, and it frightened me.

''Tis only talk,' he assured me, grinning. 'And I'd think it unlikely that the priests would welcome a heathen like myself into their number. Besides, my ghost will be busy enough, watching over you.'

'Do you mean to haunt me, then?'

'Ay.' His eyes were very warm on mine. 'You'll not be rid of me so easily.' His gaze slid away again, this time beyond my shoulder to the altar. 'What a mystery is death,' he said, slowly. ' "The undiscovered country," Shakespeare called it, and we do fear to travel to new lands. But surely foreign shores are filled with possibilities?' He frowned. 'I met a man once, at the French King's court, who claimed he'd lived in Roman times, and dined at Caesar's table. I thought him mad,' he recalled, vaguely, 'and like as not he was. But what if he were not?'

I shivered again. 'Must we speak of death?'

'If it is true that men have souls that do survive them,' he went on, ignoring me, 'and if those souls are born again to life, you need not worry that my ghost will haunt you. I'll haunt you in the flesh, instead.'

My eyes were gently sceptical. 'And how would I know you, pray, in another body?'

''Tis simple.' He brought his hand up with an effort, turning his fingers round to show me the heavy crested ring he wore. 'Look you here, and remember. 'Tis the hooded hawk of the de Mornays. The hood may blind it, and yet it sees more clearly than the sighted.'

'You mean that I should trust my heart.'

'More than your heart. Your soul.' His hand lifted higher, and clasped mine strongly. 'Feel that, love. There's nothing can break that. We are two parts of the one whole, you and I. The hawk mates for life, and our lives are but beginning. Faith,' he said smiling, 'd'you think I'd let a little thing like the grave come between us?'

'I'll not lose you.' My voice wavered.

His large hand loosed its grip on mine. 'Take this ring from my finger.'

'Richard . . .'

'Take you my ring,' he repeated, 'and keep it with you.'

His tone was stubborn, and so I obeyed, sliding the

great ring from his outstretched finger. The ring was cold, as his hands were cold, and I held it tenderly in my palm, blinking back the rising wetness of my eyes.

'Remember that hawk, Mariana Farr,' he told me gently, 'and seek me not with your eyes, but with your soul. The soul sees what truly matters.'

A single tear spilled hotly from my eye and trailed a path down my cheek, and he caught it with one finger. I tried to smile at him but could not, and as my mouth began to tremble a flash of pain burned briefly in his eyes and he slid his hand behind my head, drawing me down to him.

I tasted the salt on my own lips, and the bitter taste of blood on his. It was a desperate kiss, the sort of kiss that marks a lovers' parting, a kiss of sorrow and regret and a kind of blind and wordless promise. I would have risen up when it was finished, but he held me close, his hand stroking my hair.

'I'll hurt your chest,' I protested, but he shook his head.

'I am past pain,' he lied, 'and I've always had a fancy to die in my lover's arms. 'Tis most romantic.' His words slurred every so slightly, and after a few minutes the movement of his hand on my hair slowed, then stopped altogether.

My own chest tightened. 'Don't leave me.' The plea broke from me in a tortured whisper that I could not stop. 'Oh, please, Richard . . . please stay . . .'

'Don't be afraid,' he told me, brushing my hair with a kiss. 'I am indestructible, remember? I do but sleep a little while.'

I raised my head and looked at him. Even in that poor light, I could see the truth that I had dreaded. 'No,' I whispered painfully. 'Oh, please God, no. Richard . . .'

'Another time,' he promised. He smiled and closed his eyes.

After a long moment I turned my face against his shoulder and let the sorrow claim me in great racking sobs, feeling nothing save the hollow ache of grief. I tried desperately to hold him, but he would not stay. The fine thick coat beneath my cheek stiffened, grew colder, and finally turned to flat, unyielding stone. I clenched my hand more tightly round his ring, but that, too, dissolved into emptiness. Behind my closed eyelids, the light changed subtly and I felt the first faint touch of sunlight warm upon my skin.

I was alone in the church.

I don't know how long I lay there, with my face upon the damp stone floor, grieving against the wishes of a man who had been dead for more than three centuries. At length I pushed myself, slowly, to my feet, brushing the lingering tears from my face with an absent hand and lifting my eyes to the sad-eyed saints in the glowing window above me.

'Julia.' The voice, coming from the shadowed porch behind me, made me jump. 'Julia,' Mrs Hutherson said again, quietly authoritative, 'it's time for us to go.'

I turned round, confused.

'There'll be Holy Communion at eight o'clock,' she explained, 'and it's nearly seven, now.'

Of course, I thought. Sunday morning. I did not think to question Alfreda Hutherson's presence in the church – it seemed quite logical that she should be there, waiting. I had no urge to question anything. The open wound of grief had numbed my mind. Blankly, I nodded at her, and took a few dragging steps along the nave towards the altar, reading the worn names beneath my feet. 'Where is he?' I asked.

'There.' She pointed. 'Beside his father.'

'There is no name.'

'Yes, well,' she smiled faintly, stepping forward, 'there is an explanation. It was the Plague, you see. A month from Richard's death the Plague came to Exbury, and the village mason was among the many who died. It was more than a year before they found another mason, and by that time Richard's nephew Arthur was installed at the manor house, and did not wish to spend his money to have the stone carved.'

'The Plague came here?'

'Oh, yes. It was quite devastating. One out of every three people died of it, I believe. Nearly wiped the village from the map.'

'But Mariana lived.' I smiled humourlessly at the cold stone slab beneath my feet.

'Yes. Of course,' she qualified, 'she was not here, then. She went away, with Caroline, for several months.'

'I see.' I was only half listening. 'What happened to the ring?'

'Which ring?'

'Richard's silver ring, with the crest upon it. He gave it to Mariana, to remember him by.'

'Oh, that.' She nodded. 'Come, and I'll show you.'

I followed her out of the stale, silent church, and into the clear morning sunlight. The rain had stopped at last, and the world was fresh and clean and sweetly scented. High overhead the hawk was sailing, shrill-voiced and graceful, feathers spread to catch the rising currents in the air. By the churchyard wall, Mrs Hutherson stopped walking and pointed downwards. 'There,' she said. 'That's where the ring is, now.'

We were standing on Mariana's grave.

'She wore it always,' she continued. 'On a chain around her neck. John Howard found it when she died, and had her buried with it.'

'John . . .' I shook my head slightly, trying to clear my muddled thoughts. 'But John Howard died in infancy. Jabez killed him. I saw it happen.'

'Yes.' She slanted an odd look at me. 'Curious, isn't it? Come along, now. It's time you had a cup of good, strong tea, and something to eat.'

I obeyed mechanically, without really thinking, and a short while later found myself once again ensconced in my chair in the manor house kitchen, facing Mrs Hutherson across the familiar teapot. The breakfast she made me was large and appetizing, but I chewed my food without tasting it, my mind drifting stubbornly back to that single point.

'John Howard died,' I said again. And yet, John Howard had lived to bury Mariana, some sixty years later. And John Howard had once owned the lap-desk that I had bought at the estate sale, the lap-desk that had held the gilt bracelet ringed with blue-eyed birds of paradise . . .

'Five people knew of the child's death,' she pointed out, counting them off on her fingers. 'Jabez Howard, who also died that night. Mariana and Caroline, who concealed it. And Richard de Mornay's two servants, the steward and the maid, both of whom kept the secret.'

I shook my head. 'But why? Why would anyone bother to . . .' The answer struck me suddenly, and I lifted my eyes, startled. 'Oh, Lord.'

Mrs Hutherson refilled my teacup. 'Could you not feel the child, inside you?'

'No. I mean, I didn't pay much attention to it.'

'Caroline knew.' Her tone was firm. 'She even helped in her own way. She went away with Mariana, into the country, just the two of them. And when they returned to Exbury in the spring, to Greywethers, they brought with them a baby called John. There was hardly anyone left who could remember the child, or judge with certainty his age. So Mariana kept Richard's baby, and her reputation, and Caroline – Caroline kept her Johnnie.'

I stared silently into my untouched cup of tea. 'I'd love to have seen him,' I said, finally. 'Richard's child.'

'You can see him, if you want to.'

'How?'

'My dear,' her eyes were kind, 'you are not stuck in time, though it may seem that way. It's true your recollections have all followed a chronological order – what happened in September then, will happen in September now, that's true. But you have already skipped ahead, on one occasion.'

I blinked at her. 'I have?'

'The stables,' she said. 'Remember? You went inside the stables once, and saw Richard's horse. Well, that was a memory out of order. It happened in May, as I recall, but at that time in 1665 Mariana hadn't even arrived in Exbury.' She looked at me to make certain I was following along. 'The scene that you remembered was a later one, from the following year.'

I tried to remember the exact incident. I had gone inside the stables, and I had seen Navarre standing in his stall. That much I remembered. And then . . .

'Someone was whistling,' I recalled suddenly. 'Outside. It sounded like Evan Gilroy.'

'Anyhow,' she went on, 'it is possible to see episodes from different times in your life as Mariana Farr, if you want to. Just try it, and you'll see. But,' she warned, 'you haven't much time left.'

'What do you mean?'

She levelled her gaze on mine. 'You remember I told you that your journey was a circle?'

'Yes.' I nodded. 'You said that I had to go all the way round before I'd understand the purpose of it all.'

'Right. Well, the circle is almost closed. And in a short while, perhaps a very short while, you won't be able to live Mariana's life anymore.'

I stared at her. 'You mean I'll forget what happened?'

'Heavens, no.' She hastened to reassure me. 'No, those memories are a part of your essential make-up, Julia, you'll never forget them. You just won't be able to *live* them anymore, you understand?'

'No, I don't.'

'It's too easy, you see, to get trapped in the past. The past is very seductive. People always talk about the mists of time, you know, but really it's the present that's in a mist, uncertain. The past is quite clear, and warm, and comforting. That's why people often get stuck there.'

I struggled to absorb the thought, unhappy.

'It's better this way,' she told me gently. 'Really it is. Otherwise you might go on reliving that single summer, year after year, when you ought to be getting on with life in the here and now.'

'And how much longer will it be,' I asked, 'before the circle closes, as you say?'

Mrs Hutherson smiled. 'Not long. You'll know the moment, when it comes. Are you finished with your breakfast? Yes? Well, then it's time you were home, in bed. You'll feel better once you've slept, and so, for that matter, will I.' She stifled a yawn. 'I've had a busy night, keeping up with you.'

Of course, I thought, a little shamefaced. Someone must have been following me around, opening the doors of the manor house for me, seeing that I came to no harm. Someone had even gone to the bother of oiling the lock on the courtyard door, in preparation for my coming, so that my key would turn.

I apologized for putting her to such trouble, but she brushed the apology aside.

'I found it fascinating, to tell the truth,' she admitted. 'You never spoke aloud, if you want to know. You only stood, and looked, and reacted. And in the Cavalier bedroom you were the very image of the ghost I'd seen all those years ago. It was Richard's return that you saw, wasn't it, that caused you such pain?'

I nodded. 'He fell from his horse, you see. He fell, and then . . .' I bit my lip, the pain resurfacing, and she leaned across the table to cover my hand with her strong one.

'I am so sorry, my dear. I forget that you lost him only this morning.'

I smiled, gathering the pieces of my composure round me like a shield. 'It's odd,' I told her, 'that his burial wasn't noted in the church register.'

'Not so odd, really.' She rose to clear the table, practical as always. 'It was a time of great confusion, the Plague Year. It's hard to keep a written record when the world is tumbling down around you. Besides, it's all worked out for the best, this way.'

'How's that?'

'It was better, I think, that you did not know ahead of time what happened to Mariana and Richard,' she explained mildly. 'Better to find out certain things by living them, not by reading them in a book. Would you have been as anxious to go back, do you think, if you had known that Richard would die young?'

'Perhaps not.' I considered the logic of her argument, and accepted it. 'May I ask you something?'

She smiled. 'If it concerns Geoffrey, I'm still not interfering on that front.'

'It's nothing to do with Geoff. Actually, it's about you.'

'Oh?'

'The other day, when we were talking, you were about to say something. About you and Jabez Howard, and how you knew his temper.'

She hesitated, but only for a moment. 'He was my brother.'

I stared at her, realization dawning. 'Then that makes you . . . you must have been . . .'

'So you see,' she said, 'why I had to help you through this. I'd left you once, when you needed me. Left you to the mercy of my brother, and as a spirit I could only watch and suffer with you when you suffered. This life is my way of making up for that.'

It should have been a glorious reunion. I should have hugged her, kissed her, wept over her. But I merely sat in my chair, and she went on wiping dishes, and somehow the love and comfort and understanding flowed between us anyway, like waves washing back and forth along a windswept beach. There would be time for talking later. For now, the knowing was enough.

The plain truth was, I had no more emotion to give at the moment. My grief for Richard was still a living pain, my nerves were strung like tightropes and my eyes were raw and dry with weariness and unshed tears.

When I finally left the kitchen, instead of leaving by the back door, I went back through the main passageway and out into the courtyard. The air was still, there, and nothing moved. The ivy on the wall had changed colour in the autumn air, no longer green alone, but green tinged with vivid crimson and gold, so bright it almost hurt the eyes to look at it. I pushed aside the ivy and stooped, looking for the door.

It had been oiled, as I suspected. Not just the lock, but the hinges as well. My key was still protruding from the lock, and when I turned and withdrew it the oil came with it and clung to my fingers. I pulled open the little door and stepped out into the lane, closing my hand possessively round the key.

Richard had given me that key, I reminded myself, and I would not part with it. Richard . . .

I blinked the tears away, stoically, and turned my steps towards home, stumbling a little on the uneven ground of the roughened fields. A face swam before my eyes, a dark achingly handsome face with serious, forest-green eyes. 'Which one of us do you see?' Geoff had asked me. 'Geoff, or Richard?'

I was further than ever from being able to answer him.

Chapter Thirty-Three

I believe I knew, even in the moment before I closed my eyes, that it would be my last journey back.

Only a few hours had passed since my return to Greywethers, but it had seemed an intolerable length of time. I had gone immediately to bed, trying my best to heed the advice of Mrs Hutherson and the voice of my own weariness, and there I had lain, staring at the ceiling, while the sun passed above the house and spilled through the dancing poplar leaves that screened my bedroom window.

Sleep would not come. The thought of that invisible circle, closing in its unrelenting arc, spawned a sense of urgency that had made me increasingly restless. That same urgency had brought me now to this spot, outside the house, and I knew better than to question it.

Behind my back the poplar shivered as the clouds passed over the midday sun, and a faint breath of anticipation went rippling through the grass at my feet, and out across the wide fields.

This was the garden where the Green Lady stood. Not the dovecote garden that Iain had created among the rubble, but the original old kitchen garden, long grown over, where Mariana's ghost had lingered all those years. Until the moment of my birth. It was a fitting place, I thought, to finish things.

I squared my stance and clenched my fists, lifting my face towards the sun with my eyes tightly closed. The light breeze ruffled my hair while I waited, forcing all thoughts from my mind but one . . .

There was no dizziness this time, nor noise. Time flowed smoothly backwards like a river to the sea, and drew me in its sure and golden wake.

'Mariana.'

I opened my eyes, and turned to face the lad who came now across the yard towards me. He was a tall youth, tall and square and solid, with bright fair hair and eyes as blue as the autumn sky.

I had searched often for his father in him, hoping to find some part of Richard still preserved, but he was not there. Which was as well for John, I reasoned. No-one had ever called him less than Jabez Howard's rightful son, and no-one ever would while I had breath to deny it.

'Cousin,' he called me, halting his approach a few yards distant. 'It is done. I have left the fastening loose – if you do change your mind, I can reverse it.'

I smiled at him, resolute. 'I shall not change my mind.'

'It seems a terrible waste,' he said, with a shrug of his broad shoulders, 'but you must do as you will.'

My smile held steady as my gaze moved past him to the abandoned dovecote. The birds had gone just that morning, taken in sacks by the servants of Sir George Staynor, new lord of Crofton Hall and all its lands. Sir George was a retired military man, and had set upon his new estate with true campaign vigour, seeking to restore wealth to the noble manor that Arthur de Mornay had despoiled.

Declaring the old dovecote ill-repaired and inconvenient, Sir George had ordered the construction of a new and larger pigeon house nearer the Hall, with a fish-pond and warren close by, and had sent five men to relocate the birds. I was not sorry to witness their departure. When the last squab had been bundled off I had sent John to nail the trapdoor closed.

Perhaps, I reasoned, the birds would not nest easily in the new dovecote. And if, in trying to return to their old nests, they found their entry barred, they might perhaps choose freedom as a better way. Perhaps. At any rate, I would not have them back again, imprisoned in my yard to wait for death. The trap would work no more.

There was only one occupant remaining in the dim and dusty nesting holes: a single key, and that placed there by my own hand. All else was silent, dead and empty.

John came across the grass to stand beside me, looking down into my face with a serious, critical eye. 'You did not sleep last night,' he said.

'I dreamed.'

'They were waking dreams, I think,' he accused me, gently. 'I heard you walk the floor. My mother had such dreams, when she did live, but then she was a nervous woman.'

'You make too great a fuss, John. 'Tis only the one night.'

'Ay. The same night every year. Perhaps one day I'll learn the reason for it.'

I smiled and touched his cheek. 'Perhaps. But not today.' Something fell jingling from my upraised wrist, and he caught it deftly in his hand.

'You ought to have this clasp replaced,' he told me, 'or else you'll lose this bracelet, and I cannot imagine you without it.'

I looked down at the timeworn birds of paradise that had ringed my wrist for sixteen years – John's entire lifetime – and smiled sadly. 'I cannot afford a new clasp.'

'Nonsense.' He closed his hand around the bracelet. 'I'll see to it myself, this afternoon. The goldsmith is a decent man, and will offer me good trade, I think. I would not see you lose a thing you treasure so.'

My heart swelled with love unspoken. I yearned to tell him that, of the gifts Richard had given me, I treasured him above all . . . but the words would not, could not, form themselves. 'You take good care of me, John,' I said.

'We take care of each other.'

They had been good years, I reflected, lean but peaceful, and filled with roses more than rain. The house that had once held me prisoner had come to be my home, its angry shadows gentled by the passing years. We were just the two of us, now. Caroline had lasted seven winters, but she had not the will to live for long, and her passing was as that of a shadow upon the wall, when the lamps are all extinguished.

Together John and I had worked the land and kept the house, and through it all I'd watched him grow to manhood.

The Manor had not fared so well. Arthur de Mornay had plundered the house of all its riches, and let the rest fall into ruin while he diced and whored and played at cards. I had been glad to see him sell the Hall. But I was gladder still to know Navarre was not among the things he sold.

The great grey horse had languished after Richard's death. When I had returned to Exbury in the spring, after giving birth to John, I had chanced to see Navarre afield, and the change in the beast had shattered me. He had looked gaunt and close to death, his noble head bent low and listless, his great legs weighted to the ground.

I had tried, in my own way, to comfort him, braving a charge of trespass by visiting the stables of the manor house, when the stable-boy was gone. I had brought treats for the ailing stallion, and talked to him, and done my best to cheer him, but though he recognized me he had no will to change, his dull sad eyes compounding my own grief.

And then one day, while I was visiting the stables, both horse and I heard someone whistling outside, and even as I started guiltily I knew the whistle was familiar . . .

And Evan Gilroy had come boldly round the stable door. As recognition flashed between us, he had raised a warning finger to his lips. 'Take care, mistress,' he murmured softly. I would not have known him but for the eyes, and his voice. He was completely transfigured, with fashionable whiskers and a periwig that cascaded to his deliberately stooped shoulders. 'I've come to collect Navarre,' he told me, in a voice both plain and firm. His eyes moved past me to the horse, and I watched his expression change. 'Oh, Christ,' he said, softly 'what have they done to you?'

I understood his meaning. Navarre had been so nearly an extension of his handsome owner, that it seemed a brutal desecration of Richard himself, that his animal should be so used after his death.

Evan moved past me to stroke the stallion's neck. At the touch, Navarre's ears had twitched, turning to catch the familiar voice. The liquid eyes had shown a glimmer of something akin to hope, and a faint tremor of excitement rippled through the horse's muscles, beneath my calming hand. I almost sobbed aloud, to see the transformation.

And so it was done. Our parting had been a brief one, with little time for talk.

'What news of Rachel?' I had asked him. 'Is she with you?'

'She is not. I left her safely with my people, north of Bristol. We have been married these eight months.'

'Oh, Evan,' I could not keep the pleasure from my voice, 'I am glad.'

'Would you could share our happiness,' he said, gently. 'You know he loved you.'

'Yes.'

'He meant to marry you.'

'I know.'

He had smiled at me then, a small tight smile that pained him. 'Rachel and I are bound for the north,' he told me. 'For Scotland. We think to make a new start there, away from all the shades that haunt us here.'

I had forced a smile, and wished him well, though my heart had ached within me. And then he had left, upon the great grey stallion, and I thought I saw some remnant of the old pride in the horse's gait.

The theft was soon discovered, but the thief was never found. While Arthur de Mornay's men had searched the local road, Navarre was galloping free upon the highway to Bristol, bearing Evan Gilroy upon his back and, with him, my love to Rachel. I would not see them again.

The recollection made me smile sadly, and close by my shoulder I heard John give a heavy sigh. I turned to face him, and found him looking down at me with mingled wonder and frustration.

'You are a riddle, Cousin, that I one day would unravel.' He bent and kissed my cheek. 'You will not work too hard, while I am in the village? You seem to tire easily, these days.'

'The curse of age.' My smile deepened. 'But for your sake, I will not overtire myself. I would but stand a little longer, and watch the fields awhile.'

John looked at me again, hesitating as if he would say something, or ask a question, but then the moment passed. Smiling, he turned and left me, and I swung my gaze back over the wide, rolling carpet of gold and green, blaming the dazzling sunlight for the sudden misting of my vision . . .

Sharply, intrusively, the loud and brutal ringing broke the silence. I blinked, and was no longer Mariana, but Julia again, with the shrill voice of the telephone calling me through the open kitchen door. It seemed to take a very great effort to move my feet from the spot on which they stood, as though I had somehow taken root there and could not be shifted. The phone went on ringing while I walked slowly back to answer it.

'You took your time,' my brother's voice teased, and I slumped against the wall, rubbing my forehead with tired fingers.

'Yes, well,' I answered, 'I was busy.'

'Gardening, again?'

'Something like that.'

'Are you all right?' His tone sharpened. 'Your voice sounds queer.' And then before I could reply, 'You've been back again, haven't you? What's happened now?'

'I'll tell you all about it, Tom, I promise. Only not now. I don't want to talk about anything, now. I just want to go to bed, and sleep.'

'Do you need company? I could shuffle my sermons a little, and come down. Or maybe Vivien—'

'No.' The flat refusal sounded rude, but I couldn't help it. 'I don't want anyone, Tom. Really I don't. I just want to be alone.'

'But Julia—'

'Oh, Tommy, please!' I lost my patience, briefly. 'Just leave it, can't you?'

He left it, and rang off with an apology. 'Ring me when you're feeling better, love,' he invited, and I felt like an ungrateful shrew as I replaced the receiver.

I wandered back into the kitchen and stood looking out the window at the place where I had been standing, there in the garden where a sad young woman had stood and watched and grown old, waiting for a lover who never came.

Or perhaps, I thought, he had returned to her after all, as he had come to me in the beginning – a tall, silent figure on a grey horse, slipping in and out of the shadows beneath the sheltering oak, tantalizingly near yet ever out of reach.

How many seasons had passed, how many snows had come and gone, and flowers bloomed to die beneath the summer sun, while Mariana and her Richard had waited, locked helplessly in time . . . waited for that one moment when their souls could come together once again in an ecstasy of earthly love?

And now that moment had arrived, and I could find no pleasure in it, no resolution, only a dull sense of disappointment and the weariness of wasted effort.

Turning from the window, I made my way upstairs with dragging steps and fell upon the bed fully clothed. There, in the semi-darkness of the silent room, sleep came to me at last – a dark, deep sleep, deep as an abyss, with no dreams in it. The time for dreams was past.

Chapter Thirty-Four

The weather held fair the following day, and I went to lunch in London. It was an impulsive, unnecessary trip, a hastily-arranged meeting with my editor to discuss a non-existent problem with the book. Had I been truthful with myself, I might have admitted that I was only only trying to avoid my own house, in a somewhat childish attempt to postpone the inevitable. If I was away from home, and had no recollections of Mariana's life, that was no tragedy. Or so my reasoning ran. But if I was at Greywethers, and no living memories came, I was not sure that I could bear it.

I had already borne the loss of Richard, and in a different sense, of Rachel; it seemed unfair to me that I should also lose the life in which I'd known them. And yet I knew that I would lose it. Indeed, if Mrs Hutherson was to be believed, then I *must* lose it. Such was the fate to which I'd been born; the fate which had called me home, across the years, to Exbury, and Greywethers, and Geoff . . .

The soul sees what truly matters, Richard had promised me, and I sought comfort in that promise. No doubt, in time, the sharpness of my pain would fade. In time I would not mind so much that Geoff could not remember, as I remembered. I would find happiness within the present tense, be glad that I had found him twice in separate lifetimes, and let it rest at that.

He had kept his part of the bargain, after all. He had said he would return to me, and seek me out, and that I would know him. He had not promised more.

It did me good to be in London, among the bustling shops and businesses, to sit with my editor in the expensively sleek restaurant and watch the flood of humanity pour past the windows, shoulder to shoulder in vivacious and colourful variety. I could not have lived in London anymore. It was no longer part of me, nor I of it, but being there for those few hours brought order to my life, and charged me with a new and vital energy.

As I drove my car bumping over the little bridge on my homeward journey, I felt alive again and almost peaceful. My house rose proudly from the fields to greet me, solid and unchanging beneath the wide September sky. I drew along the drive, past balding trees that dropped their leaves upon my windshield, and parked the car in the old stables.

I had company, waiting for me. Vivien called to me and waved, swinging her legs as she sat upon the dovecote wall. The evening air was crisp and chill, and she wore a bright red jumper over her jeans, her fair hair gathered back in a dishevelled plait.

'We helped ourselves to coffee,' she explained with a welcoming grin. 'I didn't think you'd mind. The kitchen door was open.'

Beside her, Iain stopped working and leaned on his rake, pushing the russet hair from his forehead with a gloved hand. 'I would've made a sandwich,' he said, good-naturedly, 'but she wouldn't let me.'

'Small wonder,' Vivien said drily. 'I've seen you make a sandwich. You'd think no-one had ever fed you.'

He gave her a look. 'I've been hard at work, my love. I need my sustenance.'

He had been hard at work, indeed. The garden lay in tatters at his feet, the brown and withered flowers cast in piles upon the faded grass. The only thing he'd left was the single, climbing rose, its dead and twisted fingers clinging to the crumbling stone, just hips and thorns remaining. It had been such a lovely garden, this past summer. I looked away from it, and smiled at Vivien.

'I think I'll make a cup of coffee for myself,' I said. 'Anyone want seconds?'

'A foolish question,' Iain grinned, and handed me his cup. Vivien came with me into the house, but when I would have rinsed her cup as well, she shook her head.

'I can't stop long,' she apologized. 'I have to work tonight. But I've a question to ask you, if you've got a minute.'

I set the kettle on the stove, curious. 'All right.'

'I wanted you to be the first to know,' she began, twisting her fingers awkwardly. 'Well, not *exactly* the first . . . Iain knows, of course, and my Aunt Freda, but no-one else.' She took a deep breath, smiled, and plunged ahead. 'I'm getting married.'

'Vivien!' I nearly dropped a coffee mug, delighted. 'That's wonderful!'

'And I'd like you to be my maid of honour.'

'Of course,' I said instantly. 'I'd love to. And Geoff will be best man, I suppose.'

She crinkled her forehead. 'Why Geoff?'

'Well,' I faltered, 'I just thought . . . with he and Iain being so close, I thought that *naturally* . . .'

Vivien's expression relaxed, but she sent me a queer look before replying. 'I'm not marrying Iain, Julia.

You've got it all wrong, somehow. I'm marrying Tom.'

'Tom?'

'Your brother.' She nodded. 'He asked me yesterday. He was going to tell you himself, I think, but he said you weren't feeling well.'

'I had a headache,' I said vaguely. I was beginning to get one, now. 'You're marrying Tom?' I checked again, unable to believe it.

'Yes.' Vivien's flushed smile had given way now to a puzzled, hurt expression. 'We thought you'd be pleased.'

'I am.' I forced a smile. 'Really, I am. I'm just surprised, that's all.'

She grinned, shamefaced. 'We were rather cloak and dagger about the whole thing, weren't we? I'm not sure why. It was part of the fun of it, I think, sneaking off with no-one knowing. We both have to be so respectable most of the time.'

'Well, you fooled me,' I said honestly. 'I can't believe my mother didn't say something, either. She's terrible at keeping secrets.'

'She doesn't know,' Vivien told me, hesitating. 'I haven't met your parents, yet.'

Tom must be head over heels, I thought in amazement, to propose marriage without first vetting the girl through the family. It seemed there were some corners of my brother that I barely knew, for all our intimacy. Vivien bit her lip, watching my face.

'Do you think they'll like me?' she asked.

'My parents?' I smiled at the thought. 'They'll be over the moon. They've been pestering Tom to marry since he came down from Oxford, and you're very much their type. You'll like them, too, I think,' I added. 'They're rather odd, but lovable.'

'Like Tom.'

I grinned. 'Not quite as odd as that.'

'And you're not upset? About us getting married, I mean.'

'Of course not. Why should I be upset?' Why, indeed, I asked myself, my gaze straying out the window to the man bent working in the garden by the crumbled dovecote wall. Why should I think that destiny was perfect? After all, Rachel and Evan had gone off together, loved each other, presumably grown old together. Maybe fate had reserved a different twist for them, this time round.

Richard and I, once separated, had been brought together. Perhaps Rachel and Evan, in this second life, must live apart . . .

The kettle screamed upon the stove, and I looked away from the window with a start, reaching to switch off the burner and fill the coffee cups. Vivien was watching me, silently, wearing again that look of puzzled concern.

'Oh,' she said suddenly. 'I nearly forgot. Geoff rang you.'

I lifted my head. 'Here?'

'While I was getting the coffee,' she nodded. 'About an hour ago. It was a rotten connection, I could barely hear him, but I promised I'd give you the message.'

'He's still in France?'

'I think so. Somewhere in the Pyrenees, I think he said. Anyhow, he said to tell you he'd ring again this evening.'

I stirred the coffee, thoughtfully. 'Did you tell him you were getting married?'

'No,' she said, grinning. 'It must have slipped my mind. But then, he was on a bit of a high, himself, so I let him do most of the talking. There's no out-talking Geoff, once he gets going.'

I smiled. 'So I've learned. Did he say when he was likely to ring back?'

'No. Only that I wasn't to drag you off to the pub this evening, until after he'd called.' She checked her watch, and grimaced. 'Lord, I must be going. Ned will have my hide. Look, I'm sorry to have sprung this on you out of nowhere . . .'

'I'm thrilled,' I told her firmly. 'Honestly.'

'And you will stand up for me? I promise I won't make you wear some ghastly dress, or anything.'

'I'll be there with bells on,' I said, and sealed the promise with a hug. 'I hope my brother appreciates his good fortune.'

Vivien smiled, and shook her head. 'I'm the one who's lucky,' she told me 'And I'll be getting a sister, on top of it all. I always wanted a sister.'

A shadow flitted by the door, and I fancied for a moment that it was Rachel who stood before me, and not Vivien. Rachel, with her soft, quick smile and laughing eyes, and the fair hair tumbled anyhow about her shoulders. But as I blinked, she vanished.

'You will stop by the Lion, later?' Vivien paused on the doorstep, turning back. 'After Geoff rings? I'll treat you to a bottle of my best Bordeaux, in honour of the occasion. And I'm sure the lads will want to celebrate.'

I promised her I'd be there, and she went off happily, calling a farewell to Iain as she headed off across the field towards the village. Perhaps in sympathy for the stoic Scotsman, I fixed a plate of sandwiches and pickles, and gathering up the coffee mugs in my free hand I went out again to the dovecote, crossing the grass slowly so as not to spill anything.

He stopped work when he saw me coming, straightening his bent back and stretching. He pulled the gloves from his hands and set them neatly on the rough wall beside him, then reached to take his plate and mug from my careful grasp.

'You're an angel,' he thanked me, tucking in. 'She told you about the wedding, then?'

I nodded. 'Yes.'

'She's got good taste. I like your brother.'

I glanced at him, looking for some sign of emotion behind that impassive façade. 'I suppose you'll miss her, though, when she's gone.'

He shrugged. 'Hampshire's not so very far away, and I fancy we'll see plenty of them.' He set his plate upon the wall. 'She'd hoped you'd be excited.'

'I am,' I said, but my voice was flat.

He pulled a crumpled packet of cigarettes from his shirt pocket, shook one loose and lit it. Over the brief flare of the match, the grey eyes flicked towards me, unconvinced. 'Then d'you mind telling me why you look as though you've just lost your best friend?'

'I don't know.' I sighed, and leaned my back against the wall, gazing out at the line of distant hills. The sun was fading in the west, setting off a glowing burst of dying colours that spread across the rolling grass, bowed low beneath the breeze. I looked down, at the ruined garden. 'I really don't know,' I said again. 'It's just been a wretched couple of days, what with the rain, and everything dying, and . . .' My voice trailed off. It was impossible to explain. 'This was such a beautiful garden,' I said.

He seemed to understand. 'It will be again,' he told me. 'Next year. That's the wonderful thing about gardens, they always grow back.'

'I suppose so.' I sighed again. 'But I wish they wouldn't die.'

He was silent a moment, gazing down at his feet with a contemplative air, and then he kicked gently at a loose clod of earth, turning it over with the toe of his boot to expose its underbelly of tangled white roots.

'It's still there, you see,' he pointed out. 'Bulbs and roots, just waiting to grow. You have to learn to look with more than just your eyes, Julia.' He took a deep pull on the cigarette and exhaled, slowly. 'Try looking with your soul, instead. The soul sees what truly matters.'

For a long minute, nothing moved. Then he lifted his head and his eyes met mine across the stillness of the dead garden. Across the centuries. Behind us, in the house, the telephone began to ring, but I made no move to answer it. I went on staring at him, wordlessly, my heart rising in my throat.

'Could you not see it?' he asked me, gently. 'Christ, I'd have thought it was that obvious. Freda had to threaten violence, once or twice, to make me hold my tongue.'

My own voice came with difficulty. 'She knew?'

'Oh, aye. She knew the moment Geoff first brought me home from Cambridge. Hell of a time I had, that summer. I thought I must be going mad . . . well,' he smiled faintly, blowing smoke, 'you know what it's like.'

'Yes.'

We might have been discussing the weather. He hadn't moved to touch me – he looked the same old Iain, leaning square against the dovecote wall, his hair turned copper by the setting sun that caught the stubborn angle of his jaw. Unhurried, he lifted the cigarette. 'Afterwards, I went to Paris, worked for Morland,' he went on. 'I was curious, about what Richard did in Paris, in his exile. I had some small adventures, over there, but all I really felt was loneliness, and of course, there was no you.'

'So you came back.' I almost whispered the words.

'Aye. I bought the cottage, settled in and waited for you to turn up. I knew you would.'

His gaze slid sideways to mine, a glancing touch, then passed on to where the oak tree stood in shadows in the hollow. The telephone, forgotten, gave a final dying ring that faded softly into silence. I scarcely noticed.

'Why didn't you say anything?' I asked him.

'I wanted to.' This time the grey eyes didn't look away. 'Believe me, I wanted to. I've been to hell and back, this summer. But Freda said you'd get it right, in time, if I would only wait.'

'Iain . . .'

'Ordinarily,' he went on, evenly, 'I'm a patient man. But I think I've waited long enough.' He pitched the cigarette away and came towards me with slow, deliberate steps. 'Time we both stopped waiting, and began to live.'

The tone, the stance, were briefly Richard's, but it was Iain who came to me, Iain who stood before me with his broad shoulders blocking out the light. How could I have been so blind, I wondered, not to have seen it long before? Everything I wanted, all that I had ever been or could ever hope to be, was there in those steady grey eyes.

For a long, aching minute, he just stood there looking down at me, silent and serious. And in my eyes he saw his answer, for at last he smiled, and took my face in his strong hands, tracing my cheekbone with a delicate touch.

'These are your beautiful days, Julia Beckett,' he promised me softly. And as he lowered his head to mine and kissed me, a flock of starlings rose beating from the hollow in a shifting, glorious crowd, wheeled once against the blood-red sky, and then was gone.

The circle was closed.

THE END

THE HUNGRY TIDE
by Valerie Wood

In the slums of Hull, at the turn of the eighteenth century, lived Will and Maria Foster, constantly fighting a war against poverty, disease, and crime. Will was a whaler, wedded to the sea, and when tragedy struck, crippling him for life, it was John Rayner, nephew of the owner of the whaling fleet, who was to rescue the family. Will had saved the boy's life on an arctic voyage and they were offered work and a home on the headlands of Holderness, on the estate owned by the wealthy Rayner family. And there, Will's third child was born - Sarah, a bright and beautiful girl who was to prove the strength of the family.

As John Rayner, heir to the family lands and ships, watched Sarah grow into a serene and lovely woman, he became increasingly aware of his love for her, a love that was hopeless, for the gulf of wealth and social standing between them made marriage impossible.

Against the background of the sea, the wide skies of Holderness, and the frightening crumbling of the land that meant so much to them, their love story was played out to its final climax.

The Hungry Tide is the first winner of the Catherine Cookson Prize which was set up in 1992 to celebrate the achievement of Dame Catherine Cookson.

0 552 14118 6

EPTEMBER STARLINGS
y Ruth Hamilton

Laura Starling, now wealthy and successful, has survived a bitter past. She fled from a tyrannical mother into the clutches of a sadistic man. She endured poverty, fear and pain. Then along came Ben Starling, older, wiser, who smoothed her path and gave her love and security.

But now Ben has become a stranger who has slipped beyond her reach. As her stability threatens to disintegrate once more, a thin, waif-like girl from Liverpool thrusts her way into Laura's life – a girl who is to prove a link with the past. But no one can help Laura make the decisions that will alter the course of her existence. As the September starlings gather, Laura realises she must take courage and forge her own future.

0 552 14139 9

THE YEAR OF THE VIRGINS
by Catherine Cookson

It had never been the best of marriages and over recent years it had become effectively a marriage in name and outward appearance only. Yet, in the autumn of 1960, Winifred and Daniel Coulson presented an acceptable façade to the outside world, for Daniel had prospered sufficiently to allow them to live at Wearcill House, a mansion situated in the most favoured outskirt of the Tyneside town of Fellburn.

Of their children, it was Donald on whom Winifred doted to the point of obsession, and now he was to be married, Winifred's prime concern was whether Donald was entering wedlock with an unbesmirched purity of body and spirit, for amidst the strange workings of her mind much earlier conceptions of morality and the teachings of the church held sway.

There was something potentially explosive just below the surface of life at Wearcill House, but when that explosion came it was in a totally unforeseeable and devastating form, plunging the Coulsons into an excoriating series of crises out of which would come both good and evil, as well as the true significance of the year of the virgins.

'The power and mastery are astonishing'
Elizabeth Buchan, *Sunday Times*

0 552 13247 0

A SELECTION OF FINE NOVELS
AVAILABLE FROM CORGI BOOKS

THE PRICES SHOWN BELOW WERE CORRECT AT THE TIME OF GOING TO
PRESS. HOWEVER TRANSWORLD PUBLISHERS RESERVE THE RIGHT TO
SHOW NEW RETAIL PRICES ON COVERS WHICH MAY DIFFER FROM
THOSE PREVIOUSLY ADVERTISED IN THE TEXT OR ELSEWHERE.

☐	14036 8	MAGGIE MAY	*Lyn Andrews* £3.99
☐	14044 9	STARLIGHT	*Louise Brindley* £3.99
☐	13952 1	A DURABLE FIRE	*Brenda Clarke* £4.99
☐	13621 2	THE GILLYVORS	*Catherine Cookson* £4.99
☐	13303 5	THE HOUSE OF WOMEN	*Catherine Cookson* £4.99
☐	13302 7	MY BELOVED SON	*Catherine Cookson* £4.99
☐	13683 2	THE RAG NYMPH	*Catherine Cookson* £4.99
☐	13247 0	THE YEAR OF THE VIRGINS	*Catherine Cookson* £4.99
☐	13686 7	THE SHOEMAKER'S DAUGHTER	*Iris Gower* £4.99
☐	13687 5	HONEY'S FARM	*Iris Gower* £4.99
☐	13977 7	SPINNING JENNY	*Ruth Hamilton* £4.99
☐	14139 9	THE SEPTEMBER STARLINGS	*Ruth Hamilton* £4.99
☐	13872 X	LEGACY OF LOVE	*Caroline Harvey* £4.99
☐	13917 3	A SECOND LEGACY	*Caroline Harvey* £4.99
☐	14138 0	PROUD HARVEST	*Janet Haslam* £4.99
☐	14045 7	THE SUGAR PAVILION	*Rosalind Laker* £5.99
☐	14002 3	FOOL'S CURTAIN	*Claire Lorrimer* £4.99
☐	13737 5	EMERALD	*Elisabeth Luard* £5.99
☐	13910 6	BLUEBIRDS	*Margaret Mayhew* £4.99
☐	13904 1	VOICES OF SUMMER	*Diane Pearson* £4.99
☐	10375 6	CSARDAS	*Diane Pearson* £5.99
☐	13987 4	ZADRUGA	*Margaret Pemberton* £4.99
☐	13870 3	THE RAINBOW THROUGH THE RAIN	*Elvi Rhodes* £4.99
☐	13636 0	CARA'S LAND	*Elvi Rhodes* £4.99
☐	13934 3	DAUGHTERS OF THE MOON	*Susan Sallis* £4.99
☐	14162 3	SWEETER THAN WINE	*Susan Sallis* £4.99
☐	13951 3	SERGEANT JOE	*Mary Jane Staples* £3.99
☐	14154 2	A FAMILY AFFAIR	*Mary Jane Staples* £4.99
☐	14118 6	THE HUNGRY TIDE	*Valerie Wood* £4.99
☐	14263 8	ANNIE	*Valerie Wood* £4.99